PENGUIN CLASSICS

DEBITS AND CREDITS

Rudyard Joseph Kipling was born in Bombay in 1865. His father, John Lockwood Kipling, was the author and illustrator of *Beast and Man in India* and his mother, Alice, was the sister of Lady Burne-Jones. In 1871 Kipling was brought home from India and spent five unhappy years with a foster family in Southsea, an experience he later drew on in *The Light That Failed* (1890). The years he spent at the United Services College, a school for officers' children, are depicted in *Stalky and Co.* (1899) and the character of Beetle is something of a self-portrait. It was during his time at the college that he began writing poetry and *Schoolboy Lyrics* was published privately in 1881. In the following year he started work as a journalist in India, and while there, produced a body of work, stories, sketches and poems – notably *Plain Tales from the Hills* (1888) – which made him an instant literary celebrity when he returned to England in 1889. *Barrack Room Ballads* (1892) contains some of his most popular pieces, including 'Mandalay', 'Gunga Din' and 'Danny Deever'. In this collection Kipling experimented with form and dialect, notably the cockney accent of the soldier poems, but the influence of hymns, music-hall songs, ballads and public poetry can be found throughout his verse.

In 1892 he married an American, Caroline Balestier, and from 1892 to 1896 they lived in Vermont where Kipling wrote *The Jungle Book*, published in 1894. In 1901 came *Kim* and in 1902 the *Just So Stories*. Tales of every kind – including historical and science fiction – continued to flow from his pen, but *Kim* is generally thought to be his greatest long work, putting him high among the chroniclers of British expansion.

From 1902, Kipling made his home in Sussex, but he continued to travel widely and caught his first glimpse of warfare in South Africa, where he wrote some excellent reportage on the Boer War. However, many of the views he expressed were rejected by anti-imperialists who accused him of jingoism and love of violence. Though rich and successful, he never again enjoyed the literary esteem of his early years. With the onset of the Great War, his work became a great deal more sombre. The stories he subsequently wrote, *A Diversity of Creatures* (1917), *Debits and Credits* (1926) and *Limits and Renewals* (1932), are now thought by many to contain some of his finest writing. The death of his only son in 1915 also contributed to a new inwardness of vision.

Kipling refused to accept the role of Poet Laureate and other civil honours, but he was the first English writer to be awarded the Nobel Prize, in 1907. He died in 1936 and his autobiographical fragment *Something of Myself* was published the following year.

Sandra Kemp gained her B.A. and D.Phil. from Oxford University. She is currently a Lecturer in English Literature at the University of Glasgow, having taught previously at the Universities of Southampton and Edinburgh. She is the author of *Kipling's Hidden Narratives* (1987) and has edited an anthology, *Kipling: Selected Stories* (1987).

Rudyard Kipling

DEBITS
AND CREDITS

EDITED
WITH AN INTRODUCTION AND NOTES
BY SANDRA KEMP

PENGUIN BOOKS

Penguin Books Ltd, 27 Wrights Lane, London w8 5tz (Publishing and Editorial)
and Harmondsworth, Middlesex, England (Distribution and Warehouse)
Viking Penguin Inc., 40 West 23rd Street, New York, New York 10010, USA
Penguin Books Australia Ltd, Ringwood, Victoria, Australia
Penguin Books Canada Ltd, 2801 John Street, Markham, Ontario, Canada l3r 1b4
Penguin Books (NZ) Ltd, 182–190 Wairau Road, Auckland 10, New Zealand

First published by Macmillan 1926
Published in Penguin Books 1987
Reprinted 1987

Introduction and Notes Copyright © Sandra Kemp, 1987
All rights reserved

Made and printed in Great Britain by
Richard Clay Ltd, Bungay, Suffolk
Typeset in Lasercomp Ehrhardt

Contents

DEBITS AND CREDITS

Introduction

'It must be nice to inspire affection at short notice,' wrote Kipling wistfully to his friend Rider Haggard in 1925. 'I haven't the gift. Like olives and caviare and asafoetida, I'm an acquired taste stealing slowly on the senses.'[1]

Kipling, of course, had won instant acclaim when his work first appeared in Britain. Few writers have achieved such immediate popularity. By the mid-1920s, however, the situation had changed. When *Debits and Credits* was published in 1926, Kipling's critical reputation was at its lowest. 'Chiefly Debits' was the verdict of Robert Wolf, reviewing the volume for the *Nation*; in the *New Republic* Edmund Wilson referred to the 'stock opinion' that Kipling was 'written out'; the other reviews modulated between the indifferent and the apologetic. Indeed, despite Kipling's meteoric rise to fame in the 1890s – 'He must have felt like a comet trying to lose its tail,' recalled Jerome K. Jerome – for the literary world Kipling was now the outworn voice of racism and jingoism, aptly caricatured in Max Beerbohm's 'On the Shelf'.[2] When Kipling died ten years later he was buried in Poets' Corner in Westminster Abbey, but there were no writers among his pall-bearers and few in the congregation. His funeral passed almost unnoticed. As T. S. Eliot perceived, Kipling had become 'a neglected celebrity ... a laureate without laurels', and latterly this misfortune had attached itself to his personal life as well.[3] The years 1923 to 1925, when nine of the fourteen stories in *Debits and Credits* and all but two of the poems were written or revised, saw a sense of the frustrations and futilities of old age closing in on Kipling.[4] There was continued and inconsolable grief at the death of his son John in the Battle of Loos in 1915; his daughter Elsie's marriage in 1924 which left Bateman's, the family home, 'resonant, silent and enormously empty'; and during the whole of this period, there was increasing distance from his wife Carrie, along with Kipling's deepening fear that his prolonged and undiagnosed illness might be cancer. In 1925 he wrote to Ernest Snow: 'You have my acutest sympathy over what you delicately call the "nuisance" of growing old. A train has to stop at some place or other. I only wish it wasn't such an ugly and lonesome place, don't you?' [5] In 1923 Kipling had published a history of his son's regiment, *The Irish Guards in the Great War*, a painful and arduous task to which he'd set himself in 1917. His work on the history, and his own visits to the battle-fields, provided material for many of his war stories. Background material also came from Kipling's work on the Imperial War Graves Commission. Kipling chose the inscription 'Their Name Liveth for Evermore' that was placed in every cemetery. Later Kipling was among the founders of a Masonic Lodge at St Omer connected with the Commission which he named 'The Builders of Silent Cities'.

These private concerns carry over into and deeply inform the writings. *Debits and Credits* opens with 'The Enemies to Each Other', a tale of disenchanted marital love, and closes with 'The Gardener', a moving and compassionate story of the death of a son. Eleven of the stories deal with discords within marriage and adulterous love, three are concerned with cancer, and seven with the war. In 'The Prophet and the Country', the dawn wind that in the earlier stories is a harbinger of mystic experience – what Kipling described as his 'fortunate hour'[6] – now preludes only the passage of a hearse: 'Time was when such nights, and the winds that heralded their dawns, had been fortunate and blessed; but those Gates, I thought, were forever shut' the narrator remarks sadly.

At the same time, however, the tone of anguish is counter-pointed by a sense of strange expectation that informs the larger design of the stories and poems in *Debits and Credits*. For this volume seems to mark a special place in Kipling's writings. As well as resignation and withdrawal there is, paradoxically, artistic and personal renewal. As M. H. Hirst pointed out in the *Central Literary Magazine* in January 1927, an 'unexpected ecstasy' contrasts with the shattered body – 'bent in two directions' – that haunts the volume.[7] As with the dying poet's own epitaph-making in Yeats's 'Under Ben Bulben' – 'Cast a cold eye / On life, on death. / Horseman, pass by!' – the question of literary reputation recurs throughout *Debits and Credits*. In this volume the concealed autobiographical elements, the references to Kipling's own art, and the musings on the past reputation, translation and current reception of classic texts – the Bible, Horace, Jane Austen – hint that Kipling was in the process of assessing his own literary career. In this respect the title, *Debits and Credits*, is strongly suggestive of an old man reviewing his own works. Significantly, at the time Kipling was assembling the stories and poems in *Debits and Credits* he was being pressed to authorize the founding of the Kipling Society – a body that would ensure the continuity of his writings. Almost as if warning himself – and us – not to take all this too seriously, however, in 'The Propagation of Knowledge', the last Stalky story and the last story written for this collection, we are reminded that 'the pearls of English Literature existed only to be wrenched from their settings and cast before young men rooting for marks'. But, as Angus Wilson points out in his biography of Kipling, from the time of Kipling's experimenting with Horace as a distraction during the war years, and the consequent beautifully imitative 'Epitaphs of War', a greater note of literary scholarship runs through the writings.[8] The pre-war years also saw Kipling in a new relationship with the universities – no longer mocking the education he himself had not had, but accepting with pleasure honorary doctorates from Oxford and the Sorbonne, and in 1923, becoming Rector of St Andrews University.

Throughout *Debits and Credits* the idea of literary stocktaking is also endorsed by the way in which the stories and poems reveal Kipling's continued preoccupation with certain key themes. Like the earlier collections, this volume contains tales of magic and the supernatural ('The Wish House', 'A Madonna of the Trenches'); historical material ('The Eye of Allah'): farces and fantasies ('The Prophet and the Country', 'The Bull that Thought', 'On the Gate'); and tales concerning the war ('In the Interests of the Brethren', 'The Janeites', 'Sea Constables', 'A Friend of the Family', 'The Gardener'). There are also two new Stalky stories ('The United Idolaters' and 'The Propagation of Knowledge'). Indeed, as J. M. S. Tompkins points out in her influential study *The Art of Rudyard Kipling*:

9

'Kipling's tales hook into each other in all directions; if one is lifted up for inspection, several others come with it.'[9] So, for example, 'The Prophet and the Country', a bizarre tale set in America at the time of Prohibition which cautions against forms of extremism in national life, recalls earlier farces such as 'The Puzzler', 'The Vortex' and 'Aunt Ellen'. The retributory manoeuvres of 'Sea Constables' and 'A Friend of the Family' – the former a tale of hatred of the neutral who trades petrol to the enemy during the war; the latter a story of ironic revenge perpetrated by a war veteran – remind the reader of 'Mary Postgate' and 'Swept and Garnished', earlier tales of war-violence and revenge. 'The Eye of Allah', like 'Marklake Witches' before it, and 'Unprofessional', written several years later, deals with the problems of scientific advance and the related theme of the artist and doctor. 'The Gardener' is in the tradition of some of the most poignant of Kipling's stories – 'The Story of Muhammad Din', 'Without Benefit of Clergy' and 'They' – concerning the death of a child; and 'The United Idolaters' and 'The Propagation of Knowledge', the two new Stalky stories, for all their hyperbole and exaggeration, reiterate Kipling's unchanged vision of what a man should be: 'It [*Stalky and Co.*] is still read, and I maintain it is a truly valuable collection of tracts' Kipling wrote in his autobiography.[10]

In their separate ways these themes are the 'debits' and 'credits' that persisted throughout Kipling's work to the end, but one of the most striking aspects of this volume is its vivid affirmation and celebration of the techniques of Kipling's craft. The nine-year gap between the publication of *Debits and Credits* and its predecessor, *A Diversity of Creatures*, suggests that Kipling was pausing before setting out into the next phase of his literary career. *Debits and Credits* is characterized by a self-consciousness about writing and poetic inspiration which has been ignored by those who have persisted in regarding Kipling solely as the voice of imperialism, even against the evidence of the stories. Indeed, as John Rouse points out in, *The Literary Reputation of Rudyard Kipling*, by the time *Debits and Credits* was published it is as if reading Kipling had become a kind of rite with set subjects and conventional phrases, with no longer any need to read the stories at all. 'Mr Kipling, fiercely attired in white drill and a pith helmet, writing to prove . . . the futility of literature as opposed to life as lived by the Overseas Man on whose doings he gloats' is the image presented by the *Saturday Review*, despite significant changes in the form and content of these stories.[11] For example, as C. A. Bodelsen comments in *Aspects of Kipling's Art*, in 'The Bull that Thought', a story located at the centre of the collection, the words 'art' and 'artist' occur fourteen times during the course of the story and the bullfighting scenes are described in terms which suggest a work of art and include a disquisition on its principles, its inspiration, and the conditions necessary for its production. In the story itself, three comparisons with circumstances before and after the war emphasize the need for a widening of vision and new fictional strategies to express sufferings hitherto unimaginable and the irrevocably altered conditions of life.[12] 'After the War,' the narrator says 'spaciously', 'everything is credible.' It is possible, as we shall see, that Kipling himself is reflected in the image of the bull that refined itself in the process of recreating its art.

Kipling's early stories had been characterized by the single omniscient narrator that so irritated many of his readers. In general they were short extrovert pieces that reflected a passing moment or mood. Among his early reviewers, Oscar Wilde memorably remarked: 'One feels as if one were seated under a palm-tree reading life by superb flashes of vulgarity'.[13] Nevertheless, these stories were also characterized by their knife-edge alternations between fantastic and real worlds, their evasiveness and reticence, their contrasting styles and tones, and their conclusions, which are often ambivalent or equivocal, retraversing uncertainties rather than ironing them out.

From about 1904, however, Kipling seemed to be looking for a change: 'a sort of balance to, as well as seal upon, some aspects of my "Imperialist" output in the past'. In *Rewards and Fairies* Kipling self-consciously sought structures that would increase the complexity of his writing: 'I worked the material in three or four overlaid tints and textures, which might or might not reveal themselves according to the shifting light of sex, youth and experience'.[14] So, in 'The Knife and the Naked Chalk', 'Cold Iron', 'The House Surgeon' and 'The Dog Hervey', the

stories both enact and ask of the reader acts of insight pene-
trating towards the less apparent. Thought, feeling and imagination interweave: the movements represent a regress which does
not stop at coherent or elegant answers, and the narratives are
closer to poetic fantasy. For the mind open to ambiguity and
depth, there is no fixity or resting place.

From this point onwards Kipling also lengthened the
time-span of his stories, moving from brief incidents to long
periods in the lives of his characters – achieving an effect described by J. M. S. Tompkins as that of a compressed
novel.[15] He also experimented with more conscious symbolic
effects: parallelisms between the frame and the story itself;
significant words and phrases; multiple narration, and the
rigorous editing out of anything he considered superfluous.
'I wrote [in 'The Eye of Allah'] about a medieval artist, a
monastery, and the premature discovery of the microscope',
Kipling tells us in his autobiography. 'Again and again it went
dead under my hand, and for the life of me I could not see
why. I put it away and waited. Then my Daemon said ...
"Treat it as an illuminated manuscript". I had ridden off on
hard black-and-white decoration, instead of pumicing the
whole thing ivory-smooth, and loading it with thick colour
and gilt.'[16] 'A tale from which pieces have been raked out is
like a fire that has been poked,' Kipling remarks elsewhere in
Something of Myself.[17] But sometimes, as C. S. Lewis complains of 'Mrs Bathurst', a story of the destructive power of
love written in 1904, 'the final effect is of a narrative so
compressed that the completed version is not quite told'. The
bewilderment and indignation of many of Kipling's readers
is epitomized in the words of Lord Radcliffe's address to the
Kipling Society in October 1966: 'Kipling's late manner ...
often fails to make effect ... by the sheer complexity of the
structure ... After all, prose must remain an art of com-
munication ... The artist has no right to retire so far that
only through prayer and fasting can his voice be heard.'[18]

'The Bull that Thought' comes closer than any of Kipling's
stories to defending this right. Twice during the course of the
story the artist proclaims his refusal to repeat himself, and both
the frame and the narrative itself reaffirm Kipling's delight in

the story well told and his conviction of its importance. As the narrator and Monsieur Voiron sit talking they drink a wine 'composed of the whispers of angels' wings, the breath of Eden, and the foam and pulse of Youth renewed'.

On one level 'The Bull that Thought' is a story about a bull and a bull-fight. Despite the linear progression of the narrative, however, on another level, in semi-concealed parallelisms and cross-references between the discussions that form the opening and closing frame to the story and the story itself, Kipling is experimenting with a new sophistication of multiple-mirroring: the narrator beats the speed-record and Chisto achieves his ambition of success in the arena; both narrator and Chisto experience a return to youth and to the exuberance of early years, and the analogy between the car and the bull suggests amoral or primal energy contained or controlled. What is also new here is the imaginative oddness of the story. In contrast to 'They', where, as one might expect, the anima or dispenser of inspiration is a child – subtle, gentle and elusive – in 'The Bull that Thought' the bull's mixture of fine sensibility and utter callousness shocks and offends: 'My God, he was cruel! . . . He was playing for a laugh from the spectators which would synchronize with the fracture of the human morale' Monsieur Voiron says. The 'mathematically straight' road of the story's frame seems important here: the 'straight' power of the car is contrasted with the devious twistings of the bull and his infinite cunning. Apis uses the side-kick, which is strictly dishonourable, and on several occasions perpetrates murder as accident: 'In that instant, by that stumble, he produced the impression that his adorable assassination was a mere bestial blunder'. Divorced from morality, the bull becomes the instinctual artist who can play with all his passions and moods: he lives 'so many lives in one' because the daemon is not linked to a concept of single or unified personality. Apis's antics suggest that the creative act is not simply rational – that art originates from a chaos deeper than intellectual control. His movements mime the deceit of all fictions: the artifice and circumlocution of narrative patterns. Like Yeats, who wrote in 'Nineteen Hundred and Nineteen' of 'the weasel's twist, the weasel's tooth', Kipling was fascinated by the cruel, murderous and dark side of the creative imagination. As the bull performs his dance of death, Kipling seems to be inverting the process where most images of creativity euphemistically conceal their own powers of terror and destruction.

At the same time, however, the movement from potential tragedy to full-blooded comedy at the end of the story suggests a further transformation. As a final 'twist' in the narrative, the 'passion that arrives after experience' brings with it a humorous irony, and comedy is seen as the inspired relaxation of genius. As Chisto and Apis perform their dance of life in the midst of the carnage of the bull-ring, the new imaginative tact combined with 'a certain Rabelaisian abandon' triumphantly affirm the artist's power and self-healing.

In this story the sense of affirmation and triumph derive in part from the balancing of tragic and comic modes: neither is given undue weighting. And if, on the one hand, *Debits and Credits* refers to Kipling's retrospective weighing up of his own career, the title also suggests the notion of balance or inclusiveness. The emphasis is not now on absolutes – justice, retribution, revenge – but on a desire to embrace and accommodate all, especially those who, in Kipling's view, had fought with 'beasts' more terrible than those of St Paul at Ephesus (I Corinthians 15:32). In 1919 Kipling is reported to have said that 'he would not be surprised if in a few years the monastic life was revived – as men were seeking relief from the burden of a hard world and turning ... to spiritual matters'.[19] As Kipling seeks to counter the desolation of the 'suffering vacant days', there are more and more echoes of the language and concepts of the New Testament in his writing. So in *Debits and Credits*, 'Samuel Two, Double Fourteen ...! "Yet doth He devise means ... that His banished be not expelled from Him"', cited in 'On the Gate', becomes a key text. And the 'Marvellous mercy and infinite love' located in the epigraph to 'A Madonna of the Trenches' is a touchstone both in *Debits and Credits* and in *Limits and Renewals*, Kipling's last collection of stories.

The *descente aux enfers* had been imaginatively anticipated in the early stories of psychic and psychological trauma, but the suffering related to the experiences of war is at once more terrible and more complex. 'Oh, there was fun in Hell, those days, wasn't there, boys?' quips Bevin in 'A Friend of the Family', but, after the event, the shattered war veterans find themselves dealing with imaginal processes which have restructured their daily lives into new shapes – surreal or emotional tableaux. 'Ye-es,' says Pole (in the same story), 'The trouble is there hasn't been any judgement taken or executed. That's why the world is where it is now. We didn't need anything but justice – afterwards. Not gettin' that, the bottom fell out of things, naturally.'

In *Debits and Credits* Kipling turns to Freemasonry to find an image for the restorative balance he seeks. Kipling himself became a mason early in life, joining the lodge at Lahore at the age of twenty in 1886. Although he was an active mason for only three years, Kipling remained a subscribing member of certain lodges until his death in 1936. There had been scattered references to freemasonry in his early works, but 'In the Interests of the Brethren', 'The Janeites' and 'A Madonna of the Trenches' are actually set in the fictional lodge 'Faith and Works 5837'. 'I sat between a one-footed R.A.M.C. Corporal and a Captain of the Territorials, who, he told me, had "had a brawl" with a bomb, which had sent him in two directions' the narrator tells us in 'In the Interests of the Brethren'. This is the first story in which we meet injured and shell-shocked men. Located in London during the First World War, the narrative portrays a Masonic Lodge of Instruction which has offered its hospitality to the injured Masons in local hospitals. The presiding officers are selected from among the crippled and the wounded and perform the ceremony as best they can: 'it's the Spirit, not the Letter, that giveth life' Burges says.

'In the Interests of the Brethren' is not really a story: it is more like a narrative tableau of exhausted veterans seeking momentary respite from the pressures of war – a context which enables Kipling to demonstrate his respect for Masonry as a powerful source of healing and consolation: 'The Fatherhood of God, an' the Brotherhood of Man; an' what more in Hell *do* you want?' Here admission is open to all irrespective of race or caste, and Kipling emphasizes the companionship and security offered by its inclusive closed circle.

Elsewhere Kipling further strengthens the idea of 'debits'

and 'credits' as harmony and counterpoise through the inclusion of a fantasy written many years earlier and revised for this volume. Contrary to what one might expect in 'A Tale of '16', the emphasis in 'On the Gate' is upon forgiveness and redemption. The narrative takes the form of a conversation between Azrael, the angel of death, and St Peter, as they supervise 'volunteer staff' laid on to deal with the 'incoming multitude' seeking admission at heaven's gates during the war. Intent upon exploring the mystery of divine grace, all forms of judgement and punishment are seen to be alien to Heaven's enterprise, and Kipling abandons his earlier criticism of particular Christian denominations: in this story Bradlaugh, Bunyan and Calvin join forces as 'pickets' at the gates of hell. Judas Iscariot and Mary Magdalene are also enlisted in the cause: they work with St Christopher, St Paul and St Luke along the 'convoy' guiding weak souls past 'the voluble and insinuating spirits who strove to draw them aside'. But supervising all, 'on The Gate twenty-two hours out of the twenty-four', is St Peter himself who, because of his own betrayal of Christ, most fully comprehends the need for absolute compassion: 'oh, my child, *you* don't know what it is to need forgiveness. Be gentle with 'em – be very gentle with 'em!' Every soul that is safely admitted into heaven demonstrates the extent of divine mercy. Even the 'Deserter; spy; murderer', whose case nearly defeats St Peter, is saved by the recollection of God's word: 'Yet doth He devise means . . . that His banished be not expelled from Him'. Such is the force of these words that Satan himself – 'that only One of all created beings who is doomed to perish utterly' – can take comfort from them and feels able to hope for mercy at the end.

Throughout the story the mystery of forgiveness and acceptance is conveyed through elements of the comic and the mock-heroic. One of the most moving descriptions is St Peter's assessment of St Christopher: 'St Christopher, of course, will pass anything that looks wet and muddy.' In a parody of Civil Service bureaucracy, no souls are admitted to Heaven until they have been interviewed by the 'Assessors on the Board of Admission', and until the appropriate form has been filled in and checked. Heaven itself is humorously presented as an enormous Office of Death with prefabricated temporary structures to deal with the extra demand, where advance warning of each death is transmitted via S.O.S. signals on a wireless installation with less than perfect reception: 'Waves are always jamming here' a Seraph says. While St Peter and Azrael embark on 'an inter-departmental inspection', 'Normal Civil Death, K.G., K.T., K.P., P.C.' complains about having to 'give up two-thirds of my Archives Basement (E.7–E.64) to the Polish Civilian Casualty Check and Audit . . . And they've just been cross-indexed too!'

The narrative also mocks the language and figures of conventional religion, but at times the delicate and tender word-play is strangely moving: 'Which Department is Q.M.A.?' said Death. St Peter chuckled. 'It's not a department. It's a Ruling. *"Quia multum amavit"*.[20] A most useful Ruling.'

Perhaps most interesting of all, the story is also significant for its portrayal of the 'high' figures of Western religious tradition as ordinary people. St Ignatius Loyola is 'an officer and a gentleman to boot'; St Paul is a problem case who needs praise and special handling: 'Perhaps a well-timed reference to his seamanship in the Mediterranean'; Judas Iscariot is volatile and oriental: 'This way, please. Many mansions, gentlemen! Go-od billets! Don't you notice these low people, Sar'; and the saints and angels are presented in their human aspect rather than the heavenly: exhausted, overworked and subjected to extreme pressures and strains.

On the one hand, as Tompkins suggests, the story demonstrates that there is enough hell on earth to suspend the notion of retribution: 'What further payment should be exacted from those who were muddy and wet and did not desert?'[21] On the other hand, the story also seeks to locate religion firmly in the world of ordinary reality, which, though painful, has its own supports, as the accompanying poem, 'The Supports', indicates:

> But the everyday affair of business, meals and clothing
> Builds a bulkhead 'twixt Despair and the Edge of Nothing.

In view of the range and complexity of these stories, Edmund Wilson's remarks on the subject-matter in his 1926 review –

'how simple his ideas remain, how banal' – seem puzzling. But Wilson has fascinating things to say about what he regards as significant 'credits' in the technique and style, attributing to Kipling the invention of 'the whole genre of vernacular stories – I mean the kind in which we are made to see some comedy or tragedy through the half-obscuring veil of the special slang and technical vocabulary of the person who is telling it' and commenting also on Kipling's 'unrivalled collection of . . . marvellous language exhibits: the kitchen chatter of a Sussex cook, the eloquence of a Middle Western realtor and several varieties of war slang'. 'I cannot believe that James Joyce . . . would ever have written the Cyclops chapter of *Ulysses*, if he had never read Kipling' is his triumphant conclusion.[22]

Wilson's commentary is important because the decreasing popularity of Kipling's writing in the twenties was partly due to the belief that literary 'modernism' had passed him by; that he was unfashionable and uninteresting in an era that produced Joyce and Virginia Woolf. With its 'special slang and technical vocabulary', Kipling's modernism was different from the language games and metafictional practices of high modernism, but there are striking similarities as well.

'It is as if Eliot has strung his images like beads onto a thread and then removed the thread, leaving the images glittering in a void, mysteriously and violently yoked together' remarked one reviewer of *The Waste Land*, and the same could be said of the cross-references and related themes and images in *Debits and Credits*. Indeed, as Lisa Lewis points out in her study of the links between the stories in Kipling's *Debits and Credits*: 'Jewellery is used as a metaphor for literature in 'The Enemies to Each Other', where the storytellers are called "the stringers of the pearls of words" . . . There seems to be a hint here of Kipling's intention; one can see the tales as pearls, the book as the necklace or setting'. W. W. Robson was one of the first to draw attention to stories by Kipling 'totally different from the conventional account of him', and Robson opens his discussion of 'Kipling's Later Stories' with the statement that 'the mode of the tale ["They"] is nearer to "Burnt Norton" than to *The Turn of the Screw*'. Along the same lines, C. A. Bodelsen remarks: 'The late stories are closer to poetry like T. S. Eliot's

Four Quartets than to the tales in Kipling's earlier manner . . .
The new type was to be, as de Saussure said about language,
"un système où tout se tient", a whole which is more than the
sum of its parts, because the effect of each of these depends on
interaction with the others.'[23] Among the examples cited in
Lisa Lewis's account are the metaphors of locked and unlocked
doors and of drapery and clothing, linked with the theme of
secret and illicit love; motifs of labels, numbers and official
documents linked with the theme of the law, and the religious
theme linked with that of artistic creation. The manuscripts of
Debits and Credits in Durham University Library, and Professor
Carrington's notes from Carrie Kipling's *Diaries*, support the
thesis that most of the stories and poems were carefully revised
or redrafted to fit an overall scheme.

In *The Art of Rudyard Kipling*, Tompkins has shown that in
the 'collections of his middle and later life, Kipling seemed to
have intended his first and last tales to serve as the pillars of an
archway . . . framing the life we see between them'.[24] Lisa
Lewis notes a powerful movement between the first story, 'The
Enemies to Each Other' which is centred on the Adam and Eve
creation myth, and the final story, 'The Gardener', which is a
tale of the resurrection.[25] But there is also another set of rela-
tionships, one of Kipling's most subversive narrative strategies:
the way he uses the adulterous passion of ordinary, and even
unlikeable, women to image divine and transcendent love —
what he considered to be 'uncovenanted mercies' in God's
scheme for mankind. 'The Wish House', 'A Madonna of the
Trenches' and 'The Gardener' reach out tentatively towards a
spiritual vision of the redemptive possibilities of love, and hint
at deep and intuitive levels of religious experience which
transcend the languages of dogma and creed. In these stories
love is selfless and triumphant, and although they suggest that
no simple affirmation is possible in a world in which people
suffer so terribly, they show how far Kipling has advanced
since the early stories with their glib and patronizing attitudes
to women, and their emphasis upon the destructive power of
love — its violence and irrationality. As Carrington suggests,
these stories point to a third possible interpretation of the title:
Debits and Credits as 'the part played in love or friendship by

the one who gives and the one who takes, a relationship often seen in reverse when seen with intimate understanding'.[26]

In 'The Wish House' most of the narrative is taken up by the 'back-lookin's' of two women, Mrs Ashcroft and Mrs Fettley. They speak in Sussex dialect and their tale is full of local detail. During the course of the conversation, knowing this will be the last time they meet, for Grace Ashcroft is dying of cancer and Liz Fettley is going blind, each tells a story of illicit and unrequited love. Mrs Fettley speaks first. But Mrs Ashcroft's tale is at once more tragic and more complex. She too has remained passionately in love with a man long after he has tired of her, and when she returned home from London once to find him critically ill, she made a pact with a 'Token' at a 'Wish House' to 'take everythin' bad that's in store for my man, 'Arry Mockler, for love's sake'. This, she explains to her friend, is why he has enjoyed continued good health – 'wonderful fleshed up an' restored back' – whereas she has been continually troubled by a 'long-standing-ulcer' which has now become cancerous. ''Twas *so*. Year in, year out . . . 'e got 'is good from me 'thout knowin' – for years and years,' she says triumphantly.

The whole setting of the conversation and the narratives of the past suggest that, within the apparently male-orientated world, it is women's love and vision and caring which, in secret and selfless ways, sustains and supports: 'No odds twixt boys now an' forty years back. 'Take all an' give naught – an' we to put up with it!' 'We only go through this world once,' says Mrs Ashcroft. 'But don't it lay heavy on ye, sometimes?' her friend replies. Both before and after she visits the Wish House Grace Ashcroft accepts suffering as a part of love and faces it courageously. ''Tis like a tooth,' her friend comments. 'It must rage and rugg till it tortures itself quiet.' But she herself knows better: 'I knowed it must go on burnin' till it burned me out,' she says. In this way the sudden transforming power of intense feeling is converted into a sacrificial passion: her love is purified by the intensity of her pain.

In the poems which preface and conclude the story the emphasis is also upon the strength of women's love and their capacity to bear suffering. 'Late Came the God' describes how 'the God' tries to punish woman for the 'wrong' she has committed, but her suffering miraculously creates a love which is 'Resolute, selfless, divine'. At the end of the poem the situation is reversed and the retributive God is seen as wholly inferior to the woman: 'What is God beside Woman? Dust and derision'. Love and suffering are also linked in 'Rahere': the eye of love transforms the leper, 'faceless, fingerless, obscene', into something without 'blemish':

> 'Tis a motion of the Spirit that revealeth God to man
> In the shape of Love exceeding, which regards not taint or fall,
> Since in perfect Love, saith Scripture, can be no excess at all.

In the story itself it is also significant that it is a child's experience of love and selfless caring which inspires the adult's. Mrs Ashcroft has been no paragon of virtue: 'You pray no man'll ever deal with you like you've dealed with some' her husband tells her on his death-bed; and at one point in the story she asks Liz Fettley, 'if you'll believe it', and receives the reply: 'I do. I lay you're further off lyin' now than in all your life, Gra'.' But Sophy Ellis shows her how suffering can be a credential of sincerity and ultimately of love. The child's demand for belief and trust in the irrational and the imaginative (the trust in the Wish House) suggests the reappearance of the child-spirit of 'They', now forced to play her part not in the remote and magical 'House Beautiful', but on a council estate. She teaches Grace Ashcroft how to transform selfish passion and egotistical suffering into selfless and redemptive love.

At the end of the story Grace Ashcroft remains concerned that the pain she has endured will continue to keep Harry alive and in health: 'I don't want no more'n this – *if* de pain is taken into de reckonin'.' But we are never entirely sure of the real motivation for her actions. Nor do we know whether the incident at the Wish House actually took place or was simply imagined. Like the woman in 'Late Came the God', 'alone, without hope of regard or reward; but uncowed' she is not concerned with her own praise or punishment.

In 'A Madonna of the Trenches', as in 'The Wish House', we find 'Marvellous Mercy and infinite love' daringly associated with a vision of a mistress, but now also linked with the idea of the resurrection. When Sergeant Godsoe hears from Bella Armine that she will shortly die of cancer, he times his suicide to correspond with the day of her death (the twenty-first of the month). He does this not only so that they will be together in eternity, but so that they can make love together in death: 'an' he killin' 'imself so's to carry on with 'er for all Eternity – an' she 'oldin' out 'er arms for it! I want to know where I'm *at*!'

The tale is narrated by Godsoe's nephew, Clem, who witnesses the 'resurrection' of the lovers. Although he later discovers that Bella Armine died at home in London, he remains convinced that he did see her with Sergeant Godsoe in the trenches.

The most striking aspect of this story is its treatment of the physical body. There are repeated references to the frozen bodies of the dead soldiers used for making the trenches at 'French End an' Butcher's Row': 'There's nothing on earth creaks like they do! And – and when it thaws we – we've got to slap 'em back with a spa-ade!' But these are contrasted with the still warm bodies of the dead woman and Sergeant Godsoe and the hut warmed by the braziers, and their association with the idea of the resurrection. When Clem jokingly tells his uncle that he thinks he has seen Aunty Armine in the trenches, Godsoe is not surprised. Later he quotes to his nephew from the Church of England Service: 'If, after the manner of men I have fought with beasts at Ephesus, what advantageth it me, if the dead rise not?' The implication is that he and Aunty Armine will now be rewarded for their patient and unselfish love ('this must be only the second time we've been alone together in all these years'), and that they will consummate their love in death and throughout eternity: '"Why, Bella!" 'e says. "Oh Bella!" 'e says. "Thank Gawd!" . . . Then he comes out an' says: "Come in, my dear"; an' she stoops an' goes into the dug-out with that look on her face – An' then 'e shuts the door from inside an' starts wedgin' it up.'

In this daring image Kipling brings together the two traditions of transcendental love, the 'sacred' and the 'profane' ('Mary' and 'Isolde'): a vision of perfect love, not in traditional terms as virgin love but as a love that is both spiritual and sexual: 'The reel thing's life an' death. It *begins* at death, d'ye see?' The persistent but puzzled allusions throughout the story to the resurrection of the body emphasize how incomprehensible these ideas are, particularly as they are expressed by the shocked and sceptical young narrator: 'What a bloody mix-up things are . . . if the dead *do* rise, why, what in 'ell becomes of me an' all I've believed in all me life?' Clem's apparent 'conversion' as a result of it all – ' 'Fore it ended, I knew what reel things reely mean!' – and at the same time his refusal to accept the full implications of what he has seen, is imagined in the story's implicit equation of 'shell-shock' with 'belief', and shows the need for the intervention of the 'mercy and love' mentioned in the epigraph and in the story itself.

In 'A Madonna of the Trenches', as in 'The Wish House', the poem and the dramatic extract which preface and conclude the story also endorse the positive aspects of the uncovenanted and the illegal. Contempt for the conventional is expressed in the lightly mocking rhythms of 'Gipsy Vans':

> Unless you come of the gipsy stock
> That steals by night and day,
> Lock your heart with a double lock
> And throw the key away.

And in 'Gow's Watch' the princess who has seen perfect love is impatient with the demands of this world: 'God and my Misery! I have seen Love at last. / What shall content me after?' Like the mysterious resurrection of the lovers in the story, these perspectives undermine what we would like to call 'reality': 'You see' – he half lifted himself off the sofa – 'there wasn't a single gor-dam thing left abidin' for me to take hold of, here or hereafter. If the dead *do* rise – and I saw 'em – why – why *anything* can 'appen. Don't you understand?'

In 'The Gardener' the emphasis is once again on the uncovenanted and the unconventional. Helen Turrell brings Michael, her illegitimate son, back to the village where she has always lived, and is obliged to pretend that he is her nephew.

Introduction

At the beginning of the story Kipling shows how the internalizing and the struggling to contain and measure love against conventional standards fracture the relationship between mother and son. They both suffer; they inflict pain on each other, and Helen feels a terrible sense of isolation because of her need to sustain the pretence outwardly, while strengthening their relationship in private. When Michael is six years old he is allowed to call Helen 'Mummy' at home. She perpetuates the lie by explaining to her friends and neighbours that Michael does this because she feels he must miss having a real mother. When Michael discovers this he feels angry and betrayed: 'You've hurted me in my insides and I'll hurt you back. I'll hurt you as long as I live.' Twelve years later Michael's sudden death in the war drives Helen even further into herself. Her particular circumstances prevent her from expressing her sorrow or from finding relief in the public rituals devised to meet it. Like the speaker in the poem which follows the story, she finds the intense inwardness of grief becomes an obsession, a secret 'burden':

> One grief on me is laid
>   Each day of every year,
> Wherein no soul can aid,
>   Whereof no soul can hear:
> Whereto no end is seen
>   Except to grieve again –
> Ah, Mary Magdalene,
>   Where is there greater pain?

In the story itself Helen's deep inner distress is mirrored in the surreal quality of her perceptions which are at once disturbed and psychologically acute: the village of Hagenzeele becomes 'a razed city full of whirling lime-dust and blown papers'; the Military Cemetery a 'waist-high wilderness as of weeds stricken dead, rushing at her'. Like a shell in a munition factory – 'the wretched thing was never left alone for a single second' – she feels as if she is being 'manufactured' by the processes of grief. As in the stories of breakdown and neurosis, and the shell-shock stories, however, this disorientation marks the beginning of the process of healing.

Introduction

The degree of Helen's love and loss is measured at the end of the story against that of Mrs Scarsworth and is heightened by the comparison. The two women meet on a 'pilgrimage' to Hagenzeele Third War Cemetery in France. Mrs Scarsworth's case is remarkably similar to Helen's. She too has been isolated by her own illicit love and oppressive lying: 'When I don't tell lies I've got to act 'em and I've got to think 'em always.' But there is something profoundly distasteful in her 'commissions' to take photos for other bereaved relatives, and in her attitude to the dead. Despite Mrs Scarsworth's later confession – 'there's *one*, d'you see, and – and he was more to me than anything else in the world' – it seems that her love and grief are self-centred, even superficial, and cannot be shared or alleviated by Helen's instinctive sympathy. By contrast, complete acknowledgement of Helen's love and grief is registered at the end of the story. Unable to find Michael's grave among the twenty-one thousand of Hagenzeele Third, she seeks help from the only other person present, 'evidently a gardener':

She went towards him, her paper in her hand. He rose at her approach and without prelude or salutation asked: 'Who are you looking for?'

'Lieutenant Michael Turrell – my nephew,' said Helen slowly and word for word, as she had many thousands of times in her life.

The man lifted his eyes and looked at her with infinite compassion before he turned from the fresh-sown grass toward the naked black crosses.

'Come with me,' he said, 'and I will show you where your son lies.'

When Helen left the Cemetery she turned for a last look. In the distance she saw the man bending over his young plants; and she went away, supposing him to be the gardener.

Here both context and wording recall John 20:15 and the Biblical reference points to the identification of Christ and 'the gardener' in the story: 'Jesus saith unto her Woman, why weepest thou? whom seekest thou? She, supposing him to be the gardener, saith unto him, Sir, if you have borne him hence, tell me where thou hast laid him, and I will take him away.' Christ is seen here helping without being known, and the substitution of the word 'son' for 'nephew' is a subtle and moving revelation of divine compassion: the lifting of the burden depends upon an imaginative understanding of the inner person not possible in conventional human terms, and requires divine love and understanding.

Kipling's search for such deeper understanding is a central concern of *Debits and Credits*, but so, too, is his constant awareness of mysteries that cannot adequately be explained, and experiences which cannot fully be understood. 'But the pain *do* count, don't ye think, Liz? The pain *do* count to keep 'Arry – where I want 'im. Say it can't be wasted, like,' Grace Ashcroft asks Liz Fettley in 'The Wish House'. So strong in her love and devotion, yet she fears betrayal by the very powers she has proven to be real. At the end of 'The Gardener', Helen Turrell's experience balances understanding and misunderstanding, gain and loss, for she leaves still 'supposing him to be the gardener'. Despite the Biblical allusion, the gardener could simply be a Belgian gardener who says 'son' by way of habit, as most people visiting the cemetery would be searching for the graves of their sons. The equivocation of tone here reminds us of 'They', the story of the loss of a daughter, echoed by this story of the death of a son. And how significant that in 'The Gardener', the accompanying poem ends on a note of certainty while the story itself finishes on a note of poignant pathos. Together they reflect that fundamental ambivalence or 'two-sidedness' evident throughout Kipling's writings: for Mary Magdalene in the poem, who loves the lost and defeated Christ, there is the triumph of the resurrection: but for Helen Turrell there is only the unknown lifting of the burden of grief in a world where the dead do not return.

Acknowledgement

The editor would like to thank Lisa Lewis and Donald Mackenzie for their help in compiling the notes to the stories.

Further Reading

The official biography is C. E. Carrington's *Rudyard Kipling. His Life and Work* (1955); this remains the most reliable and useful account. Morton Cohen's *Rudyard Kipling to Rider Haggard: The Record of a Friendship* (1965), an edition of Kipling's letters to Haggard and of the material in Haggard's *Diaries* pertaining to Kipling, contains fascinating information on the composition of the stories and on Kipling's views on writing. *Something of Myself* (1936), Kipling's autobiography, is also useful in this respect. Harold Orel's *Rudyard Kipling: Interviews and Recollections* (two vols, 1983) is a colourful selection of reminiscences.

Of the critical material relevant to *Debits and Credits*, J. M. S. Tompkins' *The Art of Rudyard Kipling* (1959) and W. W. Robson's 'Kipling's Later Stories' (published in Andrew Rutherford, ed., *Kipling's Mind and Art*, 1964) remain the most influential. C. A. Bodelsen's *Aspects of Kipling's Art* (1964) and Elliott L. Gilbert's *The Good Kipling* (1972) both contain excellent analyses of individual stories. There is detailed discussion of the stories in *Debits and Credits* in my own study, *Kipling's Hidden Narratives* (1987). Roger Lancelyn Green's *The Critical Heritage* (1971) collects reviews and criticism of Kipling's writings from 1886 to 1936. Norman Page's *The Kipling Companion* (1984) contains much useful information. For detailed notes on the individual stories, see R. E. Harbord's *The Reader's Guide to Rudyard Kipling's Work* (eight vols, 1961–72).

J. McGregor Stewart's *Rudyard Kipling: A Bibliographical Catalogue* (1959) remains the best bibliography of Kipling's own work. There is an annotated bibliography of writings about Kipling in *English Literature in Transition* (1960), with a supplement (1965). Recent Kipling criticism is listed in the *Year's Work in English Studies* and in *Victorian Studies*.

Note on the Text

The text of this edition is that of the first English edition published by Macmillan in 1926.

Debits and Credits consists of fourteen stories and twenty-one poems. All of the stories and two of the poems ('The Vineyard' and 'The Supports') had previously appeared in periodicals. 'The Supports' and two of the stories ('In the Interests of the Brethren' and 'The Janeites') were issued prior to the 1926 collection as separate items. Details of such periodical and separate item issue are given in the Notes. There are manuscripts of *Debits and Credits* at Durham University Library. These were presented by Mrs Kipling in 1937 under terms which permit consultation but not copying or quotation. Further information on the dates of composition of the stories and poems in *Debits and Credits* is contained in notes taken from Mrs Kipling's *Diaries* by C. E. Carrington during his work on the official biography of Kipling. The *Diaries* have since been destroyed and Carrington's notes, now in the Kipling Society Library, London, are also under an interdict which forbids citation.

The first American edition of *Debits and Credits* was published in 1926 by Doubleday, Page.

DEBITS AND CREDITS

The Enemies to Each Other

With Apologies to the Shade of
Mirza Mirkhond [1]

It is narrated (and God knows best the true state of the case) by Abu Ali Jafir Bin Yakub-ul-isfahani [2] that when, in His determinate Will, The Benefactor had decided to create the Greatest Substitute (Adam), He despatched, as is known, the faithful and the excellent Archangel Jibrail [3] to gather from Earth clays, loams, and sands endowed with various colours and attributes, necessary for the substance of our pure Forefather's body. Receiving the Command and reaching the place, Jibrail put forth his hand to take them, but Earth shook and lamented and supplicated him. Then said Jibrail: 'Lie still and rejoice, for out of thee He will create that than which (there) is no handsomer thing – to wit a Successor and a Wearer of the Diadem over thee through the ages.' Earth said: 'I adjure thee to abstain from thy purpose, lest evil and condemnation of that person who is created out of me should later overtake him, and the Abiding (sorrow) be loosed upon my head. I have no power to resist the Will of the Most High, but I take refuge with Allah from thee.' So Jibrail was moved by the lamentations and helplessness of Earth, and returned to the Vestibule of the Glory with an empty hand.

After this, by the Permission, the Just and Terrible Archangel Michael [4] next descended, and he, likewise, hearing and seeing the abjection of Earth, returned with an empty hand. Then was sent the Archangel Azrael, [5] and when Earth had once again implored God, and once again cried out, he closed his hand upon her bosom and tore out the clays and sands necessary.

Upon his return to the Vestibule it was asked if Earth had

again taken refuge with Allah or not? Azrael said: 'Yes.' It was answered: 'If it took refuge with Me why didst thou not spare?' Azrael answered: 'Obedience (to Thee) was more obligatory than Pity (for it).' It was answered: 'Depart! I have made thee the Angel of Death to separate the souls from the bodies of men.' Azrael wept, saying: 'Thus shall all men hate me.' It was answered: 'Thou hast said that Obedience is more obligatory than Pity. Mix thou the clays and the sands and lay them to dry between Tayif[6] and Mecca till the time appointed.' So, then, Azrael departed and did according to the Command. But in his haste he perceived not that he had torn out from Earth clays and minerals that had lain in her at war with each other since the first; nor did he withdraw them and set them aside. And in his grief that he should have been decreed the Separator of Companions, his tears mingled with them in the mixing, so that the substance of Adam's body was made unconformable and ill-assorted, pierced with burning drops, and at issue with itself before there was (cause of) strife.

This, then, lay out to dry for forty years between Tayif and Mecca and, through all that time, the Beneficence of the Almighty leavened it and rained upon it the Mercy and the Blessing, and the properties necessary to the adornment of the Successorship. In that period, too, it is narrated that the Angels passed to and fro above it, and among them Eblis[7] the Accursed, who smote the predestined Creation while it was drying, and it rang hollow. Eblis then looked more closely and observing that of which it was composed to be diverse and ill-assorted and impregnated with bitter tears, he said: 'Doubt not I shall soon attain authority over this; and his ruin shall be easy.' (This, too, lay in the foreknowledge of The Endless.)

When time was that the chain of cause and effect should be surrendered to Man's will, and the vessels of desire and intention entrusted to his intelligence, and the tent of his body illuminated by the lamp of vitality, the Soul was despatched, by Command of the Almighty, with the Archangel Jibrail, towards that body. But the Soul being thin and subtle refused, at first, to enter the thick and diverse clays, saying: 'I have fear of that (which is) to be.' This it cried twice, till it received the Word:

'*Enter unwillingly, and unwillingly depart.*' Then only it entered. And when that agony was accomplished, the Word came: '*My Compassion exceedeth My Wrath.*'[8] It is narrated that these were the first words of which our pure Forefather had cognizance.

Afterwards, by the operation of the determinate Will, there arose in Adam a desire for a companion, and an intimate and a friend in the Garden of the Tree. It is narrated that he first took counsel of Earth (which had furnished) his body. Earth said: 'Forbear. Is it not enough that one should have dominion over me?' Adam answered: 'There is but one who is One in Earth or Heaven. All paired things point to the Unity, and my soul, which came not from thee, desires unutterably.' Earth said: 'Be content in innocence, and let thy body, which I gave unwillingly, return thus to (me) thy mother.' Adam said: 'I am motherless. What should I know?'

At that time came Eblis the Accursed who had long prepared an evil stratagem and a hateful device against our pure Forefather, being desirous of his damnation, and anxious to multiply causes and occasions thereto. He addressed first his detestable words to the Peacock among the birds of the Garden, saying: 'I have great amity towards thee because of thy beauty; but, through no fault of mine, I am forbidden the Garden. Hide me, then, among thy tail-feathers that I may enter it, and worship both thee and our Lord Adam, who is Master of thee.' The Peacock said: 'Not by any contrivance of mine shalt thou enter, lest a judgment fall on my beauty and my excellence. But there is in the Garden a Serpent of loathsome aspect who shall make thy path easy.' He then despatched the Serpent to the Gate and after conversation and by contrivance and a malign artifice, Eblis hid himself under the tongue of the Serpent, and was thus conveyed past the barrier. He then worshipped Adam and ceased not to counsel him to demand a companion and an intimate that the delights might be increased, and the succession assured to the Regency of Earth. For he foresaw that, among multitudes, many should come to him. Adam therefore made daily supplication for that blessing. It was answered him: 'How knowest thou if the gratification of thy desire be a blessing or a curse?' Adam said: 'By no means; but I will abide the chance.'

Then the somnolence fell upon him, as is narrated; and upon waking he beheld our Lady Eve (upon whom be the Mercy and the Forgiveness). Adam said: 'O my Lady and Light of my Universe, who art thou?' Eve said: 'O my Lord and Summit of my Contentment, who art thou?' Adam said: 'Of a surety I am thine.' Eve said: 'Of a surety I am thine.' Thus they ceased to inquire further into the matter, but were united, and became one flesh and one soul, and their felicity was beyond comparison or belief or imagination or apprehension.

Thereafter, it is narrated that Eblis the Stoned consorted with them secretly in the Garden, and the Peacock with him; and they jested and made mirth for our Lord Adam and his Lady Eve and propounded riddles and devised occasions for the stringing of the ornaments and the threading of subtleties. And upon a time when their felicity was at its height, and their happiness excessive, and their contentment expanded to the uttermost, Eblis said: 'O my Master and my Mistress declare to us, if it pleases, some comparison or similitude that lies beyond the limits of possibility.' Adam said: 'This is easy. That the Sun should cease in Heaven or that the Rivers should dry in the Garden is beyond the limits of possibility.' And they laughed and agreed, and the Peacock said: 'O our Lady, tell us now something of a jest as unconceivable and as beyond belief as this saying of thy Lord.' Our Lady Eve then said: 'That my Lord should look upon me otherwise than is his custom is beyond this saying.' And when they had laughed abundantly, she said: 'O our Servitors, tell us now something that is further from possibility or belief than my saying.' Then the Peacock said: 'O our Lady Eve, except that thou shouldst look upon thy Lord otherwise than is thy custom, there is nothing further than thy saying from possibility or belief or imagination.' Then said Eblis: 'Except that the one of you should be made an enemy to the other, there is nothing, O my Lady, further than thy saying from possibility, or belief, or imagination, or apprehension.' And they laughed immoderately all four together in the Garden.

But when the Peacock had gone and Eblis had seemed to depart, our Lady Eve said to Adam: 'My Lord and Disposer of my Soul, by what means did Eblis know our fear?' Adam said: 'O my Lady, what fear?' Eve said: 'The fear which was in our hearts from the first, that the one of us might be made an enemy to the other.' Then our pure Forefather bowed his head on her bosom and said: 'O Companion of my Heart, this has been my fear also from the first, but how didst thou know?' Eve said: 'Because I am thy flesh and thy soul. What shall we do?'

Thus, then, they came at moonrise to the Tree that had been forbidden to them, and Eblis lay asleep under it. But he waked merrily and said: 'O my Master and my Mistress, this is the Tree of Eternity. By eating her fruit, felicity is established for ever among mankind; nor after eating it shall there be any change whatever in the disposition of the hearts of the eaters.'

Eve then put out her hand to the fruit, but Adam said: 'It is forbidden. Let us go.' Eve said: 'O my Lord and my Sustainer, upon my head be it, and upon the heads of my daughters after me. I will first taste of this Tree, and if misfortune fall on me, do thou intercede for me; or else eat likewise, so that eternal bliss may come to us together.'

Thus she ate, and he after her; and at once the ornaments of Paradise disappeared from round them, and they were delivered to shame and nudity and abjection. Then, as is narrated, Adam accused Eve in the Presence; but our Lady Eve (upon whom be the Pity and the Recompense) accepted (the blame of) all that had been done.

When the Serpent and the Peacock had each received their portion for their evil contrivances (for the punishment of Eblis was reserved) the Divine Decree of Expulsion was laid upon Adam and Eve in these words: '*Get ye down, the one of you an enemy to the other.*' [9] Adam said: 'But I have heard that Thy Compassion exceeds Thy Wrath.' It was answered: 'I have spoken. The Decree shall stand in the place of all curses.' So they went down, and the barriers of the Garden of the Tree were made fast behind them.

It is further recorded by the stringers of the pearls of words and the narrators of old, that when our pure Forefather the Lord Adam and his adorable consort Eve (upon whom be the

Glory and the Sacrifice) were thus expelled, there was lamentation among the beasts in the Garden whom Adam had cherished and whom our Lady Eve had comforted. Of those unaffected there remained only the Mole, whose custom it was to burrow in earth and to avoid the light of the Sun. His nature was malignant and his body inconspicuous but, by the Power of the Omnipotent, Whose Name be exalted, he was then adorned with eyes far-seeing both in the light and the darkness.

When the Mole heard the Divine Command of Expulsion, it entered his impure mind that he would extract profit and advancement from a secret observation and a hidden espial. So he followed our Forefather and his august consort, under the earth, and watched those two in their affliction and their abjection and their misery, and the Garden was without his presence for that time.

When his watch was complete and his observation certain, he turned him swiftly underneath the Earth and came back saying to the Guardians of the Gate: 'Make room! I have a sure and a terrible report.' So his passage was permitted, and he lay till evening in the Garden. Then he said: 'Can the Accursed by any means escape the Decree?' It was answered: 'By no means can they escape or avoid.' Then the Mole said: 'But I have seen that they have escaped.' It was answered: 'Declare thy observation.' The Mole said: 'The enemies to each other have altogether departed from Thy worship and Thy adoration. Nor are they in any sort enemies to each other, for they enjoy together the most perfect felicity, and moreover they have made them a new God.' It was answered: 'Declare the shape of the God.' The Mole said: 'Their God is of small stature, pinkish in colour, unclothed, fat and smiling. They lay it upon the grass and, filling its hands with flowers, worship it and desire no greater comfort.' It was answered: 'Declare the name of the God.' The Mole said: 'Its name is Quabil (Cain), and I testify upon a sure observation that it is their God and their Uniter and their Comforter.' It was answered: 'Why hast thou come to Us?' The Mole said: 'Through my zeal and my diligence; for honour and in hope of reward.' It was answered: 'Is this, then, the best thou canst do with the eyes which We gave thee?' The Mole said: 'To the extreme of my ability!' It was answered: 'There is no need. Thou hast not added to their burden, but to thine own. Be darkened henceforward, upon Earth and under Earth. It is not good to spy upon any creature of God to whom alleviation is permitted.' So, then, the Mole's eyes were darkened and contracted, and his lot was made miserable upon and under the Earth to this day.

But to those two, Adam and Eve, the alleviation was permitted, till Habil and Quabil and their sisters Labuda and Aqlemia had attained the age of maturity. Then there came to the Greatest Substitute and his Consort, from out of Kabul the Stony, that Peacock, by whose contrivance Eblis the Accursed had first obtained admission into the Garden of the Tree. And they made him welcome in all their ways and into all their imaginings; and he sustained them with false words and flagitious counsels, so that they considered and remembered their forfeited delights in the Garden both arrogantly and impenitently.

Then came the Word to the Archangel Jibrail the Faithful, saying: 'Follow those two with diligence, and interpose the shield of thy benevolence where it shall be necessary; for though We have surrendered them for awhile (to Eblis) they shall not achieve an irremediable destruction.' Jibrail therefore followed our First Substitute and the Lady Eve – upon whom is the Grace and a Forgetfulness – and kept watch upon them in all the lands appointed for their passage through the world. Nor did he hear any lamentations in their mouths for their sins. It is recorded that for an hundred years they were continuously upheld by the Peacock under the detestable power of Eblis the Stoned, who by means of magic multiplied the similitudes of meat and drink and rich raiment about them for their pleasure, and came daily to worship them as Gods. (This also lay in the predestined Will of the Inscrutable.) Further, in that age, their eyes were darkened and their minds were made turbid, and the faculty of laughter was removed from them. The Excellent Archangel Jibrail, when he perceived by observation that they had ceased to laugh, returned and bowed himself among the Servitors and cried: 'The last evil has fallen upon Thy creatures whom I guard! They have ceased to laugh and are made even with the ox and the camel.' It was answered: 'This also was foreseen. Keep watch.'

After yet another hundred years Eblis, whose doom is assured, came to worship Adam as was his custom and said: 'O my Lord and my Advancer and my Preceptor in Good and Evil, whom has thou ever beheld in all thy world, wiser and more excellent than thyself?' Adam said: 'I have never seen such an one.' Eblis asked: 'Hast thou ever conceived of such an one?' Adam answered: 'Except in dreams I have never conceived of such an one.' Eblis then answered: 'Disregard dreams. They proceed from superfluity of meat. Stretch out thy hand upon the world which thou hast made and take possession.' So Adam took possession of the mountains which he had levelled and of the rivers which he had diverted and of the upper and lower Fires which he had made to speak and to work for him, and he named them as possessions for himself and his children for ever. After this, Eblis asked: 'O, my Upholder and Crown of my Belief, who has given thee these profitable things?' Adam said: 'By my Hand and my Head, I alone have given myself these things.' Eblis said: 'Praise we the Giver!' So, then, Adam praised himself in a loud voice, and built an Altar and a Mirror behind the Altar; and he ceased not to adore himself in the Mirror, and to extol himself daily before the Altar, by the name and under the attributes of the Almighty.

The historians assert that on such occasions it was the custom of the Peacock to expand his tail and stand beside our First Substitute and to minister to him with flatteries and adorations.

After yet another hundred years, the Omnipotent Whose Name be exalted, put a bitter remorse into the bosom of the Peacock, and that bird closed his tail and wept upon the mountains of Serendib.[10] Then said the Excellent and Faithful Archangel Jibrail: 'How has the Vengeance overtaken thee, O thou least desirable of fowl?' The Peacock said: 'Though I myself would by no means consent to convey Eblis into the Garden of the Tree, yet as is known to thee and to the All Seeing, I referred him to the Serpent for a subtle device, by whose malice and beneath whose tongue did Eblis secretly enter that Garden. Wherefore did Allah change my attuned voice to a harsh cry and my beauteous legs to unseemly legs, and hurled me into the district of Kabul the Stony. Now I fear that He will also deprive me of my tail, which is the ornament of my days and the delight of my eye. For that cause and in that fear I am penitent, O Servant of God.' Jibrail then said: 'Penitence lies not in confession, but in restitution and visible amendment.' The Peacock said: 'Enlighten me in that path and prove my sincerity.' Jibrail said: 'I am troubled on account of Adam who, through the impure magic of Eblis, has departed from humility, and worships himself daily at an Altar and before a Mirror, in such and such a manner.' The Peacock said: 'O Courier of the Thrones, hast thou taken counsel of the Lady Eve?' Jibrail asked: 'For what reason?' The Peacock said: 'For the reason that when the Decree of Expulsion was issued against those two, it was said: "*Get ye down, the one of you an enemy unto the other*," and this is a sure word.' Jibrail answered: 'What will that profit?' The Peacock said: 'Let us exchange our shapes for a time and I will show thee that profit.'

Jibrail then exacted an oath from the Peacock that he would return him his shape at the expiration of a certain time without dishonour or fraud, and the exchange was effected, and Jibrail retired himself into the shape of the Peacock, and the Peacock lifted himself into the illustrious similitude of Jibrail and came to our Lady Eve and said: 'Who is God?' The Lady Eve answered him: 'His name is Adam.' The Peacock said: 'How is he God?' The Lady Eve answered: 'For that he knows both Good and Evil.' The Peacock asked: 'By what means attained he to that knowledge?' The Lady Eve answered: 'Of a truth it was I who brought it to him between my hands from off a Tree in the Garden.' The Peacock said: 'The greater then thy modesty and thy meekness, O my Lady Eve,' and he removed himself from her presence, and came again to Jibrail a little before the time of the evening prayer. He said to that excellent and trusty one: 'Continue, I pray, to serve in my shape at the time of the Worship at the Altar.' So Jibrail consented and preened himself and spread his tail and pecked between his claws, after the manner of created Peacocks, before the Altar until the entrance of our pure Forefather and his august consort. Then he perceived by observation that when Adam kneeled at the Mirror to adore himself the Lady Eve abode unwillingly, and in time she asked: 'Have I then no part in this worship?' Adam answered: 'A great and a redoubtable part hast thou, O my Lady, which is to praise and worship me constantly.' The Lady Eve said: 'But I weary of this worship. Except thou build me an Altar and make a Mirror to me also I will in no wise be present at this worship, nor in thy bed.' And she withdrew her presence. Adam then said to Jibrail whom he esteemed to be the Peacock: 'What shall we do? If I build not an Altar, the Woman who walks by my side will be a reproach to me by day and a penance by night, and peace will depart from the earth.' Jibrail answered, in the voice of the Peacock: 'For the sake of Peace on earth build her also an Altar.' So they built an Altar with a Mirror in all respects conformable to the Altar which Adam had made, and Adam made proclamation from the ends of the earth to the ends of the earth that there were now two Gods upon earth – the one Man, and the other Woman.

Then came the Peacock in the likeness of Jibrail to the Lady Eve and said: 'O Lady of Light, why is thy Altar upon the left hand and the Altar of my Lord upon the right?' The Lady Eve said: 'It is a remediable error,' and she remedied it with her own hands, and our pure Forefather fell into a great anger. Then entered Jibrail in the likeness of the Peacock and said to Adam: 'O my Lord and Very Interpreter, what has vexed thee?' Adam said: 'What shall we do? The Woman who sleeps in my bosom has changed the honourable places of the Altars, and if I suffer not the change she will weary me by night and day, and there will be no refreshment upon earth.' Jibrail said, speaking in the voice of the Peacock: 'For the sake of refreshment suffer the change.' So they worshipped at the changed Altars, the Altar to the Woman upon the right, and to the Man upon the left.

Then came the Peacock, in the similitude of Jibrail the Trusty One, to our Lady Eve and said: 'O Incomparable and All-Creating, art thou by chance the mother of Quabil and Habil

(Cain and Abel)?' [11] The Lady Eve answered: 'By no chance but by the immutable ordinance of Nature am I their Mother.' The Peacock said, in the voice of Jibrail: 'Will they become such as Adam?' The Lady Eve answered: 'Of a surety, and many more also.' The Peacock, as Jibrail, said: 'O Lady of Abundance, enlighten me now which is the greater, the mother or the child?' The Lady Eve answered: 'Of a surety, the mother.' The disguised Peacock then said: 'O my Lady, seeing that from thee alone proceed all the generations of Man who calls himself God, what need of any Altar to Man?' The Lady Eve answered: 'It is an error. Doubt not it shall be rectified,' and at the time of the Worship she smote down the left-hand Altar. Adam said: 'Why is this, O my Lady and my Co-equal?' The Lady Eve answered: 'Because it has been revealed that in Me is all excellence and increase, splendour, terror, and power. Bow down and worship.' Adam answered: 'O my Lady, but thou art Eve my mate and no sort of goddess whatever. This have I known from the beginning. Only for Peace' sake I suffered thee to build an Altar to thyself.' The Lady Eve answered: 'O my Lord, but thou art Adam my mate, and by many universes removed from any sort of Godhead, and this have I known from the first. Nor for the sake of any peace whatever will I cease to proclaim it.' She then proclaimed it aloud, and they reproached each other and disputed and betrayed their thoughts and their inmost knowledges until the Peacock lifted himself in haste from their presence and came to Jibrail and said: 'Let us return each to his own shape; for Enlightenment is at hand.'

So restitution was made without fraud or dishonour and they returned to the temple each in his proper shape with his attributes, and listened to the end of that conversation between the First Substitute and his august Consort who ceased not to reprehend each other upon all matters within their observation and their experience and their imagination.

When the steeds of recrimination had ceased to career across the plains of memory, and when the drum of evidence was no longer beaten by the drumstick of malevolence, and the bird of argument had taken refuge in the rocks of silence, the Excellent and Trustworthy Archangel Jibrail bowed himself before our pure Forefather and said: 'O my Lord and Fount of all Power and Wisdom, is it permitted to worship the Visible God?'

Then by the operation of the Mercy of Allah, the string was loosed in the throat of our First Substitute and the oppression was lifted from his lungs and he laughed without cessation and said: 'By Allah I am no God but the mate of this most detestable Woman whom I love, and who is necessary to me beyond all the necessities.' But he ceased not to entertain Jibrail with tales of the follies and the unreasonableness of our Lady Eve till the night time.

The Peacock also bowed before the Lady Eve and said: 'Is it permitted to adore the Source and the Excellence?' and the string was loosened in the Lady Eve's throat and she laughed aloud and merrily and said: 'By Allah I am no goddess in any sort, but the mate of this mere Man whom, in spite of all, I love beyond and above my soul.' But she detained the Peacock with tales of the stupidity and the childishness of our pure Forefather till the Sun rose.

Then Adam entered, and the two looked upon each other laughing. Then said Adam: 'O my Lady and Crown of my Torments, is it peace between us?' And our Lady Eve answered: 'O my Lord and sole Cause of my Unreason, it is peace till the next time and the next occasion.' And Adam said: 'I accept, and I abide the chance.' Our Lady Eve said: 'O Man, wouldst thou have it otherwise upon any composition?' Adam said: 'O Woman, upon no composition would I have it otherwise – not even for the return to the Garden of the Tree; and this I swear on thy head and the heads of all who shall proceed from thee.' And Eve said: 'I also.' So they removed both Altars and laughed and built a new one between.

Then Jibrail and the Peacock departed and prostrated themselves before the Throne and told what had been said. It was answered: 'How left ye them?' They said: 'Before one Altar.' It was answered: 'What was written upon the Altar?' They said:

The Enemies to Each Other

'The Decree of Expulsion as it was spoken –' "*Get ye down, the one of you an enemy unto the other.*"'

And it was answered: 'Enough! It shall stand in the place of both Our Curse and Our Blessing.'[12]

❴ Sea Constables ❵

A Tale of '15

The Changelings

Or ever the battered liners sank
    With their passengers to the dark,
I was head of a Walworth Bank,
    And you were a grocer's clerk.[1]

I was a dealer in stocks and shares,
    And you in butters and teas,
And we both abandoned our own affairs
    And took to the dreadful seas.

Wet and worry about our ways –
    Panic, onset, and flight –
Had us in charge for a thousand days
    And a thousand-year-long night.

We saw more than the nights could hide –
    More than the waves could keep –
And – certain faces over the side
    Which do not go from our sleep.

We were more tired than words can tell
    While the pied craft[2] fled by,
And the swinging mounds of the Western swell
    Hoisted us Heavens-high . . .[3]

Now there is nothing – not even our rank –
    To witness what we have been;
And I am returned to my Walworth Bank,
    And you to your margarine!

Sea Constables

A Tale of '15

The head-waiter of the Carvoitz almost ran to meet Portson and his guests as they came up the steps from the palm-court where the string band plays.

'Not seen you since – oh, ever so long,' he began. '*So* glad to get your wire. Quite well – eh?'

'Fair to middling, Henri,' Portson shook hands with him. 'You're looking all right, too. Have you got us our table?'

Henri nodded toward a pink alcove, kept for mixed doubles, which discreetly commanded the main dining-room's glitter and blaze.

'Good man!' said Portson. 'Now, this is serious, Henri. We put ourselves unreservedly in your hands. We're weather-beaten mariners – though we don't look it, and we haven't eaten a Christian meal in months. Have you thought of all that, Henri, mon ami?'

'The menu, I have compose it myself,' Henri answered with the gravity of a high priest.

It was more than a year since Portson – of Portson, Peake and Ensell, Stock and Share Brokers – had drawn Henri's attention to an apparently extinct Oil Company which, a little later, erupted profitably; and it may be that Henri prided himself on paying all debts in full.

The most recent foreign millionaire and the even more recent foreign actress at a table near the entrance clamoured for his attention while he convoyed the party to the pink alcove. With his own hands he turned out some befrilled electrics and lit four pale rose-candles.

'Bridal!' someone murmured. 'Quite bridal!'

'*So* glad you like. There is nothing too good.' Henri slid

away, and the four men sat down. They had the coarse-grained complexions of men who habitually did themselves well, and an air, too, of recent, red-eyed dissipation. Maddingham, the eldest, was a thick-set middle-aged presence, with crisped grizzled hair, of the type that one associates with Board Meetings. He limped slightly. Tegg, who followed him, blinking, was neat, small, and sandy, of unmistakable Navy cut, but sheepish aspect. Winchmore, the youngest, was more on the lines of the conventional pre-war 'nut', but his eyes were sunk in his head and his hands black-nailed and roughened. Portson, their host, with Vandyke beard and a comfortable little stomach, beamed upon them as they settled to their oysters.

'*That's* what I mean,' said the carrying voice of the foreign actress, whom Henri had just disabused of the idea that she had been promised the pink alcove. 'They ain't *alive* to the war yet. Now, what's the matter with those four dubs yonder joining the British Army or – or *doing* something?'

'Who's your friend?' Maddingham asked.

'I've forgotten her name for the minute,' Portson replied, 'but she's the latest thing in imported patriotic piece-goods. She sings "Sons of the Empire, Go Forward!" at the Palemseum. It makes the aunties weep.'

'That's Sidney Latter. She's not half bad.' Tegg reached for the vinegar. 'We ought to see her some night.'

'Yes. We've a lot of time for that sort of thing,' Maddingham grunted. 'I'll take your oysters, Portson, if you don't want 'em.'

'Cheer up, Papa Maddingham! 'Soon be dead!' [4] Winchmore suggested.

Maddingham glared at him. 'If I'd had you with me for *one* week, Master Winchmore –'

'Not the least use,' the boy retorted. 'I've just been made a full-lootenant. I have indeed. I couldn't reconcile it with my conscience to take *Etheldreda* out any more as a plain sub. She's too flat in the floor.'

'Did you get those new washboards of yours fixed?' Tegg cut in.

'Don't talk shop already,' [5] Portson protested. 'This is Vesiga soup. [6] I don't know what he's arranged in the way of drinks.'

'Pol Roger '04,' said the waiter.

'Sound man, Henri,' said Winchmore. 'But,' he eyed the waiter doubtfully, 'I don't quite like ... What's your alleged nationality?'

''Henri's nephew, monsieur,' the smiling waiter replied, and laid a gloved hand on the table. It creaked corkily at the wrist. 'Bethisy-sur-Oise,' he explained. 'My uncle he buy me *all* the hand for Christmas. It is good to hold plates only.'

'Oh! Sorry I spoke,' said Winchmore.

'Monsieur is right. But my uncle is very careful, even with neutrals.' He poured the champagne.

'Hold a minute,' Maddingham cried. 'First toast of obligation: For what we are going to receive, thank God and the British Navy.'

'Amen!' said the others with a nod toward Lieutenant Tegg, of the Royal Navy afloat, and, occasionally, of the Admiralty ashore.

'Next! "Damnation to all neutrals!"'[7] Maddingham went on.

'Amen! Amen!' they answered between gulps that heralded the sole à la Colbert. Maddingham picked up the menu. 'Suprème of chicken,' he read loudly. 'Filet béarnaise, Woodcock and Richebourg '74, Pêches Melba, Croûtes Baron. I couldn't have improved on it myself; though one might,' he went on – 'one *might* have substituted quail *en casserole* for the woodcock.'

'Then there would have been no reason for the Burgundy,' said Tegg with equal gravity.

'You're right,' Maddingham replied.

The foreign actress shrugged her shoulders. 'What *can* you do with people like that?' she said to her companion. 'And yet *I*'ve been singing to 'em for a fortnight.'

'I left it all to Henri,' said Portson.

'My Gord!' the eavesdropping woman whispered. 'Get on to that! Ain't it typical? They leave everything to Henri in this country.'

'By the way,' Tegg asked Winchmore after the fish, 'where did you mount that one-pounder of yours after all?'

'Midships. *Etheldreda* won't carry more weight forward. She's wet enough as it is.'

'Why don't you apply for another craft?' Portson put in. 'There's a chap at Southampton just now, down with pneumonia and —'

'No, thank you. I know *Etheldreda*. She's nothing to write home about, but when she feels well she can shift a bit.'

Maddingham leaned across the table. 'If she does more than eleven in a flat calm,' said he, 'I'll   I'll give you *Hilarity*.'

''Wouldn't be found dead in *Hilarity*,' was Winchmore's grateful reply. 'You don't mean to say you've taken her into real wet water, Papa? Where did it happen?'

The other laughed. Maddingham's red face turned brick colour, and the veins on the cheekbones showed blue through a blurr of short bristles.

'He's been convoying neutrals — in a tactful manner,' Tegg chuckled.

Maddingham filled his glass and scowled at Tegg. 'Yes,' he said, 'and here's special damnation to me Lords of the Admiralty. A more muddle-headed set of brass-bound apes —'

'My! My! My!' Winchmore chirruped soothingly. 'It don't seem to have done you any good, Papa. Who were you conveyancing?'

Maddingham snapped out a ship's name and some details of her build.

'Oh, but that chap's a friend of *mine*!' cried Winchmore. 'I ran across him — the — not so long ago, hugging the Scotch coast — out of his course, he said, owing to foul weather and a new type of engine — a Diesel. That's him, ain't it — the complete neutral?' He mentioned an outstanding peculiarity of the ship's rig.

'Yes,' said Portson. 'Did you board him, Winchmore?'

'No. There'd been a bit of a blow the day before and old *Ethel*'s only dinghy had dropped off the hooks. But he signalled me all his symptoms. He was as communicative as — as a lady in the Promenade. (Hold on, Nephew of my Uncle! I'm going to have some more of that Béarnaise fillet.) His smell attracted me. I chaperoned him for a couple of days.'

'Only two days. *You* hadn't anything to complain of,' said Maddingham wrathfully.

'I didn't complain. If he chose to hug things, 'twasn't any of my business. I'm not a Purity League. 'Didn't care what he hugged, so long as I could lie behind him and give him first chop at any mines that were going. I steered in his wake (I really *can* steer a bit now, Portson) and let him stink up the whole of the North Sea. I thought he might come in useful for bait. No Burgundy, thanks, Nephew of my Uncle. I'm sticking to the Jolly Roger.'

'Go on, then – before you're speechless. Was he any use as bait?' Tegg demanded.

'We never got a fair chance. As I told you, he hugged the coast till dark, and then he scraped round Gilarra Head and went up the bay nearly to the beach.'

''Lights out?' Maddingham asked.

Winchmore nodded. 'But I didn't worry about that. I was under his stern. As luck 'ud have it, there was a fishing-party in the bay, and we walked slam into the middle of 'em – a most ungodly collection of local talent. 'First thing I knew a steam-launch fell aboard us, and a boy – a nasty little Navy boy, Tegg – wanted to know what I was doing. I told him, and he cursed me for putting the fish down just as they were rising. Then the two of us (he was hanging on to my quarter with a boat-hook) drifted on to a steam trawler and our friend the Neutral and a ten-oared cutter full of the military, all mixed up. They were subs from the garrison out for a lark. Uncle Newt explained over the rail about the weather and his engine-troubles, but they were all so keen to carry on with their fishing, they didn't fuss. They told him to clear off.'

'Was there anything on the move round Gilarra at that time?' Tegg inquired.

'Oh, they spun me the usual yarns about the water being thick with 'em, and asked me to help; but I couldn't stop. The cutter's stern-sheets were piled up with mines, like lobster-pots, and from the way the soldiers handled 'em I thought I'd better get out. So did Uncle Newt. *He* didn't like it a bit. There were a couple of shots fired at something just as we cleared the

Head, and one dropped rather close to him. (These duck-shoots in the dark are dam' dangerous, y'know.) He lit up at once – tail-light, head-light, and side-lights. I had no more trouble with him the rest of the night.'

'But what about the report that you sawed off the steam-launch's boat-hook?' Tegg demanded suddenly.

'What! You don't mean to say that little beast of a snotty reported it? He was scratchin' poor old *Ethel*'s paint to pieces. I never reported what he said to *me*. And he called me a damned amateur, too! Well! Well! War's war. I missed all that fishing-party that time. My orders were to follow Uncle Newt. So I followed – and poor *Ethel* without a dry rag on her.'

Winchmore refilled his glass.

'Well, don't get poetical,' said Portson. 'Let's have the rest of your trip.'

'There wasn't any rest,' Winchmore insisted pathetically. 'There was just good old *Ethel* with her engines missing like sin, and Uncle Newt thumping and stinking half a mile ahead of us, and me eating bread and Worcester sauce. I do when I feel that way. Besides, I wanted to go back and join the fishing-party. Just before dark I made out *Cordelia* – that Southampton ketch that old Jarrott fitted with oil auxiliaries for a family cruiser last summer. She's a beamy bus, but she *can* roll, and she was doing an honest thirty degrees each way when I overhauled her. I asked Jarrott if he was busy. He said he wasn't. But he was. He's like me and Nelson when there's any sea on.'

'But Jarrott's a Quaker. 'Has been for generations. Why does he go to war?' said Maddingham.

'If it comes to that,' Portson said, 'why do any of us?'

'Jarrott's a mine-sweeper,' Winchmore replied with deep feeling. 'The Quaker religion (I'm not a Quaker, but I'm *much* more religious than any of you chaps give me credit for) has decided that mine-sweeping is life-saving. Consequently' – he dwelt a little on the word – 'the profession is crowded with Quakers – specially off Scarborough. 'See? Owin' to the purity of their lives, they "*all* go to Heaven when they die – Roll, Jordan, Roll!"'

*

'Disgustin',' said the actress audibly as she drew on her gloves. Winchmore looked at her with delight. 'That's a peach-Melba, too,' he said.

'And David Jarrott's a mine-sweeper,' Maddingham mused aloud. 'So you turned our Neutral over to him, Winchmore, did you?'

'Yes, I did. It was the end of my beat – I wish I didn't feel so sleepy – and I explained the whole situation to Jarrott, over the rail. 'Gave him all my silly instructions – those latest ones, y'know. I told him to do nothing to imperil existing political relations. I told him to exercise tact. I – I told him that in my capac'ty as Actin' Lootenant, you see: Jarrott's only a Lootenant-Commander – at fifty-four, too! Yes, I handed my Uncle Newt over to Jarrott to chaperone, and I went back to my – I can say it perfectly – pis-ca-to-rial party in the bay. Now I'm going to have a nap. In ten minutes I shall be on deck again. This is my first civilized dinner in nine weeks, so I don't apologize.'

He pushed his plate away, dropped his chin on his palm and closed his eyes.

'Lyndnoch and Jarrott's Bank, established 1793,' said Maddingham half to himself. 'I've seen old Jarrott in Cowes week bullied by his skipper and steward till he had to sneak ashore to sleep. And now he's out mine-sweeping with *Cordelia*! What's happened to his I shall forget my own name next – Belfast-built two-hundred tonner?'

'*Goneril*,' said Portson. 'He turned her over to the Service in October. She's – she was *Culana*.'

'*She* was *Culana*, was she? My God! I never knew that. Where did it happen?'

'Off the same old Irish corner I was watching last month. My young cousin was in her; so was one of the Raikes boys. A whole nest of mines, laid between patrols.'

'I've heard there's some dirty work going on there now,' Maddingham half whispered.

'You needn't tell *me* that,' Portson returned. 'But one gets a little back now and again.'

'What are you two talking about?' said Tegg, who seemed to be dozing too.

'*Culana*,' Portson answered as he lit a cigarette.

'Yes, that was rather a pity. But . . . What about this Newt of ours?'

'*I* took her over from Jarrott next day – off Margate,' said Portson. 'Jarrott wanted to get back to his mine-sweeping.'

'Every man to his taste,' said Maddingham. 'That never appealed to me. Had they detailed you specially to look after the Newt?'

'Me among others,' Portson admitted. 'I was going down Channel when I got my orders, and so I went on with him. Jarrott had been tremendously interested in his course up to date – specially off the Wash. He'd charted it very carefully and he said he was going back to find out what some of the kinks and curves meant. Has he found out, Tegg?'

Tegg thought for a moment. '*Cordelia* was all right up to six o'clock yesterday evening,' he said.

''Glad of that. Then I did what Winchmore did. I lay behind this stout fellow and saw him well into the open.'

'Did you say anything to him?' Tegg asked.

'Not a thing. He kept moving all the time.'

''See anything?' Tegg continued.

'No. He didn't seem to be in demand anywhere in the Channel, and, when I'd got him on the edge of soundings, I dropped him – as per your esteemed orders.'

Tegg nodded again and murmured some apology.

'Where did *you* pick him up, Maddingham?' Portson went on.

Maddingham snorted.

'Well north and west of where you left him heading up the Irish Channel and stinking like a taxi. I hadn't had my breakfast. My cook was seasick; so were four of my hands.'

'I can see that meeting. Did you give him a gun across the bows?' Tegg asked.

'No, no. Not *that* time. I signalled him to heave to. He had his papers ready before I came over the side. You see,' Maddingham said pleadingly, 'I'm new to this business. Perhaps I wasn't as polite to him as I should have been if I'd had my breakfast.'

'He deposed that Maddingham came alongside swearing like a bargee,' said Tegg.

'Not in the least. This is what happened.' Maddingham turned to Portson. 'I asked him where he was bound for and he told me – Antigua.'

'Hi! Wake up, Winchmore. You're missing something.' Portson nudged Winchmore, who was slanting sideways in his chair.

'Right! All right! I'm awake,' said Winchmore stickily. 'I heard every word.'

Maddingham went on. 'I told him that this wasn't his way to Antigua –'

'Antigua. Antigua!' Winchmore finished rubbing his eyes. '"There was a young bride of Antigua –"' [8]

'Hsh! Hsh!' said Portson and Tegg warningly.

'Why? It's the proper one. "Who said to her spouse, 'What a pig you are!'"'

'Ass!' Maddingham growled and continued: 'He told me that he'd been knocked out of his reckoning by foul weather and engine-trouble, owing to experimenting with a new type of Diesel engine. He was perfectly frank about it.'

'So he was with me,' said Winchmore. 'Just like a real lady. I hope you were a real gentleman, Papa.'

'I asked him what he'd got. He didn't object. He had some fifty thousand gallon of oil for his new Diesel engine, and the rest was coal. He said he needed the oil to get to Antigua with, he was taking the coal as ballast, and he was coming back, so he told me, with coconuts. When he'd quite finished, I said: "What sort of damned idiot do you take me for?" He said: "I haven't decided yet!" Then I said he'd better come into port with me, and we'd arrive at a decision. He said that his papers were in perfect order and that my instructions – mine, please! – were not to imperil political relations. I hadn't received these asinine instructions, so I took the liberty of contradicting him – perfectly politely, as I told them at the Inquiry afterward. He was a small-boned man with a grey beard, in a glengarry, and he picked his teeth a lot. He said: "The last time I met you, Mister Maddingham, you were going to Carlsbad, and you told me all about your blood-pressures in the wagon-lit before we tossed for upper berth. Don't you think you are a little old to buccaneer about the sea this way?" I couldn't recall his face – he must have been some fellow that I'd travelled with some time or other. I told him I wasn't doing this for amusement – it was business. Then I ordered him into port. He said: "S'pose I don't go?" I said: "Then I'll sink you." Isn't it extraordinary how natural it all seems after a few weeks? If anyone had told me when I commissioned *Hilarity* last summer what I'd be doing this spring I'd – I'd ... God! It *is* mad, isn't it?'

'Quite,' said Portson. 'But not bad fun.'

'Not at all, but that's what makes it all the madder. Well, he didn't argue any more. He warned me I'd be hauled over the coals for what I'd done, and I warned him to keep two cables ahead of me and not to yaw.'

'Jaw?' said Winchmore sleepily.

'No. Yaw,' Maddingham snarled. 'Not to look as if he even wanted to yaw. I warned him that, if he did, I'd loose off into him, end-on. But I was absolutely polite about it. 'Give you my word, Tegg.'

'I believe you. Oh, I believe you,' Tegg replied.

'Well, so I took him into port – and that was where I first ran across our Master Tegg. He represented the Admiralty on that beach.'

The small blinking man nodded. 'The Admiralty had that honour,' he said graciously.

Maddingham turned to the others angrily. 'I'd been rather patting myself on the back for what I'd done, you know. Instead of which, they held a court-martial –'

'*We* called it an Inquiry,' Tegg interjected.

'*You* weren't in the dock. They held a court-martial on me to find out how often I'd sworn at the poor injured Neutral, and whether I'd given him hot-water bottles and tucked him up at night. It's all very fine to laugh, but they treated me like a pickpocket. There were two fat-headed civilian judges and that blackguard Tegg in the conspiracy. A cursed lawyer defended my Neutral and he made fun of *me*. He dragged in everything the Neutral had told him about my blood-pressures on the Carlsbad trip. And that's what you get for trying to serve your country in your old age!' Maddingham emptied and refilled his glass.

'We *did* give you rather a grilling,' said Tegg placidly. 'It's the national sense of fair play.'

'I could have stood it all if it hadn't been for the Neutral. We dined at the same hotel while this court-martial was going on, and he used to come over to my table and sympathize with me! He told me that I was fighting for his ideals and the uplift of democracy, but I must respect the Law of Nations!'

'And we respected 'em,' said Tegg. 'His papers were perfectly correct; the Court discharged him. We had to consider existing political relations. I *told* Maddingham so at the hotel and he –'

Again Maddingham turned to the others. 'I couldn't make up my mind about Tegg at the Inquiry,' he explained. 'He had the air of a decent sailor-man, but he talked like a poisonous politician.'

'I was,' Tegg returned. 'I had been ordered to change into that rig. So I changed.'

Maddingham ran one fat square hand through his crisped hair and looked up under his eyebrows like a shy child, while the others lay back and laughed.

'I suppose I ought to have been on to the joke,' he stammered, 'but I'd blacked myself all over for the part of Lootenant-Commander R.N.V.R. in time of war, and I'd given up thinking as a banker. If it had been put before me as a business proposition I might have done better.'

'I thought you were playing up to me and the judges all the time,' said Tegg. 'I never dreamed you took it seriously.'

'Well, I've been trained to look on the law as serious. I've had to pay for some of it in my time, you know.'

'I'm sorry,' said Tegg. 'We were obliged to let that oil beggar go – for reasons, but, as I told Maddingham, the night the award was given, *his* duty was to see that he was properly directed to Antigua.'

'Naturally,' Portson observed. 'That being the Neutral's declared destination. And what did Maddingham do? Shut up, Maddingham!'

Said Tegg, with downcast eyes: 'Maddingham took my hand and squeezed it; he looked lovingly into my eyes (he *did*!); he turned plum-colour, and he said: "I will" – just like a bridegroom at the altar. It makes me feel shy to think of it even now. I didn't see him after that till the evening when *Hilarity* was pulling out of the Basin, and Maddingham was cursing the tugmaster.'

'I was in a hurry,' said Maddingham. 'I wanted to get to the Narrows and wait for my Neutral there. I dropped down to Biller and Grove's yard that tide (they've done all my work for years) and I jammed *Hilarity* into the creek behind their slip, so the Newt didn't spot me when he came down the river. Then I pulled out and followed him over the Bar. He stood nor-west at once. I let him go till we were well out of sight of land. Then I overhauled him, gave him a gun across the bows and ran alongside. I'd just had my lunch, and I wasn't going to lose my temper *this* time. I said: "Excuse me, but I understand you are bound for Antigua?" He was, he said, and as he seemed a little nervous about my falling aboard him in that swell, I gave *Hilarity* another sheer in – she's as handy as a launch – and I said: "May I suggest that this is not the course for Antigua?" By that time he had his fenders overside, and all hands yelling at me to keep away. I snatched *Hilarity* out and began edging in again. He said: "I'm trying a sample of inferior oil that I have my doubts about. If it works all right I shall lay my course for Antigua, but it will take some time to test the stuff and adjust the engines to it." I said: "Very good, let me know if I can be of any service," and I offered him *Hilarity* again once or twice – he didn't want her – and then I dropped behind and let him go on. Wasn't that proper, Portson?'

Portson nodded. 'I know that game of yours with *Hilarity*,' he said. 'How the deuce do you do it? My nerve always goes at close quarters in any sea.'

'It's only a little trick of steering,' Maddingham replied with a simper of vanity. 'You can almost shave with her when she feels like it. I had to do it again that same evening, to establish a moral ascendancy. He wasn't showing any lights, and I nearly tripped over him. He was a scared Neutral for three minutes, but I got a little of my own back for that damned court-martial. *But* I was perfectly polite. I apologized profusely. I didn't even ask him to show his lights.'

'But did he?' said Winchmore.

'He did – every one; and a flare now and then,' Maddingham replied. 'He held north all that night, with a falling barometer and a rising wind and all the other filthy things. Gad, how I hated him! Next morning we got it, good and tight from the nor-nor-west out of the Atlantic, off Carso Head. He dodged into a squall, and then he went about. We weren't a mile behind, but it was as thick as a wall. When it cleared, and I couldn't see him ahead of me, I went about too, and followed the rain. I picked him up five miles down wind, legging it for all he was worth to the south'ard – nine knots, I should think. *Hilarity* doesn't like a following sea. We got pooped a bit, too, but by noon we'd struggled back to where we ought to have been – two cables astern of him. Then he began to signal, but his flags being end-on to us, of course, we had to creep up on his beam – well abeam – to read 'em. *That* didn't restore his morale either. He made out he'd been compelled to put back by stress of weather before completing his oil tests. I made back I was sorry to hear it, but would be greatly interested in the results. Then I turned in (I'd been up all night) and my lootenant took on. He was a widower (by the way) of the name of Sherrin, aged forty-seven. He'd run a girls' school at Weston-super-Mare after he'd left the Service in 'ninety-five, and he believed the English were the Lost Tribes.'

'What about the Germans?' said Portson.

'Oh, they'd been misled by Austria, who was the Beast with Horns in Revelations. Otherwise he was rather a dull dog. He set the tops'ls in his watch. *Hilarity* won't steer under any canvas, so we rather sported round our friend that afternoon, I believe. When I came up after dinner, she was biting his behind, first one side, then the other. Let's see – that would be about thirty miles east-sou-east of Harry Island. We were running as near as nothing south. The wind had dropped, and there was a useful cross-rip coming up from the south-east. I took the wheel and, the way I nursed him from starboard, he had to take the sea over his port bow. I had my sciatica on me – buccaneering's no game for a middle-aged man – but I gave that fellow sprudel![10] By Jove; I washed him out! He stood it as long as he could, and then he made a bolt for Harry Island. I had to ride in his pocket most of the way there because I didn't know that coast. We had charts, but Sherrin never understood 'em, and I couldn't leave the wheel. So we rubbed along together, and about midnight this Newt dodged in over the tail of Harry Shoals and anchored, if you please, in the lee of the Double Ricks. It was dead calm there, except for the swell, but there wasn't much room to manoeuvre in, and *I* wasn't going to anchor. It looked too like a submarine rendezvous. But first, I came alongside and asked him what his trouble was. He told me he had overheated his something-or-other bulb. I've never been shipmates with Diesel engines, but I took his word for it, and I said I 'ud stand by till it cooled. Then he told me to go to hell.'

'If you were inside the Double Ricks in the dark, you were practically there,' said Portson.

'That's what *I* thought. I was on the bridge, rabid with sciatica, going round and round like a circus-horse in about three acres of water, and wondering when I'd hit something. Ridiculous position. Sherrin saw it. He saved me. He said it was an ideal place for submarine attacks, and we'd better begin to repel 'em at once. As I said, I couldn't leave the wheel, so Sherrin fought the ship – both quick-firers and the maxims. He tipped 'em well down into the sea or well up at the Ricks as we went round and round. We made rather a row; and the row the gulls made when we woke 'em was absolutely terrifying. 'Give you my word!'

'And then?' said Winchmore.

'I kept on running in circles through this ghastly din. I took one sheer over toward his stern – I thought I'd cut it too fine, but we missed it by inches. Then I heard his capstan busy, and in another three minutes his anchor was up. He didn't wait to stow. He hustled out as he was – bulb or no bulb. He passed within ten feet of us (I was waiting to fall in behind him) and he shouted over the rail: "You think you've got patriotism. All you've got is uric acid and rotten spite!" I expect he was a little bored. I waited till we had cleared Harry Shoals before I went below, and then I slept till 9 a.m. He was heading north this time, and after I'd had breakfast and a smoke I ran alongside and asked him where he was bound for now. He was wrapped in a comforter, evidently suffering from a bad cold. I couldn't quite catch what he said, but I let him croak for a few minutes and fell back. At 9 p.m. he turned round and headed south (I was getting to know the Irish Channel by then) and I followed. There was no particular sea on. It was a little chilly, but as he didn't hug the coast I hadn't to take the wheel. I stayed below most of the night and let Sherrin suffer. Well, Mr Newt kept up this game all the next day, dodging up and down the Irish Channel. And it was infernally dull. He threw up the sponge off Cloone Harbour. That was on Friday morning. He signalled: "Developed defects in engine-room. Antigua trip abandoned." Then he ran into Cloone and tied up at Brady's Wharf. You know you can't repair a dinghy at Cloone! I followed, of course, and berthed behind him. After lunch I thought I'd pay him a call. I wanted to look at his engines. I don't understand Diesels, but Hyslop, my engineer, said they must have gone round 'em with a hammer, for they were pretty badly smashed up. Besides that, they had offered all their oil to the Admiralty agent there, and it was being shifted to a tug when I went aboard him. So I'd done my job. I was just going back to *Hilarity* when his steward said he'd like to see me. He was lying in his cabin breathing pretty loud – wrapped up in rugs and his eyes sticking out like a rabbit's. He offered me drinks. I couldn't accept 'em, of course. Then he said: "Well, Mr Maddingham, I'm all in." I said I was glad to hear it. Then he told me he was seriously ill with a sudden attack of bronchial pneumonia, and he asked me to run him across to England to see his doctor in town. I said, of course, that was out of the question, *Hilarity* being a man-of-war in commission. He couldn't see it. He asked what had that to do with it? He thought this war was some sort of joke, and I had to repeat it all over again. He seemed rather afraid of dying (it's no game for a middle-aged man, of course) and he hoisted himself up on one elbow and began calling me a murderer. I explained to him – perfectly politely – that I wasn't in this job for fun. It was business. My orders were to see that he went to Antigua, and now that he wasn't going to Antigua, and had sold his oil to us, that finished it as far as I was concerned. (Wasn't that perfectly correct?) He said: "But that finishes me, too. I can't get any doctor in this God-forsaken hole. I made sure you'd treat me properly as soon as I surrendered." I said there wasn't any question of surrender. If he'd been a wounded belligerent, I might have taken him aboard, though I certainly shouldn't have gone a yard out of my course to land him anywhere; but as it was, he was a neutral – altogether outside the game. You see my point? I tried awfully hard to make him understand it. He went on about his affairs all being at loose ends. He was a rich man – a million and a quarter, he said – and he wanted to redraft his will before he died. I told him a good many people were in his position just now – only they weren't rich. He changed his tack then and appealed to me on the grounds of our common humanity. "Why, if you leave me now, Mr Maddingham," he said, "you condemn me to death, just as surely as if you hanged me."'

'This *is* interesting,' Portson murmured. 'I never imagined you in this light before, Maddingham.'

'I was surprised at myself – 'give you my word.[11] But I was perfectly polite. I said to him: "Try to be reasonable, sir. If you had got rid of your oil where it was wanted, you'd have condemned lots of people to death just as surely as if you'd drowned 'em." "Ah, but I didn't," he said. "That ought to count in my favour." "That was no thanks to you," I said. "You weren't given the chance. This is war, sir. If you make up your mind to that, you'll see that the rest follows." "I didn't imagine you'd take it as seriously as all that," he said – and he said it quite seriously, too. "Show a little consideration. Your side's bound to win anyway." I said: "Look here! I'm a middle-aged man, and I don't suppose my conscience is any clearer than yours in many respects, but this is business. I can do nothing for you."'

'You got that a bit mixed, I think,' said Tegg critically.

'*He* saw what I was driving at,' Maddingham replied, 'and he was the only one that mattered for the moment. "Then I'm a dead man, Mr Maddingham," he said. "That's *your* business," I said. "Good afternoon." And I went out.'

'And?' said Winchmore, after some silence.

'He died. I saw his flag half-masted next morning.'

There was another silence. Henri looked in at the alcove and smiled. Maddingham beckoned to him.

'But why didn't you lend him a hand to settle his private affairs?' said Portson.

'Because I wasn't acting in my private capacity. I'd been on the bridge for three nights and –' Maddingham pulled out his watch – 'this time tomorrow I shall be there again – confound it! Has my car come, Henri?'

'Yes, Sare Francis. I am sorry.' They all complimented Henri on the dinner, and when the compliments were paid he expressed himself still their debtor. So did the nephew.

'Are you coming with me, Portson?' said Maddingham as he rose heavily.

'No. I'm for Southampton, worse luck! My car ought to be here, too.'

'I'm for Euston and the frigid calculating North,' said Winchmore with a shudder. 'One common taxi, please, Henri.'

Tegg smiled. 'I'm supposed to sleep in just now, but if you don't mind, I'd like to come with you as far as Gravesend, Maddingham.'

'Delighted. There's a glass all round left still,' said Maddingham. 'Here's luck! The usual, I suppose? "Damnation to all neutrals!"'

The Vineyard

At the eleventh hour he came,[12]
But his wages were the same
As ours who all day long had trod
The wine-press of the Wrath of God.

When he shouldered through the lines
Of our cropped and mangled vines,
His unjaded eye could scan
How each hour had marked its man.

(Children of the morning-tide
With the hosts of noon had died;
And our noon contingents lay
Dead with twilight's spent array.)

Since his back had felt no load
Virtue still in him abode;
So he swiftly made his own
Those last spoils we had not won.

We went home, delivered thence,
Grudging him no recompense
Till he portioned praise or blame
To our works before he came.

Till he showed us for our good —
  Deaf to mirth, and blind to scorn —
How we might have best withstood
  Burdens that he had not borne!

'In the Interests of the Brethren'

'Banquet Night'

'Once in so often,' King Solomon said,
  Watching his quarrymen drill the stone,[1]
'We will club our garlic and wine and bread
  And banquet together beneath my Throne.
And all the Brethren shall come to that mess
As Fellow-Craftsmen – no more and no less.

'Send a swift shallop to Hiram of Tyre,
  Felling and floating[2] our beautiful trees,
Say that the Brethren and I desire
  Talk with our Brethren who use the seas.
And we shall be happy to meet them at mess
As Fellow-Craftsmen – no more and no less.

'Carry this message to Hiram Abif –
  Excellent Master of forge and mine:
I and the Brethren would like it if
  He and the Brethren will come to dine
(Garments from Bozrah[3] or morning-dress)
As Fellow-Craftsmen – no more and no less.

'God gave the Hyssop and Cedar[4] their place
  Also the Bramble, the Fig and the Thorn   [5]
But that is no reason to black a man's face
  Because he is not what he hasn't been born.
And, as touching the Temple, I hold and profess
We are Fellow-Craftsmen – no more and no less.'

So it was ordered and so it was done,
  And the hewers of wood and the Masons of Mark,
With foc'sle hands of the Sidon run
  And Navy Lords from the *Royal Ark*,

63

Came and sat down and were merry at mess
As Fellow-Craftsmen – no more and no less.

The Quarries are hotter than Hiram's forge,
*   No one is safe from the dog-whips' reach.*
It's mostly snowing up Lebanon gorge,
*   And it's always blowing off Joppa beach;* [6]
But once in so often, the messenger brings
Solomon's mandate: 'Forget these things!
Brother to Beggars and Fellow to Kings,
Companion of Princes – forget these things!
Fellow-Craftsman, forget these things!'

'In the Interests of the Brethren'

I was buying a canary in a birdshop when he first spoke to me and suggested that I should take a less highly coloured bird. 'The colour is in the feeding,' said he. 'Unless you know how to feed 'em, it goes. Canaries are one of our hobbies.'

He passed out before I could thank him. He was a middle-aged man with grey hair and a short, dark beard, rather like a Sealyham terrier in silver spectacles. For some reason his face and his voice stayed in my mind so distinctly that, months later, when I jostled against him on a platform crowded with an Angling Club going to the Thames, I recognized, turned, and nodded.

'I took your advice about the canary,' I said.

'Did you? Good!' he replied heartily over the rod-case on his shoulder, and was parted from me by the crowd.

A few years ago I turned into a tobacconist's to have a badly stopped pipe cleaned out.

'Well! Well! And how did the canary do?' said the man behind the counter. We shook hands,[7] and 'What's your name?' we both asked together.

His name was Lewis Holroyd Burges, of 'Burges and Son', as I might have seen above the door – but Son had been killed in Egypt. His hair was whiter than it had been, and the eyes were sunk a little.

'Well! Well! To think,' said he, 'of one man in all these millions turning up in this curious way, when there's so many who don't turn up at all – eh?' (It was then that he told me of Son Lewis's death and why the boy had been christened Lewis.) 'Yes. There's not much left for middle-aged people just at present. Even one's hobbies – We used to fish together. And the same with canaries! We used to breed 'em for colour – deep orange was our speciality. That's why I spoke to you, if you remember; but I've sold all my birds. Well! Well! And now we must locate your trouble.'

He bent over my erring pipe and dealt with it skilfully as a surgeon. A soldier came in, spoke in an undertone, received a reply, and went out.

'Many of my clients are soldiers nowadays, and a number of 'em belong to the Craft,' said Mr Burges. 'It breaks my heart to give them the tobaccos they ask for. On the other hand, not one man in five thousand has a tobacco-palate. Preference, yes. Palate, no. Here's your pipe, again. It deserves better treatment than it's had. There's a procedure, a ritual, in all things. Any time you're passing by again, I assure you, you will be welcome. I've one or two odds and ends that may interest you.'

I left the shop with the rarest of all feelings on me – the sensation which is only youth's right – that I might have made a friend. A little distance from the door I was accosted by a wounded man who asked for 'Burges's'. The place seemed to be known in the neighbourhood.

I found my way to it again, and often after that, but it was not till my third visit that I discovered Mr Burges held a half interest in Ackerman and Pernit's, the great cigar-importers, which had come to him through an uncle whose children now lived almost in the Cromwell Road, and said that the uncle had been on the Stock Exchange.

'*I*'m a shopkeeper by instinct,' said Mr Burges. 'I like the ritual of handling things. The shop has done me well. I like to do well by the shop.'

It had been established by his grandfather in 1827, but the fittings and appointments must have been at least half a century older. The brown and red tobacco- and snuff-jars, with Crowns, Garters, and names of forgotten mixtures in gold leaf; the polished 'Oronoque' tobacco-barrels on which favoured customers sat; the cherry-black mahogany counter, the delicately moulded shelves, the reeded cigar-cabinets, the German-silver-mounted scales, and the Dutch brass roll and cake-cutter, were things to covet.

'They aren't so bad,' he admitted. 'That large Bristol jar hasn't any duplicate to my knowledge. Those eight snuff-jars

on the third shelf – they're Dollin's ware; he used to work for
Wimble in Seventeen-Forty – are absolutely unique. Is there
anyone in the trade now could tell you what "Romano's Hol-
lande" was? Or "Scholten's"? Here's a snuff-mull of George
the First's time; and here's a Louis Quinze – what am I talking
of? Treize, Treize,[8] of course – grater for making bran-snuff.
They were regular tools of the shop in my grandfather's day.
And who on earth to leave 'em to outside the British Museum
now, *I* can't think!'

His pipes – I would this were a tale for virtuosi – his amazing
collection of pipes was kept in the parlour, and this gave me the
privilege of making his wife's acquaintance. One morning, as I
was looking covetously at a jacaranda-wood 'cigarro' – *not* cigar
– cabinet with silver lock-plates and drawer-knobs of Spanish
work, a wounded Canadian came into the shop and disturbed
our happy little committee.

'Say,' he began loudly, 'are you the right place?'

'Who sent you?' Mr Burges demanded.

'A man from Messines.[9] But *that* ain't the point! I've got no
certificates, nor papers – nothin', you understand. I left my
Lodge owin' 'em seventeen dollars back-dues. But this man at
Messines told me it wouldn't make any odds with *you*.'

'It doesn't,' said Mr Burges. 'We meet tonight at 7 p.m.'

The man's face fell a yard. 'Hell!' said he. 'But I'm in
hospital – I can't get leaf.'

'*And* Tuesdays and Fridays at 3 p.m.,' Mr Burges added
promptly. 'You'll have to be proved, of course.'

'Guess I can get by *that* all right,' was the cheery reply.
'Toosday, then.' He limped off, beaming.

'Who might that be?' I asked.

'I don't know any more than you do – except he must be a
Brother. London's full of Masons now. Well! Well! We must
do what we can these days. If you'll come to tea this evening,
I'll take you on to Lodge afterwards. It's a Lodge of Instruction.'

'Delighted. Which is your Lodge?' I said, for up till then he
had not given me its name.

'"Faith and Works 5837"[10] – the third Saturday of every

month. Our Lodge of Instruction meets nominally every Thursday, but we sit oftener than that now because there are so many Visiting Brothers in town.' Here another customer entered, and I went away much interested in the range of Brother Burges's hobbies.

At tea-time he was dressed as for Church, and wore gold pince-nez in lieu of the silver spectacles. I blessed my stars that I had thought to change into decent clothes.

'Yes, we owe that much to the Craft,' he assented. 'All Ritual is fortifying. Ritual's a natural necessity for mankind. The more things are upset, the more they fly to it.[11] I abhor slovenly Ritual anywhere. By the way, would you mind assisting at the examinations, if there are many Visiting Brothers tonight? You'll find some of 'em very rusty but – it's the Spirit, not the Letter, that giveth life.[12] The question of Visiting Brethren is an important one. There are so many of them in London now, you see; and so few places where they can meet.'

'You dear thing!' said Mrs Burges, and handed him his locked and initialed apron-case.

'Our Lodge is only just round the corner,' he went on. 'You mustn't be too critical of our appurtenances. The place was a garage once.'

As far as I could make out in the humiliating darkness, we wandered up a mews and into a courtyard. Mr Burges piloted me, murmuring apologies for everything in advance.

'You mustn't expect –' he was still saying when we stumbled up a porch and entered a carefully decorated ante-room hung round with Masonic prints. I noticed Peter Gilkes and Barton Wilson, fathers of 'Emulation' working, in the place of honour; Kneller's Christopher Wren; Dunkerley, with his own Fitz-George book-plate below and the bend sinister on the Royal Arms; Hogarth's caricature of Wilkes, also his disreputable 'Night'; and a beautifully framed set of Grand Masters, from Anthony Sayer down.

'Are these another hobby of yours?' I asked.

'Not this time,' Mr Burges smiled. 'We have to thank Brother Lemming for them.' He introduced me to the senior partner of Lemming and Orton, whose little shop is hard to find, but whose words and cheques in the matter of prints are widely circulated.

'The frames are the best part of 'em,' said Brother Lemming after my compliments. 'There are some more in the Lodge Room. Come and look. We've got the big Desaguliers there that nearly went to Iowa.'[13]

I had never seen a Lodge Room better fitted. From mosaicked floor to appropriate ceiling, from curtain to pillar, implements to seats, seats to lights, and little carved music-loft at one end, every detail was perfect in particular kind and general design. I said what I thought of them all, many times over.

'I told you I was a Ritualist,' said Mr Burges. 'Look at those carved corn-sheaves and grapes on the back of these Wardens' chairs. That's the old tradition – before Masonic furnishers spoilt it. I picked up that pair in Stepney ten years ago – the same time I got the gavel.' It was of ancient, yellowed ivory, cut all in one piece out of some tremendous tusk. 'That came from the Gold Coast,' he said. 'It belonged to a Military Lodge there in 1794. You can see the inscription.'

'If it's a fair question,' I began, 'how much –'

'It stood us,' said Brother Lemming, his thumbs in his waistcoat pockets, 'an appreciable sum of money when we built it in 1906, even with what Brother Anstruther – he was our contractor – cheated himself out of. By the way, that ashlar[14] there is pure Carrara, he tells me. I don't understand marbles myself. Since then I expect we've put in – oh, quite another little sum. Now we'll go to the examination-room and take on the Brethren.'

He led me back, not to the ante-room, but a convenient chamber flanked with what looked like confessional-boxes (I found out later that that was what they had been, when first picked up for a song near Oswestry). A few men in uniform were waiting at the far end. 'That's only the head of the procession. The rest are in the ante-room,' said an officer of the Lodge.

Brother Burges assigned me my discreet box, saying: 'Don't be surprised. They come all shapes.'

'Shapes' was not a bad description, for my first penitent was

all head-bandages – escaped from an Officers' Hospital, Pen-
tonville way. He asked me in profane Scots how I expected a
man with only six teeth and half a lower lip to speak to any
purpose, so we compromised on the signs. The next – a New
Zealander from Taranaki – reversed the process, for he was
one-armed, and that in a sling. I mistrusted an enormous Sergeant-Major of Heavy Artillery, who struck me as much too
glib, so I sent him on to Brother Lemming in the next box, who
discovered he was a Past District Grand Officer. My last man
nearly broke me down altogether. Everything seemed to have
gone from him.

'I don't blame yer,' he gulped at last. 'I wouldn't pass my
own self on my answers, but I give yer my word that so far as
I've had any religion, it's been all the religion I've had. For
God's sake, let me sit in Lodge again, Brother!'

When the examinations were ended, a Lodge Officer came
round with our aprons – no tinsel or silver-gilt confections, but
heavily-corded silk with tassels and – where a man could prove
he was entitled to them – levels, of decent plate. Someone in
front of me tightened a belt on a stiffly silent person in civil
clothes with discharge-badge. ''Strewth! This is comfort again,'
I heard him say. The companion nodded. The man went on
suddenly: 'Here! What're you doing? Leave off! You promised
not to! Chuck it!' and dabbed at his companion's streaming
eyes.

'Let him leak,' said an Australian signaller. 'Can't you see
how happy the beggar is?'

It appeared that the silent Brother was a 'shell-shocker' whom
Brother Lemming had passed, on the guarantee of his friend
and – what moved Lemming more – the threat that, were he
refused, he would have fits from pure disappointment. So the
'shocker' went happily and silently among Brethren evidently
accustomed to these displays.

We fell in, two by two, according to tradition, fifty of us at
least, and were played into Lodge by what I thought was an
harmonium, but which I discovered to be an organ of repute. It
took time to settle us down, for ten or twelve were cripples and
had to be helped into long or easy chairs. I sat between a one-

footed R. A. M. C. Corporal and a Captain of Territorials, who, he told me, had 'had a brawl' with a bomb, which had bent him in two directions. 'But that's first-class Bach the organist is giving us now,' he said delightedly. 'I'd like to know him. *I* used to be a piano-thumper of sorts.'

'I'll introduce you after Lodge,' said one of the regular Brethren behind us – a plump, torpedo-bearded man, who turned out to be a doctor. 'After all, there's nobody to touch Bach, is there?' Those two plunged at once into musical talk, which to outsiders is as fascinating as trigonometry.

Now a Lodge of Instruction is mainly a parade-ground for Ritual. It cannot initiate or confer degrees, but is limited to rehearsals and lectures. Worshipful Brother Burges, resplendent in Solomon's Chair (I found out later where that, too, had been picked up), briefly told the Visiting Brethren how welcome they were and always would be, and asked them to vote what ceremony should be rendered for their instruction.

When the decision was announced he wanted to know whether any Visiting Brothers would take the duties of Lodge Officers. They protested bashfully that they were too rusty. 'The very reason why,' said Brother Burges, while the organ Bached softly. My musical Captain wriggled in his chair.

'One moment, Worshipful Sir.' The plump Doctor rose. 'We have here a musician for whom place and opportunity are needed. Only,' he went on colloquially, 'those organ-loft steps are a bit steep.'

'How much,' said Brother Burges with the solemnity of an initiation, 'does our Brother weigh?'

'Very little over eight stone,' said the Brother. 'Weighed this morning, Worshipful Sir.'

The Past District Grand Officer, who was also a Battery-Sergeant-Major, waddled across, lifted the slight weight in his arms and bore it to the loft, where, the regular organist pumping, it played joyously as a soul caught up to Heaven by surprise.

When the visitors had been coaxed to supply the necessary officers, a ceremony was rehearsed. Brother Burges forbade the regular members to prompt. The visitors had to work entirely by themselves, but, on the Battery-Sergeant-Major taking a hand, he was ruled out as of too exalted rank. They floundered badly after that support was withdrawn.

The one-footed R.A.M.C. on my right chuckled.

'D'you like it?' said the Doctor to him.

'*Do* I? It's Heaven to me, sittin' in Lodge again. It's all comin' back now, watching their mistakes. I haven't much religion, but all I had I learnt in Lodge.' Recognizing me, he flushed a little as one does when one says a thing twice over in another's hearing. 'Yes, "veiled in all'gory and illustrated in symbols" – the Fatherhood of God, an' the Brotherhood of Man; an' what more in Hell *do* you want? . . . Look at 'em!' He broke off giggling. 'See! See! They've tied the whole thing into knots. *I* could ha' done it better myself – my one foot in France. Yes, I should think they *ought* to do it again!'

The new organist covered the little confusion that had arisen with what sounded like the wings of angels.

When the amateurs, rather red and hot, had finished, they demanded an exhibition-working of their bungled ceremony by Regular Brethren of the Lodge. Then I realized for the first time what word-and-gesture-perfect Ritual can be brought to mean. We all applauded, the one-footed Corporal most of all.

'We *are* rather proud of our working, and this is an audience worth playing up to,' the Doctor said.

Next the Master delivered a little lecture on the meanings of some pictured symbols and diagrams. His theme was a well-worn one, but his deep holding voice made it fresh.

'Marvellous how these old copybook-headings persist,' the Doctor said.

'*That's* all right!' the one-footed man spoke cautiously out of the side of his mouth like a boy in form. 'But they're the kind o' copybook-headin's we shall find burnin' round our bunks in Hell. Believe me-ee! I've broke enough of 'em to know. Now, h'sh!' He leaned forward, drinking it all in.

Presently Brother Burges touched on a point which had given rise to some diversity of Ritual. He asked for information. 'Well, in Jamaica, Worshipful Sir,' a Visiting Brother began, and explained how they worked that detail in his parts. Another and another joined in from different quarters of the Lodge (and the world), and when they were well warmed the Doctor sidled softly round the walls and, over our shoulders, passed us cigarettes.

'A shocking innovation,' he said, as he returned to the Captain-musician's vacant seat on my left. 'But men can't really talk without tobacco, and we're only a Lodge of Instruction.'

'An' I've learned more in one evenin' here than ten years.' The one-footed man turned round for an instant from a dark, sour-looking Yeoman in spurs who was laying down the law on Dutch Ritual. The blue haze and the talk increased, while the organ from the loft blessed us all.

'But this is delightful,' said I to the Doctor. 'How did it all happen?'

'Brother Burges started it. He used to talk to the men who dropped into his shop when the war began. He told us sleepy old chaps in Lodge that what men wanted more than anything else was Lodges where they could sit – just sit and be happy like we are now. He was right too. We're learning things in the war. A man's Lodge means more to him than people imagine. As our friend on your right said just now, very often Masonry's the only practical creed we've ever listened to since we were children.[15] Platitudes or no platitudes, it squares with what everybody knows ought to be done.' He sighed. 'And if this war hasn't brought home the Brotherhood of Man to us all, I'm – a Hun!'

'How did you get your visitors?' I went on.

'Oh, I told a few fellows in hospital near here, at Burges's suggestion, that we had a Lodge of Instruction and they'd be welcome. And they came. And they told their friends. And *they* came! That was two years ago – and now we've Lodge of Instruction two nights a week, and a matinée nearly every Tuesday and Friday for the men who can't get evening leave. Yes, it's all very curious. I'd no notion what the Craft meant – and means – till this war.'

'Nor I, till this evening,' I replied.

'Yet it's quite natural if you think. Here's London – all England – packed with the Craft from all over the world, and

nowhere for them to go. Why, our weekly visiting attendance
for the last four months averaged just under a hundred and
forty. Divide by four – call it thirty-five Visiting Brethren a
time. Our record's seventy-one, but we have packed in as many
as eighty-four at Banquets. You can see for yourself what a
potty little hole we are!'

'Banquets too!' I cried. 'It must cost like anything. May the
Visiting Brethren –'

The Doctor – his name was Keede – laughed. 'No, a Visiting
Brother may *not*.'

'But when a man has had an evening like this, he wants to –'

'That's what they all say. That makes our difficulty. They
do exactly what you were going to suggest, and they're offended
if we don't take it.'

'Don't you?' I asked.

'My dear man – what *does* it come to? They can't all stay to
Banquet. Say one hundred suppers a week – fifteen quid – sixty a
month – seven hundred and twenty a year. How much are
Lemming and Orton worth? And Ellis and McKnight – that long
big man over yonder – the provision dealers? How much d'you
suppose could Burges write a cheque for and not feel? 'Tisn't as
if he had to save for anyone now. I assure you we have no scruple
in calling on the Visiting Brethren when we want anything. We
couldn't do the work otherwise. Have you noticed how the Lodge
is kept – brass-work, jewels, furniture, and so on?'

'I have indeed,' I said. 'It's like a ship. You could eat your
dinner off the floor.'

'Well, come here on a bye-day and you'll often find half-a-
dozen Brethren, with eight legs between 'em, polishing and
ronuking and sweeping everything they can get at. I cured a
shell-shocker this spring by giving him our jewels to look after.
He pretty well polished the numbers off 'em, but – it kept him
from fighting Huns in his sleep. And when we need Masters to
take our duties – two matinées a week is rather a tax – we've the
choice of P.M.'s from all over the world. The Dominions are
much keener on Ritual than an average English Lodge. Besides
that – Oh, we're going to adjourn. Listen to the greetings.
They'll be interesting.'

The crack of the great gavel brought us to our feet, after some surging and plunging among the cripples. Then the Battery-Sergeant-Major, in a trained voice, delivered hearty and fraternal greetings to 'Faith and Works' from his tropical District and Lodge. The others followed, without order, in every tone between a grunt and a squeak. I heard 'Hauraki', 'Inyanga-Umbezi', 'Aloha', 'Southern Lights' (from somewhere Punta Arenas way), 'Lodge of Rough Ashlars' (and that Newfoundland Naval Brother looked it), two or three Stars of something or other, half-a-dozen cardinal virtues, variously arranged, hailing from Klondyke to Kalgoorlie, one Military Lodge on one of the fronts, thrown in with a severe Scots burr by my friend of the head-bandages, and the rest as mixed as the Empire itself. Just at the end there was a little stir. The silent Brother had begun to make noises; his companion tried to soothe him.

'Let him be! Let him be!' the Doctor called professionally. The man jerked and mouthed, and at last mumbled something unintelligible even to his friend, but a small dark P.M. pushed forward importantly.

'It iss all right,' he said. 'He wants to say –' he spat out some yard-long Welsh name, adding, 'That means Pembroke Docks, Worshipful Sir. We haf good Masons in Wales, too.' The silent man nodded approval.

'Yes,' said the Doctor, quite unmoved. 'It happens that way sometimes. *Hespere panta fereis*,[16] isn't it? The Star brings 'em all home. I must get a note of that fellow's case after Lodge. I saw you didn't care for music,' he went on, 'but I'm afraid you'll have to put up with a little more. It's a paraphrase from Micah.[17] Our organist arranged it. We sing it antiphonally, as a sort of dismissal.'

Even I could appreciate what followed. The singing seemed confined to half-a-dozen trained voices answering each other till the last line, when the full Lodge came in. I give it as I heard it:

> 'We have showèd thee, O Man,
>   What is good.
> What doth the Lord require of us?

Or Conscience' self desire of us?
    But to do justly –
    But to love mercy,
   And to walk humbly with our God,
    As every Mason should.'

Then we were played and sung out to the quaint tune of the 'Entered Apprentices' Song'.[18] I noticed that the regular Brethren of the Lodge did not begin to take off their regalia till the lines:

    'Great Kings, Dukes, and Lords
    Have laid down their swords.'

They moved into the ante-room, now set for the Banquet, on the verse:

    'Antiquity's pride
    We have on our side,
    Which maketh men just in their station.'

The Brother (a big-boned clergyman) that I found myself next to at table told me the custom was 'a fond thing vainly invented' on the strength of some old legend. He laid down that Masonry should be regarded as an 'intellectual abstraction'. An Officer of Engineers disagreed with him, and told us how in Flanders, a year before, some ten or twelve Brethren held Lodge in what was left of a Church. Save for the Emblems of Mortality and plenty of rough ashlars, there was no furniture.

'I warrant you weren't a bit the worse for that,' said the Clergyman. 'The idea should be enough without trappings.'

'But it wasn't,' said the other. 'We took a lot of trouble to make our regalia out of camouflage-stuff that we'd pinched, and we manufactured our jewels from old metal. I've got the set now. It kept us happy for weeks.'

'Ye were absolutely irregular an' unauthorized. Whaur was your Warrant?' said the Brother from the Military Lodge. 'Grand Lodge ought to take steps against –'

'If Grand Lodge had any sense,' a private three places up

76

our table broke in, 'it 'ud warrant travelling Lodges at the front and attach first-class lecturers to 'em.'

'Wad ye confer degrees promiscuously?' said the scandalized Scot.

'Every time a man asked, of course. You'd have half the Army in.'

The speaker played with the idea for a little while, and proved that, on the lowest scale of fees, Grand Lodge would get huge revenues.

'I believe,' said the Engineer Officer thoughtfully, 'I could design a complete travelling Lodge outfit under forty pounds weight.'

'Ye're wrong. I'll prove it. We've tried ourselves,' said the Military Lodge man; and they went at it together across the table, each with his own note-book.

The 'Banquet' was simplicity itself. Many of us ate in haste so as to get back to barracks or hospitals, but now and again a Brother came in from the outer darkness to fill a chair and empty a plate. These were Brethren who had been there before and needed no examination.

One man lurched in – helmet, Flanders mud, accoutrements and all – fresh from the leave-train.

''Got two hours to wait for my train,' he explained. 'I remembered your night, though. My God, this *is* good!'

'What is your train and from what station?' said the Clergyman precisely. 'Very well. What will you have to eat?'

'Anything. Everything. I've thrown up a month's rations in the Channel.'

He stoked himself for ten minutes without a word. Then, without a word, his face fell forward. The Clergyman had him by one already limp arm and steered him to a couch, where he dropped and snored. No one took the trouble to turn round.

'Is that usual too?' I asked.

'Why not?' said the Clergyman. 'I'm on duty tonight to wake them for their trains. They do not respect the Cloth on those occasions.' He turned his broad back on me and continued his discussion with a Brother from Aberdeen by way of Mitylene where, in the intervals of mine-sweeping, he had evolved a complete theory of the Revelations of St John [19] the Divine in the Island of Patmos.

I fell into the hands of a Sergeant-Instructor of Machine Guns – by profession a designer of ladies' dresses. He told me that Englishwomen as a class 'lose on their corsets what they make on their clothes', and that 'Satan himself can't save a woman who wears thirty-shilling corsets under a thirty-guinea costume.' Here, to my grief, he was buttonholed by a zealous Lieutenant of his own branch, and became a Sergeant again all in one click.

I drifted back and forth, studying the prints on the walls and the Masonic collection in the cases, while I listened to the inconceivable talk all round me. Little by little the company thinned, till at last there were only a dozen or so of us left. We gathered at the end of a table near the fire, the night-bird from Flanders trumpeting lustily into the hollow of his helmet, which someone had tipped over his face.

'And how did it go with you?' said the Doctor.

'It was like a new world,' I answered.

'That's what it *is* really.' Brother Burges returned the gold pince-nez to their case and reshipped his silver spectacles. 'Or that's what it might be made with a little trouble. When I think of the possibilities of the Craft at this juncture I wonder –' He stared into the fire.

'I wonder, too,' said the Sergeant-Major slowly, 'but – on the whole – I'm inclined to agree with you. We could do much with Masonry.'

'As an aid – as an aid – not as a substitute for Religion,' the Clergyman snapped.

'Oh, Lord! Can't we give Religion a rest for a bit?' the Doctor muttered. 'It hasn't done so – I beg your pardon all round.'

The Clergyman was bristling. 'Kamerad!' the wise Sergeant-Major went on, both hands up. 'Certainly not as a substitute for a creed, but as an average plan of life. What I've seen at the front makes me sure of it.'

Brother Burges came out of his muse. 'There ought to be a dozen – twenty – other Lodges in London every night; conferring degrees too, as well as instruction. Why shouldn't the

78

young men join? They practise what we're always preaching.
Well! Well! We must all do what we can. What's the use of old
Masons if they can't give a little help along their own lines?'

'Exactly,' said the Sergeant-Major, turning on the Doctor.
'And what's the darn use of a Brother if he isn't allowed to
help?'

'Have it your own way then,' said the Doctor testily. He had
evidently been approached before. He took something the Sergeant-Major handed to him and pocketed it with a nod. 'I was
wrong,' he said to me, 'when I boasted of our independence.
They get round us sometimes. This,' he slapped his pocket,
'will give a banquet on Tuesday. We don't usually feed at
matinées. It will be a surprise. By the way, try another sandwich.
The ham are best.' He pushed me a plate.

'They are,' I said. 'I've only had five or six. I've been looking
for them.'

''Glad you like them,' said Brother Lemming. 'Fed him
myself, cured him myself — at my little place in Berkshire. His
name was Charlemagne. By the way, Doc, am I to keep another
one for next month?'

'Of course,' said the Doctor with his mouth full. 'A little
fitter than this chap, please. And don't forget your promise
about the pickled nasturtiums. They're appreciated.' Brother
Lemming nodded above the pipe he had lit as we began a
second supper. Suddenly the Clergyman, after a glance at the
clock, scooped up half-a-dozen sandwiches from under my nose,
put them into an oiled paper bag, and advanced cautiously
towards the sleeper on the couch.

'They wake rough sometimes,' said the Doctor. 'Nerves,
y'know.' The Clergyman tip-toed directly behind the man's
head, and at arm's length rapped on the dome of the helmet.
The man woke in one vivid streak, as the Clergyman stepped
back, and grabbed for a rifle that was not there.

'You've barely half an hour to catch your train.' The
Clergyman passed him the sandwiches. 'Come along.'

'You're uncommonly kind and I'm very grateful,' said the
man, wriggling into his stiff straps. He followed his guide into
the darkness after saluting.

'Who's that?' said Lemming.

''Can't say,' the Doctor returned indifferently. 'He's been here before. He's evidently a P.M. of sorts.'

'Well! Well!' said Brother Burges, whose eyelids were drooping. 'We must all do what we can. Isn't it almost time to lock up?'

'I wonder,' said I, as we helped each other into our coats, 'what would happen if Grand Lodge knew about all this.'

'About what?' Lemming turned on me quickly.

'A Lodge of Instruction open three nights and two afternoons a week – and running a lodging-house as well. It's all very nice, but it doesn't strike me somehow as regulation.'

'The point hasn't been raised yet,' said Lemming. 'We'll settle it after the war. Meantime we shall go on.'

'There ought to be scores of them,' Brother Burges repeated as we went out of the door. 'All London's full of the Craft, and no places for them to meet in. Think of the possibilities of it! Think what could have been done *by* Masonry *through* Masonry *for* all the world. I hope I'm not censorious, but it sometimes crosses my mind that Grand Lodge may have thrown away its chance in the war almost as much as the Church has.'

''Lucky for you the Padre is taking that chap to King's Cross,' said Brother Lemming, 'or he'd be down your throat. What really troubles him is our legal position under Masonic Law. I think he'll inform on us one of these days. Well, good night, all.' The Doctor and Lemming turned off together.

'Yes,' said Brother Burges, slipping his arm into mine. 'Almost as much as the Church has. But perhaps I'm too much of a Ritualist.'

I said nothing. I was speculating how soon I could steal a march on the Clergyman and inform against 'Faith and Works No. 5837 E.C.'.

⦃ The United Idolaters ⦄

To the Companions
Horace, Ode 17, Bk V [1]

How comes it that, at even-tide,
  When level beams should show most truth,
Man, failing, takes unfailing pride
  In memories of his frolic youth?

Venus and Liber fill their hour;
  The games engage, the law-courts prove;
Till hardened life breeds love of power
  Or Avarice, Age's final love.

Yet at the end, these comfort not –
  Nor any triumph Fate decrees –
Compared with glorious, unforgot-
  ten innocent enormities

Of frontless days before the beard,
  When, instant on the casual jest,
The God Himself of Mirth appeared
  And snatched us to His heaving breast.

And we – not caring who He was
  But certain He would come again –
Accepted all He brought to pass
  As Gods accept the lives of men . . .

Then He withdrew from sight and speech,
  Nor left a shrine. How comes it now
While Charon's keel grates on the beach,
  He calls so clear: 'Rememberest thou?'

The United Idolaters

His name was Brownell and his reign was brief. He came from
the Central Anglican Scholastic Agency, a soured, clever, red-
dish man picked up by the Head at the very last moment of
the summer holidays in default of Macrea (of Macrea's House)
who wired from Switzerland that he had smashed a knee
mountaineering, and would not be available that term.

Looking back at the affair, one sees that the Head should
have warned Mr Brownell of the College's [2] outstanding peculiarity, instead of leaving him to discover it for himself the first
day of the term, when he went for a walk to the beach, and saw
'Potiphar' Mullins, Head of Games, smoking without conceal
on the sands. 'Pot', having the whole of the Autumn Football
challenges, acceptances, and Fifteen reconstructions to work
out, did not at first comprehend Mr Brownell's shrill cry of:
'You're smoking! You're smoking, sir!' but he removed his
pipe, and answered, placably enough: 'The Army Class is
allowed to smoke, sir.'

Mr Brownell replied: 'Preposterous!'

Pot, seeing that this new person was uninformed, suggested
that he should refer to the Head.

'You may be sure I shall – sure I shall, sir! Then we shall see!'

Mr Brownell and his umbrella scudded off, and Pot returned
to his match-plannings. Anon, he observed, much as the
Almighty might observe black-beetles, two small figures coming
over the Pebble-ridge a few hundred yards to his right. They
were a Major and his Minor, the latter a new boy and, as such,
entitled to his brother's countenance for exactly three days –
after which he would fend for himself. Pot waited till they
were well out on the great stretch of mother-o'-pearl sands;
then caused his ground-ash to describe a magnificent whirl of
command in the air.

'Come on,' said the Major. 'Run!'

'What for?' said the Minor, who had noticed nothing.

''Cause we're wanted. Leg it!'

'Oh, I can do *that*,' the Minor replied and, at the end of the sprint, fetched up a couple of yards ahead of his brother, and much less winded.

''Your Minor?' said Pot, looking over them, seawards.

'Yes, Mullins,' the Major replied.

'All right. Cut along!' They cut on the word.

'Hi! Fludd Major! Come back!'

Back fled the elder.

'Your wind's bad. Too fat. You grunt like a pig. 'Mustn't do it! Understand? Go away!'

'What was all that for?' the Minor asked on the Major's return.

'To see if we could run, you fool!'

'Well, I ran faster than you, anyhow,' was the scandalous retort.

'Look here, Har – Minor, if you go on talking like this, you'll get yourself kicked all round Coll. An' you mustn't stand like you did when a Prefect's talkin' to you.'

The Minor's eyes opened with awe. 'I thought it was only one of the masters,' said he.

'Masters! It was Mullins – Head o' Games. You *are* a putrid young ass!'

By what seemed pure chance, Mr Brownell ran into the School Chaplain, the Reverend John Gillett, beating up against the soft, September rain that no native ever troubled to wear a coat for.

'I was trying to catch you after lunch,' the latter began. 'I wanted to show you our objects of local interest.'

'Thank you! I've seen all *I* want,' Mr Brownell answered. 'Gillett, *is* there anything about me which suggests the Congenital Dupe?'

'It's early to say, yet,' the Chaplain answered. 'Who've you been meeting?'

'A youth called Mullins, I believe.' And, indeed, there was Potiphar, ground-ash, pipe, and all, quarter-decking serenely below the Pebble-ridge.

'Oh! I see. Old Pot – our Head of Games.'

'He was smoking. He's smoking *now*! Before those two little boys, too!' Mr Brownell panted. 'He had the audacity to tell me that –'

'Yes,' the Reverend John cut in. 'The Army Class is allowed to smoke – not in their studies, of course, but within limits, out of doors. You see we have to compete against the Crammers' establishments, where smoking's usual.'

This was true! Of the only school in England was this the cold truth, and for the reason given, in that unprogressive age.

'Good Heavens!' said Mr Brownell to the gulls and the gray sea. 'And I was never warned!'

'The Head *is* a little forgetful. *I* ought to have – But it's all right,' the Chaplain added soothingly. 'Pot won't – er – give you away.'

Mr Brownell, who knew what smoking led to, testified out of his twelve years' experience of what he called the Animal Boy. He left little unexplored or unexplained.

'There may be something in what you say,' the Reverend John assented. 'But as a matter of fact, their actual smoking doesn't amount to much. They talk a great deal about their brands of tobacco. Practically, it makes them rather keen on putting down smoking among the juniors – as an encroachment on their privilege, you see. They lick 'em twice as hard for it as *we'd* dare to.'

'Lick!' Mr Brownell cried. 'One expels! One expels! *I* know the end of these practices.' He told his companion, in detail, with anecdotes and inferences, a great deal more about the Animal Boy.

'Ah!' said the Reverend John to himself. 'You'll leave at the end of the term; but you'll have a deuce of a time first.' Aloud: 'We-ell, I suppose no one can be sure of any school's tendency at any given moment, but, personally, I should incline to believe that we're reasonably free from the – er – monastic microbes of – er – older institutions.'

'But a school's a school. You can't get out of *that*! It's preposterous! You must admit *that*,' Mr Brownell insisted.

They were within hail of Pot by now, and the Reverend John asked him how Affairs of State stood.

'All right, thank you, sir. How are you, sir?'

'Loungin' round and sufferin', my son. What about the dates of the Exeter and Tiverton matches?'

'As late in the term as we can get 'em, don't you think, sir?'

'Quite! Specially Blundell's. They're our dearest foe,' he explained to the frozen Mr Brownell. 'Aren't we rather light in the scrum just now, Mullins?'

''Fraid so, sir: but Packman's playin' forward this term.'

'*At* last!' cried the Reverend John. (Packman was Pot's second-in-command, who considered himself a heaven-born half-back, but Pot had been working on him diplomatically.) 'He'll be a pillar, at any rate. Lend me one of your fuzees, please. I've only got matches.'

Mr Brownell was unused to this sort of talk. 'A bad beginning to a bad business,' he muttered as they returned to College.

Pot finished out his meditations; from time to time rubbing up the gloss on his new seven-and-sixpenny silver-mounted, rather hot, myall-wood [3] pipe, with its very thin crust in the bowl.

As the Studies brought back brackets and pictures for their walls, so did they bring odds and ends of speech – theatre, opera, and music-hall gags – from the great holiday world; some of which stuck for a term, and others were discarded. Number Five was unpacking, when Dick Four (King's House) of the red nose and dramatic instincts, who with Pussy and Tertius [4] inhabited the study below, loafed up and asked them 'how their symptoms seemed to segashuate'. They said nothing at the time, for they knew Dick had a giddy uncle who took him to the Pavilion and the Cri, and all would be explained later. But, before they met again, Beetle came across two fags at war in a box-room, one of whom cried to the other: 'Turn me loose, or I'll knock the natal stuffin' out of you.' Beetle demanded why he, being offal, presumed to use this strange speech. The fag said it came out of a new book about rabbits and foxes and turtles and niggers, which was in his locker. (*Uncle Remus* [5] was a popular holiday gift-book in Shotover's year: when Cetewayo lived in the Melbury Road, Arabi Pasha in Egypt, and Spofforth on the Oval.) Beetle had it out and read for some time, standing by the window, ere he carried it off to Number Five and began at once to give a wonderful story of a Tar Baby. Stalky tore it from him because he sputtered incoherently; McTurk, for the same cause, wrenching it from Stalky. There was no prep that night. The book was amazing, and full of quotations that one could hurl like javelins. When they came down to prayers, Stalky, to show he was abreast of the latest movement, pounded on the door of Dick Four's study shouting a couplet that pleased him:

> 'Ti-yi! Tungalee!
> I eat um pea! I pick um pea!'

Upon which Dick Four, hornpiping and squinting, and not at all unlike a bull-frog, came out and answered from the bottom of his belly, whence he could produce incredible noises:

> 'Ingle-go-jang, my joy, my joy!
> Ingle-go-jang, my joy!
> *I'm* right at home, my joy, my joy! –'

The chants seemed to answer the ends of their being created for the moment. They all sang them the whole way up the corridor, and, after prayers, bore the burdens dispersedly to their several dormitories where they found many who knew the book of the words, but who, boylike, had waited for a lead ere giving tongue. In a short time the College was as severely infected with *Uncle Remus* as it had been with *Pinafore* and *Patience*. King realized it specially because he was running Macrea's House in addition to his own and, Dick Four said, was telling his new charges what he thought of his 'esteemed colleague's' methods of House-control.

The Reverend John was talking to the Head in the latter's study, perhaps a fortnight later.

'If you'd only wired *me*,' he said. 'I could have dug up something that might have tided us over. This man's dangerous.'

'*Mea culpa!*' the Head replied. 'I had so much on hand. Our Governing Council alone – But what do *We* make of him?'

'Trust Youth! *We* call him "Mister".'

'"Mister Brownell"?'

'Just "Mister". It took *Us* three days to plumb his soul.'

'And he doesn't approve of Our institutions? You say he is On the Track – eh? He suspects the worst?'

The School Chaplain nodded.

'We-ell. *I* should say that that was the one tendency we had *not* developed. Setting aside we haven't even a curtain in a dormitory, let alone a lock to any form-room door – there has to be tradition in these things.'

'So I believe. So, indeed, one knows. And – 'tisn't as if I ever preached on personal purity either.'

The Head laughed. 'No, or you'd join Brownell at term-end. By the way, what's this new line of Patristic discourse you're giving us in church? I found myself listening to some of it last Sunday.'

'Oh! My early Christianity sermons? I bought a dozen ready made in Town just before I came down. Someone who knows his Gibbon must have done 'em. Aren't they good?' The Reverend John, who was no hand at written work, beamed self-approvingly. There was a knock and Pot entered.

The weather had defeated him, at last. All footer-grounds, he reported, were unplayable, and must be rested. His idea, to keep things going, was Big and Little Side Paper-chases thrice a week. For the juniors, a shortish course on the Burrows, which he intended to oversee personally the first few times, while Packman lunged Big Side across the inland and upland ploughs, for proper sweats. There was some question of bounds that he asked authority to vary; and, would the Head please say which afternoons would interfere least with the Army Class, Extra Tuition.

As to bounds, the Head left those, as usual, entirely to Pot. The Reverend John volunteered to shift one of his extra-Tu classes from four to five p.m. till after prayers – nine to ten. The whole question was settled in five minutes.

'*We* hate paper-chases, don't we, Pot?' the Headmaster asked as the Head of Games rose.

'Yes, sir, but it keeps 'em in training. Good night, sir.'

'To go back –' drawled the Head when the door was well shut. 'No-o. I do *not* think so! . . . Ye-es! He'll leave at the end of the term ... A-aah! How does it go? "Don't 'spute wid de squinch-owl. Jam de shovel in de fier." Have you come across that extraordinary book, by the way?'

'Oh, yes. *We*'ve got it badly too. It has some sort of elemental appeal, I suppose.'

Here Mr King came in with a neat little scheme for the reorganization of certain details in Macrea's House, where he had detected reprehensible laxities. The Head sighed. The Reverend John only heard the beginnings of it. Then he slid out softly. He remembered he had not written to Macrea for quite a long time.

The first Big Side Paper-chase, in blinding wet, was as vile as even the groaning and bemired Beetle had prophesied. But Dick Four had managed to run his own line when it skirted Bideford, and turned up at the Lavatories half an hour late cherishing a movable tumour beneath his sweater.

'Ingle-go-jang!' he chanted, and slipped out a warm but coy land-tortoise.

'My Sacred Hat!' cried Stalky. 'Brer Terrapin! Where you catchee? What you makee-do *aveck*?'

This was Stalky's notion of how they talked in *Uncle Remus*; and he spake no other tongue for weeks.

'I don't know yet; but I had to get him. 'Man with a barrow full of 'em in Bridge Street. 'Gave me my choice for a bob. Leave him alone, you owl! He won't swim where you've been washing your filthy self! "*I*'m right at home, my joy, my joy."'

Dick's nose shone like Bardolph's as he bubbled in the bath.

Just before tea-time, he, 'Pussy', and Tertius broke in upon Number Five, processionally, singing:

> 'Ingle-go-jang, my joy, my joy!
> Ingle-go-jang, my joy!
> I'm right at home, my joy, my joy!
> Ingle-go-jang, my joy.'

Brer Terrapin, painted *or* and *sable* [6] – King's House-colours – swung by a neatly contrived belly-band from the end of a broken jumping-pole. They thought rather well of taking him in to tea. They called at one or two studies on the way, and were warmly welcomed; but when they reached the still shut doors of the dining-hall (Richards, ex-Petty Officer, R.N., was always unpunctual – but they needn't have called him 'Stinking Jim') the whole school shouted approval. After the meal, Brer Terrapin was borne the round of the form-rooms from Number One to Number Twelve, in an unbroken roar of homage.

'Tomorrow,' Dick Four announced, 'we'll sacrifice to him. Fags in blazin' paper-baskets!' and with thundering 'Ingle-go-jangs' the Idol retired to its shrine.

It had been a satisfactory performance. Little Hartopp, surprised labelling 'rocks' in Number Twelve, which held the Natural History Museum, had laughed consumedly; and the Reverend John, just before prep, complimented Dick that he had not a single dissenter to his following. In this respect the affair was an advance on Byzantium and Alexandria which, of course, were torn by rival sects led by militant Bishops or zealous heathen. *Vide*, (Beetle), *Hypatia*,[7] and (if Dick Four ever listened, instead of privily swotting up his Euclid, in Church) the Reverend John's own sermons. Mr King, who had heard the noise but had not appeared, made no comment till dinner, when he told the Common Room ceiling that he entertained the lowest opinion of Uncle Remus's buffoonery, but opined that it might interest certain types of intellect. Little Hartopp, School Librarian, who had, by special request, laid in an extra copy of the book, differed acridly. He had, he said, heard or overheard every salient line of *Uncle Remus* quoted, appositely too, by boys whom he would not have credited with intellectual interests. Mr King repeated that he was wearied by the senseless and childish repetitions of immature minds. He recalled the *Patience* epidemic. Mr Prout did not care for *Uncle Remus* – the dialect put him off – but he thought the Houses were getting a bit out of hand. There was nothing one could lay hold of, of course – 'As yet,' Mr Brownell interjected darkly. 'But this larking about in form-rooms,' he added, 'had potentialities which, if *he* knew anything of the Animal Boy, would develop – or had developed.'

'I shouldn't wonder,' said the Reverend John. 'This is the first time to my knowledge that Stalky has ever played second-fiddle to any one. Brer Terrapin was entirely Dick Four's notion. By the way, he was painted *your* House-colours, King.'

'Was he?' said King artlessly. 'I have always held that our Dickson Quartus had the rudiments of imagination. We will look into it – look into it.'

'In our loathsome calling, more things are done by judicious letting alone than by any other,' the Reverend John grunted.

'I can't subscribe to that,' said Mr Prout. '*You* haven't a House,' and for once Mr King backed Prout.

'Thank Heaven I haven't! Or I should be like you two. Leave 'em alone! Leave 'em alone! Haven't you ever seen puppies fighting over a slipper for hours?'

'Yes, but Gillett admits that Dickson Quartus was the only begetter of this manifestation. I wasn't aware that the – er – Testacean had been tricked out in *my* colours,' said King.

And at that very hour, Number Five Study – 'prep' thrown to the winds – were toiling inspiredly at a Tar Baby made up of Beetle's sweater, and half-a-dozen lavatory-towels; a condemned cretonne curtain and, ditto, baize table-cloth for 'natal stuffin''; an ancient, but air-tight puntabout-ball for the head; all three play-box ropes for bindings; and most of Richards' weekly blacking-allowance for Prout's House's boots, to give tone to the whole.

'Gummy!' said Beetle when their curtain-pole had been taken down and Tar Baby hitched to the end of it by a loop in its voluptuous back. 'It looks pretty average indecent, somehow.'

'You can use it this way, too,' Turkey demonstrated, handling the curtain-pole like a flail. 'Now, shove it in the fireplace to dry an' we'll wash up.'

'But – but,' said Stalky, fascinated by the unspeakable front and behind of the black and bulging horror. 'How *come* he lookee so hellish?'

'Dead easy! If you do anything with your whole heart, Ruskin says, you always pull off something dam'-fine. Brer Terrapin's only a natural animal; but Tar Baby's Art,'[8] McTurk explained.

'I see! "If you're anxious for to shine in the high aesthetic

line." [9] Well, Tar Baby's the filthiest thing *I*'ve ever seen in
my life,' Stalky concluded. 'King'll be rabid.'

The United Idolaters set forth, side by side, at five o'clock
next afternoon; Brer Terrapin, wide awake, and swimming hard
into nothing; Tar Baby lurching from side to side with a las-
civious abandon that made Foxy, the School Sergeant, taking
defaulters' drill in the Corridor, squawk like an outraged hen.
And when they ceremoniously saluted each other, like aristo-
cratic heads on revolutionary pikes, it beat the previous day's
performance out of sight and mind. The very fags, offered up,
till the bottoms of the paper-baskets carried away, as heave-
offerings before them, fell over each other for the honour; and
House by House, when the news spread, dropped its doings,
and followed the Mysteries – not without song . . .

Some say it was a fag of Prout's who appealed for rescue
from Brer Terrapin to Tar Baby; others, that the introits to the
respective creeds ('Ingle-go-jang' – 'Ti-yi-Tungalee!') carried
in themselves the seeds of dissent. At any rate, the cleavage
developed as swiftly as in a new religion, and by tea-time when
they were fairly hoarse, the rolling world was rent to the death
between Ingles *versus* Tungles, and Brer Terrapin had swept
out Number Eleven form-room to the War-cry: 'Here I come
a-bulgin' and a-bilin'.' Prep stopped further developments, but
they agreed that, as a recreation for wet autumn evenings, the
jape was unequalled, and called for its repetition on Saturday.

That was a brilliant evening, too. Both sides went into prayers
practically re-dressing themselves. There was a smell of singed
fag down the lines and a watery eye or so; but nothing to which
the most fastidious could have objected. The Reverend John
hinted something about roof-lifting noises.

'Oh, *no*, Padre, Sahib. We were only billin' an' cooin' a bit,'
Stalky explained. 'We haven't really begun. There's goin' to be
a tug-o'-war next Saturday with Miss Meadow's bed-cord –'

'"Which in dem days would ha' hilt a mule",' the Reverend
John quoted. 'Well, I've got to be impartial. I wish you both
good luck.'

The week, with its three paper-chases, passed uneventfully,
but for a certain amount of raiding and reprisals on new lines

that might have warned them they were playing with fire. The Juniors had learned to use the sacred war-chants as signals of distress; oppressed Ingles squealing for aid against oppressing Tungles, and *vice versa*; so that one never knew when a peaceful form-room would flare up in song and slaughter. But not a soul dreamed, for a moment, that that Saturday's jape would develop into – what it did! They were rigidly punctilious about the ritual; exquisitely careful as to the weights on Miss Meadow's bed-cord, kindly lent by Richards, who said he knew nothing about mules, but guaranteed it would hold a barge's crew; and if Dick Four chose to caparison himself as Archimandrite of Joppa, black as burned cork could make him, why, Stalky, in a nightgown kilted up beneath his sweater, was equally the Pope Symmachus, just converted from heathendom but given to alarming relapses.

It began after tea – say 6.50 p.m. It got into its stride by 7.30 when Turkey, with pillows bound round the ends of forms, invented the Royal Battering-Ram Corps. It grew and – it grew till a quarter to nine when the Prefects, most of whom had fought on one side or the other, thought it time to stop and went in with ground-ashes and the bare hand for ten minutes. . . .

Honours for the action were not awarded by the Head till Monday morning when he dealt out one dozen lickings to selected seniors, eight 'millies' (one thousand), fourteen 'usuals' (five hundred lines), minor impositions past count, and a stoppage of pocket-money on a scale and for a length of time unprecedented in modern history.

He said the College was within an ace of being burned to the ground when the gas-jet in Number Eleven form-room – where they tried to burn Tar Baby, fallen for the moment into the hands of the enemy – was wrenched off, and the lit gas spouted all over the ceiling till someone plugged the pipe with dormitory soap. He said that nothing save his consideration for their future careers kept him from expelling the wanton ruffians who had noosed all the desks in Number Twelve and swept them up in one crackling mound, barring a couple that had pitch-poled through the window. This, again, had been no man's design but the inspiration of necessity when Tar Baby's bodyguard, surrounded but defiant, was only rescued at the last minute by Turkey's immortal flank-attack with the battering-rams that carried away the door of Number Nine. He said that the same remarks applied to the fireplace and mantelpiece in Number Seven which everybody had seen fall out of the wall of their own motion after Brer Terrapin had hitched Miss Meadow's bed-cord to the bars of the grate.

He said much more, too; but as King pointed out in Common Room that evening, his canings were inept, he had *not* confiscated the Idols and, above all, had not castigated, as King would have castigated, the disgusting childishness of all concerned.

'Well,' said Little Hartopp. 'I saw the Prefects choking them off as we came into prayers. You've reason to reckon that in the scale of suffering.'

'And more than half the damage was done under *your* banner, King,' the Reverend John added.

'That doesn't affect my judgment; though, as a matter of fact, I believe Brer Terrapin triumphed over Tar Baby all along the line. Didn't he, Prout?'

'It didn't seem to me a fitting time to ask. The Tar Babies were handicapped, of course, by not being able to – ah – tackle a live animal.'

'I confess,' Mr Brownell volunteered, 'it was the studious perversity of certain aspects of the orgy which impressed *me*. And yet, what can one exp –'

'How do you mean?' King demanded. 'Dickson Quartus may be eccentric, but –'

'I was alluding to the vile and calculated indecency of that black doll.'

Mr Brownell had passed Tar Baby going down to battle, all round and ripe, before Turkey had begun to use it as Bishop Odo's [10] holy-water sprinkler.

'It is possible you didn't –'

'*I* never noticed anything,' said Prout. 'If there had been, I should have been the first –'

Here Little Hartopp sniggered, which did not cool the air.

'Peradventure,' King began with due intake of the breath. 'Peradventure even *I* might have taken cognizance of the matter both for my own House's sake and for my colleague's . . . No! Folly I concede. Utter childishness and complete absence of discipline in *all* quarters, as the natural corollary to dabbling in so-called transatlantic humour, I frankly admit. But that there was anything esoterically obscene in the outbreak I absolutely deny.'

'They've been fighting for weeks over those things,' said Mr Prout. ''Silly, of course, but I don't see how it can be dangerous.'

'Quite true. Any House-master of experience knows *that*, Brownell,' the Reverend John put in reprovingly.

'Given a normal basis of tradition and conduct – certainly,' Mr Brownell answered. 'But with such amazing traditions as exist here, no man with any experience of the Animal Boy can draw your deceptive inferences. That's all *I* mean.'

Once again, and not for the first time, but with greater heat he testified what smoking led to – what, indeed, he was morally certain existed in full blast under their noses . . .

Gloves were off in three minutes. Pessimists, no more than poets, love each other and, even when they work together, it is one thing to pessimize congenially with an ancient and tried associate who is also a butt, and another to be pessimized over by an inexperienced junior, even though the latter's college career may have included more exhibitions – nay, even pothuntings – than one's own. The Reverend John did his best to pour water on the flames. Little Hartopp, perceiving that it was pure oil, threw in canfuls of his own, from the wings. In the end, words passed which would have made the Common Room uninhabitable for the future, but that Macrea had written (the Reverend John had seen the letter) saying that his knee was fairly re-knit and he was prepared to take on again at half-term. This happened to be the only date since the Creation beyond which Mr Brownell's self-respect would not permit him to stay one hour. It solved the situation, amid puffings and blowings and bitter epigrams, and a most distinguished stateliness of bearing all round, till Mr Brownell's departure.

*

'My dear fellow!' said the Reverend John to Macrea, on the first night of the latter's return. 'I *do* hope there was nothing in my letters to you – you asked me to keep you posted – that gave you any idea King wasn't doing his best with your House according to his lights?'

'Not in the least,' said Macrea. 'I've the greatest respect for King, but after all, one's House is one's House. One can't stand it being tinkered with by well-meaning outsiders.'

To Mr Brownell on Bideford station-platform, the Reverend John's last words were:

'Well, well. You mustn't judge us too harshly I dare say there's a great deal in what you say. Oh, Yes! King's conduct was inexcusable, absolutely inexcusable! About the smoking? Lamentable, but we must all bow down, more or less, in the House of Rimmon.[11] *We* have to compete with the Crammers' Shops.'

To the Head, in the silence of his study, next day: 'He didn't seem to me the kind of animal who'd keep to advantage in our atmosphere. Luckily he lost his temper (King and he are own brothers) and he couldn't withdraw his resignation.'

'Excellent. After all, it's only a few pounds to make up. I'll slip it in under our recent – er – barrack damages. And what do *We* think of it all, Gillett?'

'*We* do not think at all – any of us,' said the Reverend John. 'Youth is its own prophylactic, thank Heaven.'

And the Head, not usually devout, echoed, 'Thank Heaven!'

'It was worth it,' Dick Four pronounced on review of the profit-and-loss account with Number Five in his study.

'Heap-plenty-*bong-assez*,' Stalky assented.

'But why didn't King ra'ar up an' cuss Tar Baby?' Beetle asked.

'You preter-pluperfect, fat-ended fool!' Stalky began –

'Keep your hair on! We *all* know the Idolaters wasn't our Uncle Stalky's idea. But why didn't King –'

'Because Dick took care to paint Brer Terrapin King's House-colours. You can always conciliate King by soothin' his putrid *esprit-de-maisong*. Ain't that true, Dick?'

Dick Four, with the smile of modest worth unmasked, said it was so.

'An' now,' Turkey yawned, 'King an' Macrea'll jaw for the rest of the term how he ran his house when Macrea was tryin' to marry fat widows in Switzerland. Mountaineerin'! 'Bet Macrea never went near a mountain.'

''One good job, though. I go back to Macrea for Maths. He *does* know something,' said Stalky.

'Why? Didn't "Mister" know anythin'?' Beetle asked.

''Bout as much as *you*,' was Stalky's reply.

'*I* don't go about pretending to. What was he like?'

'"Mister"? Oh, rather like King – King and water.'

Only water was not precisely the fluid that Stalky thought fit to mention.

The Centaurs

Up came the young Centaur-colts [12] from the plains they were
                                     fathered in –
  Curious, awkward, afraid.
Burrs in their hocks and their tails, they were gathered in
  Mobs and run up to the yard to be made.

Starting and shying at straws, with sidelings and plungings,
  Buckings and whirlings and bolts;
Greener than grass, but full-ripe for their bridlings and lungings,
  Up to the yards and to Chiron [13] they bustled the colts . . .

First the light web and the cavesson; then the linked keys
  To jingle and turn on the tongue. Then, with cocked ears,
The hour of watching and envy, while comrades at ease
  Passaged and backed, making naught of these terrible gears.

Next, over-pride and its price at the low-seeming fence,
  Too oft and too easily taken – the world-beheld fall!
And none in the yard except Chiron to doubt the immense,
  Irretrievable shame of it all! . . .

Last, the trained squadron, full-charge – the sound of a going
  Through dust and spun clods, and strong kicks, pelted in as
                                    they went,
And repaid at top-speed; till the order to halt without slowing
  Brought every colt on his haunches – and Chiron content!

The Wish House

'Late Came the God'

Late came the God, having sent his forerunners who were
                                                    not regarded –
  Late, but in wrath;
Saying: 'The wrong shall be paid, the contempt be rewarded
  On all that she hath.'
He poisoned the blade and struck home, the full bosom receiving
The wound and the venom in one, past cure or relieving.

He made treaty with Time to stand still that the grief might
                                                    be fresh –
Daily renewed and nightly pursued through her soul to her flesh –
Mornings of memory, noontides of agony, midnights unslaked
                                                    for her,
Till the stones of the Streets of her Hells and her Paradise ached
                                                    for her.[1]

So she lived while her body corrupted upon her.
  And she called on the Night[2] for a sign, and a Sign was allowed,
And she builded an Altar and served by the light of her Vision –
  Alone, without hope of regard or reward, but uncowed,
Resolute, selfless, divine.
  These things she did in Love's honour . . .
What is a God beside Woman? Dust and derision!

The Wish House

The new Church Visitor had just left after a twenty minutes' call. During that time, Mrs Ashcroft[3] had used such English as an elderly, experienced, and pensioned cook should, who had seen life in London. She was the readier, therefore, to slip back into easy, ancient Sussex[4] ('t's softening to 'd's as one warmed) when the 'bus brought Mrs Fettley from thirty miles away for a visit, that pleasant March Saturday. The two had been friends since childhood; but, of late, destiny had separated their meetings by long intervals.

Much was to be said, and many ends, loose since last time, to be ravelled up on both sides, before Mrs Fettley, with her bag of quilt-patches, took the couch beneath the window commanding the garden, and the football-ground in the valley below.

'Most folk got out at Bush Tye for the match there,' she explained, 'so there weren't no one for me to cushion agin, the last five mile. An' she *do* just-about bounce ye.'

'You've took no hurt,' said her hostess. 'You don't brittle by agein', Liz.'

Mrs Fettley chuckled and made to match a couple of patches to her liking. 'No, or I'd ha' broke twenty year back. You can't ever mind when I was so's to be called round, can ye?'

Mrs Ashcroft shook her head slowly – she never hurried – and went on stitching a sack-cloth lining into a list-bound rush tool-basket. Mrs Fettley laid out more patches in the Spring light through the geraniums on the window-sill, and they were silent awhile.

'What like's this new Visitor o' yourn?' Mrs Fettley inquired, with a nod towards the door. Being very short-sighted, she had, on her entrance, almost bumped into the lady.

Mrs Ashcroft suspended the big packing-needle judicially on high, ere she stabbed home. 'Settin' aside she don't bring much news with her yet, I dunno as I've anythin' special agin her.'

'Ourn, at Keyneslade,' said Mrs Fettley, 'she's full o' words an' pity, but she don't stay for answers. Ye can get on with your thoughts while she clacks.'

'This 'un don't clack. She's aimin' to be one o' those High Church nuns, like.'

'Ourn's married, but, by what they say, she've made no great gains of it . . .' Mrs Fettley threw up her sharp chin. 'Lord! How they dam' cherubim do shake the very bones o' the place!'

The tile-sided cottage trembled at the passage of two specially chartered forty-seat charabancs [5] on their way to the Bush Tye match; a regular Saturday 'shopping' 'bus, for the county's capital, fumed behind them; while, from one of the crowded inns, a fourth car backed out to join the procession, and held up the stream of through pleasure-traffic.

'You're as free-tongued as ever, Liz,' Mrs Ashcroft observed.

'Only when I'm with you. Otherwhiles, I'm Granny – three times over. I lay that basket's for one o' your gran'chiller – ain't it?'

''Tis for Arthur – my Jane's eldest.'

'But he ain't workin' nowheres, is he?'

'No. 'Tis a picnic-basket.'

'You're let off light. My Willie, he's allus at me for money for them aireated wash-poles folk puts up in their gardens to draw the music from Lunnon, like. An' I give it 'im – pore fool me!'

'An' he forgets to give you the promise-kiss after, don't he?' Mrs Ashcroft's heavy smile seemed to strike inwards.

'He do. 'No odds 'twixt boys now an' forty year back. 'Take all an' give naught – an' we to put up with it! Pore fool we! Three shillin' at a time Willie'll ask me for!'

'They don't make nothin' o' money these days,' Mrs Ashcroft said.

'An' on'y last week,' the other went on, 'me daughter, she ordered a quarter pound suet at the butchers's; an' she sent it back to 'im to be chopped. She said she couldn't bother with choppin' it.'

'I lay he charged her, then.'

'I lay he did. She told me there was a whisk-drive that afternoon at the Institute, an' she couldn't bother to do the choppin'.'

'Tck!'

Mrs Ashcroft put the last firm touches to the basket-lining. She had scarcely finished when her sixteen-year-old grandson, a maiden of the moment in attendance, hurried up the garden-path shouting to know if the thing were ready, snatched it, and made off without acknowledgment. Mrs Fettley peered at him closely.

'They're goin' picnickin' somewheres,' Mrs Ashcroft explained.

'Ah,' said the other, with narrowed eyes. 'I lay *he* won't show much mercy to any he comes across, either. Now 'oo the dooce do he remind me of, all of a sudden?'

'They must look arter theirselves – 'same as we did.' Mrs Ashcroft began to set out the tea.

'No denyin' *you* could, Gracie,' said Mrs Fettley.

'What's in your head now?'

'Dunno . . . But it come over me, sudden-like – about dat woman from Rye – I've slipped the name – Barnsley, wadn't it?'

'Batten – Polly Batten, you're thinkin' of.'

'That's it – Polly Batten. That day she had it in for you with a hay-fork – 'time we was all hayin' at Smalldene – for stealin' her man.'

'But you heered me tell her she had my leave to keep him?' Mrs Ashcroft's voice and smile were smoother than ever.

'I did – an' we was all looking that she'd prod the fork spang through your breasts when you said it.'

'No-oo. She'd never go beyond bounds – Polly. She shruck too much for reel doin's.'

'Allus seems to *me*,' Mrs Fettley said after a pause, 'that a man 'twixt two fightin' women is the foolishest thing on earth. 'Like a dog bein' called two ways.'

'Mebbe. But what set ye off on those times, Liz?'

'That boy's fashion o' carryin' his head an' arms. I haven't rightly looked at him since he's growed. Your Jane never showed it, but – *him*! Why, 'tis Jim Batten and his tricks come to life again! . . . Eh?'

'Mebbe. There's some that would ha' made it out so – bein' barren-like, themselves.'

'Oho! Ah well! Dearie, dearie me, now! . . . An' Jim Batten's been dead this –'

'Seven and twenty year,' Mrs Ashcroft answered briefly. 'Won't ye draw up, Liz?'

Mrs Fettley drew up to buttered toast, currant bread, stewed tea, bitter as leather, some home-preserved pears, and a cold boiled pig's tail to help down the muffins. She paid all the proper compliments.

'Yes. I dunno as I've ever owed me belly much,' said Mrs Ashcroft thoughtfully. 'We only go through this world once.'

'But don't it lay heavy on ye, sometimes?' her guest suggested.

'Nurse says I'm a sight liker to die o' me indigestion than me leg.' For Mrs Ashcroft had a long-standing ulcer on her shin, which needed regular care from the Village Nurse, who boasted (or others did, for her) that she had dressed it one hundred and three times already during her term of office.

'An' you that *was* so able, too! It's all come on ye before your full time, like. *I*'ve watched ye goin'.' Mrs Fettley spoke with real affection.

'Somethin's bound to find ye sometime. I've me 'eart left me still,' Mrs Ashcroft returned.

'You was always big-hearted enough for three. That's somethin' to look back on at the day's eend.'

'I reckon you've *your* back-lookin's, too,' was Mrs Ashcroft's answer.

'You know it. But I don't think much regardin' such matters excep' when I'm along with you, Gra'. 'Takes two sticks to make a fire.'

Mrs Fettley stared, with jaw half-dropped, at the grocer's bright calendar on the wall. The cottage shook again to the roar of the motor-traffic, and the crowded football-ground below the garden roared almost as loudly; for the village was well set to its Saturday leisure.

Mrs Fettley had spoken very precisely for some time without interruption, before she wiped her eyes. 'And,' she concluded, 'they read 'is death-notice to me, out o' the paper last month. O' course it wadn't any o' *my* becomin' concerns – let be I 'adn't set eyes on him for so long. O' course I couldn't say nor show nothin'. Nor I've no rightful call to go to Eastbourne to see 'is grave, either. I've been schemin' to slip over there by the 'bus some day; but they'd ask questions at 'ome past endurance. So I 'aven't even *that* to stay me.'

'But you've 'ad your satisfactions?'

'Godd! Yess! Those four years 'e was workin' on the rail near us. An' the other drivers they gave him a brave funeral, too.'

'Then you've naught to cast-up about. 'Nother cup o' tea?'

The light and air had changed a little with the sun's descent, and the two elderly ladies closed the kitchen-door against chill. A couple of jays squealed and skirmished through the undraped apple-trees in the garden. This time, the word was with Mrs Ashcroft, her elbows on the tea-table, and her sick leg propped on a stool . . .

'Well I never! But what did your 'usband say to that?' Mrs Fettley asked, when the deep-toned recital halted.

''E said I might go where I pleased for all of 'im. But seein' 'e was bedrid, I said I'd 'tend 'im out. 'E knowed I wouldn't take no advantage of 'im in that state. 'E lasted eight or nine week. Then he was took with a seizure-like; an' laid stone-still for days. Then 'e propped 'imself up abed an' says: "You pray no man'll ever deal with you like you've dealed with some." "An' you?" I says, for *you* know, Liz, what a rover 'e was. "It cuts both ways," says 'e, "but *I*'m death-wise, an' I can see what's comin' to you." He died a-Sunday an' was buried a-Thursday . . . An' yet I'd set a heap by him – one time or – did I ever?'

'You never told me that before,' Mrs Fettley ventured.

'I'm payin' ye for what ye told me just now. Him bein' dead, I wrote up, sayin' I was free for good, to that Mrs Marshall in Lunnon – which gave me my first place as kitchen-maid – Lord, how long ago! She was well pleased, for they two was both gettin' on, an' I knowed their ways. You remember, Liz, I used to go to 'em in service between whiles, for years – when we wanted money, or – or my 'usband was away – on occasion.'

''E *did* get that six months at Chichester, didn't 'e?' Mrs Fettley whispered. 'We never rightly won to the bottom of it.'

''E'd ha' got more, but the man didn't die.'

''None o' your doin's, was it, Gra'?'

'No! 'Twas the woman's husband this time. An' so, my man bein' dead, I went back to them Marshalls, as cook, to get me legs under a gentleman's table again, and be called with a handle to me name. That was the year you shifted to Portsmouth.'

'Cosham,' Mrs Fettley corrected. 'There was a middlin' lot o' new buildin' bein' done there. My man went first, an' got the room, an' I follered.'

'Well, then, I was a year-abouts in Lunnon, all at a breath, like, four meals a day an' livin' easy. Then, 'long towards autumn, they two went travellin', like, to France; keepin' me on, for they couldn't do without me. I put the house to rights for the caretaker, an' then I slipped down 'ere to me sister Bessie – me wages in me pockets, an' all 'ands glad to be'old of me.'

'That would be when I was at Cosham,' said Mrs Fettley.

'*You* know, Liz, there wasn't no cheap-dog pride to folk, those days, no more than there was cinemas nor whisk-drives. Man or woman 'ud lay hold o' any job that promised a shillin' to the backside of it, didn't they? I was all peaked up after Lunnon, an' I thought the fresh airs 'ud serve me. So I took on at Smalldene, obligin' with a hand at the early potato-liftin', stubbin' hens, an' such-like. They'd ha' mocked me sore in my kitchen in Lunnon, to see me in men's boots, an' me petticoats all shorted.'

'Did it bring ye any good?' Mrs Fettley asked.

''Twadn't for that I went. You know, 's'well's me, that na'un happens to ye till it *'as* 'appened. Your mind don't warn

ye before'and of the road ye've took, till you're at the far eend
of it. We've only a backwent view of our proceedin's.'

''Oo was it?'

''Arry Mockler.' Mrs Ashcroft's face puckered to the pain
of her sick leg.

Mrs Fettley gasped. ''Arry? Bert Mockler's son! An' *I* never
guessed!'

Mrs Ashcroft nodded. 'An' I told myself – *an'* I beleft it –
that I wanted field-work.'

'What did ye get out of it?'

'The usuals. Everythin' at first – worse than naught after. I
had signs an' warnings a-plenty, but I took no heed of 'em. For
we was burnin' rubbish one day, just when we'd come to know
how 'twas with – with both of us. 'Twas early in the year for
burnin', an' I said so. "No!" says he. "The sooner dat old
stuff's off an' done with," 'e says, "the better." 'Is face was
harder'n rocks when he spoke. Then it come over me that I'd
found me master, which I 'adn't ever before. I'd allus owned
'em, like.'

'Yes! Yes! They're yourn or you're theirn,' the other sighed.
'I like the right way best.'

'I didn't. But 'Arry did . . . 'Long then, it come time for me
to go back to Lunnon. I couldn't. I clean couldn't! So, I took
an' tipped a dollop o' scaldin' water out o' the copper one
Monday mornin' over me left 'and and arm. Dat stayed me
where I was for another fortnight.'

'Was it worth it?' said Mrs Fettley, looking at the silvery scar
on the wrinkled fore-arm.

Mrs Ashcroft nodded. 'An' after that, we two made it up
'twixt us so's 'e could come to Lunnon for a job in a liv'ry-stable
not far from me. 'E got it. *I* 'tended to that. There wadn't no
talk nowhere. His own mother never suspicioned how 'twas. He
just slipped up to Lunnon, an' there we abode that winter,
not 'alf a mile 'tother from each.'

'Ye paid 'is fare an' all, though'; Mrs Fettley spoke con-
vincedly.

Again Mrs Ashcroft nodded. 'Dere wadn't much I didn't do
for him. 'E was me master, an' – O God, help us! – we'd laugh

over it walkin' together after dark in them paved streets, an' me
corns fair wrenchin' in me boots! I'd never been like that before.
Ner he! Ner he!'

Mrs Fettley clucked sympathetically.

'An' when did ye come to the eend?' she asked.

'When 'e paid it all back again, every penny. Then I knowed,
but I wouldn't *suffer* meself to know. "You've been mortal kind
to me," he says. "Kind!" I said. " 'Twixt *us*?" But 'e kep' all on
tellin' me 'ow kind I'd been an' 'e'd never forget it all his days.
I held it from off o' me for three evenin's, because I would *not*
believe. Then 'e talked about not bein' satisfied with 'is job in
the stables, an' the men there puttin' tricks on 'im, an' all they
lies which a man tells when 'e's leavin' ye. I heard 'im out,
neither 'elpin' nor 'inderin'. At the last, I took off a liddle
brooch which he'd give me an' I says: "Dat'll do. *I* ain't askin'
na'un'." An' I turned me round an' walked off to me own
sufferin's. 'E didn't make 'em worse. 'E didn't come nor write
after that. 'E slipped off 'ere back 'ome to 'is mother again.'

'An' 'ow often did ye look for 'en to come back?' Mrs Fettley
demanded mercilessly.

'More'n once – more'n once! Goin' over the streets we'd
used, I thought de very pave-stones 'ud shruck out under me
feet.'

'Yes,' said Mrs Fettley. 'I dunno but dat don't 'urt as much
as aught else. An' dat was all ye got?'

'No. 'Twadn't. That's the curious part, if you'll believe it,
Liz.'

'I do. I lay you're further off lyin' now than in all your life,
Gra'.'

'I am . . . An' I suffered, like I'd not wish my most arrantest
enemies to. God's Own Name! I went through the hoop that
spring! One part of it was headaches which I'd never known all
me days before. Think o' *me* with an 'eddick! But I come to be
grateful for 'em. They kep' me from thinkin' . . .'

' 'Tis like a tooth,' Mrs Fettley commented. 'It must rage an'
rugg till it tortures itself quiet on ye; an' then – then there's
na'un left.'

'*I* got enough lef' to last me all *my* days on earth. It come about through our charwoman's liddle girl – Sophy Ellis was 'er name – all eyes an' elbers an' hunger. I used to give 'er vittles. Otherwhiles, I took no special notice of 'er, an' a sight less, o' course, when me trouble about 'Arry was on me. But – you know how liddle maids first feel it sometimes – she come to be crazy-fond o' me, pawin' an' cuddlin' all whiles; an' I 'adn't the 'eart to beat 'er off . . . One afternoon, early in spring 'twas, 'er mother 'ad sent 'er round to scutchel up what vittles she could off of us. I was settin' by the fire, me apern over me head, half-mad with the 'eddick, when she slips in. I reckon I was middlin' short with 'er. "Lor!" she says. "Is *that* all? I'll take it off you in two-twos!" I told her not to lay a finger on me, for I thought she'd want to stroke my forehead; an' – I ain't that make. "*I* won't tech ye," she says, an' slips out again. She 'adn't been gone ten minutes 'fore me old 'eddick took off quick as bein' kicked. So I went about my work. Prasin'ly, Sophy comes back, an' creeps into my chair quiet as a mouse. 'Er eyes was deep in 'er 'ead an' 'er face all drawed. I asked 'er what 'ad 'appened. "Nothin'," she says. "On'y *I*'ve got it now." "Got what?" I says. "Your 'eddick," she says, all hoarse an' sticky-lipped. "I've took it on me." "Nonsense," I says, "it went of itself when you was out. Lay still an' I'll make ye a cup o' tea." "'Twon't do no good," she says, "till your time's up. 'Ow long do *your* 'eddicks last?" "Don't talk silly," I says, "or I'll send for the Doctor." It looked to me like she might be hatchin' de measles. "Oh, Mrs Ashcroft," she says, stretchin' out 'er liddle thin arms. "I *do* love ye." There wasn't any holdin' agin that. I took 'er into me lap an' made much of 'er. "Is it truly gone?" she says. "Yes," I says, "an' if 'twas you took it away, I'm truly grateful." "'*Twas* me," she says, layin' 'er cheek to mine. "No one but me knows how." An' then she said she'd changed me 'eddick for me at a Wish 'Ouse.'

'Whatt?' Mrs Fettley spoke sharply.

'A Wish House. No! *I* 'adn't 'eard o' such things, either. I couldn't get it straight at first, but, puttin' all together, I made out that a Wish 'Ouse 'ad to be a house which 'ad stood unlet an' empty long enough for Some One, like, to come an' in'abit there. She said, a liddle girl that she'd played with in the livery-stables where 'Arry worked 'ad told 'er so. She said the girl 'ad belonged in a caravan that laid up, o' winters, in Lunnon. Gipsy, I judge.'

'Ooh! There's no sayin' what Gippos know, but *I*'ve never 'eard of a Wish 'Ouse, an' I know – some things,' said Mrs Fettley.

'Sophy said there was a Wish 'Ouse in Wadloes Road – just a few streets off, on the way to our green-grocer's. All you 'ad to do, she said, was to ring the bell an' wish your wish through the slit o' the letter-box. I asked 'er if the fairies give it 'er? "Don't ye know," she says, "there's no fairies in a Wish 'Ouse? There's on'y a Token."'⁶

'Goo' Lord A'mighty! Where did she come by *that* word?' cried Mrs Fettley; for a Token is a wraith of the dead or, worse still, of the living.

'The caravan-girl 'ad told 'er, she said. Well, Liz, it troubled me to 'ear 'er, an' lyin' in me arms she must ha' felt it. "That's very kind o' you," I says, holdin' 'er tight, "to wish me 'eddick away. But why didn't ye ask somethin' nice for yourself?" "You can't do that," she says. "All you'll get at a Wish 'Ouse is leave to take someone else's trouble. I've took Ma's 'eadaches, when she's been kind to me; but this is the first time I've been able to do aught for you. Oh, Mrs Ashcroft, I *do* just-about love you." An' she goes on all like that. Liz, I tell you my 'air e'en a'most stood on end to 'ear 'er. I asked 'er what like a Token was. "I dunno," she says, "but after you've ringed the bell, you'll 'ear it run up from the basement, to the front door. Then say your wish," she says, "an' go away." "The Token don't open de door to ye, then?" I says. "Oh no," she says. "You on'y 'ear gigglin', like, be'ind the front door. Then you say you'll take the trouble off of 'ooever 'tis you've chose for your love; an' ye'll get it," she says. I didn't ask no more – she was too 'ot an' fevered. I made much of 'er till it come time to light de gas, an' a liddle after that, 'er 'eddick – mine, I suppose – took off, an' she got down an' played with the cat.'

'Well I never!' said Mrs Fettley. 'Did – did ye foller it up, anyways?'

'She askt me to, but I wouldn't 'ave no such dealin's with a child.'

'What *did* ye do, then?'

''Sat in me own room 'stid o' the kitchen when me 'eddicks come on. But it lay at de back o' me mind.'

''Twould. Did she tell ye more, ever?'

'No. Besides what the Gippo girl 'ad told 'er, she knew naught, 'cept that the charm worked. An', next after that – in May 'twas – I suffered the summer out in Lunnon. 'Twas hot an' windy for weeks, an' the streets stinkin' o' dried 'orse-dung blowin' from side to side an' lyin' level with the kerb. We don't get that nowadays. I 'ad my 'ol'day just before hoppin',[7] an' come down 'ere to stay with Bessie again. She noticed I'd lost flesh, an' was all poochy under the eyes.'

'Did ye see 'Arry?'

Mrs Ashcroft nodded. 'The fourth – no, the fifth day. Wednesday 'twas. I knowed 'e was workin' at Smalldene again. I asked 'is mother in the street, bold as brass. She 'adn't room to say much, for Bessie – you know 'er tongue – was talkin' full-clack. But that Wednesday, I was walkin' with one o' Bessie's chillern hangin' on me skirts, at de back o' Chanter's Tot. Prasin'ly, I felt 'e was be'ind me on the footpath, an' I knowed by 'is tread 'e'd changed 'is nature. I slowed, an' I heard 'im slow. Then I fussed a piece with the child, to force him past me, like. So 'e '*ad* to come past. 'E just says "Good-evenin'"', and goes on, tryin' to pull 'isself together.'

'Drunk, was he?' Mrs Fettley asked.

'Never! S'runk an' wizen; 'is clothes 'angin' on 'im like bags, an' the back of 'is neck whiter'n chalk. 'Twas all I could do not to oppen my arms an' cry after him. But I swallered me spittle till I was back 'ome again an' the chillern abed. Then I says to Bessie, after supper, "What in de world's come to 'Arry Mockler?" Bessie told me 'e'd been a-Hospital for two months, 'long o' cuttin' 'is foot wid a spade, muckin' out the old pond at Smalldene. There was poison in de dirt, an' it rooshed up 'is leg, like, an' come out all over him. 'E 'adn't been back to 'is job – carterin' at Smalldene – more'n a fortnight. She told me the Doctor said he'd go off, likely, with the November frostes; an' 'is mother 'ad told 'er that 'e didn't rightly eat nor sleep, an' sweated 'imself into pools, no odds 'ow chill 'e lay. An' spit terrible o' mornin's. "Dearie me," I says. "But, mebbe, hoppin' 'll set 'im right again," an' I licked me thread-point an' I fetched me needle's eye up to it an' I threads me needle under de lamp, steady as rocks. An' dat night (me bed was in de wash-house) I cried an' I cried. An' *you* know, Liz – for you've been with me in my throes – it takes summat to make me cry.'

'Yes; but chile-bearin' is on'y just pain,' said Mrs Fettley.

'I come round by cock-crow, an' dabbed cold tea on me eyes to take away the signs. Long towards nex' evenin' – I was settin' out to lay some flowers on me 'usband's grave, for the look o' the thing – I met 'Arry over against where the War Memorial is now. 'E was comin' back from 'is 'orses, so 'e couldn't *not* see me. I looked 'im all over, an' "'Arry," I says twix' me teeth, "come back an' rest-up in Lunnon." "I won't take it," he says, "for I can give ye naught." "I don't ask it," I says. "By God's Own Name, I don't ask na'un! On'y come up an' see a Lunnon doctor." 'E lifts 'is two 'eavy eyes at me: "'Tis past that, Gra'," 'e says. "I've but a few months left." "'Arry!" I says. "*My* man!" I says. I couldn't say no more. 'Twas all up in me throat. "Thank ye kindly, Gra'," 'e says (but 'e never says "my woman"), an' 'e went on up-street an' 'is mother – Oh, damn 'er! – she was watchin' for 'im, an' she shut de door be'ind 'im.'

Mrs Fettley stretched an arm across the table, and made to finger Mrs Ashcroft's sleeve at the wrist, but the other moved it out of reach.

'So I went on to the churchyard with my flowers, an' I remembered my 'usband's warnin' that night he spoke. 'E *was* death-wise, an' it '*ad* 'appened as 'e said. But as I was settin' down de jam-pot on the grave-mound, it come over me there was one thing I *could* do for 'Arry. Doctor or no Doctor, I thought I'd make a trial of it. So I did. Nex' mornin', a bill came down from our Lunnon green-grocer. Mrs Marshall, she'd lef' me petty cash for suchlike – o' course – but I tole Bess 'twas for me to come an' open the 'ouse. So I went up, afternoon train.'

'An' – but I know you 'adn't – 'adn't you no fear?'

'What for? There was nothin' front o' me but my own shame

an' God's croolty. I couldn't ever get 'Arry – 'ow *could* I? I knowed it must go on burnin' till it burned me out.'

'Aie!' said Mrs Fettley, reaching for the wrist again, and this time Mrs Ashcroft permitted it.

'Yit 'twas a comfort to know I could try *this* for 'im. So I went an' I paid the green-grocer's bill, an' put 'is receipt in me hand-bag, an' then I stepped round to Mrs Ellis – our char – an' got the 'ouse-keys an' opened the 'ouse. First, I made me bed to come back to (God's Own Name! Me bed to lie upon!). Nex' I made me a cup o' tea an' sat down in the kitchen thinkin', till 'long towards dusk. Terrible close, 'twas. Then I dressed me an' went out with the receipt in me 'and-bag, feignin' to study it for an address, like. Fourteen, Wadloes Road, was the place – a liddle basement-kitchen 'ouse, in a row of twenty-thirty such, an' tiddy strips o' walled garden in front – the paint off the front doors, an' na'un done to na'un since ever so long. There wasn't 'ardly no one in the streets 'cept the cats. 'Twas 'ot, too! I turned into the gate bold as brass; up de steps I went an' I ringed the front-door bell. She pealed loud, like it do in an empty house. When she'd all ceased, I 'eard a cheer, like, pushed back on de floor o' the kitchen. Then I 'eard feet on de kitchen-stairs, like it might ha' been a heavy woman in slippers. They come up to de stair-head, acrost the hall – I 'eard the bare boards creak under 'em – an' at de front door dey stopped. I stooped me to the letter-box slit, an' I says: "Let me take everythin' bad that's in store for my man, 'Arry Mockler, for love's sake." [8] Then, whatever it was 'tother side de door let its breath out, like, as if it 'ad been holdin' it for to 'ear better.'

'Nothin' was *said* to ye?' Mrs Fettley demanded.

'Na'un. She just breathed out – a sort of *A-ah*, like. Then the steps went back an' downstairs to the kitchen – all draggy – an' I heard the cheer drawed up again.'

'An' you abode on de doorstep, throughout all, Gra'?'

Mrs Ashcroft nodded.

'Then I went away, an' a man passin' says to me: "Didn't you know that house was empty?" "No," I says. "I must ha' been give the wrong number." An' I went back to our 'ouse, an' I went to bed; for I was fair flogged out. 'Twas too 'ot to sleep more'n snatches, so I walked me about, lyin' down betweens, till crack o' dawn. Then I went to the kitchen to make me a cup o' tea, an' I hitted meself just above the ankle on an old roastin'-jack o' mine that Mrs Ellis had moved out from the corner, her last cleanin'. An' so – nex' after that – I waited till the Marshalls come back o' their holiday.'

'Alone there? I'd ha' thought you'd 'ad enough of empty houses,' said Mrs Fettley, horrified.

'Oh, Mrs Ellis an' Sophy was runnin' in an' out soon's I was back, an' 'twixt us we cleaned de house again top-to-bottom. There's allus a hand's turn more to do in every house. An' that's 'ow 'twas with me that autumn an' winter, in Lunnon.'

'Then na'un hap – overtook ye for your doin's?'

Mrs Ashcroft smiled. 'No. Not then. 'Long in November I sent Bessie ten shillin's.'

'You was allus free-'anded,' Mrs Fettley interrupted.

'An' I got what I paid for, with the rest o' the news. She said the hoppin' 'ad set 'im up wonderful. 'E'd 'ad six weeks of it, and now 'e was back again carterin' at Smalldene. No odds to me 'ow it 'ad 'appened – 'slong's it 'ad. But I dunno as my ten shillin's eased me much. 'Arry bein' *dead*, like, 'e'd ha' been mine, till Judgment. 'Arry bein' alive, 'e'd like as not pick up with some woman middlin' quick. I raged over that. Come spring, I 'ad somethin' else to rage for. I'd growed a nasty little weepin' boil, like, on me shin, just above the boot-top, that wouldn't heal no shape. It made me sick to look at it, for I'm clean-fleshed by nature. Chop me all over with a spade, an' I'd heal like turf. Then Mrs Marshall she set 'er own doctor at me. 'E said I ought to ha' come to him at first go-off, 'stead o' drawin' all manner o' dyed stockin's over it for months. 'E said I'd stood up too much to me work, for it was settin' very close atop of a big swelled vein, like, behither the small o' me ankle. "Slow come, slow go," 'e says. "Lay your leg up on high an' rest it," he says, "an 'twill ease off. Don't let it close up too soon. You've got a very fine leg, Mrs Ashcroft," 'e says. An' he put wet dressin's on it.'

''E done right.' Mrs Fettley spoke firmly. 'Wet dressin's to wet wounds. They draw de humours, same's a lamp-wick draws de oil.'

'That's true. An' Mrs Marshall was allus at me to make me set down more, an' dat nigh healed it up. An' then after a while they packed me off down to Bessie's to finish the cure; for I ain't the sort to sit down when I ought to stand up. You was back in the village then, Liz.'

'I was. I was, but – never did I guess!'

'I didn't desire ye to.' Mrs Ashcroft smiled. 'I saw 'Arry once or twice in de street, wonnerful fleshed up an' restored back. Then, one day I didn't see 'im, an' 'is mother told me one of 'is 'orses 'ad lashed out an' caught 'im on the 'ip. So 'e was abed an' middlin' painful. An' Bessie, she says to his mother, 'twas a pity 'Arry 'adn't a woman of 'is own to take the nursin' off 'er. And the old lady *was* mad! She told us that 'Arry 'ad never looked after any woman in 'is born days, an' as long as she was atop the mowlds, she'd contrive for 'im till 'er two 'ands dropped off. So I knowed she'd do watch-dog for me, 'thout askin' for bones.'

Mrs Fettley rocked with small laughter.

'That day,' Mrs Ashcroft went on, 'I'd stood on me feet nigh all the time, watchin' the doctor go in an' out; for they thought it might be 'is ribs, too. That made my boil break again, issuin' an' weepin'. But it turned out 'twadn't ribs at all, an' 'Arry 'ad a good night. When I heard that, nex' mornin', I says to meself, "I won't lay two an' two together *yit*. I'll keep me leg down a week, an' see what comes of it." It didn't hurt me that day, to speak of – 'seemed more to draw the strength out o' me like – an' 'Arry 'ad another good night. That made me persevere; but I didn't dare lay two an' two together till the week-end, an' then, 'Arry come forth e'en a'most 'imself again – na'un hurt outside ner in of him. I nigh fell on me knees in de wash-house when Bessie was up-street. "I've got ye now, my man," I says. "You'll take your good from me 'thout knowin' it till my life's end. O God send me long to live for 'Arry's sake!" I says. An' I dunno that didn't still my ragin's.'

'For good?' Mrs Fettley asked.

'They come back, plenty times, but, let be how 'twould, I

knowed I was doin' for 'im. I *knowed* it. I took an' worked me pains on an' off, like regulatin' my own range, till I learned to 'ave 'em at my commandments. An' that was funny, too. There was times, Liz, when my trouble 'ud all s'rink an' dry up, like. First, I used to try an' fetch it on again; bein' fearful to leave 'Arry alone too long for anythin' to lay 'old of. Prasin'ly I come to see that was a sign he'd do all right awhile, an' so I saved myself.'

''Ow long for?' Mrs Fettley asked, with deepest interest.

'I've gone de better part of a year onct or twice with na'un more to show than the liddle weepin' core of it, like. *All* s'rinked up an' dried off. Then he'd inflame up – for a warnin' – an' I'd suffer it. When I couldn't no more – an' I '*ad* to keep on goin' with my Lunnon work – I'd lay me leg high on a cheer till it eased. Not too quick. I knowed by the feel of it, those times, dat 'Arry was in need. Then I'd send another five shillin's to Bess, or somethin' for the chillern, to find out if, mebbe, 'e'd took any hurt through my neglects. 'Twas *so*! Year in, year out, I worked it dat way, Liz, an' 'e got 'is good from me 'thout knowin' – for years and years.'

'But what did *you* get out of it, Gra'?' Mrs Fettley almost wailed. 'Did ye see 'im reg'lar?'

'Times – when I was 'ere on me 'ol'days. An' more, now that I'm 'ere for good. But 'e's never looked at me, ner any other woman 'cept 'is mother. 'Ow I used to watch an' listen! So did she.'

'Years an' years!' Mrs Fettley repeated. 'An' where's 'e workin' at now?'

'Oh, 'e's give up carterin' quite a while. He's workin' for one o' them big tractorizin' firms – plowin' sometimes, an' sometimes off with lorries – fur as Wales, I've 'eard. He comes 'ome to 'is mother 'tween whiles; but I don't set eyes on him now, fer weeks on end. No odds! 'Is job keeps 'im from continuin' in one stay anywheres.'

'But – just for de sake o' sayin' somethin' – s'pose 'Arry *did* get married?' said Mrs Fettley.

Mrs Ashcroft drew her breath sharply between her still even and natural teeth. '*Dat* ain't been required of me,' she answered. 'I reckon my pains 'ull be counted agin that. Don't *you*, Liz?'

'It ought to be, dearie. It ought to be.'

'It *do* 'urt sometimes. You shall see it when Nurse comes. She thinks I don't know it's turned.'

Mrs Fettley understood. Human nature seldom walks up to the word 'cancer'.

'Be ye certain sure, Gra'?' she asked.

'I was sure of it when old Mr Marshall 'ad me up to 'is study an' spoke a long piece about my faithful service. I've obliged 'em on an' off for a goodish time, but not enough for a pension. But they give me a weekly 'lowance for life. I knew what *that* sinnified – as long as three years ago.'

'Dat don't *prove* it, Gra'.'

'To give fifteen bob a week to a woman 'oo'd live twenty year in the course o' nature? It *do*!'

'You're mistook! You're mistook!' Mrs Fettley insisted.

'Liz, there's *no* mistakin' when the edges are all heaped up, like – same as a collar. You'll see it. An' I laid out Dora Wickwood, too. *She* 'ad it under the arm-pit, like.'

Mrs Fettley considered awhile, and bowed her head in finality.

''Ow long d'you reckon 'twill allow ye, countin' from now, dearie?'

'Slow come, slow go. But if I don't set eyes on ye 'fore next hoppin', this'll be goodbye, Liz.'

'Dunno as I'll be able to manage by then – not 'thout I have a liddle dog to lead me. For de chillern, dey won't be troubled, an' – O Gra'! – I'm blindin' up – I'm blindin' up!'

'Oh, *dat* was why you didn't more'n finger with your quilt-patches all this while! I was wonderin' ... But the pain *do* count, don't ye think, Liz? The pain *do* count to keep 'Arry – where I want 'im. Say it can't be wasted, like.'

'I'm sure of it – sure of it, dearie. You'll 'ave your reward.'

'I don't want no more'n this – *if* de pain is taken into de reckonin'.'

''Twill be – 'twill be, Gra'.'

There was a knock on the door.

'That's Nurse. She's before 'er time,' said Mrs Ashcroft. 'Open to 'er.'

The young lady entered briskly, all the bottles in her bag clicking. 'Evenin', Mrs Ashcroft,' she began. 'I've come raound a little earlier than usual because of the Institute dance to-na-ite. You won't ma-ind, will you?'

'Oh, no. Me dancin' days are over.' Mrs Ashcroft was the self-contained domestic at once. 'My old friend, Mrs Fettley 'ere, has been settin' talkin' with me a while.'

'I hope she 'asn't been fatiguing you?' said the Nurse a little frostily.

'Quite the contrary. It 'as been a pleasure. Only – only – just at the end I felt a bit – a bit flogged out like.'

'Yes, yes.' The Nurse was on her knees already, with the washes to hand. 'When old ladies get together they talk a deal too much, I've noticed.'

'Mebbe we do,' said Mrs Fettley, rising. 'So, now, I'll make myself scarce.'

'Look at it first, though,' said Mrs Ashcroft feebly. 'I'd like ye to look at it.'

Mrs Fettley looked, and shivered. Then she leaned over, and kissed Mrs Ashcroft once on the waxy yellow forehead, and again on the faded grey eyes.

'It *do* count, don't it – de pain?' [9] The lips that still kept trace of their original moulding hardly more than breathed the words.

Mrs Fettley kissed them and moved towards the door.

Rahere

Rahere, King Henry's Jester,[10] feared by all the Norman Lords
For his eye that pierced their bosoms, for his tongue that shamed
their swords;
Feed and flattered by the Churchmen – well they knew how deep
he stood
In dark Henry's crooked counsels – fell upon an evil mood.

Suddenly, his days before him and behind him seemed to stand
Stripped and barren, fixed and fruitless, as those leagues of
naked sand
When St Michael's ebb slinks outward to the bleak horizon-bound,
And the trampling wide-mouthed waters are withdrawn from
sight and sound.

Then a Horror of Great Darkness[11] sunk his spirit and, anon,
(Who had seen him wince and whiten as he turned to walk alone)
Followed Gilbert the Physician, and muttered in his ear,
'Thou hast it, O my brother?' 'Yea, I have it,' said Rahere.

'So it comes,' said Gilbert smoothly, 'man's most immanent distress.
'Tis a humour of the Spirit which abhorreth all excess;
And, whatever breed the surfeit – Wealth, or Wit, or Power, or Fame
(And thou hast each) the Spirit laboureth to expel the same.

'Hence the dulled eye's deep self-loathing – hence the loaded
leaden brow;
Hence the burden of Wanhope that aches thy soul and body now.
Ay, the merriest fool must face it, and the wisest Doctor learn;
For it comes – it comes,' said Gilbert, 'as it passes – to return.'

But Rahere was in his torment, and he wandered, dumb and far,
Till he came to reeking Smithfield where the crowded gallows are.
(Followed Gilbert the Physician) and beneath the wry-necked dead,
Sat a leper and his woman, very merry, breaking bread.

He was cloaked from chin to ankle – faceless, fingerless, obscene –
Mere corruption swaddled man-wise, but the woman whole and clean;
And she waited on him crooning, and Rahere beheld the twain,
Each delighting in the other, and he checked and groaned again.

'So it comes, – it comes,' said Gilbert, 'as it came when Life began.
'Tis a motion of the Spirit that revealeth God to man
In the shape of Love exceeding, which regards not taint or fall,
Since in perfect Love,[12] saith Scripture, can be no excess at all.

'Hence the eye that sees no blemish – hence the hour that holds
                                                    no shame.
Hence the Soul assured the Essence and the Substance are the same.
Nay, the meanest need not miss it, though the mightier pass it by;
For it comes – it comes,' said Gilbert, 'and, thou seest, it does not die!'

The Survival

Horace, Ode 22, Bk V

Securely, after days
　Unnumbered, I behold
Kings mourn that promised praise
　Their cheating bards foretold.

Of earth-constricting wars,
　Of Princes passed in chains,
Of deeds out-shining stars,
　No word or voice remains.

Yet furthest times receive
　And to fresh praise restore,
Mere flutes that breathe at eve,
　Mere seaweed on the shore.

A smoke of sacrifice;
　A chosen myrtle-wreath;
An harlot's altered eyes;
　A rage 'gainst love or death;

Glazed snow beneath the moon;
　The surge of storm-bowed trees –
The Caesars perished soon,
　And Rome Herself: But these

Endure while Empires fall
　And Gods for Gods make room . . .[1]
Which greater God than all
　Imposed the amazing doom?

The Janeites

Jane lies in Winchester   blessed be her shade!
Praise the Lord for making her, and her for all she made!
And while the stones of Winchester, or Milsom Street, remain,
Glory, love, and honour unto England's Jane!

In the Lodge of Instruction² attached to 'Faith and Works No 5837 E.C.,' which has already been described, Saturday afternoon was appointed for the weekly clean-up, when all visiting Brethren were welcome to help under the direction of the Lodge Officer of the day: their reward was light refreshment and the meeting of companions.

This particular afternoon – in the autumn of '20 – Brother Burges, P.M., was on duty and, finding a strong shift present, took advantage of it to strip and dust all hangings and curtains, to go over every inch of the Pavement – which was stone, not floorcloth – by hand; and to polish the Columns, Jewels, Working outfit and organ. I was given to clean some Officer's Jewels – beautiful bits of old Georgian silver-work humanized by generations of elbow-grease – and retired to the organ loft; for the floor was like the quarter-deck of a battleship on the eve of a ball. Half-a-dozen brethren had already made the Pavement as glassy as the aisle of Greenwich Chapel; the brazen chapiters winked like pure gold at the flashing Marks on the Chairs; and a morose one-legged brother was attending to the Emblems of Mortality with, I think, rouge.

'They ought,' he volunteered to Brother Burges as we passed, 'to be betwixt the colour of ripe apricots an' a half-smoked meerschaum. That's how we kept 'em in my Mother-Lodge – a treat to look at.'

'I've never seen spit-and-polish to touch this,' I said.

'Wait till you see the organ,' Brother Burges replied. 'You

could shave in it when they've done. Brother Anthony's in charge up there – the taxi-owner you met here last month. I don't think you've come across Brother Humberstall,[3] have you?'

'I don't remember –' I began.

'You wouldn't have forgotten him if you had. He's a hair-dresser now, somewhere at the back of Ebury Street. 'Was Garrison Artillery. 'Blown up twice.'

'Does he show it?' I asked at the foot of the organ-loft stairs.

'No-o. Not much more than Lazarus[4] did, I expect.' Brother Burges fled off to set someone else to a job.

Brother Anthony, small, dark, and hump-backed, was hissing groom-fashion while he treated the rich acacia-wood panels of the Lodge organ with some sacred, secret composition of his own. Under his guidance Humberstall, an enormous, flat-faced man, carrying the shoulders, ribs, and loins of the old Mark '14 Royal Garrison Artillery, and the eyes of a bewildered retriever, rubbed the stuff in. I sat down to my task on the organ-bench, whose purple velvet cushion was being vacuum-cleaned on the floor below.

'Now,' said Anthony, after five minutes' vigorous work on the part of Humberstall. '*Now* we're gettin' somethin' worth lookin' at! Take it easy, an' go on with what you was tellin' me about that Macklin man.'

'I – I 'adn't anything against 'im,' said Humberstall, 'excep' he'd been a toff by birth; but that never showed till he was bosko absoluto. Mere bein' drunk on'y made a common 'ound of 'im. But when bosko, it all came out. Otherwise, he showed me my duties as mess-waiter very well on the 'ole.'

'Yes, yes. But what in 'ell made you go *back* to your Circus? The Board gave you down-an'-out fair enough, you said, after the dump went up at Eatables?'

'Board or no Board, *I* 'adn't the nerve to stay at 'ome – not with mother chuckin' 'erself round all three rooms like a rabbit every time the Gothas tried to get Victoria; an' sister writin' me aunts four pages about it next day. Not for *me*, thank you! till the war was over. So I slid out with a draft – they wasn't particular in '17, so long as the tally was correct – and I joined up again with our Circus somewhere at the back of Lar Pug Noy,[5] I think it was.' Humberstall paused for some seconds and his brow wrinkled. 'Then I – I went sick, or somethin' or other, they told me; but I know *when* I reported for duty, our Battery Sergeant Major says that I wasn't expected back, an' – an', one thing leadin' to another – to cut a long story short – I went up before our Major – Major – I shall forget my own name next – Major –'

'Never mind,' Anthony interrupted. 'Go on! It'll come back in talk!'

''Alf a mo'. 'Twas on the tip o' my tongue then.'

Humberstall dropped the polishing-cloth and knitted his brows again in most profound thought. Anthony turned to me and suddenly launched into a sprightly tale of his taxi's collision with a Marble Arch refuge on a greasy day after a three-yard skid.

''Much damage?' I asked.

'Oh no! Ev'ry bolt an' screw an' nut on the chassis strained; *but* nothing carried away, you understand me, an' not a scratch on the body. You'd never 'ave guessed a thing wrong till you took 'er in hand. It *was* a wop too: 'ead-on – like this!' And he slapped his tactful little forehead to show what a knock it had been.

'Did your Major dish you up much?' he went on over his shoulder to Humberstall who came out of his abstraction with a slow heave.

'We-ell! He told me I wasn't expected back either; an' he said 'e couldn't 'ang up the 'ole Circus till I'd rejoined; an' he said that my ten-inch Skoda which I'd been Number Three of, before the dump went up at Eatables, had 'er full crowd. But, 'e said, as soon as a casualty occurred he'd re-member me. "Meantime," says he, "I particularly want you for actin' mess-waiter."

'"Beggin' your pardon, sir," I says perfectly respectful; "but I didn't exactly come back for *that*, sir."

'"Beggin' *your* pardon, 'Umberstall," says 'e, "but I 'appen to command the Circus! Now, you're a sharp-witted man," he says; "an' what we've suffered from fool-waiters in Mess 'as been somethin' cruel. You'll take on, from now – under instruction to Macklin 'ere." So this man, Macklin, that I was tellin' you about, showed me my duties . . . 'Ammick! I've got it! 'Ammick was our Major, an' Mosse was Captain!' Humberstall celebrated his recapture of the name by labouring at the organ-panel on his knee.

'Look out! You'll smash it,' Anthony protested.

'Sorry! Mother's often told me I didn't know my strength. Now, here's a curious thing. This Major of ours – it's all comin' back to me – was a high-up divorce-court lawyer; an' Mosse, our Captain, was Number One o' Mosse's Private Detective Agency. You've heard of it? 'Wives watched while you wait, an' so on. Well, these two 'ad been registerin' together, so to speak, in the Civil line for years on end, but hadn't ever met till the War. Consequently, at Mess their talk was mostly about famous cases they'd been mixed up in. 'Ammick told the Law-courts' end o' the business, an' all what had been left out of the pleadin's; an' Mosse 'ad the actual facts concernin' the errin' parties – in hotels an' so on. I've heard better talk in our Mess than ever before or since. It comes o' the Gunners bein' a scientific corps.'

'That be damned!' said Anthony. 'If anythin' 'appens to 'em they've got it all down in a book. There's no book when your lorry dies on you in the 'Oly Land. *That's* brains.'

'Well, *then*,' Humberstall continued, 'come on this secret society business that I started tellin' you about. When those two – 'Ammick an' Mosse – 'ad finished about their matrimonial relations – and, mind you, they weren't radishes – they seldom or ever repeated – they'd begin, as often as not, on this Secret Society woman I was tellin' you of – this Jane.[6] She was the only woman I ever 'eard 'em say a good word for. 'Cordin' to them Jane was a none-such. *I* didn't know then she was a Society. 'Fact is, I only 'ung out 'arf an ear in their direction at first, on account of bein' under instruction for mess-duty to this Macklin man. What drew *my* attention to her was a new Lieutenant joinin' up. We called 'im "Gander" on account of his profeel, which was the identical bird. 'E'd been a nactuary[7] – workin' out 'ow long civilians 'ad to live. Neither 'Ammick nor Mosse wasted words on 'im at Mess. They went on talking as usual, an' in due time, *as* usual, they got back to Jane.

Gander cocks one of his big chilblainy ears an' cracks his cold finger-joints. "By God! Jane?" says 'e. "Yes, Jane," says 'Ammick pretty short an' senior. "Praise 'Eaven!" says Gander. "It was 'Bubbly' where I've come from down the line." (Some damn review or other, I expect.) Well, neither 'Ammick nor Mosse was easy-mouthed, or for that matter mealy-mouthed; but no sooner 'ad Gander passed that remark than they both shook 'ands with the young squirt across the table an' called for the port back again. It *was* a password, all right! Then they went at it about Jane – all three, regardless of rank. That made me listen. Presently, I 'eard 'Ammick say –'

''Arf a mo',' Anthony cut in. 'But what was *you* doin' in Mess?'

'Me an' Macklin was refixin' the sand-bag screens to the dug-out passage in case o' gas. We never knew when we'd cop it in the 'Eavies, don't you see. But we knew we 'ad been looked for for some time, an' it might come any minute. But, as I was sayin', 'Ammick says what a pity 'twas Jane 'ad died barren. "I deny that," says Mosse. "I maintain she was fruitful in the 'ighest sense o' the word." An' Mosse knew about such things, too. "I'm inclined to agree with 'Ammick," says young Gander. "Any'ow, she's left no direct an' lawful prog'ny." I remember every word they said, on account o' what 'appened subsequently. I 'adn't noticed Macklin much, or I'd ha' seen he was bosko absoluto. Then 'e cut in, leanin' over a packin'-case with a face on 'im like a dead mackerel in the dark. "Pa-hardon me, gents," Macklin says, "but this *is* a matter on which I *do* 'appen to be moderately well-informed. She *did* leave lawful issue in the shape o' one son; an' 'is name was 'Enery James."

'"By what sire! Prove it," says Gander, before 'is senior officers could get in a word.

'"I will," says Macklin, surgin' on 'is two thumbs. *An'*, mark you, none of 'em spoke! I forget whom he said was the sire of this 'Enery James-man; but 'e delivered 'em a lecture on this Jane-woman for more than a quarter of an hour. I know the exact time, because my old Skoda was on duty at ten-minute intervals reachin' after some Jerry formin'-up area; and her blast always put out the dug-out candles. I relit 'em once, an' again at the end. In conclusion, this Macklin fell flat forward on 'is face, which was how 'e generally wound up 'is notion of a perfect day. Bosko absoluto!

'"Take 'im away," says 'Ammick to me. "'E's sufferin' from shell-shock."

'To cut a long story short, *that* was what first put the notion into my 'ead. Wouldn't it you? Even 'ad Macklin been a 'igh-up Mason —'

'Wasn't 'e, then?' said Anthony, a little puzzled.

'"E'd never gone beyond the Blue Degrees, 'e told me. Any'ow, 'e'd lectured 'is superior officers up an' down; 'e'd as good as called 'em fools most o' the time, in 'is toff's voice. I 'eard 'im an' I saw 'im. An' all he got was — me told off to put 'im to bed! And all on account o' Jane! Would *you* have let a thing like that get past you? Nor me, either! Next mornin', when his stummick was settled, I was at him full-cry to find out 'ow it was worked. Toff or no toff, 'e knew his end of a bargain. First, 'e wasn't takin' any. He said I wasn't fit to be initiated into the Society of the Janeites. That only meant five bob more — fifteen up to date.

'"Make it one Bradbury[8]," 'e says. "It's dirt-cheap. You saw me 'old the Circus in the 'ollow of me 'and?"

'No denyin' it. I 'ad. So, for one pound, he communicated me the Pass-word of the First Degree which was *Tilniz an' trap-doors*.[9]

'"I know what a trap-door is," I says to 'im, "but what in 'ell's *Tilniz?*"

'"You obey orders," 'e says, "an' next time I ask you what you're thinkin' about you'll answer, '*Tilniz an' trap-doors*,' in a smart and soldierly manner. I'll spring that question at me own time. All you've got to do is to be distinck."

'We settled all this while we was skinnin' spuds for dinner at the back o' the rear-truck under our camouflage-screens. Gawd, 'ow that glue-paint did stink! Otherwise, 'twasn't so bad, with the sun comin' through our pantomime-leaves, an' the wind marcelling the grasses in the cutting. Well, one thing leading to another, nothin' further 'appened in this direction till the afternoon. We 'ad a high standard o' livin' in Mess — an' in the

Group, for that matter. I was takin' away Mosse's lunch – dinner 'e would never call it – an' Mosse was fillin' 'is cigarette-case previous to the afternoon's duty. Macklin, in the passage, comin' in as if 'e didn't know Mosse was there, slings 'is question at me, an' I give the countersign in a low but quite distinck voice, makin' as if I 'adn't seen Mosse. Mosse looked at me through and through, with his cigarette-case in his 'and. Then 'e jerks out 'arf a dozen – best Turkish – on the table an' exits. I pinched 'em an' divvied with Macklin.

'"You see 'ow it works," says Macklin. "Could you 'ave invested a Bradbury to better advantage?"

'"So far, no," I says. "Otherwise, though, if they start provin' an' tryin' me, I'm a dead bird. There must be a lot more to this Janeite game."

'"'Eaps an' 'eaps," he says. "But to show you the sort of 'eart I 'ave, I'll communicate you all the 'Igher Degrees among the Janeites, includin' the Charges, for another Bradbury; but you'll 'ave to work, Dobbin."'

''Pretty free with your Bradburys, wasn't you?' Anthony grunted disapprovingly.

'What odds? *Ac*-tually, Gander told us, we couldn't expect to av'rage more than six weeks' longer apiece, an', any'ow, *I* never regretted it. But make no mistake – the preparation was somethin' cruel. In the first place, I come under Macklin for direct instruction *re* Jane.'

'Oh! Jane *was* real, then?' Anthony glanced for an instant at me as he put the question. 'I couldn't quite make that out.'

'Real!' Humberstall's voice rose almost to a treble. 'Jane? Why, she was a little old maid 'oo'd written 'alf a dozen books about a hundred years ago. 'Twasn't as if there was anythin' *to* 'em, either. *I* know. I had to read 'em. They weren't adventurous, nor smutty, nor what you'd call even interestin' – all about girls o' seventeen (they begun young then, I tell you), not certain 'oom they'd like to marry; an' their dances an' card-parties an' picnics, and their young blokes goin' off to London on 'orseback for 'air-cuts an' shaves. It took a full day in those days, if you went to a proper barber. They wore wigs, too, when they was chemists or clergymen. All that interested me on account o' me

126

profession, an' cuttin' the men's 'air every fortnight. Macklin used to chip me about bein' an 'air-dresser. 'E *could* pass remarks, too!'

Humberstall recited with relish a fragment of what must have been a superb commination-service, ending with, 'You lazy-minded, lousy-headed, long-trousered, perfumed perookier.'[10]

'An' you took it?' Anthony's quick eyes ran over the man.

'Yes. I was after my money's worth; an' Macklin, havin' put 'is 'and to the plough, wasn't one to withdraw it. Otherwise, if I'd pushed 'im, I'd ha' slew 'im. Our Battery Sergeant Major nearly did. For Macklin had a wonderful way o' passing remarks on a man's civil life; an' he put it about that our B.S.M. had run a dope an' dolly-shop with a Chinese woman, the wrong end o' Southwark Bridge. Nothin' you could lay 'old of, o' course; but —' Humberstall let us draw our own conclusions.

'That reminds me,' said Anthony, smacking his lips. 'I 'ad a bit of a fracas with a fare in the Fulham Road last month. He called me a paras-tit-ic Forder. I informed 'im I was owner-driver, an' 'e could see for 'imself the cab was quite clean. That didn't suit 'im. 'E said it was crawlin'.'

'What happened?' I asked.

'One o' them blue-bellied Bolshies of post-war Police (neglectin' point-duty, as usual) asked us to flirt a little quieter. My joker chucked some Arabic at 'im. That was when we signed the Armistice. 'E'd been a Yeoman — a perishin' Gloucestershire Yeoman — that I'd helped gather in the orange crop with at Jaffa, in the 'Oly Land!'

'And after that?' I continued.

'It 'ud be 'ard to say. I know 'e lived at Hendon or Cricklewood. I drove 'im there. We must 'ave talked Zionism or somethin', because at seven next mornin' him an' me was tryin' to get petrol out of a milkshop at St Albans. They 'adn't any. In lots o' ways this war has been a public noosance, as one might say, but there's no denyin' it 'elps you slip through life easier. The dairyman's son 'ad done time on Jordan with camels. So he stood us rum an' milk.'

'Just like 'avin' the Password, eh?' was Humberstall's comment.

'That's right! Ours was *Imshee kelb*.[11] Not so 'ard to remember as your Jane stuff.'

'Jane wasn't so very 'ard – not the way Macklin used to put 'er,' Humberstall resumed. 'I 'ad only six books to remember. I learned the names by 'eart as Macklin placed 'em. There was one, called *Persuasion*, first; an' the rest in a bunch, except another about some Abbey or other[12] – last by three lengths. But, as I was sayin', what beat me was there was nothin' *to* 'em nor *in* 'em. Nothin' at all, believe me.'

'You seem good an' full of 'em, any'ow,' said Anthony.

'I mean that 'er characters was no *use*! They was only just like people you run across any day. One of 'em was a curate – the Reverend Collins – always on the make an' lookin' to marry money. Well, when I was a Boy Scout, 'im or 'is twin brother was our troop-leader. An' there was an upstandin' 'ard-mouthed Duchess or a Baronet's wife that didn't give a curse for anyone 'oo wouldn't do what she told 'em to; the Lady – Lady Catherine (I'll get it in a minute) De Bugg. Before Ma bought the 'air-dressin' business in London I used to know of an 'olesale grocer's wife near Leicester (I'm Leicestershire myself) that might 'ave been 'er duplicate. And – oh yes – there was a Miss Bates;[13] just an old maid runnin' about like a hen with 'er 'ead cut off, an' her tongue loose at both ends. I've got an aunt like 'er. Good as gold – but, *you* know.'

'Lord, yes!' said Anthony, with feeling. 'An' did you find out what *Tilniz* meant? I'm always huntin' after the meanin' of things meself.'

'Yes, 'e was a swine of a Major-General, retired, and on the make. They're all on the make, in a quiet way, in Jane. 'E was so much of a gentleman by 'is own estimation that 'e was always be'avin' like a hound. *You* know the sort. 'Turned a girl out of 'is own 'ouse because she 'adn't any money – *after*, mark you, encouragin' 'er to set 'er cap at his son, because 'e thought she had.'

'But that 'appens all the time,' said Anthony. 'Why, me own mother –'

'That's right. So would mine. But this Tilney was a man, an'
some'ow Jane put it down all so naked it made you ashamed. I
told Macklin that, an' he said I was shapin' to be a good Janeite.
'Twasn't *his* fault if I wasn't. 'Nother thing, too; 'avin' been at
the Bath Mineral Waters 'Ospital in 'Sixteen, with trench-feet,
was a great advantage to me, because I knew the names o' the
streets where Jane 'ad lived. There was one of 'em – Laura, I
think, or some other girl's name – which Macklin said was 'oly
ground. "If you'd been initiated *then*," he says, "you'd ha' felt
your flat feet tingle every time you walked over those sacred
pavin'-stones."

'"My feet tingled right enough," I said, "but not on account
of Jane. Nothin' remarkable about that," I says.

'"'Eaven lend me patience!" he says, combin' 'is 'air with 'is
little hands. "Every dam' thing about Jane is remarkable to a
pukka Janeite! It was there," he says, "that Miss What's-her-
Name" (he had the name; I've forgotten it) "made up 'er
engagement again, after nine years, with Captain T'other
Bloke."[14] An' he dished me out a page an' a half of one of the
books to learn by 'eart – *Persuasion*, I think it was.'

''You quick at gettin' things off by 'eart?' Anthony demanded.

'Not as a rule. I was then, though, or else Macklin knew 'ow
to deliver the Charges properly. 'E said 'e'd been some sort o'
schoolmaster once, and he'd make my mind resume work or
break 'imself. That was just before the Battery Sergeant Major
'ad it in for him on account o' what he'd been sayin' about the
Chinese wife an' the dolly-shop.'

'What did Macklin really say?' Anthony and I asked together.
Humberstall gave us a fragment. It was hardly the stuff to let
loose on a pious post-war world without revision.

'And what had your B. S. M. been in civil life?' I asked at the
end.

''Ead-embalmer to an 'olesale undertaker in the Midlands,'
said Humberstall; 'but, o' course, *when* he thought 'e saw his
chance he naturally took it. He came along one mornin' lickin'
'is lips. "You don't get past me this time," 'e says to Macklin.
"You're for it, Professor."

'"'Ow so, me gallant Major," says Macklin; "an' what for?"

'"For writin' obese[15] words on the breech o' the ten-inch,"
says the B.S.M. She was our old Skoda that I've been tellin'
you about. We called 'er "Bloody Eliza". She 'ad a badly wore
obturator an' blew through a fair treat. I knew by Macklin's
face the B.S.M. 'ad dropped it somewhere, but all he
vow'saifed was, "Very good, Major. We will consider it in
Common Room." The B.S.M. couldn't ever stand Macklin's
toff's way o' puttin' things; so he goes off rumblin' like 'ell's
bells in an 'urricane, as the Marines say. Macklin put it to
me at once, what had I been doin'? Some'ow he could read
me like a book.

'Well, all *I*'d done — an I told 'im *he* was responsible for it —
was to chalk the guns. 'Ammick never minded what the men
wrote up on 'em. 'E said it gave 'em an interest in their job.
You'd see all sorts of remarks chalked on the side-plates or the
gear-casin's.'

'What sort of remarks?' said Anthony keenly.

'Oh! 'Ow Bloody Eliza, or Spittin' Jim — that was our old
Mark Five Nine-point-two — felt that morning, an' such things.
But it 'ad come over me — more to please Macklin than anythin'
else — that it was time we Janeites 'ad a look in. So, as I was
tellin' you, I'd taken an' rechristened all three of 'em, on my
own, early that mornin'. Spittin' Jim I 'ad chalked "The Reverend Collins" — that Curate I was tellin' you about; an' our
cut-down Navy Twelve, "General Tilney", because it was
worse wore in the groovin' than anything *I*'d ever seen. The
Skoda (an' that was where *I* dropped it) I 'ad chalked up "The
Lady Catherine De Bugg". I made a clean breast of it all to
Macklin. He reached up an' patted me on the shoulder. "You
done nobly," he says. "You're bringin' forth abundant fruit,
like a good Janeite. But I'm afraid your spellin' has misled our
worthy B.S.M. *That's* what it is," 'e says, slappin' 'is little leg.
"'Ow might you 'ave spelt De Burgh for example?"

'I told 'im. 'Twasn't right; an' 'e nips off to the Skoda to
make it so. When 'e comes back, 'e says that the Gander 'ad
been before 'im an' corrected the error. But we two come up
before the Major, just the same, that afternoon after lunch;
'Ammick in the chair, so to speak, Mosse in another, an' the

B.S.M. chargin' Macklin with writin' obese words on His Majesty's property, on active service. When it transpired that me an' not Macklin was the offendin' party, the B.S.M. turned 'is hand in and sulked like a baby. 'E as good as told 'Ammick 'e couldn't hope to preserve discipline unless examples was made – meanin', o' course, Macklin.'

'Yes, I've heard all that,' said Anthony, with a contemptuous grunt. 'The worst of it is, a lot of it's true.'

'''Ammick took 'im up sharp about Military Law, which he said was even more fair than the civilian article.'

'My Gawd!' This came from Anthony's scornful midmost bosom.

'"Accordin' to the unwritten law of the 'Eavies," says 'Ammick, "there's no objection to the men chalkin' the guns, if decency is preserved. On the other 'and," says he, "we 'aven't yet settled the precise status of individuals entitled so to do. I 'old that the privilege is confined to combatants only."

'"With the permission of the Court," says Mosse, who was another born lawyer, "I'd like to be allowed to join issue on that point. Prisoner's position is very delicate an' doubtful, an' he has no legal representative."

'"Very good," says 'Ammick. "Macklin bein' acquitted –"

'"With submission, me lud," says Mosse. "I hope to prove 'e was accessory before the fact."

'"*As* you please," says 'Ammick. "But in that case, 'oo the 'ell's goin' to get the port I'm tryin' to stand the Court?"

'"I submit," says Mosse, "prisoner, bein' under direct observation o' the Court, could be temporarily enlarged for that duty."

'So Macklin went an' got it, an' the B.S.M. had 'is glass with the rest. Then they argued whether mess servants an' non-combatants was entitled to chalk the guns ('Ammick *versus* Mosse). After a bit, 'Ammick as C.O. give 'imself best, an' me an' Macklin was severely admonished for trespassin' on combatants' rights, an' the B.S.M. was warned that if we repeated the offence 'e could deal with us summ'rily. He 'ad some glasses o' port an' went out quite 'appy. Then my turn come, while Macklin was gettin' them their tea; an' one thing leadin' to another, 'Ammick put me through all the Janeite Degrees, you might say. 'Never 'ad such a doin' in my life.'

'Yes, but what did you tell 'em?' said Anthony. 'I can't ever *think* my lies quick enough when I'm for it.'

'No need to lie. I told 'em that the backside view o' the Skoda, when she was run up, put Lady De Bugg into my 'ead. They gave me right there, but they said I was wrong about General Tilney. 'Cordin' to them, our Navy twelve-inch ought to 'ave been christened Miss Bates. I said the same idea 'ad crossed my mind, till I'd seen the General's groovin'. Then I felt it had to be the General or nothin'. But they give me full marks for the Reverend Collins – our Nine-point-two.'

'An' you fed 'em *that* sort o' talk?' Anthony's fox-coloured eyebrows climbed almost into his hair.

'While I was assistin' Macklin to get tea – yes. Seein' it was an examination, I wanted to do 'im credit as a Janeite.'

'An' – an' what did they say?'

'They said it was 'ighly creditable to us both. I don't drink, so they give me about a hundred fags.'

'Gawd! What a Circus you must 'ave been,' was Anthony's gasping comment.

'It *was* a 'appy little Group. I wouldn't 'a changed with any other.'

Humberstall sighed heavily as he helped Anthony slide back the organ-panel. We all admired it in silence, while Anthony repocketed his secret polishing mixture, which lived in a tin tobacco-box. I had neglected my work for listening to Humberstall. Anthony reached out quietly and took over a Secretary's Jewel and a rag. Humberstall studied his reflection in the glossy wood.

'Almost,' he said critically, holding his head to one side.

'Not with an Army. You could with a Safety, though,' said Anthony. And, indeed, as Brother Burges had foretold, one might have shaved in it with comfort.

'Did you ever run across any of 'em afterwards, any time?' Anthony asked presently.

'Not so many of 'em left to run after, now. With the 'Eavies it's mostly neck or nothin'. We copped it. In the neck. In due time.'

'Well, *you* come out of it all right.' Anthony spoke both stoutly and soothingly; but Humberstall would not be comforted.

'That's right; but I almost wish I 'adn't,' he sighed. 'I was 'appier there than ever before or since. Jerry's March push in 'Eighteen did us in; an' yet, 'ow could we 'ave expected it? 'Ow *could* we 'ave expected it? We'd been sent back for rest an' runnin'-repairs, back pretty near our base; an' our old loco' that used to shift us about o' nights, she'd gone down the line for repairs. But for 'Ammick we wouldn't even 'ave 'ad our camouflage-screens up. He told our Brigadier that, whatever 'e might be in the Gunnery line, as a leadin' Divorce lawyer he never threw away a point in argument. So 'e 'ad us all screened in over in a cuttin' on a little spur-line near a wood; an' e' saw to the screens 'imself. The leaves weren't more than comin' out then, an' the sun used to make our glue-paint stink. Just like actin' in a theatre, it was! But 'appy. *But* 'appy! I expect if we'd been caterpillars, like the new big six-inch hows, they'd ha' remembered us. But we was the old La Bassee '15 Mark o' Heavies that ran on rails – not much more good than scrap-iron that late in the war. An', believe me, gents – or Brethren, as I should say – we copped it cruel. Look 'ere! It was in the afternoon, an' I was watchin' Gander instructin' a class in new sights at Lady Catherine. All of a sudden I 'eard our screens rip overhead, an' a runner on a motor-bike come sailin', sailin' through the air – like that bloke that used to bicycle off Brighton Pier – and landed one awful wop almost atop o' the class. "'Old 'ard," says Gander. "That's no way to report. What's the fuss?" "Your screens 'ave broke my back, for one thing," says the bloke on the ground; "an' for another, the 'ole front's gone." "Nonsense," says Gander. 'E 'adn't more than passed the remark when the man was vi'lently sick an' conked out. 'E 'ad plenty papers on 'im from Brigadiers and C.O.s reporting 'emselves cut off 'an askin' for orders. 'E was right both ways –his back an' our front. The 'ole Somme front washed out as clean as kiss-me-'and!' His huge hand smashed down open on his knee.

'We 'eard about it at the time in the 'Oly Land. Was it reelly as quick as all that?' said Anthony.

'Quicker! Look 'ere! The motor-bike dropped in on us about four pip-emma. After that, we tried to get orders o' some kind or other, but nothin' came through excep' that all available transport was in use and not likely to be released. *That* didn't 'elp us any. About nine o'clock comes along a young Brass 'At in brown gloves. We was quite a surprise to 'im. 'E said they were evacuating the area and we'd better shift. "Where to?" says 'Ammick, rather short.

'"Oh, somewhere Amiens way," he says. "Not that I'd guarantee Amiens for any length o' time; but Amiens might do to begin with." I'm giving you the very words. Then 'e goes off swingin' 'is brown gloves, and 'Ammick sends for Gander and orders 'im to march the men through Amiens to Dieppe; book thence to New'aven, take up positions be'ind Seaford, an' carry on the war. Gander said 'e'd see 'im damned first. 'Ammick says 'e'd see 'im court-martialled after. Gander says what 'e meant to say was that the men 'ud see all an' sundry damned before they went into Amiens with their gunsights wrapped up in their putties. 'Ammick says 'e 'adn't said a word about putties, an' carryin' off the gunsights was purely optional. "Well, anyhow," says Gander, "putties *or* drawers, they ain't goin' to shift a step unless you lead the procession."

'"Mutinous 'ounds," says 'Ammick. "But we live in a democratic age. D'you suppose they'd object to kindly diggin' 'emselves in a bit?" "Not at all," says Gander. "The B.S.M.'s kept 'em at it like terriers for the last three hours." "That bein' so," says 'Ammick, "Macklin'll now fetch us small glasses o' port." Then Mosse comes in – he could smell port a mile off – an' he submits we'd only add to the congestion in Amiens if we took our crowd there, whereas, if we lay doggo where we was, Jerry might miss us, though he didn't seem to be missin' much that evenin'.

'The 'ole country was pretty noisy, an' our dumps we'd lit ourselves flarin' Heavens high as far as you could see. Lyin' doggo was our best chance. I believe we might ha' pulled it off, if we'd been left alone, but along towards midnight – there was some small stuff swishin' about, but nothin' particular – a nice little bald-headed old gentleman in uniform pushes into the

dug-out wipin' his glasses an' sayin' 'e was thinkin' o' formin' a
defensive flank on our left with 'is battalion which 'ad just
come up. 'Ammick says 'e wouldn't form much if 'e was 'im.
"Oh, don't say *that*," says the old gentleman, very shocked.
"One must support the Guns, mustn't one?" 'Ammick says we
was refittin' an' about as effective, just then, as a public lav'tory.
"Go into Amiens," he says, "an' defend 'em there." "Oh no,"
says the old gentleman, "me an' my laddies *must* make a defensive flank for you," an' he flips out of the dug-out like a
performin' bullfinch, chirruppin' for his "laddies". Gawd
in 'Eaven knows what sort o' push they was – little boys mostly
– but they 'ung on to 'is coat-tails like a Sunday-school treat, an'
we 'eard 'em muckin' about in the open for a bit. Then a pretty
tight barrage was slapped down for ten minutes, an' 'Ammick
thought the laddies had copped it already. "It'll be our turn
next," says Mosse. "There's been a covey o' Gothas messin'
about for the last 'alf-hour – lookin' for the Railway Shops, I
expect. They're just as likely to take us." "Arisin' out o' that,"
says 'Ammick, "one of 'em sounds pretty low down now. We're
for it, me learned colleagues!" "Jesus!" says Gander, "I believe
you're right, sir." And that was the last word *I* 'eard on the
matter.'

'Did they cop you then?' said Anthony.

'They did. I expect Mosse was right, an' they took us for the
Railway Shops. When I come to, I was lyin' outside the cuttin',
which was pretty well filled up. The Reverend Collins was all
right; but Lady Catherine and the General was past prayin' for.
I lay there, takin' it in, till I felt cold an' I looked at meself.
Otherwise, I 'adn't much on excep' me boots. So I got up an'
walked about to keep warm. Then I saw somethin' like a
mushroom in the moonlight. It was the nice old gentleman's
bald 'ead. I patted it. 'Im and 'is laddies 'ad copped it right
enough. Some battalion run out in a 'urry from England, I
suppose. They 'adn't even begun to dig in – pore little perishers!
I dressed myself off 'em there, an' topped off with a British
warm. Then I went back to the cuttin' an' someone says to me:
"Dig, you ox, dig! Gander's under." So I 'elped shift things till
I threw up blood an' bile mixed. Then I dropped, an' they

brought Gander out – dead – an' laid 'im next me. 'Ammick 'ad gone too – fair tore in 'alf, the B.S.M. said; but the funny thing was he talked quite a lot before 'e died, an' nothin' to 'im below 'is stummick, they told me. Mosse we never found. 'E'd been standing by Lady Catherine. She'd up-ended an' gone back on 'em, with 'alf the cuttin' atop of 'er, by the look of things.'

'And what come to Macklin?' said Anthony.

'Dunno . . . 'E was with 'Ammick. I expect I must ha' been blown clear of all by the first bomb; for I was the on'y Janeite left. We lost about half our crowd, either under, or after we'd got 'em out. The B.S.M. went off 'is rocker when mornin' came, an' he ran about from one to another sayin': "That was a good push! That was a great crowd! Did ye ever know any push to touch 'em?" An' then 'e'd cry. So what was left of us made off for ourselves, an' I came across a lorry, pretty full, but they took me in.'

'Ah!' said Anthony with pride. '"They all take a taxi when it's rainin'." 'Ever 'eard that song?'

'They went a long way back. Then I walked a bit, an' there was a hospital-train fillin' up, an' one of the Sisters – a grey-headed one – ran at me wavin' 'er red 'ands an' sayin' there wasn't room for a louse in it. I was past carin'. But she went on talkin' and talkin' about the war, an' her pa in Ladbroke Grove, an' 'ow strange for 'er at 'er time of life to be doin' this work with a lot o' men, an' next war, 'ow the nurses 'ud 'ave to wear khaki breeches on account o' the mud, like the Land Girls; an' that reminded 'er, she'd boil me an egg if she could lay 'ands on one, for she'd run a chicken-farm once. You never 'eard any-thin' like it – outside o' Jane. It set me off laughin' again. Then a woman with a nose an' teeth on 'er, marched up. "What's all this?" she says. "What do you want?" "Nothing," I says, "only make Miss Bates, there, stop talkin' or I'll die." "Miss Bates?" she says. "What in 'Eaven's name makes you call 'er that?" "Because she is," I says. "D'you know what you're sayin'?" she says, an' slings her bony arm round me to get me off the ground. "'Course I do," I says, "an' if you knew Jane you'd know too." "That's enough," says she. "You're comin' on this

train if I have to kill a Brigadier for you," an' she an' an ord'ly
fair hove me into the train, on to a stretcher close to the cookers.
That beef-tea went down well! Then she shook 'ands with me
an' said I'd hit off Sister Molyneux in one, an' then she pinched
me an extra blanket. It was 'er own 'ospital pretty much. I
expect she was the Lady Catherine de Burgh of the area. Well,
an' so, to cut a long story short, nothing further transpired.'

''Adn't you 'ad enough by then?' asked Anthony.

'I expect so. Otherwise, if the old Circus 'ad been carryin'
on, I might 'ave 'ad another turn with 'em before Armistice.
Our B.S.M. was right. There never was a 'appier push. 'Ammick
an' Mosse an' Gander an' the B.S.M. an' that pore little
Macklin-man makin' an' passin' an' raisin' me an' gettin' me on
to the 'ospital train after 'e was dead, all for a couple of
Bradburys. I lie awake nights still, reviewing matters. There
never was a push to touch ours – never!'

Anthony handed me back the Secretary's Jewel resplendent.

'Ah,' said he. 'No denyin' that Jane business was more useful
to you than the Roman Eagles or the Star an' Garter. 'Pity
there wasn't any of you Janeites in the 'Oly Land. *I* never come
across 'em.'

'Well, as pore Macklin said, it's a very select Society, an'
you've got to be a Janeite in your 'eart, or you won't have any
success. An' yet he made *me* a Janeite! I read all her six books
now for pleasure 'tween times in the shop; an' it brings it all
back – down to the smell of the glue-paint on the screens. You
take it from me, Brethren, there's no one to touch Jane when
you're in a tight place. Gawd bless 'er, whoever she was.'

Worshipful Brother Burges, from the floor of the Lodge,
called us all from Labour to Refreshment. Humberstall hove
himself up – so very a cart-horse of a man one almost expected
to hear the harness creak on his back – and descended the steps.

He said he could not stay for tea because he had promised
his mother to come home for it, and she would most probably
be waiting for him now at the Lodge door.

'One or other of 'em always comes for 'im. He's apt to miss
'is gears sometime,' Anthony explained to me, as we followed.

'Goes on a bust, d'you mean?'

''Im! He's no more touched liquor than 'e 'as women since 'e was born. No, 'e's liable to a sort o' quiet fits, like. They came on after the dump blew up at Eatables. But for them, 'e'd ha' been Battery Sergeant Major.'

'Oh!' I said. 'I couldn't make out why he took on as mess-waiter when he got back to his guns. That explains things a bit.'

''Is sister told me the dump goin' up knocked all 'is Gunnery instruction clean out of 'im. The only thing 'e stuck to was to get back to 'is old crowd. Gawd knows 'ow 'e worked it, but 'e did. He fair deserted out of England to 'em, she says; an' when they saw the state 'e was in, they 'adn't the 'eart to send 'im back or into 'ospital. They kep' 'im for a mascot, as you might say. That's *all* dead-true. 'Is sister told me so. But I can't guarantee that Janeite business, excep' 'e never told a lie since 'e was six. 'Is sister told me so. What do *you* think?'

'He isn't likely to have made it up out of his own head,' I replied.

'But people don't get so crazy-fond o' books as all that, do they? 'E's made 'is sister try to read 'em. She'd do anythin' to please him. But, as I keep tellin' 'er, so'd 'is mother. D'you 'appen to know anything about Jane?'

'I believe Jane was a bit of a match-maker in a quiet way when she was alive, and I know all her books are full of match-making,' I said. '*You'd* better look out.'

'Oh, *that's* as good as settled,' Anthony replied, blushing.

Jane's Marriage

Jane went to Paradise:
   That was only fair.
Good Sir Walter[16] met her first,
   And led her up the stair.
Henry[17] and Tobias,[18]
   And Miguel[19] of Spain,
Stood with Shakespeare at the top
   To welcome Jane –

Then the Three Archangels
   Offered out of hand,
Anything in Heaven's gift
   That she might command.
Azrael's eyes upon her,
   Raphael's wings above,
Michael's sword against her heart,
   Jane said: 'Love.'

Instantly the under-
   standing Seraphim
Laid their fingers on their lips
   And went to look for him.
Stole across the Zodiac,
   Harnessed Charles's Wain,
And whispered round the Nebulae
   'Who loved Jane?'

In a private limbo
   Where none had thought to look,
Sat a Hampshire gentleman
   Reading of a book,
It was called *Persuasion*,
   And it told the plain
Story of the love between
   Him and Jane.

He heard the question
   Circle Heaven through –

Closed the book and answered:
  'I did – and do!'
Quietly but speedily
  (As Captain Wentworth moved)
Entered into Paradise
  The man Jane loved!

The Portent
Horace, Ode 20, Bk V

Oh, late withdrawn from human-kind
  And following dreams we never knew!
Varus, what dream has Fate assigned
  To trouble you?

Such virtue as commends the law
  Of Virtue to the vulgar horde
Suffices not. You needs must draw
  A righteous sword;

And, flagrant in well-doing, smite
  The priests of Bacchus at their fane,
Lest any worshipper invite
  The God again.

Whence public strife and naked crime
  And – deadlier than the cup you shun –
A people schooled to mock, in time,
  All law – not one.

Cease, then, to fashion State-made sin,
  Nor give thy children cause to doubt
That Virtue springs from iron within[1] –
  Not lead without.

The Prophet and the Country

North of London stretches a country called 'The Midlands', filled with brick cities, all absolutely alike, but populated by natives who, through heredity, have learned not only to distinguish between them but even between the different houses; so that at meals and at evening multitudes return, without confusion or scandal, each to the proper place.

 Last summer, desperate need forced me to cross that area, and I fell into a motor-licence 'control' which began in a market-town filled with unherded beeves[2] carrying red numbered tickets on their rumps. An English-speaking policeman inspected my licence on a bridge, while the cattle blundered and blew round the car. A native in plain clothes lolled out an enormous mulberry-coloured tongue, with which he licked a numbered label, precisely like one of those on the behinds of the bullocks, and made to dab it on my wind-screen. I protested. 'But it will save you trouble,' he said. 'You're liable to be held up for your licence from now on. This is your protection. Everybody does it.'

'Oh! If that's the case –' I began weakly.

He slapped it on the glass and I went forward – the man was right – all the cars I met were 'protected' as mine was – till I reached some county or other which marked the limit of the witch-doctoring, and entered, at twilight, a large-featured land where the Great North Road ran, bordered by wide way-wastes, between clumps of old timber.

Here the car, without warning, sobbed and stopped. One does not expect the make-and-break of the magneto[3] – that tiny two-inch spring of finest steel – to fracture; and by the time we had found the trouble, night shut down on us. A rounded pile of woods ahead took one sudden star to its forehead and faded out; the way-waste melted into the darker velvet of the hedge; another star reflected itself in the glassy

black of the bitumened road; and a weak moon struggled up out
of a mist-patch from a valley. Our lights painted the grass
unearthly greens, and the tree-boles bone-white. A church clock
struck eleven, as I curled up in the front seat and awaited the
progress of Time and Things, with some notion of picking up a
tow towards morning. It was long since I had spent a night in
the open, and the hour worked on me. Time was when such
nights, and the winds that heralded their dawns, had been
fortunate and blessed; but those Gates, I thought, were for
ever shut . . .

I diagnosed it as a baker's van on a Ford chassis, lit with
unusual extravagance. It pulled up and asked what the trouble
might be. The first sentence sufficed, even had my lights not
revealed the full hairless face, the horn-rimmed spectacles, the
hooded boots below, and the soft hat, fashioned on no block
known to the Eastern trade, above, the yellow raincoat. I explained the situation. The resources of Mr Henry Ford's
machines did not run to spare parts of my car's type, but – it
was a beautiful night for camping-out. He himself was independent of hotels. His outfit was a caravan hired these months past
for tours of Great Britain. He had been alone since his wife
died, of duodenal ulcer, five years ago. Comparative Ethnology[4] was his present study. No, not a professor, nor,
indeed, ever at any College, but a 'realtor' – a dealer in real
estate in a suburb of the great and cultured centre of Omaha,
Nebraska. Had I ever heard of it? I had once visited the very
place and there had met an unforgettable funeral-furnisher;
but I found myself (under influence of the night and my
Demon) denying all knowledge of the United States. I had, I
said, never left my native land; but the passion of my life had
ever been the study of the fortunes and future of the U.S.A.;
and to this end I had joined three Societies, each of which
regularly sent me all its publications.

He jerked her on to the grass beside my car, where our
mingled lights slashed across the trunks of a little wood; and I
was invited into his pitch-pine-lined caravan, with its over-
powering electric installation, its flap-table, typewriter, drawers
and lockers below the bunk. Then he spoke, every word well-

relished between massy dentures; the inky-rimmed spectacles obscuring the eyes and the face as expressionless as the unrelated voice.

He spoke in capital letters, a few of which I have preserved, on our National Spirit, which, he had sensed, was Homogeneous and in Ethical Contact throughout – Unconscious but Vitally Existent. That was his Estimate of our Racial Complex. It was an Asset, but a Democracy postulating genuine Ideals should be more multitudinously-minded and diverse in Outlook. I assented to everything in a voice that would have drawn confidences from letter-boxes.

He next touched on the Collective Outlook of Democracy, and thence glanced at Herd Impulse, and the counterbalancing necessity for Individual Self-expression. Here he began to search his pockets, sighing heavily from time to time.

'Before my wife died, sir, I was rated a one-hundred-percent American. I am now – but ... Have you ever in Our Literature read a book called *The Man Without a Country*?[5] I'm him!' He still rummaged, but there was a sawing noise behind the face.

'And you may say, first and last, drink did it!' he added. The noise resumed. Evidently he was laughing, so I laughed too. After all, if a man must drink what better lair than a caravan? At his next words I repented.

'On my return back home after her burial, I first received my Primal Urge towards Self-Expression. Till then I had never realized myself ... Ah!'

He had found it at last in a breast pocket – a lank and knotty cigar.

'And what, sir, is your genuine Opinion of Prohibition?'[6] he asked when the butt had been moistened to his liking.

'Oh! – er! It's a – a gallant adventure!' I babbled, for somehow I had tuned myself to listen-in to tales of other things. He turned towards me slowly.

'The Revelation *qua* Prohibition that came to me on my return back home from her funeral was *not* along those lines. This is the Platform *I* stood on.' I became, thenceforward, one of vast crowds being addressed from that Platform.

'There are Races, sir, which have been secluded since their origin from the microbes – the necessary and beneficent microbes – of Civ'lization. Once those microbes are introdooced to 'em, those races re-act precisely in proportion to their previous immunity *or* Racial Virginity. Measles, which I've had twice and never laid by for, are as fatal to the Papuan as pneumonic plague to the White. Alcohol, for them, is disaster, degeneration, and death. Why? You can't get ahead of Cause and Effect. Protect any race from its natural and God-given bacteria and you automatically create the culture for its decay, when that protection is removed. That, sir, is my Thesis.'

The unlit cigar between his lips circled slowly, but I had no desire to laugh.

'The virgin Red Indian fell for the Firewater of the Paleface as soon as it was presented to him. For Firewater, sir, he parted with his lands, his integrity, an' his future. What is he now? An Ethnological Survival under State Protection. You get me? Immunize, or virg'nize, the Cit'zen of the United States to alcohol, an' you as surely redooce him to the mental status an' outlook of that Redskin. *That* is the Ne-mee-sis of Prohibition. And the Process has begun, sir. Haven't you noticed it already' – he gulped – 'among Our People?'

'Well,' I said. 'Men don't always act as they preach, of course.'

'You won't abrade *my* National Complex. What's the worst you've seen in connection with Our People – and Rum?' The round lenses were full on me. I chanced it.

'I've seen one of 'em on a cross-Channel boat, talking Prohibition in the bar – pretty full. He had three drinks while I listened.'

'I thought you said you'd never quit England?' he replied.

'Oh, we don't count France,' I amended hastily.

'Then was you ever at Monte Carlo? No? Well, I was – this spring. One of our tourist steamers unloaded three hundred of 'em at the port o' Veel Franshe; and they went off to Monte Carlo to dine. I saw 'em, sir, come out of the dinner-hall of that vast Hotel opp'site the Cassino there, not drunk, but all – *all* havin' drink taken. In that hotel lounge after that meal, I saw an elderly cit'zen up an' kiss eight women, none of 'em specially young, sittin' in a circle on the settees; the rest of his crowd applaudin'. Folk just shrugged their shoulders, and the French nigger on the door, I heard him say: "It's only the Yanks tankin' up." It galled me. As a one-hundred-per-cent American, it galled me unspeakably. And *you've* observed the same thing durin' the last few years?'

I nodded. The face was working now in the yellow lights reflected from the close-buttoned raincoat. He dropped his hand on his knee and struck it again and again, before he steadied himself with the usual snap and grind of his superb dentist-work.

'My Rev'lation *qua* the Peril of Prohibition was laid on me on my return back home in the hour of my affliction. I'd been discussin' Prohibition with Mrs Tarworth only the week before. Her best friend, sir, a neighbour of ours, had filled one of the vases in our parlour with chrysanthemums out of a bust wreath. I can't ever smell to those flowers now 'thout it all comin' back. Yes, sir, in my hour of woe it was laid on me to warn my land of the Ne-mee-sis of Presumption. There's only one Sin in the world – and that is Presumption. Without strong Presumption, sir, we'd never have fixed Prohibition the way we did . . . An' when I retired that night I reasoned it out that there was but one weapon for me to work with to convey my message to my native land. That, sir, was the Movies. [7] So I reasoned it. I reasoned it so-oo! Now the Movies wasn't a business I'd ever been interested in, though a regular attendant . . . Well, sir, within ten days after I had realized the Scope an' Imperativeness of my Rev'lation, I'd sold out an' re-invested so's everything was available. I quit Omaha, sir, the freest – the happiest – man in the United States.'

A puff of air from the woods licked through the open door of the caravan, trailing a wreath of mist with it. He pushed home the door.

'So you started in on Anti-Prohibition films?' I suggested.

'Sir? – More! It was laid on me to feature the Murder of Immunized America by the Microbe of Modern Civ'lization which she had presumptuously defied. That text inspired all the titling. Before I arrived at the concept of the Appeal, I was months studyin' the Movie business in every State of Our Union, in labour and trava-il. The Complete Concept, sir, with its Potential'ties, came to me of a Sunday afternoon in Rand Park, Keokuk, Iowa – the centre of our native pearl-button industry. As a boy, sir, I used to go shell-tongin' after mussels, in a shanty-boat on the Cumberland River, Tennessee, always hopin' to find a thousand dollar pearl. (The shell goes to Keokuk for manufacture.) I found my pearl in Keokuk – where my Concept came to me! Excuse me!'

He pulled out a drawer of card-indexed photographs beneath the bunk, ran his long fingers down the edges, and drew out three.

The first showed the head of an elderly Red Indian chief in full war-paint, the lined lips compressed to a thread, eyes wrinkled, nostrils aflare, and the whole face lit by so naked a passion of hate that I started.

'That,' said Mr Tarworth, 'is the Spirit of the Tragedy – both of the Red Indians who initially, and of our Whites who subsequently, sold 'emselves and their heritage for the Fire-water of the Paleface. The Captions run in diapason with that note throughout. But for a Film Appeal, you must have a balanced *leet-motif* interwoven with the footage. Now this close-up of the Red Man I'm showin' you, punctuates the action of the dramma. He recurs, sir, watchin' the progressive de-gradation of his own people, from the advent of the Paleface with liquor, up to the extinction of his race. After that, you see him, again, more and more dominant, broodin' over an' rejoicin' in the downfall of the White American artificially virg'nized [8] against Alcohol – the identical cycle repeated. I got this shot of Him in Oklahoma, one of our Western States, where there's a crowd of the richest Red Indians (drawin' oil-royalties) on earth. But they've got a Historical Society that chases 'em into paint and feathers to keep up their race-pride, *and* for the Movies. He was an Episcopalian and owns a Cadillac, I was told. The sun in his eyes makes him look that way. He's indexed as "Rum-in-the-Cup" (that's the element of Popular Appeal), but, say' – the voice softened with the pride of artistry – 'ain't He just *it* for my purposes?'

He passed me the second photo. The cigar rolled again and he held on:

'Now in every Film Appeal, you must balance your *leet-motif* by balancin' the Sexes. The American Woman, sir, handed Prohibition to Us while our boys were away savin' *you*. I know the type – 'born an' bred with it. She watches throughout the film what She's brought about – watches an' watches till the final Catastrophe. She's Woman Triumphant, balanced against Rum-in-the-Cup – the Degraded Male. I hunted the whole of the Middle West for Her in vain, 'fore I remembered – not Jordan, but Abanna and Parphar[9] – Mrs Tarworth's best friend at home. I was then in Texarkhana, Arkansas, fixin' up a deal I'll tell you about; but I broke for Omaha that evenin' to get a shot of Her. When I arrived so sudden she – she – thought, I guess, I meant to make her Number Two. That's Her. You wouldn't realize the Type, but it's *it*.'

I looked; saw the trained sweetness and unction in the otherwise hardish, ignorant eyes; the slightly open, slightly flaccid mouth; the immense unconscious arrogance, the immovable certitude of mind, and the other warning signs in the poise of the broad-cheeked head. He was fingering the third photo.

'And when the American Woman realizes the Scope an' the Impact an' the Irrevocability of the Catastrophe which she has created by Her Presumption, She – She registers Despair. That's Her – at the finale.'

It was cruelty beyond justification to have pinned down any living creature in such agony of shame, anger, and impotence among life's wreckage. And this was a well-favoured woman, her torment new-launched on her as she stood gripping the back of a stamped-velvet chair.

'And so you went back to Texarkhana without proposing,' I began.

'Why, yes. There was only forty-seven minutes between trains. I told her so. But I got both shots.'

I must have caught my breath, for, as he took the photo back again, he explained: 'In the Movie business we don't employ the actool. This is only the Basis we build on to the nearest professional type. That secures controlled emphasis of expression. She's only the Basis.'

'I'm glad of that,' I said. He lit his cigar, and relaxed beneath the folds of the loose coat.

'Well, sir, having secured my *leet-motifs* and Sex-balances, the whole of the footage coverin' the downfall of the Red Man was as good as given me by a bust Congregational Church that had been boosting Prohibition near Texarkhana. That was why I'd gone there. One of their ladies, who was crazy about Our National dealin's with the Indian, had had the details documented in Washington; an' the resultant film must have cost her any God's dollars you can name. It was all there – the Red Man partin' with his lands and furs an' women to the early settlers for Rum; the liquor-fights round the tradin'-posts; the Government Agents swindlin' 'em with liquor; an' the Indians goin' mad from it; the Black Hawk War;[10] the winnin' of the West – by Rum mainly – the whole jugful of Shame. But that film failed, sir, because folk in Arkansas said it was an aspersion on the National Honour, and, anyway, buying land needful for Our inevitable development was more Christian than the bloody wars of Monarchical Europe. The Congregationalists wanted a new organ too; so I traded a big Estey organ for their film. My notion was to interweave it with parallel modern instances, from Monte Carlo and the European hotels, of White American Degradation; the Main Caption bein': "The Firewater of the Paleface Works as Indifferently as Fate." An' old Rum-in-the-Cup's close-up shows broodin' – broodin' – broodin' – through it all! You sense my Concept?'

He relighted his cigar.

'*I* saw it like a vision. But, from there on, I had to rely on my own Complex for intuition. I cut out all modern side-issues – the fight against Prohibition; bootlegging; home-made Rum manufacture; wood-alcohol tragedies, an' all that dope. 'Dunno as I didn't elim'nate to excess. The Revolt of the Red Blood Corpuscles should ha' been stressed.'

'What's *their* share in it?'

'Vital! They clean up waste and deleterious matter in the

humane system. Under the microscope they rage like lions. Deprive 'em of their job by sterilizin' an' virginizing the system, an' the Red Blood Corpuscules turn on the humane system an' destroy it bodily. Mentally, too, mebbe. Ain't that a hell of a thought?'

'Where did you get it from?'

'It came to me – with the others,' he replied as simply as Ezekiel might have told a fellow-captive beside Chebar.[11] 'But it's too high for a Democracy. So I cut it right out. For Film purposes I assumed that, at an unspecified date, the United States had become virg'nized to liquor. The Taint was out of the Blood, and, apparently, the Instinct had aborted. "The Triumph of Presumption" is the Caption. But from there on, I fell down because, for the film Appeal, you cannot present such an Epoch without featurin' confirmatory exhibits which, o' course, haven't as yet materialized. That meant that the whole Cultural Aspect o' that Civ'lization of the Future would have to be built up at Hollywood; an' half a million dollars wouldn't cover it. "The Vision of Virg'nized Civ'lization." A hell of a proposition! But it don't matter now.'

He dropped his head and was still for a little.

'Never mind,' I said. 'How does the idea work out – in your mind?'

'In my mind? As inevitably, sir, as the Red Man's Fall through Rum. My notion was a complete Cultural Exposay of a She-dom'nated Civ'lization, built on a virginal basis *qua* alcohol, with immensely increased material Productivity (say, there'd be money in that from big Businesses demonstratin' what they'll prodooce a hundred years hence), *and* a side-wipe at the practically non-existent birth-rate.'

'Why that, too?' I asked.

He gave me the reason – a perfectly sound one – which has nothing to do with the tale, and went on:

'After that Vision is fully realized, the End comes – as remorselessly for the White as for the Red. How? The American Woman – you will recall the first close-up of that lady I showed you, interweavin' throughout the narr'tive – havin' accomplished all she set out to do, wishes to demonstrate to the world the Inteegral Significance of Her Life-work. Why not? She's never been blamed in Her life. So delib'rately, out of High Presumption, the American Woman withdraws all inhibit'ry legislation, all barriers against Alcohol – to show what She has made of Her Men. The Captions here run – "The Zeenith of Presumption. America Stands by Herself – Guide and Saviour of Humanity." "Let Evil do Its Damnedest! We are above It." Say, ain't that a hell of a thought?'

'A bit extravagant, isn't it?'

'Extrav'gance? In the life of actool men an' women? It don't exist. Well, anyway, that's my top-note before the *day-bakkle*. There's an interval while the Great World-Wave is gatherin' to sweep aside the Children of Presumption. Nothin' eventuates for a while. The Machine of Virg'nized Civ'lization functions by its own stored energy. And then, sir – *then* the World-Wave crashes down on the White as it crashed on the Red Skin! (All this while old Rum-in-the-Cup is growin' more an' more dom'nant, as I told you.) But now, owin' to the artificialized mentality of the victims and the immune pop'lation, its effects are Cataclysmic. "The Alcohol Appeal, held back for five Generations, wakes like a Cyclone." That's the Horror I'm stressin'. And Europe, and Asia, and the Ghetto exploit America – cold. "A Virg'nized People let go all holts, and part with their All." It is no longer a Dom'nation – but an Obsession. Then a *Po*-ssesion! Then come the Levelled Bay'nets of Europe. Why so? Because the liquor's peddled out, sir, under armed European guards to the elderly, pleadin' American Whites who pass over their title-deeds – their businesses, fact'ries, canals, sky-scrapers, town-lots, farms, little happy-lookin' homes – everything – for it. You can see 'em wadin' into the ocean, from Oyster Bay to Palm Beach, under great flarin' sunsets of National Decay, to get at the stuff sooner. And Europe's got 'em by the gullet – peddlin' out the cases, or a single bottle at a time, to each accordin' to his need – under the Levelled Bay'nets of Europe.'

'But why lay all the responsibility on Europe?' I broke in. 'Surely some progressive American Liquor Trust would have been in the game from the first?'

'Sure! But the Appeal is National, and there are some things, sir, that the American People will *not* stand for. It was Europe or nothing. Otherwise, I could not have stressed the effect of the Levelled Bay'nets of Europe. You see those bay'nets keepin' order in the vast cathedrals of the new religions – the broken whisky bottles round the altar – the Priest himself, old and virg'nized, pleadin' and prayin' with his flock till, in the zeenith of his agony an' his denunciations, he too falls an' wallows with the rest of 'em! Extrav'gant? No! Logic. An' so it spreads, from West to East, from East to West up to the dividin' line where the European and the Asiatic Liquor Trust has parcelled out the Land o' Presumption. No paltry rum-peddlin' at tradin'-posts *this* time, but mile-long electric freight-trains, surgin' and swoopin' from San Francisco an' Boston with their seven thousand ton of alcohol, till they meet head-on at the Liquor Line, an' you see the little American People fawnin' an' pleadin' round their big wheels an' tryin' to slip in under the Levelled Bay'nets of Europe to handle and touch the stuff, even if they can't drink it. It's horrible – horrible! "The Wages of Sin!" [12] "The Death of the She-Dom'nated Sons of Presumption!"'

He stood up, his head high in the caravan's resonant roof, and mopped his face.

'Go on!' I said.

'There ain't much more. You see the devirg'nized European an' the immemorially sophisticated Asiatic, who can hold their liquor, spreadin' out an' occupyin' the land (the signs in the streets register that) like – like a lavva-flow in Honolulu. There's jest a hint, too, of the Return of the Great Scourge, an' how it fed on all this fresh human meat. Jest a few feet of the flesh rottin' off the bones – 'same as when Syph'lis originated in the Re-nay-sanse Epoch. Last of all – date not specified – will be the herdin' of the few survivin' Americans into their reservation in the Yellowstone Park [13] by a few slouchin', crippled, remnants of the Redskins. 'Get me? "Presumption's Ultimate Reward". "The Wheel Comes Full Circle". An' the final close-up of Rum-in-the-Cup with his Hate-Mission accomplished.'

He stooped again to the photos in the bunk-locker.

'I shot that,' he said, 'when I was in the Yellowstone. It's a document to build up my Last Note on. They're jest a party of tourists watchin' grizzly bears rakin' in the hotel dump-heaps (they keep 'em to show). That wet light hits back well off their clothes, don't it?'

I saw six or seven men and women, in pale-coloured raincoats, gathered, with no pretence at pose, in a little glade. One man was turning up his collar, another stooping to a bootlace, while a woman opened her umbrella over him. They faced towards a dimly defined heap of rubbish and tins; and they looked un-utterably mean.

'Yes.' He took it back from me. 'That would have been the final note – the dom'nant resolvin' into a minor. But it don't matter now.'

'Doesn't it?' I said, stupidly enough.

'Not to me, sir. My Church – I'm a Fundamentalist, an' I didn't read 'em more than half the scenario – started out by disownin' me for aspersin' the National Honour. A bunch of our home papers got holt of it next. They said I was a ren'gade an' done it for dollars. An' then the ladies on the Social Betterment an' Uplift Committees took a hand. In *your* country you don't know the implications of *that*! I'm – I'm a one-hundred-per-cent American, but – I didn't know what men an' women are. I guess none of us do at home, or we'd say so, instead o' playin' at being American Cit'zens. There's no law with Us under which a man can be jailed for aspersin' the National Honour. There's no need. It got into the Legislature, an' one Senator there he spoke for an hour, demandin' to have me unanimously an' internationally disavowed by – by my Maker, I presoom. No one else stood by me. I'd been to the big Jew combines that control the Movie business in our country. I'd been to Heuvelstein – he represents sixty-seven millions dollars' interests. They say he's never read a scenario in his life. He read every last word of mine aloud. He laughed some, but he said he was doin' well in a small way, and he didn't propose to start up any pogroms against the Chosen in New York. He said I was ahead of my time. I know that. An' then – my wife's best friend was back of this – folk at home got talkin' about callin' for an inquiry into my state o' mind, an' whether I was fit to run my own affairs. I saw a lawyer or two over that, an' I came to a realizin' sense of American Law *an'* Justice. That was another of the things I didn't know. It made me sick to my stummick, sir – sick with physical an' mental terror an' dread. So I quit. I changed my name an' quit two years back. Those ancient prophets an' martyrs haven't got much on me in the things a Democracy hands you if you don't see eye to eye with it. Therefore, I have no abidin'-place except this old cara-van. Now, sir, we are like ships that pass in the night,[14] except, as I said, I'll be very pleased to tow you into Doncaster this morning. Is there anythin' about *me* strikes you in any way as deviatin' from sanity?'

'Not in the least,' I replied quickly. 'But what have you done with your scenario?'

'Deposited it in the Bank of England at London.'

'Would you sell it?'

'*No*, sir.'

'Couldn't it be produced here?'

'I am a one-hundred-per-cent American. The way *I* see it, I could not be a party to an indirect attack on my Native Land.'

Once again he ground his jaws. There did not seem to be much left to say. The heat in the shut caravan was more and more oppressive. Time had stood still with me listening. I was aware now that the owls had ceased hooting and that a night had gone out of the world. I rose from the bunk. Mr Tarworth, carefully rebuttoning his raincoat, opened the door.

'Good Lord Gord Almighty!' he cried, with a child's awed reverence. 'It's sun-up. Look!'

Daylight was just on the heels of dawn, with the sun fol-lowing. The icy-blackness of the Great North Road banded itself with smoking mists that changed from solid pearl to writhing opal, as they lifted above hedge-row level. The dew-wet leaves of the upper branches turned suddenly into diamond facets, and that wind, which runs before the actual upheaval of the sun, swept out of the fragrant lands to the East, and touched my cheek – as many times it had touched it before, on the edge, or at the ends, of inconceivable experiences.

My companion breathed deeply, while the low glare searched

the folds of his coat and the sags and wrinkles of his face. We heard the far-away pulse of a car through the infinite, clean-born, light-filled stillness. It neared and stole round the bend – a motor-hearse on its way to some early or distant funeral, one side of the bright oak coffin showing beneath the pall, which had slipped a little. Then it vanished in a blaze of wet glory from the sun-drenched road, amid the songs of a thousand birds.

Mr Tarworth laid his hand on my shoulder.

'Say, Neighbour,' he said. 'There's somethin' very soothin' in the Concept of Death after all.'

Then he set himself, kindly and efficiently, to tow me towards Doncaster, where, when the day's life should begin again, one might procure a new magneto make-and-break – that tiny two-inch spring of finest steel, failure of which immobilizes any car.

Gow's Watch [15]

Act IV Scene 4

The Head of the Bargi Pass — in snow.
Gow and Ferdinand with their Captains.

GOW (*to Ferdinand*): The Queen's host would be delivered me
today — but that these Mountain Men have sent battalia to
hold the Pass. They're shod, helmed and torqued with soft
gold. For the rest, naked. By no argument can I persuade 'em
their gilt carcasses against my bombards [16] avail not. What's to do,
Fox?

FERDINAND: Fatherless folk go furthest. These loud pagans
Are doubly fatherless. Consider; they came
Over the passes, out of all man's world —
Adúllamites, unable to endure
Its ancient pinch and belly-ache — full of revenges
Or wilfully forgetful. The land they found
Was manless — her raw airs uncloven by speech,
Earth without wheel-track, hoof-mark, hearth or ploughshare
Since God created; nor even a cave where men,
When night was a new thing, had hid themselves.

GOW: Excellent. Do I fight them, or let go?

FERDINAND: Unused earth, air and water for their spoil,
And none to make comparison of their deeds.
No unbribed dead to judge, accuse 'em or comfort —
Their present all their future and their past.
What should they know of reason — litters of folk —
New whelped to emptiness?

GOW: Nothing. They bar my path.

FERDINAND: Turn it, then — turn it.
Give them their triumph. They'll be wiser anon —
Some thirty generations hence.

GOW: Amen! I'm no disposed murderer. (*To the Mountain Men*)
Most magnificent Senors! Lords of all Suns, Moons, Firmaments
— Sole Architects of Yourselves and this present Universe! Yon
Philosopher in the hairy cloak bids me wait only a thousand
years, till ye've sorted yourselves more to the likeness of man-
kind.

THE PRIEST OF THE MOUNTAIN MEN: There are none beside
ourselves to lead the world!

GOW: That is common knowledge. I supplicate you to allow us the
head of the Pass, that we may better reach the Queen's host yonder.
Ye will not? Why?

THE PRIEST: Because it is our will. There is none other law for all
the earth.

GOW: (That a few feet of snow on a nest of rocky mountains should
have hatched this dream-people!) (*To Priest*) Ye have reason in
nature – all you've known of it . . . But – a thousand years – I fear
they will not suffice.

THE PRIEST: Go you back! We hold the passes into and out of the
world. Do you defy us?

FERDINAND: (*To Gow*) I warned you. There's none like them under
Heaven. Say it!

GOW: Defy your puissance,[17] Senors? Not I. We'll have our bombards
away, all, by noon; and our poor hosts with them. And you, Senors,
shall have your triumph upon us.

FERDINAND: Ah! That touches! Let them shout and blow their horns
half a day and they'll not think of aught else!

GOW: Fall to your riots then! Senors, ye have won. We'll leave you
the head of the Pass – for thirty generations. (*Loudly*) The mules
to the bombards and away!

FERDINAND: Most admirably you spoke to my poor text.

GOW: Maybe the better, Fox, because the discourse has drawn them
to the head of the Pass. Meantime, our main body has taken the
lower road, with all the Artillery.

FERDINAND: Had you no bombards here, then?

GOW: None, Innocence, at all! None, except your talk and theirs!

⧘ The Bull that Thought ⧙

Westward from a town by the Mouths of the Rhône, runs a road so mathematically straight, so barometrically level, that it ranks among the world's measured miles and motorists use it for records.

I had attacked the distance several times,[1] but always with a Mistral[2] blowing, or the unchancy cattle of those parts on the move. But once, running from the East, into a high-piled, almost Egyptian, sunset, there came a night which it would have been sin to have wasted. It was warm with the breath of summer in advance; moonlit till the shadow of every rounded pebble and pointed cypress wind-break lay solid on that vast flat-floored waste; and my Mr Leggatt, who had slipped out to make sure, reported that the road-surface was unblemished.

'*Now*,' he suggested, 'we might see what she'll do under strict road-conditions. She's been pullin' like the Blue de Luxe[3] all day. Unless I'm all off, it's her night out.'

We arranged the trial for after dinner – thirty kilometres as near as might be; and twenty-two of them without even a level crossing.

There sat beside me at table d'hôte an elderly, bearded Frenchman wearing the rosette of by no means the lowest grade of the Legion of Honour, who had arrived in a talkative Citroën. I gathered that he had spent much of his life in the French Colonial Service in Annam and Tonquin. When the war came, his years barring him from the front line, he had supervised Chinese wood-cutters who, with axe and dynamite, deforested the centre of France for trench-props. He said my chauffeur had told him that I contemplated an experiment. He was interested in cars – had admired mine – would, in short, be greatly indebted to me if I permitted him to assist as an ob-server. One could not well refuse; and, knowing my Mr Leggatt, it occurred to me there might also be a bet in the background.

While he went to get his coat, I asked the proprietor his name. 'Voiron – Monsieur André Voiron,' was the reply. 'And his business?' 'Mon Dieu! He is Voiron! He is all those things, there!' The proprietor waved his hands at brilliant advertisements on the dining-room walls, which declared that Voiron Frères dealt in wines, agricultural implements, chemical manures, provisions and produce throughout that part of the globe.

He said little for the first five minutes of our trip, and nothing at all for the next ten – it being, as Leggatt had guessed, Esmeralda's night out. But, when her indicator climbed to a certain figure and held there for three blinding kilometres, he expressed himself satisfied, and proposed to me that we should celebrate the event at the hotel. 'I keep yonder,' said he, 'a wine on which I should value your opinion.'

On our return, he disappeared for a few minutes, and I heard him rumbling in a cellar. The proprietor presently invited me to the dining-room, where, beneath one frugal light, a table had been set with local dishes of renown. There was, too, a bottle beyond most known sizes, marked black on red, with a date. Monsieur Voiron opened it, and we drank to the health of my car. The velvety, perfumed liquor, between fawn and topaz, neither too sweet nor too dry, creamed in its generous glass. But I knew no wine composed of the whispers of angels' wings, the breath of Eden and the foam and pulse of Youth renewed.[4] So I asked what it might be.

'It is champagne,' he said gravely.

'Then what have I been drinking all my life?'

'If you were lucky, before the War, and paid thirty shillings a bottle, it is possible you may have drunk one of our betterclass *tisanes*.'[5]

'And where does one get this?'

'Here, I am happy to say. Elsewhere, perhaps, it is not so easy. We growers exchange these real wines among ourselves.'

I bowed my head in admiration, surrender, and joy. There stood the most ample bottle, and it was not yet eleven o'clock. Doors locked and shutters banged throughout the establishment. Some last servant yawned on his way to bed. Monsieur

Voiron opened a window and the moonlight flooded in from a small pebbled court outside. One could almost hear the town of Chambres breathing in its first sleep. Presently, there was a thick noise in the air, the passing of feet and hooves, lowings, and a stifled bark or two. Dust rose over the courtyard wall, followed by the strong smell of cattle.

'They are moving some beasts,' said Monsieur Voiron, cocking an ear. 'Mine, I think. Yes, I hear Christophe. Our beasts do not like automobiles – so we move at night. You do not know our country – the Crau, here, or the Camargue? I was – I am now, again – of it. All France is good; but this is the best.' He spoke, as only a Frenchman can, of his own loved part of his own lovely land.

'For myself, if I were not so involved in all these affairs' – he pointed to the advertisements – 'I would live on our farm with my cattle, and worship them like a Hindu. You know our cattle of the Camargue, Monsieur? No? It is not an acquaintance to rush upon lightly. There are no beasts like them. They have a mentality superior to that of others. They graze and they ruminate, by choice, facing our Mistral, which is more than some automobiles will do. Also they have in them the potentiality of thought – and when cattle think – I have seen what arrives.'

'Are they so clever as all that?' I asked idly.

'Monsieur, when your *sportif* chauffeur camouflaged your limousine so that she resembled one of your Army lorries, I would not believe her capacities. I bet him – ah – two to one – she would not touch ninety kilometres. It was proved that she could. I can give you no proof, but will you believe me if I tell you what a beast who thinks can achieve?'

'After the War,' said I spaciously, 'everything is credible.'

'That is true! Everything inconceivable has happened; but still we learn nothing and we believe nothing. When I was a child in my father's house – before I became a Colonial Administrator – my interest and my affection were among our cattle. We of the old rock live here – have you seen? – in big farms like castles. Indeed, some of them may have been Saracenic. The barns group round them – great white-walled barns, and yards solid as our houses. One gate shuts all. It is a world apart; an administration of all that concerns beasts. It was there I learned something about cattle. You see, they are our playthings in the Camargue and the Crau. The boy measures his strength against the calf that butts him in play among the manure-heaps. He moves in and out among the cows, who are – not so amiable. He rides with the herdsmen in the open to shift the herds. Sooner or later, he meets as bulls the little calves that knocked him over. So it was with me – till it became necessary that I should go to our Colonies.' He laughed. 'Very necessary. That is a good time in youth, Monsieur, when one does these things which shock our parents. Why is it always Papa who is so shocked and has never heard of such things – and Mamma who supplies the excuses? . . . And when my brother – my elder who stayed and created the business – begged me to return and help him, I resigned my Colonial career gladly enough. I returned to our own lands, and my well-loved, wicked white and yellow cattle of the Camargue and the Crau. My Faith, I could talk of them all night, for this stuff unlocks the heart, without making repentance in the morning . . . Yes! It was after the War that this happened. There was a calf, among Heaven knows how many of ours – a bull-calf – an infant indistinguishable from his companions. He was sick, and he had been taken up with his mother into the big farm-yard at home with us. Naturally the children of our herdsmen practised on him from the first. It is in their blood. The Spaniards make a cult of bull-fighting. Our little devils down here bait bulls as automatically as the English child kicks or throws balls. This calf would chase them with his eyes open, like a cow when she hunts a man. They would take refuge behind our tractors and wine-carts in the centre of the yard: he would chase them in and out as a dog hunts rats. More than that, he would study their psychology, his eyes in their eyes. Yes, he watched their faces to divine which way they would run. He himself, also, would pretend sometimes to charge directly at a boy. Then he would wheel right or left – one could never tell – and knock over some child pressed against a wall who thought himself safe. After this, he would stand over him, knowing that his companions must come to his aid; and when they were all together, waving their jackets across his eyes and pulling his tail, he would scatter them – how he would scatter them! He could kick, too, sideways like a cow. He knew his ranges as well as our gunners, and he was as quick on his feet as our Carpentier.[6] I observed him often. Christophe – the man who passed just now – our chief herdsman, who had taught me to ride with our beasts when I was ten – Christophe told me that he was descended from a yellow cow of those days that had chased us once into the marshes. "He kicks just like her," said Christophe. "He can side-kick as he jumps. Have you seen, too, that he is not deceived by the jacket when a boy waves it? He uses it to find the boy. They think they are feeling him. He is feeling them always. He thinks, that one." I had come to the same conclusion. Yes – the creature was a thinker along the lines necessary to his sport; and he was a humorist also, like so many natural murderers. One knows the type among beasts as well as among men. It possesses a curious truculent mirth – almost indecent but infallibly significant –'

Monsieur Voiron replenished our glasses with the great wine that went better at each descent.

'They kept him for some time in the yards to practise upon. Naturally he became a little brutal; so Christophe turned him out to learn manners among his equals in the grazing lands, where the Camargue joins the Crau. How old was he then? About eight or nine months, I think. We met again a few months later – he and I. I was riding one of our little half-wild horses, along a road of the Crau, when I found myself almost unseated. It was he! He had hidden himself behind a windbreak till we passed, and had then charged my horse from behind. Yes, he had deceived even my little horse! But I recognized him. I gave him the whip across the nose, and I said: "Apis,[7] for this thou goest to Arles![8] It was unworthy of thee, between us two." But that creature had no shame. He went away laughing, like an Apache. If he had dismounted me, I do not think it is I who would have laughed – yearling as he was.'

'Why did you want to send him to Arles?' I asked.

'For the bull-ring. When your charming tourists leave us, we institute our little amusements there. Not a real bull-fight, you understand, but young bulls with padded horns, and our boys from hereabouts and in the city go to play with them. Naturally, before we send them we try them in our yards at home. So we brought up Apis from his pastures. He knew at once that he was among the friends of his youth – he almost shook hands with them – and he submitted like an angel to padding his horns. He investigated the carts and tractors in the yards, to choose his lines of defence and attack. And then – he attacked with an *élan*, and he defended with a tenacity and forethought that delighted us. In truth, we were so pleased that I fear we trespassed upon his patience. We desired him to repeat himself, which no true artist will tolerate. But he gave us fair warning. He went out to the centre of the yard, where there was some dry earth; he kneeled down and – you have seen a calf whose horns fret him thrusting and rooting into a bank? He did just that, very deliberately, till he had rubbed the pads off his horns. Then he rose, dancing on those wonderful feet that twinkled, and he said: "Now, my friends, the buttons are off the foils. Who begins?" We understood. We finished at once. He was turned out again on the pastures till it should be time to amuse them at our little metropolis. But, some time before he went to Arles – yes, I think I have it correctly – Christophe, who had been out on the Crau, informed me that Apis had assassinated a young bull who had given signs of developing into a rival. That happens, of course, and our herdsmen should prevent it. But Apis had killed in his own style – at dusk, from the ambush of a wind-break – by an oblique charge from behind which knocked the other over. He had then disembowelled him. All very possible, *but* – the murder accomplished – Apis went to the bank of a wind-break, knelt, and carefully, as he had in our yard, cleaned his horns in the earth. Christophe, who had never seen such a thing, at once borrowed (do you know, it is most efficacious when taken that way?) some Holy Water from our little chapel in those pastures, sprinkled Apis (whom it did not affect), and rode in to tell me. It was obvious that a thinker of that bull's type would also be meticulous in his toilette; so, when he was sent to Arles, I warned our consignees to exercise caution with him. Happily, the change of scene, the music, the general attention, and the meeting again with old friends – all our bad boys attended – agreeably distracted him. He became for the time a pure *farceur* again; but his wheelings, his rushes, his rat-huntings were more superb than ever. There was in them now, you understand, a breadth of technique that comes of reasoned art, and, above all, the passion that arrives after experience. Oh, he had learned, out there on the Crau! At the end of his little turn, he was, according to local rules, to be handled in all respects except for the sword, which was a stick, as a professional bull who must die. He was manoeuvred into, or he posed himself in, the proper attitude; made his rush; received the point on his shoulder and then – turned about and cantered toward the door by which he had entered the arena. He said to the world: "My friends, the representation is ended. I thank you for your applause. I go to repose myself." But our Arlesians, who are – not so clever as some, demanded an encore, and Apis was headed back again. We others from his country, we knew what would happen. He went to the centre of the ring, kneeled, and, slowly, with full parade, plunged his horns alternately in the dirt till the pads came off. Christophe shouts: "Leave him alone, you straight-nosed imbeciles! Leave him before you must." But they required emotion; for Rome has always debauched her loved Provincia with bread and circuses. It was given. Have you, Monsieur, ever seen a servant, with pan and broom, sweeping round the base-board of a room? In a half-minute Apis has them all swept out and over the barrier. Then he demands once more that the door shall be opened to him. It is opened and he retires as though – which, truly, is the case – loaded with laurels.'

Monsieur Voiron refilled the glasses, and allowed himself a cigarette, which he puffed for some time.

'And afterwards?' I said.

'I am arranging it in my mind. It is difficult to do it justice. Afterwards – yes, afterwards – Apis returned to his pastures and his mistresses and I to my business. I am no longer a scandalous old "sportif" in shirt-sleeves howling encouragement to the yellow son of a cow. I revert to Voiron Frères – wines, chemical manures, *et cetera*. And next year, through some chicane which I have not the leisure to unravel, and also, thanks to our patriarchal system of paying our older men out of the increase of the herds, old Christophe possesses himself of Apis. Oh, yes, he proves it through descent from a certain cow that my father had given his father before the Republic.[9] Beware, Monsieur, of the memory of the illiterate man! An ancestor of Christophe had been a soldier under our Soult against your Beresford, near Bayonne. He fell into the hands of Spanish guerrillas. Christophe and his wife used to tell me the details on certain Saints' Days when I was a child. Now, as compared with our recent war, Soult's campaign and retreat across the Bidassoa –'

'But did you allow Christophe just to annex the bull?' I demanded.

'You do not know Christophe. He had sold him to the Spaniards before he informed me. The Spaniards pay in coin – douros of very pure silver. Our peasants mistrust our paper. You know the saying: "A thousand francs paper; eight hundred metal, and the cow is yours." Yes, Christophe sold Apis, who was then two and a half years old, and to Christophe's knowledge thrice at least an assassin.'

'How was that?' I said.

'Oh, his own kind only; and always, Christophe told me, by the same oblique rush from behind, the same sideways overthrow, and the same swift disembowelment, followed by this levitical cleaning of the horns. In human life he would have kept a manicurist – this Minotaur.[10] And so, Apis disappears from our country. That does not trouble me. I know in due time I shall be advised. Why? Because, in this land, Monsieur, not a hoof moves between Berre and the Saintes Maries without the knowledge of specialists such as Christophe. The beasts are the substance and the drama of their lives to them. So when Christophe tells me, a little before Easter Sunday, that Apis makes his début in the bull-ring of a small Catalan town on the road to Barcelona, it is only to pack my car and trundle there across the frontier with him. The place lacked importance and manufactures, but it had produced a matador of some reputation, who was condescending to show his art in his native town.

They were even running one special train to the place. Now our French railway system is only execrable, but the Spanish –'

'You went down by road, didn't you?' said I.

'Naturally. It was not too good. Villamarti was the matador's name. He proposed to kill two bulls for the honour of his birthplace. Apis, Christophe told me, would be his second. It was an interesting trip, and that little city by the sea was ravishing. Their bull-ring dates from the middle of the seventeenth century. It is full of feeling. The ceremonial too – when the horsemen enter and ask the Mayor in his box to throw down the keys of the bull-ring – that was exquisitely conceived. You know, if the keys are caught in the horseman's hat, it is considered a good omen. They were perfectly caught. Our seats were in the front row beside the gates where the bulls enter, so we saw everything.

Villamarti's first bull was not too badly killed. The second matador, whose name escapes me, killed his without distinction – a foil to Villamarti. And the third, Chisto, a laborious, middle-aged professional who had never risen beyond a certain dull competence, was equally of the background. Oh, they are as jealous as the girls of the Comédie Française, these matadors! Villamarti's troupe stood ready for his second bull. The gates opened, and we saw Apis, beautifully balanced on his feet, peer coquettishly round the corner, as though he were at home. A picador – a mounted man with the long lance-goad – stood near the barrier on his right. He had not even troubled to turn his horse, for the capeadors – the men with the cloaks – were advancing to play Apis – to feel his psychology and intentions, according to the rules that are made for bulls who do not think ... I did not realize the murder before it was accomplished! The wheel, the rush, the oblique charge from behind, the fall of horse and man were simultaneous. Apis leaped the horse, with whom he had no quarrel, and alighted, all four feet together (it was enough), between the man's shoulders, changed his beautiful feet on the carcass, and was away, pretending to fall nearly on his nose. Do you follow me? In that instant, by that stumble, he produced the impression that his adorable assassination was a mere bestial blunder. Then, Monsieur, I

166

began to comprehend that it was an artist we had to deal with. He did not stand over the body to draw the rest of the troupe. He chose to reserve that trick. He let the attendants bear out the dead, and went on to amuse himself among the capeadors. Now to Apis, trained among our children in the yards, the cloak was simply a guide to the boy behind it. He pursued, you understand, the person, not the propaganda – the proprietor, not the journal. If a third of our electors of France were as wise, my friend! . . . But it was done leisurely, with humour and a touch of truculence. He romped after one man's cloak as a clumsy dog might do, but I observed that he kept the man on his terrible left side. Christophe whispered to me: "Wait for his mother's kick. When he has made the fellow confident it will arrive." It arrived in the middle of a gambol. My God! He lashed out in the air as he frisked. The man dropped like a sack, lifted one hand a little towards his head, and – that was all. So you see, a body was again at his disposition; a second time the cloaks ran up to draw him off, but, a second time, Apis refused his grand scene. A second time he acted that his murder was accident and – he convinced his audience! It was as though he had knocked over a bridge-gate in the marshes by mistake. Unbelievable? I saw it.'

The memory sent Monsieur Voiron again to the champagne, and I accompanied him.

'But Apis was not the sole artist present. They say Villamarti comes of a family of actors. I saw him regard Apis with a new eye. He, too, began to understand. He took his cloak and moved out to play him before they should bring on another picador. He had his reputation. Perhaps Apis knew it. Perhaps Villamarti reminded him of some boy with whom he had practised at home. At any rate Apis permitted it – up to a certain point; but he did not allow Villamarti the stage. He cramped him throughout. He dived and plunged clumsily and slowly, but always with menace and always closing in. We could see that the man was conforming to the bull – not the bull to the man; for Apis was playing him towards the centre of the ring, and, in a little while – I watched his face – Villamarti knew it. But I could not fathom the creature's motive. "Wait," said old Christophe.

"He wants that picador on the white horse yonder. When he reaches his proper distance he will get him. Villamarti is his cover. He used me once that way." And so it was, my friend! With the clang of one of our own Seventy-fives, Apis dismissed Villamarti with his chest – breasted him over – and had arrived at his objective near the barrier. The same oblique charge; the head carried low for the sweep of the horns; the immense sideways fall of the horse, broken-legged and half-paralysed; the senseless man on the ground, and – behold Apis between them, backed against the barrier – his right covered by the horse; his left by the body of the man at his feet. The simplicity of it! Lacking the carts and tractors of his early parade-grounds he, being a genius, had extemporized with the materials at hand, and dug himself in. The troupe closed up again, their left wing broken by the kicking horse, their right immobilized by the man's body which Apis bestrode with significance. Villamarti almost threw himself between the horns, but – it was more an appeal than an attack. Apis refused him. He held his base. A picador was sent at him – necessarily from the front, which alone was open. Apis charged – he who, till then, you realize, had not used the horn! The horse went over backwards, the man half beneath him. Apis halted, hooked him under the heart, and threw him to the barrier. We heard his head crack, but he was dead before he hit the wood. There was no de-monstration from the audience. They, also, had begun to realize this Foch [11] among bulls! The arena occupied itself again with the dead. Two of the troupe irresolutely tried to play him – God knows in what hope! – but he moved out to the centre of the ring. "Look!" said Christophe. "Now he goes to clean himself. That always frightened me." He knelt down; he began to clean his horns. The earth was hard. He worried at it in an ecstasy of absorption. As he laid his head along and rattled his ears, it was as though he were interrogating the Devils them-selves upon their secrets, and always saying impatiently: "Yes, I know that – and *that* – and *that*! Tell me more – *more*!' In the silence that covered us, a woman cried: "He digs a grave! Oh, Saints, he digs a grave!" Some others echoed this – not loudly – as a wave echoes in a grotto of the sea.

'And when his horns were cleaned, he rose up and studied poor Villamarti's troupe, eyes in eyes, one by one, with the gravity of an equal in intellect and the remote and merciless resolution of a master in his art. This was more terrifying than his toilette.'

'And they – Villamarti's men?' I asked.

'Like the audience, were dominated. They had ceased to posture, or stamp, or address insults to him. They conformed to him.[12] The two other matadors stared. Only Chisto, the oldest, broke silence with some call or other, and Apis turned his head towards him. Otherwise he was isolated, immobile – sombre – meditating on those at his mercy. Ah!

'For some reason the trumpet sounded for the *bandilleras* – those gay hooked darts that are planted in the shoulders of bulls who do not think, after their neck-muscles are tired by lifting horses. When such bulls feel the pain, they check for an instant, and, in that instant, the men step gracefully aside. Villamarti's bandillero answered the trumpet mechanically – like one condemned. He stood out, poised the darts and stammered the usual patter of invitation . . . And after? I do not assert that Apis shrugged his shoulders, but he reduced the episode to its lowest elements, as could only a bull of Gaul. With his truculence was mingled always – owing to the shortness of his tail – a certain Rabelaisian abandon,[13] especially when viewed from the rear. Christophe had often commented upon it. Now, Apis brought that quality into play. He circulated round that boy, forcing him to break up his beautiful poses. He studied him from various angles, like an imcompetent photographer. He presented to him every portion of his anatomy except his shoulders. At intervals he feigned to run in upon him. My God, he was cruel! But his motive was obvious. He was playing for a laugh from the spectators which should synchronize with the fracture of the human morale. It was achieved. The boy turned and ran towards the barrier. Apis was on him before the laugh ceased; passed him; headed him – what do I say? – herded him off to the left, his horns beside and a little in front of his chest: he did not intend him to escape into refuge. Some of the troupe would have closed in, but Villamarti cried: "If he wants him he will take him. Stand!" They stood. Whether the boy slipped or Apis nosed him over I could not see. But he dropped, sobbing. Apis halted like a car with four brakes, struck a pose, smelt him very completely and turned away. It was dismissal more ignominious than degradation at the head of one's battalion. The representation was finished. Remained only for Apis to clear his stage of the subordinate characters.

'Ah! His gesture then! He gave a dramatic start – this Cyrano [14] of the Camargue – as though he was aware of them for the first time. He moved. All their beautiful breeches twinkled for an instant along the top of the barrier. He held the stage alone! But Christophe and I, we trembled! For, observe, he had now involved himself in a stupendous drama of which he only could supply the third act. And, except for an audience on the razor-edge of emotion, he had exhausted his material. Molière [15] himself – we have forgotten, my friend, to drink to the health of that great soul – might have been at a loss. And Tragedy is but a step behind Failure. We could see the four or five Civil Guards, who are sent always to keep order, fingering the breeches of their rifles. They were but waiting a word from the Mayor to fire on him, as they do sometimes at a bull who leaps the barrier among the spectators. They would, of course, have killed or wounded several people – but that would not have saved Apis.'

Monsieur Voiron drowned the thought at once, and wiped his beard.

'At that moment Fate – the Genius of France, if you will – sent to assist in the incomparable finale, none other than Chisto, the eldest, and I should have said (but never again will I judge!) the least inspired of all; mediocrity itself but, at heart – and it is the heart that conquers always, my friend – at heart an artist. He descended stiffly into the arena, alone and assured. Apis regarded him, his eyes in his eyes. The man took stance, with his cloak, and called to the bull as to an equal: "Now, Señor, we will show these honourable caballeros something together." He advanced thus against this thinker who at a plunge – a kick – a thrust – could, we all knew, have extinguished him. My dear friend, I wish I could convey to you something of the unaffected bonhomie, the humour, the delicacy, the consideration bordering on respect even, with which Apis, the supreme artist, responded to this invitation. It was the Master, wearied after a strenuous hour in the atelier, unbuttoned and at ease with some not inexpert but limited disciple. The telepathy was instantaneous between them. And for good reason! Christophe said to me: "All's well. That Chisto began among the bulls. I was sure of it when I heard him call just now. He has been a herdsman. He'll pull it off." There was a little feeling and adjustment, at first, for mutual distances and allowances.

'Oh, yes! And here occurred a gross impertinence of Villamarti. He had, after an interval, followed Chisto – to retrieve his reputation. My Faith! I can conceive the elder Dumas slamming his door on an intruder precisely as Apis did. He raced Villamarti into the nearest refuge at once. He stamped his feet outside it, and he snorted: "Go! I am engaged with an artist." Villamarti went – his reputation left behind for ever.

'Apis returned to Chisto saying: "Forgive the interruption. I am not always master of my time, but you were about to observe, my dear confrère . . .?" Then the play began. Out of compliment to Chisto, Apis chose as his objective (every bull varies in this respect) the inner edge of the cloak – that nearest to the man's body. This allows but a few millimetres clearance in charging. But Apis trusted himself as Chisto trusted him, and, this time, he conformed to the man, with inimitable judgment and temper. He allowed himself to be played into the shadow or the sun, as the delighted audience demanded. He raged enormously; he feigned defeat; he despaired in statuesque abandon, and thence flashed into fresh paroxysms of wrath – but always with the detachment of the true artist who knows he is but the vessel of an emotion whence others, not he, must drink. And never once did he forget that honest Chisto's cloak was to him the gauge by which to spare even a hair on the skin. He inspired Chisto too. My God! His youth returned to that meritorious beef-sticker – the desire, the grace, and the beauty of his early dreams. One could almost see that girl of the past for whom he was rising, rising to these present heights of skill and daring. It was his hour too – a miraculous hour of dawn returned to gild the sunset. All he knew was at Apis' disposition. Apis acknowledged it with all that he had learned at home, at Arles and in his lonely murders on our grazing-grounds. He flowed round Chisto like a river of death – round his knees, leaping at his shoulders, kicking just clear of one side or the other of his head; behind his back hissing as he shaved by; and once or twice – inimitable! – he reared wholly up before him while Chisto slipped back from beneath the avalanche of that instructed body. Those two, my dear friend, held five thousand people dumb with no sound but of their breathings – regular as pumps. It was unbearable. Beast and man realized together that we needed a change of note – a *détente*. They relaxed to pure buffoonery. Chisto fell back and talked to him outrageously. Apis pretended he had never heard such language. The audience howled with delight. Chisto slapped him; he took liberties with his short tail, to the end of which he clung while Apis pirouetted; he played about him in all postures; he had become the herdsman again – gross, careless, brutal, but comprehending. Yet Apis was always the more consummate clown. All that time (Christophe and I saw it) Apis drew off towards the gates of the *toril* where so many bulls enter but – have you ever heard of one that returned? *We* knew that Apis knew that as he had saved Chisto, so Chisto would save him. Life is sweet to us all; to the artist who lives many lives in one, sweetest. Chisto did not fail him. At the last, when none could laugh any longer, the man threw his cape across the bull's back, his arm round his neck. He flung up a hand at the gate, as Villamarti, young and commanding but *not* a herdsman, might have raised it, and he cried: "Gentlemen, open to me and my honourable little donkey." They opened – I have misjudged Spaniards in my time! – those gates opened to the man and the bull together, and closed behind them. And then? From the Mayor to the Guarda Civile they went mad for five minutes, till the trumpets blew and the fifth bull rushed out – an unthinking black Andalusian. I suppose someone killed him. My friend, my very dear friend, to whom I have opened my heart, I confess that I did not watch. Christophe and I, we were weeping together like children of the same Mother. Shall we drink to Her?'

Alnaschar[16] and the Oxen

There's a pasture in a valley where the hanging woods divide,
    And a Herd lies down and ruminates in peace;
Where the pheasant rules the nooning, and the owl the twilight tide,
    And the war-cries of our world die out and cease.
Here I cast aside the burden that each weary week-day brings
    And, delivered from the shadows I pursue,
On peaceful, postless Sabbaths I consider Weighty Things –
    Such as Sussex Cattle feeding in the dew![17]

At the gate beside the river where the trouty shallows brawl,
    I know the pride that Lobengula[18] felt,
When he bade the bars be lowered of the Royal Cattle Kraal,
    And fifteen mile of oxen took the veldt.
    From the walls of Bulawayo in unbroken file they came
    To where the Mount of Council cuts the blue . . .
I have only six and twenty, but the principle's the same
    With my Sussex Cattle feeding in the dew!

To a luscious sound of tearing, where the clovered herbage rips,
    Level-backed and level-bellied watch 'em move –
See those shoulders, guess that heart-girth, praise those loins, admire
                              those hips,
    And the tail set low for flesh to make above!
Count the broad unblemished muzzles, test the kindly mellow skin
    And, where yon heifer lifts her head at call,
Mark the bosom's just abundance 'neath the gay and clean-cut chin,
    And those eyes of Juno, overlooking all!

Here is colour, form and substance! I will put it to the proof
    And, next season, in my lodges shall be born
Some very Bull of Mithras,[19] flawless from his agate hoof
    To his even-branching, ivory, dusk-tipped horn.
He shall mate with block-square virgins – kings shall seek his like
                              in vain,
    While I multiply his stock a thousandfold,
Till an hungry world extol me, builder of a lofty strain
    That turns one standard ton at two years old!

Debits and Credits

There's a valley, under oakwood, where a man may dream his dream,
  In the milky breath of cattle laid at ease,
Till the moon o'ertops the alders, and her image chills the stream,
  And the river-mist runs silver round their knees!
Now the footpaths fade and vanish; now the ferny clumps deceive;
  Now the hedgerow-folk possess their fields anew;
Now the Herd is lost in darkness, and I bless them as I leave,
  My Sussex Cattle feeding in the dew!

A Madonna of the Trenches

Gipsy Vans

Unless you come of the gipsy stock
　That steals by night and day,
Lock your heart with a double lock
　And throw the key away.[1]
Bury it under the blackest stone
　Beneath your father's hearth,
And keep your eyes on your lawful own
　And your feet to the proper path.
　　Then you can stand at your door and mock
　　　When the gipsy-vans come through . . .
　　For it isn't right that the Gorgio stock
　　　Should live as the Romany do.

Unless you come of the gipsy blood
　That takes and never spares,
Bide content with your given good
　And follow your own affairs.
Plough and harrow and roll your land,
　And sow what ought to be sowed;
But never let loose your heart from your hand,
　Nor flitter it down the road!
　　Then you can thrive on your boughten food
　　　As the gipsy-vans come through . . .
　　For it isn't nature the Gorgio blood
　　　Should love as the Romany do.

Unless you carry the gipsy eyes
　That see but seldom weep,
Keep your head from the naked skies
　Or the stars'll trouble your sleep.
Watch your moon through your window-pane
　And take what weather she brews;

But don't run out in the midnight rain
 Nor home in the morning dews.
  Then you can huddle and shut your eyes
   As the gipsy-vans come through . . .
  For it isn't fitting the Gorgio ryes
   Should walk as the Romany do.

Unless you come of the gipsy race
 That counts all time the same,
Be you careful of Time and Place
 And Judgment and Good Name:
Lose your life for to live your life
 The way that you ought to do;
And when you are finished, your God and your wife
 And the Gipsies 'll laugh at you!
  Then you can rot in your burying-place
   As the gipsy-vans come through . . .
  For it isn't reason the Gorgio race
   Should die as the Romany do.

A Madonna of the Trenches

Whatever a man of the sons of men
    Shall say to his heart of the lords above,
They have shown man, verily, once and again,
    Marvellous mercy and infinite love.

O sweet one love, O my life's delight,
    Dear, though the days have divided us,
Lost beyond hope, taken far out of sight,
    Not twice in the world shall the Gods do thus.
                    Swinburne,[2] 'Les Noyades'.

Seeing how many unstable ex-soldiers came to the Lodge of Instruction[3] (attached to Faith and Works E.C. 5837) in the years after the war, the wonder is there was not more trouble from Brethren whom sudden meetings with old comrades jerked back into their still raw past. But our round, torpedo-bearded local Doctor – Brother Keede, Senior Warden – always stood ready to deal with hysteria before it got out of hand; and when I examined Brethren unknown or imperfectly vouched for on the Masonic side, I passed on to him anything that seemed doubtful. He had had his experience as medical officer of a South London Battalion, during the last two years of the war; and, naturally, often found friends and acquaintances among the visitors.

Brother C. Strangwick, a young, tallish, new-made Brother, hailed from some South London Lodge. His papers and his answers were above suspicion, but his red-rimmed eyes had a puzzled glare that might mean nerves. So I introduced him particularly to Keede, who discovered in him a Headquarters Orderly of his old Battalion, congratulated him on his return to fitness – he had been discharged for some infirmity or other – and plunged at once into Somme memories.

177

'I hope I did right, Keede,' I said when we were robing before Lodge.

'Oh, quite. He reminded me that I had him under my hands at Sampoux in 'Eighteen, when he went to bits. He was a Runner.'

'Was it shock?' I asked.

'Of sorts – but not what he wanted me to think it was. No, he wasn't shamming. He had Jumps to the limit – but he played up to mislead me about the reason of 'em . . . Well, if we could stop patients from lying, medicine would be too easy, I suppose.'

I noticed that, after Lodge-working, Keede gave him a seat a couple of rows in front of us, that he might enjoy a lecture on the Orientation of King Solomon's Temple, which an earnest Brother thought would be a nice interlude between labour and the high tea that we called our 'Banquet'. Even helped by tobacco it was a dreary performance. About half-way through, Strangwick, who had been fidgeting and twitching for some minutes, rose, drove back his chair grinding across the tesselated floor, and yelped: 'Oh, My Aunt! I can't stand this any longer.' Under cover of a general laugh of assent he brushed past us and stumbled towards the door.

'I thought so!' Keede whispered to me. 'Come along!' We overtook him in the passage, crowing hysterically and wringing his hands. Keede led him into the Tyler's Room,[4] a small office where we stored odds and ends of regalia and furniture, and locked the door.

'I'm – I'm all right,' the boy began, piteously.

''Course you are.' Keede opened a small cupboard which I had seen called upon before, mixed sal volatile and water in a graduated glass, and, as Strangwick drank, pushed him gently on to an old sofa. 'There,' he went on. 'It's nothing to write home about. I've seen you ten times worse. I expect our talk has brought things back.'

He hooked up a chair behind him with one foot, held the patient's hands in his own, and sat down. The chair creaked.

'Don't!' Strangwick squealed. 'I can't stand it! There's nothing on earth creaks like they do! And – and when it thaws we – we've got to slap 'em back with a spa-ade! 'Remember those Frenchmen's little boots under the duck-boards? . . . What'll I do? What'll I do about it?'

Someone knocked at the door, to know if all were well.

'Oh, quite, thanks!' said Keede over his shoulder. 'But I shall need this room awhile. Draw the curtains, please.'

We heard the rings of the hangings that drape the passage from Lodge to Banquet Room click along their poles, and what sound there had been, of feet and voices, was shut off.

Strangwick, retching impotently, complained of the frozen dead who creak in the frost.

'He's playing up still,' Keede whispered. '*That's* not his real trouble – any more than 'twas last time.'

'But surely,' I replied, 'men get those things on the brain pretty badly. 'Remember in October –'

'This chap hasn't, though. I wonder what's really helling him. What are you thinking of ?' said Keede peremptorily.

'French End an' Butcher's Row,' Strangwick muttered.

'Yes, there were a few there. But, suppose we face Bogey instead of giving him best every time.' Keede turned towards me with a hint in his eye that I was to play up to his leads.

'What was the trouble with French End?' I opened at a venture.

'It was a bit by Sampoux,[5] that we had taken over from the French. They're tough, but you wouldn't call 'em tidy as a nation. They had faced both sides of it with dead to keep the mud back. All those trenches were like gruel in a thaw. Our people had to do the same sort of thing – elsewhere; but Butcher's Row in French End was the – er – showpiece. Luckily, we pinched a salient from Jerry just then, an' straightened things out – so we didn't need to use the Row after November. You remember, Strangwick?'

'My God, yes! When the duckboard-slats were missin' you'd tread on 'em, an' they'd creak.'

'They're bound to. Like leather,' said Keede. 'It gets on one's nerves a bit, but –'

'Nerves? It's real! It's real!' Strangwick gulped.

'But at your time of life, it'll all fall behind you in a year or so. I'll give you another sip of – paregoric, an' we'll face it quietly. Shall we?'

Keede opened his cupboard again and administered a carefully dropped dark dose of something that was not sal volatile. 'This'll settle you in a few minutes,' he explained. 'Lie still, an' don't talk unless you feel like it.'

He faced me, fingering his beard.

'Ye-es. Butcher's Row wasn't pretty,' he volunteered. 'Seeing Strangwick here, has brought it all back to me again. 'Funny thing! We had a Platoon Sergeant of Number Two – what the deuce was his name? – an elderly bird who must have lied like a patriot to get out to the front at his age; but he was a first-class Non-Com., and the last person, you'd think, to make mistakes. Well, he was due for a fortnight's home leave in January, 'Eighteen. You were at B.H.Q. then, Strangwick, weren't you?'

'Yes. I was Orderly. It was January twenty-first'; Strangwick spoke with a thickish tongue, and his eyes burned. Whatever drug it was, had taken hold.

'About then,' Keede said. 'Well, this Sergeant, instead of coming down from the trenches the regular way an' joinin' Battalion Details after dark, an' takin' that funny little train for Arras, thinks he'll warm himself first. So he gets into a dug-out, in Butcher's Row, that used to be an old French dressing-station, and fugs up between a couple of braziers of pure charcoal! As luck 'ud have it, that was the only dug-out with an inside door opening inwards – some French anti-gas fitting, I expect – and, by what we could make out, the door must have swung to while he was warming. Anyhow, he didn't turn up at the train. There was a search at once. We couldn't afford to waste Platoon Sergeants. We found him in the morning. He'd got his gas all right. A machine-gunner reported him, didn't he, Strangwick?'

'No, sir. Corporal Grant – o' the Trench Mortars.'

'So it was. Yes, Grant – the man with that little wen on his neck. 'Nothing wrong with your memory, at any rate. What was the Sergeant's name?'

'Godsoe – John Godsoe,' Strangwick answered.

'Yes, that was it. I had to see him next mornin' – frozen stiff between the two braziers – and not a scrap of private papers on him. *That* was the only thing that made me think it mightn't have been – quite an accident.'

Strangwick's relaxing face set, and he threw back at once to the Orderly Room manner.

'I give my evidence – at the time – to you, sir. He passed – overtook me, I should say – comin' down from supports, after I'd warned him for leaf. I thought he was goin' through Parrot Trench as usual; but 'e must 'ave turned off into French End where the old bombed barricade was.'

'Yes. I remember now. You were the last man to see him alive. That was on the twenty-first of January, you say? Now, *when* was it that Dearlove and Billings brought you to me – clean out of your head?' ... Keede dropped his hand, in the style of magazine detectives, on Strangwick's shoulder. The boy looked at him with cloudy wonder, and muttered: 'I was took to you on the evenin' of the twenty-fourth of January. But you don't think I did him in, do you?'

I could not help smiling at Keede's discomfiture; but he recovered himself. 'Then what the dickens *was* on your mind that evening – before I gave you the hypodermic?'

'The – the things in Butcher's Row. They kept on comin' over me. You've seen me like this before, sir.'

'But I knew that it was a lie. You'd no more got stiffs on the brain then than you have now. You've got something, but you're hiding it.'

''Ow do *you* know, Doctor?' Strangwick whimpered.

'D'you remember what you said to me, when Dearlove and Billings were holding you down that evening?'

'About the things in Butcher's Row?'

'Oh, no! You spun me a lot of stuff about corpses creaking; but you let yourself go in the middle of it – when you pushed that telegram at me. What did you mean, f'rinstance, by asking what advantage it was for you to fight beasts of officers if the dead didn't rise?'[6]

'Did I say "Beasts of Officers"?'

'You did. It's out of the Burial Service.'

'I suppose, then, I must have heard it. As a matter of fact, I 'ave.' Strangwick shuddered extravagantly.

'Probably. And there's another thing – that hymn you were shouting till I put you under. It was something about Mercy and Love. 'Remember it?'

'I'll try,' said the boy obediently, and began to paraphrase, as nearly as possible thus: '"Whatever a man may say in his heart unto the Lord, yea verily I say unto you – Gawd hath shown man, again and again, marvellous mercy an' – an' somethin' or other love."' [7] He screwed up his eyes and shook.

'Now where did you get *that* from?' Keede insisted.

'From Godsoe – on the twenty-first Jan. . . . 'Ow could *I* tell what 'e meant to do?' he burst out in a high, unnatural key – 'Any more than I knew *she* was dead.'

'Who was dead?' said Keede.

'Me Auntie Armine.'

'The one the telegram came to you about, at Sampoux, that you wanted me to explain – the one that you were talking of in the passage out here just now when you began: "O Auntie," and changed it to "O Gawd," when I collared you?'

'That's her! I haven't a chance with you, Doctor. *I* didn't know there was anything wrong with those braziers. How could I? We're always usin' 'em. Honest to God, I thought at first go-off he might wish to warm himself before the leaf-train. I – I didn't know Uncle John meant to start – 'ouse-keepin'.' He laughed horribly, and then the dry tears came.

Keede waited for them to pass in sobs and hiccoughs before he continued: 'Why? Was Godsoe your Uncle?'

'No,' said Strangwick, his head between his hands. 'Only we'd known him ever since we were born. Dad 'ad known him before that. He lived almost next street to us. Him an' Dad an' Ma an' – an' the rest had always been friends. So we called him Uncle – like children do.'

'What sort of man was he?'

'One o' *the* best, sir. 'Pensioned Sergeant with a little money left him – quite independent – and very superior. They had a sittin'-room full o' Indian curios that him and his wife used to let sister an' me see when we'd been good.'

'Wasn't he rather old to join up?'

'That made no odds to him. He joined up as Sergeant Instructor at the first go-off, an' when the Battalion was ready he got 'imself sent along. He wangled me into 'is Platoon when I went out – early in 'Seventeen. Because Ma wanted it, I suppose.'

'I'd no notion you knew him that well,' was Keede's comment.

'Oh, it made no odds to him. He 'ad no pets in the Platoon, but 'e'd write 'ome to Ma about me an' all the doin's. You see' – Strangwick stirred uneasily on the sofa – 'we'd known him all our lives – lived in the next street an' all . . . An' him well over fifty. Oh dear me! *Oh* dear me! What a bloody mix-up things are, when one's as young as me!' he wailed of a sudden.

But Keede held him to the point. 'He wrote to your Mother about you?'

'Yes. Ma's eyes had gone bad followin' on air-raids. 'Blood-vessels broke behind 'em from sittin' in cellars an' bein' sick. She had to 'ave 'er letters read to her by Auntie. Now I think of it, that was the only thing that you might have called anything at all –'

'Was that the Aunt that died, and that you got the wire about?' Keede drove on.

'Yes – Auntie Armine – Ma's younger sister, an' she nearer fifty than forty. What a mix-up! An' if I'd been asked any time about it, I'd 'ave sworn there wasn't a single sol'tary item concernin' her that everybody didn't know an' hadn't known all along. No more conceal to her doin's than – than so much shop-front. She'd looked after sister an' me, when needful – hoopin' cough an' measles – just the same as Ma. We was in an' out of her house like rabbits. You see, Uncle Armine is a cabinet-maker, an' second-'and furniture, an' we liked playin' with the things. She 'ad no children, and when the war came, she said she was glad of it. But she never talked much of her feelin's. She kept herself to herself, you understand.' He stared most earnestly at us to help out our understandings.

'What was she like?' Keede inquired.

'A biggish woman, an' had been 'andsome, I believe, but, bein' used to her, we two didn't notice much – except, per'aps, for one thing. Ma called her 'er proper name, which was Bella; but Sis an' me always called 'er Auntie Armine. See?'

'What for?'

'We thought it sounded more like her – like somethin' movin' slow, in armour.'

'Oh! And she read your letters to your mother, did she?'

'Every time the post came in she'd slip across the road from opposite an' read 'em. An' – an' I'll go bail for it that that was all there was to it for as far back as *I* remember. Was I to swing tomorrow, I'd go bail for *that*! 'Tisn't fair of 'em to 'ave unloaded it all on me, because – because – if the dead *do* rise, why, what in 'ell becomes of me an' all I've believed all me life?[8] I want to know *that*! I – I –'

But Keede would not be put off. 'Did the Sergeant give you away at all in his letters?' he demanded, very quietly.

'There was nothin' to give away – we was too busy – but his letters about me were a great comfort to Ma. I'm no good at writin'. I saved it all up for my leafs. I got me fourteen days every six months an' one over . . . I was luckier than most, that way.'

'And when you came home, used you to bring 'em news about the Sergeant?' said Keede.

'I expect I must have; but I didn't think much of it at the time. I was took up with me own affairs – naturally. Uncle John always wrote to me once each leaf, tellin' me what was doin' an' what I was li'ble to expect on return, an' Ma 'ud 'ave that read to her. Then o' course I had to slip over to his wife an' pass her the news. An' then there was the young lady that I'd thought of marryin' if I came through. We'd got as far as pricin' things in the windows together.'

'And you didn't marry her – after all?'

Another tremor shook the boy. '*No!*' he cried. ''Fore it ended, I knew what reel things reelly mean! I – I never dreamed such things could be! . . . An' she nearer fifty than forty an' me own Aunt! . . . But there wasn't a sign nor a hint from first to last, so 'ow *could* I tell? Don't you *see* it? All she said to me after me Christmas leaf in '18, when I come to say goodbye – all Auntie Armine said to me was: "You'll be seein' Mister Godsoe soon?"

184

"Too soon for my likings," I says. "Well then, tell 'im from me," she says, "that I expect to be through with my little trouble by the twenty-first of next month, an' I'm dyin' to see him as soon as possible after that date."'

'What sort of trouble was it?' Keede turned professional at once.

'She'd 'ad a bit of a gatherin' in 'er breast,[9] I believe. But she never talked of 'er body much to anyone.'

'*I* see,' said Keede. 'And she said to you?'

Strangwick repeated: '"Tell Uncle John I hope to be finished of my drawback by the twenty-first, an' I'm dying to see 'im as soon as 'e can after that date." An' then she says, laughin': "But you've a head like a sieve. I'll write it down, an' you can give it him when you see 'im." So she wrote it on a bit o' paper an' I kissed 'er goodbye – I was always her favourite, you see – an' I went back to Sampoux. The thing hardly stayed in my mind at all, d'you see. But the next time I was up in the front line – I was a Runner, d'ye see – our platoon was in North Bay Trench an' I was up with a message to the Trench Mortar there that Corporal Grant was in charge of. Followin' on receipt of it, he borrowed a couple of men off the platoon, to slue 'er round or somethin'. I give Uncle John Auntie Armine's paper, an' I give Grant a fag, an' we warmed up a bit over a brazier. Then Grant says to me: "I don't like it"; an' he jerks 'is thumb at Uncle John in the bay studyin' Auntie's message. Well, *you* know, sir, you had to speak to Grant about 'is way of prophesyin' things – after Rankine shot himself with the Very light.'

'I did,' said Keede, and he explained to me: 'Grant had the Second Sight – confound him! It upset the men. I was glad when he got pipped. What happened after that, Strangwick?'

'Grant whispers to me: "Look, you damned Englishman. 'E's for it." Uncle John was leanin' up against the bay, an' hummin' that hymn I was tryin' to tell you just now. He looked different all of a sudden – as if 'e'd got shaved. *I* don't know anything of these things, but I cautioned Grant as to his style of speakin', if an officer 'ad 'eard him, an' I went on. Passin' Uncle John in the bay, 'e nods an' smiles, which he didn't often, an' he says, pocketin' the paper: "This suits *me*. I'm for leaf on the twenty-first, too."'

'He said that to you, did he?' said Keede.

'*Pre*cisely the same as passin' the time o' day. O' course I returned the agreeable about hopin' he'd get it, an' in due course I returned to 'Eadquarters. The thing 'ardly stayed in my mind a minute. That was the eleventh January – three days after I'd come back from leaf. You remember, sir, there wasn't anythin' doin' either side round Sampoux the first part o' the month. Jerry was gettin' ready for his March Push, an' as long as he kept quiet, we didn't want to poke 'im up.'

'I remember that,' said Keede. 'But what about the Sergeant?'

'I must have met him, on an' off, I expect, goin' up an' down, through the ensuin' days, but it didn't stay in me mind. Why needed it? And on the twenty-first Jan., his name was on the leaf-paper when I went up to warn the leaf-men. I noticed *that*, o' course. Now that very afternoon Jerry 'ad been tryin' a new trench-mortar, an' before our 'Eavies could out it, he'd got a stinker into a bay an' mopped up 'alf a dozen. They were bringin' 'em down when I went up to the supports, an' that blocked Little Parrot, same as it always did. *You* remember, sir?'

'Rather! And there was that big machine-gun behind the Half-House waiting for you if you got out,' said Keede.

'I remembered that too. But it was just on dark an' the fog was comin' off the Canal, so I hopped out of Little Parrot an' cut across the open to where those four dead Warwicks are heaped up. But the fog turned me around, an' the next thing I knew I was knee-over in that old 'alf-trench that runs west o' Little Parrot into French End. I dropped into it – almost atop o' the machine-gun platform by the side o' the old sugar boiler an' the two Zoo-ave skel'tons. That gave me my bearin's, an' so I went through French End, all up those missin' duckboards, into Butcher's Row where the *poy-looz* [10] was laid in six deep each side, an' stuffed under the duckboards. It had froze tight, an' the drippin's had stopped, an' the creakin's had begun.'

'Did that really worry you at the time?' Keede asked.

'No,' said the boy with professional scorn. 'If a Runner

starts noticin' such things he'd better chuck. In the middle of
the Row, just before the old dressin'-station you referred to,
sir, it come over me that somethin' ahead on the duckboards
was just like Auntie Armine, waitin' beside the door; an' I
thought to meself 'ow truly comic it would be if she could be
dumped where I was then. In 'alf a second I saw it was only the
dark an' some rags o' gas-screen, 'angin' on a bit of board, 'ad
played me the trick. So I went on up to the supports an' warned
the leaf-men there, includin' Uncle John. Then I went up Rake
Alley to warn 'em in the front line. I didn't hurry because I
didn't want to get there till Jerry 'ad quieted down a bit. Well,
then a Company Relief dropped in – an' the officer got the
wind up over some lights on the flank, an' tied 'em into knots,
an' I 'ad to hunt up me leaf-men all over the blinkin' shop.
What with one thing an' another, it must 'ave been 'alf-past
eight before I got back to the supports. There I run across
Uncle John, scrapin' mud off himself, havin' shaved – quite
the dandy. He asked about the Arras train, an' I said, if Jerry
was quiet, it might be ten o'clock. "Good!" says 'e. "I'll come
with you." So we started back down the old trench that used to
run across Halnaker, back of the support dug-outs. *You* know,
sir.'

Keede nodded.

'Then Uncle John says something to me about seein' Ma an'
the rest of 'em in a few days, an' had I any messages for 'em?
Gawd knows what made me do it, but I told 'im to tell Auntie
Armine I never expected to see anything like *her* up in our part
of the world. And while I told him I laughed. That's the last
time I *'ave* laughed. "Oh – you've seen 'er, 'ave you?" says he,
quite natural-like. Then I told 'im about the sand-bags an' rags
in the dark, playin' the trick. "Very likely," says he, brushin'
the mud off his puttees. By this time, we'd got to the corner
where the old barricade into French End was – before they
bombed it down, sir. He turns right an' climbs across it. "No,
thanks," says I. "I've been there once this evenin'." But he
wasn't attendin' to me. He felt behind the rubbish an' bones
just inside the barricade, an' when he straightened up, he had a
full brazier in each hand.

'"Come on, Clem," he says, an' he very rarely give me me own name. "You aren't afraid, are you?" he says. "It's just as short, an' if Jerry starts up again he won't waste stuff here. He knows it's abandoned." "Who's afraid now?" I says. "Me for one," says he. "I don't want *my* leaf spoiled at the last minute." Then 'e wheels round an' speaks that bit you said come out o' the Burial Service.'

For some reason Keede repeated it in full, slowly: 'If, after the manner of men, I have fought with beasts at Ephesus, what advantageth it me if the dead rise not?'

'That's it,' said Strangwick. 'So we went down French End together – everything froze up an' quiet, except for their creakin's. I remember thinkin' –' his eyes began to flicker.

'Don't think. Tell what happened,' Keede ordered.

'Oh! Beg y' pardon! He went on with his braziers, hummin' his hymn, down Butcher's Row. Just before we got to the old dressin'-station he stops and sets 'em down an' says: "Where did you say she was, Clem? Me eyes ain't as good as they used to be."

'"In 'er bed at 'ome," I says. "Come on down. It's perishin' cold, an' *I'm* not due for leaf."

'"Well, I am," 'e says. "*I* am . . ." An' then – 'give you me word I didn't recognize the voice – he stretches out 'is neck a bit, in a way 'e 'ad, an' he says: "Why, Bella!" 'e says. "Oh, Bella!" 'e says. "Thank Gawd!"' 'e says. Just like that! An' then I saw – I tell you I *saw* – Auntie Armine herself standin' by the old dressin'-station door where first I'd thought I'd seen her. He was lookin' at 'er an' she was lookin' at him. I saw it, an' me soul turned over inside me because – because it knocked out everything I'd believed in. I 'ad nothin' to lay 'old of, d'ye see? An' 'e was lookin' at 'er as though he could 'ave et 'er, an' she was lookin' at 'im the same way, out of 'er eyes. Then he says: "Why, Bella," 'e says, "this must be only the second time we've been alone together in all these years." An' I saw 'er half hold out her arms to 'im in that perishin' cold. An' she nearer fifty than forty an' me own Aunt! You can shop me for a lunatic tomorrow, but I saw it – I *saw* 'er answerin' to his spoken word! . . . Then 'e made a snatch to unsling 'is rifle.

Then 'e cuts 'is hand away saying: "No! Don't tempt me, Bella. We've all Eternity ahead of us. An hour or two won't make any odds." Then he picks up the braziers an' goes on to the dug-out door. He'd finished with me. He pours petrol on 'em, an' lights it with a match, an' carries 'em inside, flarin'. All that time Auntie Armine stood with 'er arms out – an' a look in 'er face! *I* didn't know such things was or could be! Then he comes out an' says: "Come in, my dear"; an' she stoops an' goes into the dug-out with that look on her face – that look on her face! An' then 'e shuts the door from inside an' starts wedgin' it up. So 'elp me Gawd, I saw an' 'eard all these things with my own eyes an' ears!'

He repeated his oath several times. After a long pause Keede asked him if he recalled what happened next.

'It was a bit of a mix-up, for me, from then on. I must have carried on – they told me I did, but – but I was – I felt a – a long way inside of meself, like – if you've ever had that feelin'. I wasn't rightly on the spot at all. They woke me up sometime next morning, because 'e 'adn't showed up at the train; an' someone had seen him with me. I wasn't 'alf cross-examined by all an' sundry till dinner-time.

'Then, I think, I volunteered for Dearlove, who 'ad a sore toe, for a front-line message. I had to keep movin', you see, because I hadn't anything to hold *on* to. Whilst up there, Grant informed me how he'd found Uncle John with the door wedged an' sand-bags stuffed in the cracks. I hadn't waited for that. The knockin' when 'e wedged up was enough for me. 'Like Dad's coffin.'

'No one told *me* the door had been wedged.' Keede spoke severely.

'No need to black a dead man's name, sir.'

'What made Grant go to Butcher's Row?'

'Because he'd noticed Uncle John had been pinchin' charcoal for a week past an' layin' it up behind the old barricade there. So when the 'unt began, he went that way straight as a string, an' when he saw the door shut, he knew. He told me he picked the sand-bags out of the cracks an' shoved 'is hand through and shifted the wedges before anyone come along.

It looked all right. You said yourself, sir, the door must 'ave blown to.'

'Grant knew what Godsoe meant, then?' Keede snapped.

'Grant knew Godsoe was for it; an' nothin' earthly could 'elp or 'inder. He told me so.'

'And then what did you do?'

'I expect I must 'ave kept on carryin' on, till Headquarters give me that wire from Ma – about Auntie Armine dyin'.'

'When had your Aunt died?'

'On the mornin' of the twenty-first. The mornin' of the 21st! That tore it, d'ye see? As long as I could think, I had kep' tellin' myself it was like those things you lectured about at Arras when we was billeted in the cellars – the Angels of Mons,[11] and so on. But that wire tore it.'

'Oh! Hallucinations! I remember. And that wire tore it?' said Keede.

'Yes! You see' – he half lifted himself off the sofa – 'there wasn't a single gor-dam thing left abidin' for me to take hold of, here or hereafter. If the dead *do* rise – and I saw 'em – why – why *anything* can 'appen. Don't you understand?'

He was on his feet now, gesticulating stiffly.

'For I saw 'er,' he repeated. 'I saw 'im an' 'er – she dead since mornin' time, an' he killin' 'imself before my livin' eyes so's to carry on with 'er for all Eternity – an' she 'oldin' out 'er arms for it! I want to know where I'm *at*! Look 'ere, you two – why stand *we* in jeopardy every hour?'

'God knows,' said Keede to himself.

'Hadn't we better ring for someone?' I suggested. 'He'll go off the handle in a second.'

'No, he won't. It's the last kick-up before it takes hold. I know how the stuff works. Hul-lo!'

Strangwick, his hands behind his back and his eyes set, gave tongue in the strained, cracked voice of a boy reciting. 'Not twice in the world shall the Gods do thus,' he cried again and again.

'And I'm damned if it's goin' to be even once for me!' he went on with sudden insane fury. '*I* don't care whether we *'ave* been pricin' things in the windows ... *Let* 'er sue if she likes!

She don't know what reel things mean. *I* do – I've 'ad occasion to notice 'em . . . *No*, I tell you! I'll 'ave 'em when I want 'em, an' be done with 'em; but not till I see that look on a face . . . that look . . . I'm not takin' any. The reel thing's life an' death. It *begins* at death, d'ye see. *She* can't understand . . . Oh, go on an' push off to Hell, you an' your lawyers. I'm fed up with it – fed up!'

He stopped as abruptly as he had started, and the drawn face broke back to its natural irresolute lines. Keede, holding both his hands, led him back to the sofa, where he dropped like a wet towel, took out some flamboyant robe from a press, and drew it neatly over him.

'Ye-es. *That's* the real thing at last,' said Keede. 'Now he's got it off his mind he'll sleep. By the way, who introduced him?'

'Shall I go and find out?' I suggested.

'Yes; and you might ask him to come here. There's no need for us to stand to all night.'

So I went to the Banquet which was in full swing, and was seized by an elderly, precise Brother from a South London Lodge who followed me, concerned and apologetic. Keede soon put him at his ease.

'The boy's had trouble,' our visitor explained. 'I'm most mortified he should have performed his bad turn here. I thought he'd put it be'ind him.'

'I expect talking about old days with me brought it all back,' said Keede. 'It does sometimes.'

'Maybe! Maybe! But over and above that, Clem's had post-war trouble, too.'

'Can't he get a job? He oughtn't to let that weigh on him, at his time of life,' said Keede cheerily.

''Tisn't that – he's provided for – but' – he coughed confidentially behind his dry hand – 'as a matter of fact, Worshipful Sir, he's – he's implicated for the present in a little breach of promise action.'

'Ah! That's a different thing,' said Keede.

'Yes. That's his reel trouble. No reason given, you understand. The young lady in every way suitable, an' she'd make

him a good little wife too, if I'm any judge. But he says she
ain't his ideel or something. 'No getting at what's in young
people's minds these days, is there?'

'I'm afraid there isn't,' said Keede. 'But he's all right now.
He'll sleep. You sit by him, and when he wakes, take him home
quietly . . . Oh, we're used to men getting a little upset here.
You've nothing to thank us for, Brother – Brother –'

'Armine,' said the old gentleman. 'He's my nephew by marriage.' [12]

'That's all that's wanted!' said Keede.

Brother Armine looked a little puzzled. Keede hastened to
explain. 'As I was saying, all he wants now is to be kept quiet
till he wakes.'

Gow's Watch [13]

Act V Scene 3

After the Battle.
The PRINCESS *by the Standard on the Ravelin.*
Enter GOW, *with the Crown of the Kingdom.*

GOW: Here's earnest of the Queen's submission.
  This by her last herald – and in haste.
PRINCESS: 'Twas ours already. Where is the woman?
GOW: 'Fled with her horse. They broke at dawn.
  Noon has not struck, and you're Queen questionless.
PRINCESS: By you – through you. How shall I honour *you*?
GOW: Me? But for what?
PRINCESS: For all – all – all –
  Since the realm sunk beneath us! Hear him! 'For what?'
  Your body 'twixt my bosom and her knife,
  Your lips on the cup she proffered for my death;
  Your one cloak over me, that night in the snows,
  We held the Pass at Bargi. Every hour
  New strengths, to this most unbelievable last.
  'Honour him?' I will honour – will honour you – . . .
  'Tis at your choice.
GOW: Child, mine was long ago.
            (*Enter* FERDINAND, *as from horse.*)
  But here's one worthy honour. Welcome, Fox!
FERDINAND: And to you, Watchdog. This day clenches all.
  We've made it and seen it.
GOW: Is the city held?
FERDINAND: Loyally. Oh, they're drunk with loyalty yonder.
  A virtuous mood. Your bombards helped 'em to it . . .
  But here's my word for you. The Lady Frances
PRINCESS: I left her sick in the city. No harm, I pray.
FERDINAND: Nothing that she called harm. In truth, so little
  That (*to* GOW) I am bidden to tell you, she'll be here
  Almost as soon as I.
GOW: She says it?
FERDINAND: Writes.
  This. (*Gives him letter.*) Yester eve.

'Twas given me by the priest –
He with her in her hour.

GOW: So? (*Reads*) So it is.
   She will be here. (*To Ferdinand*) And all is safe in the city?

FERDINAND: As thy long sword and my lean wits can make it.
   You've naught to stay for. Is it the road again?

GOW: Ay. This time, not alone ... She will be here.

PRINCESS: I am here. You have not looked at me awhile.

GOW: The rest is with you, Ferdinand ... Then free.

PRINCESS: And at my service more than ever. I claim –
   (Our wars have taught me) – being your Queen, now, claim
   You wholly mine.

GOW: Then free ... She will be here! A little while –

PRINCESS (*to* FERDINAND): He looks beyond, not at me.

FERDINAND: Weariness.
   We are not so young as once was. 'Two days' fight –
   A worthy servitor – to be allowed
   Some freedom.

PRINCESS: I have offered him all he would.

FERDINAND: He takes what he has taken.

       (*The Spirit of the* LADY FRANCES *appears to* GOW.)

GOW: Frances!

PRINCESS: Distraught!

FERDINAND: An old head-blow, may be. He has dealt in them.

GOW (*to the Spirit*): What can the Grave against us, O my Heart,
   Comfort and light and reason in all things
   Visible and invisible – my one God?
   Thou that wast I these barren unyoked years
   Of triflings now at end! Frances!

PRINCESS: She's old.

FERDINAND: True. By most reckonings old.
   They must keep other count.

PRINCESS: He kisses his hand to the air!

FERDINAND: His ring, rather, he kisses. Yes – for sure – the ring.

GOW: Dear and most dear. And now, those very arms. (*Dies.*)

PRINCESS: Oh, look! He faints. Haste, you! Unhelm him! Help!

FERDINAND: Needless. No help
   Avails against that poison. He is sped.

PRINCESS: By his own hand? *This* hour? When I had offered –

FERDINAND: He had made other choice – an old, old choice,
   Ne'er swerved from, and now patently sealed in death.

PRINCESS: He called on – the Lady Frances was it? Wherefore?

FERDINAND: Because she was his life. Forgive, my friend – (*covers
GOW's face*).
　　God's uttermost beyond me in all faith,
　　Service and passion – if I unveil at last
　　The secret. (*To the Princess*) Thought – dreamed you, it was for
　　　　　　　　　　　　　　　　　　　　　　　　　　　you
　　He poured himself – for you resoldered the Crown?
　　Struck here, held there, amended, broke, built up
　　His multiplied imaginings for *you*?
PRINCESS: I thought – I thought he –
FERDINAND: Looked beyond. *Her* wish
　　Was the sole Law he knew. *She* did not choose
　　Your House should perish. Therefore he bade it stand.
　　Enough for him when she had breathed a word:
　　'Twas his to make it iron, stone, or fire,
　　Driving our flesh and blood before his ways
　　As the wind straws. Her one face unregarded
　　Waiting you with your mantle or your glove –
　　That is the God whom he is gone to worship.
　　　　　　(*Trumpets without. Enter the Prince's Heralds.*)
　　And here's the work of Kingship begun again.
　　These from the Prince of Bargi – to whose sword
　　You owe such help as may, he thinks, be paid . . .
　　He's equal in blood, in fortune more than peer,
　　Young, most well favoured, with a heart to love –
　　And two States in the balance. Do you meet him?
PRINCESS: God and my Misery! I have seen Love at last.
　　What shall content me after?

❧ The Propagation of Knowledge ❧

The Birthright

The miracle of our land's speech – so known
And long received, none marvel when 'tis shown!

We have such wealth as Rome at her most pride
Had not or (having) scattered not so wide;
Nor with such arrant prodigality
Beneath her any pagan's foot let lie . . .
Lo! Diamond that cost some half their days
To find and t'other half to bring to blaze:
Rubies of every heat, wherethrough we scan
The fiercer and more fiery heart of man:
Emerald that with the uplifted billow vies,
And Sapphires evening remembered skies:
Pearl perfect, as immortal tears must show,
Bred, in deep waters, of a piercing woe;
And tender Turkis, so with charms y-writ,
Of woven gold, Time dares not bite on it.
Thereafter, in all manners worked and set,
Jade, coral, amber, crystal, ivories, jet, –
Showing no more than various fancies, yet,
Each a Life's token or Love's amulet . . .
Which things, through timeless arrogance of use,
We neither guard nor garner, but abuse;
So that our scholars – nay, our children – fling
In sport or jest treasure to arm a King;
And the gross crowd, at feast or market, hold
Traffic perforce with dust of gems and gold! [1]

The Propagation of Knowledge

The Army Class 'English', which included the Upper Fifth, was trying to keep awake; for 'English' (Literature – Augustan epoch – eighteenth century) came at last lesson, and that, on a blazing July afternoon, meant after everyone had been bathing. Even Mr King found it hard to fight against the snore of the tide along the Pebble Ridge, and spurred himself with strong words.

Since, said he, the pearls of English Literature existed only to be wrenched from their settings and cast before young swine [2] rooting for marks, it was his loathed business – in anticipation of the Army Preliminary Examination which, as usual, would be held at the term's end, under the auspices of an official examiner sent down *ad hoc* – to prepare for the Form a General Knowledge test-paper, which he would give them next week. It would cover their studies, up to date, of the Augustans and *King Lear*, which was the selected – and strictly expurgated – Army Exam. play for that year. Now, English Literature, as he might have told them, was *not* divided into water-tight compartments, but flowed like a river. For example, Samuel Johnson, glory of the Augustans and no mean commentator of Shakespeare, was but one in a mighty procession which –

At this point Beetle's nodding brows came down with a grunt on the desk. He had been soaking and sunning himself in the open sea-baths built out on the rocks under the cliffs, from two-fifteen to four-forty.

The Army Class took Johnson off their minds. With any luck, Beetle would last King till the tea-bell. King rubbed his hands and began to carve him. He had gone to sleep to show his contempt (*a*) for Mr King, who might or might not matter, and (*b*) for the Augustans, who none the less were not to be sneered at by one whose vast and omnivorous reading, for which such extraordinary facilities had been granted (this was because the Head had allowed Beetle the run of his library), naturally overlooked such *epigonoi*[3] as Johnson, Swift, Pope, Addison, and the like. Harrison Ainsworth and Marryat[4] doubtless appealed –

Even so, Beetle, salt-encrusted all over except his spectacles, and steeped in delicious languors, was sliding back to sleep again, when 'Taffy' Howell, the leading light of the Form, who knew his Marryat as well as Stalky did his Surtees,[5] began in his patent, noiseless whisper: '"Allow me to observe – in the most delicate manner in the world – just to hint–"'[6]

'Under pretext of studying literature, a desultory and unformed mind would naturally return, like the dog of Scripture –'

'"You're a damned trencher-scrapin', napkin-carryin', shillin'-seeking', up-an'-down-stairs &c.,"' Howell breathed.

Beetle choked aloud on the sudden knowledge that King was the ancient and eternal Chucks – later Count Shucksen – of *Peter Simple*. He had not realized it before.

'Sorry, sir. I'm afraid I've been asleep, sir,' he sputtered.

The shout of the Army Class diverted the storm. King was grimly glad that Beetle had condescended to honour truth so far. Perhaps he would now lend his awakened ear to a summary of the externals of Dr Johnson, as limned by Macaulay.[7] And he read, with intention, the just historian's outline of a grotesque figure with untied shoe-strings, that twitched and grunted, gorged its food, bit its finger-nails, and neglected its ablutions. The Form hailed it as a speaking likeness of Beetle; nor were they corrected.

Then King implored him to vouchsafe his comrades one single fact connected with Dr Johnson which might at any time have adhered to what, for decency's sake, must, Mr King supposed, be called his mind.

Beetle was understood to say that the only thing he could remember was in French.

'You add, then, the Gallic tongue to your accomplishments? The information plus the accent? 'Tis well! Admirable Crichton,[8] proceed!'

And Beetle proceeded with the text of an old Du Maurier drawing in a back-number of *Punch*:[9]

> 'De tous ces défunts cockolores
> Le moral Fénélon,
> Michel Ange et Johnson
> (Le Docteur) sont les plus awful bores.'

To which Howell, wooingly, just above his breath:
'"Oh, *won't* you come up, come up?"'

Result, as the tea-bell rang, one hundred lines, to be shown up at seven-forty-five that evening. This was meant to blast the pleasant summer interval between tea and prep. Howell, a favourite in 'English' as well as Latin, got off; but the Army Class crashed in to tea with a new Limerick.

The imposition was a matter of book-keeping, as far as Beetle was concerned; for it was his custom of rainy afternoons to fabricate a store of lines in anticipation of just these accidents. They covered such English verse as interested him at the moment, and helped to fix the stuff in his memory. After tea, he drew the required amount from his drawer in Number Five Study, thrust it into his pocket, went up to the Head's house, and settled himself in the big Outer Library[10] where, ever since the Head had taken him off all mathematics, he did précis-work and French translation. Here he buried himself in a close-printed, thickish volume which had been his chosen browse for some time. A hideous account of a hanging, drawing, and quartering had first attracted him to it; but later he discovered the book (*Curiosities of Literature*[11] was its name) full of the finest confused feeding – such as forgeries and hoaxes, Italian literary societies, religious and scholastic controversies of old when men (even that most dreary John Milton, of *Lycidas*) slanged each other, not without dust and heat,[12] in scandalous pamphlets; personal peculiarities of the great; and a hundred other fascinating inutilities. This evening he fell on a description of wandering, mad Elizabethan beggars, known as Tom-a-Bedlams, with incidental references to Edgar who plays at being a Tom-a-Bedlam in *Lear*, but whom Beetle did not consider at all funny.[13] Then, at the foot of a left-hand page, leaped out on him a verse — of incommunicable splendour, opening doors into inexplicable worlds — from a song which Tom-a-Bedlams were supposed to sing. It ran:

> With a heat of furious fancies
>   Whereof I am commander,
> With a burning spear and a horse of air,
>   To the wilderness I wander.
> With a knight of ghosts and shadows
>   I summoned am to tourney,
> Ten leagues beyond the wide world's end —
>   Methinks it is no journey.

He sat, mouthing and staring before him, till the prep-bell rang and it was time to take his lines up to King's study and lay them, as hot from the press, in the impot-basket appointed. He carried his dreams on to Number Five. They knew the symptoms of old.

'Readin' again,' said Stalky, like a wife welcoming her spouse from the pot-house.

'Look here, I've found out something —' Beetle began. 'Listen —'

'No, you don't — till afterwards. It's Turkey's prep.' This meant it was a Horace Ode through which Turkey would take them for a literal translation, and all possible pitfalls. Stalky gave his businesslike attention, but Beetle's eye was glazed and his mind adrift throughout, and he asked for things to be repeated. So, when Turkey closed the Horace, justice began to be executed.

'I'm all right,' he protested. 'I swear I heard a lot what Turkey said. Shut up! Oh, shut *up*! *Do* shut up, you putrid asses.' Beetle was speaking from the fender, his head between Turkey's knees, and Stalky largely over the rest of him.

'What's the metre of the beastly thing?' McTurk waved his Horace. 'Look it up, Stalky. Twelfth of the Third.'

'*Ionicum a minore*,' Stalky reported, closing his book in turn. 'Don't let him forget it'; and Turkey's Horace marked the metre on Beetle's skull, with special attention to elisions. It hurt.

> 'Miserar' est neq' amori dare ludum neque dulci
> Mala vino laver' aut ex –

Got it? You liar! You've no ear at all! Chorus, Stalky!'

Both Horaces strove to impart the measure, which was altogether different from its accompaniment. Presently Howell dashed in from his study below.

'Look *out*! If you make this infernal din we'll have someone up the staircase in a sec.'

'We're teachin' Beetle Horace. He was goin' to burble us some muck he'd read,' the tutors explained.

''Twasn't muck! It was about those Tom-a-Bedlams in *Lear*.'

'Oh!' said Stalky. 'Why didn't you say so?'

''Cause you didn't listen. They had drinkin'-horns an' badges, and there's a Johnson note on Shakespeare about the meanin' of Edgar sayin' "My horn's dry". But Johnson's dead-wrong about it.[14] Aubrey says –'[15]

'Who's Aubrey?' Howell demanded. 'Does King know about him?'

'Dunno. Oh yes, an' Johnson started to learn Dutch when he was seventy.'

'What the deuce for?' Stalky asked.

'For a change after his Dikker, I suppose,' Howell suggested.

'And I looked up a lot of other English stuff, too. I'm goin' to try it all on King.'

'Showin'-off as usual,' said the acid McTurk, who, like his race, lived and loved to destroy illusions.

'No. For a draw. He's an unjust dog! If you read, he says you're showin'-off. If you don't, you're a mark-huntin' Philistine. What does he want you to do, curse him?'

'Shut up, Beetle!' Stalky pronounced. 'There's more than draws in this. You've cribbed your maths off me ever since you came to Coll. You don't know what a co-sine is, even *now*. Turkey does all your Latin.'

'I like that! Who does both your *Picciolas?*'

'French don't count. It's time you began to work for your giddy livin' an' help us. *You* aren't goin' up for anythin' that matters. Play for your side, as Heffles says, or die the death! You don't want to die the death, again, do you? Now, let's hear about that stinkard Johnson swottin' Dutch. You're sure it was Sammivel, not Binjamin? You *are* so dam' inaccurate!'

Beetle conducted an attentive class on the curiosities of literature for nearly a quarter of an hour. As Stalky pointed out, he promised to be useful.

The Horace Ode next morning ran well; and King was content. Then, in full feather, he sailed round the firmament at large, and, somehow, apropros to something or other, used the word 'della Cruscan' – 'if any of you have the faintest idea of its origin.' Someone hadn't caught it correctly; which gave Beetle just time to whisper 'Bran – an' mills' to Howell, who said, promptly: 'Hasn't it somethin' to do with mills – an' bran, sir?' King cast himself into poses of stricken wonder. 'Oddly enough,' said he, 'it has.'

They were then told a great deal about some silly Italian Academy of Letters which borrowed its office furniture from the equipment of mediæval flour-mills. And: 'How has our Ap-Howell come by his knowledge?' Howell, being, indeed, Welsh, thought that it might have been something he had read in the holidays. King openly purred over him.

'If that had been *me*,' Beetle observed while they were toying with sardines between lessons, 'he'd ha' dropped on me for showin'-off.'

'See what we're savin' you from,' Stalky answered. 'I'm playin' Johnson, 'member, this afternoon.'

That, too, came cleanly off the bat; and King was gratified by this interest in the Doctor's studies. But Stalky hadn't a ghost of a notion how he had come by the fact.

'Why didn't you say your father told you?' Beetle asked at tea.

'My-y Lord! Have you ever seen the guv'nor?' Stalky collapsed shrieking among the piles of bread and butter. 'Well, look here. Taffy goes in tomorrow about those drinkin' horns an' Tom-a-Bedlams. You cut up to the library after tea, Beetle.

You know what King's English papers are like. Look out useful stuff for answers an' we'll divvy at prep.'

At prep, then, Beetle, loaded with assorted curiosities, made his forecast. He argued that there were bound to be a good many 'what-do-you-know-abouts' those infernal Augustans. Pope was generally a separate item; but the odds were that Swift, Addison, Steele, Johnson, and Goldsmith would be lumped under one head. Dryden was possible, too, though rather outside the Epoch.

'Dryden. Oh! "Glorious John!" 'Know *that* much, anyhow,' Stalky vaunted.

'Then lug in Claude Halcro in the *Pirate*,' Beetle advised. 'He's always sayin' "Glorious John". King's a hog on Scott, too.'

'No-o. I don't read Scott. You take this Hell Crow chap, Taffy.'

'Right. What about Addison, Beetle?' Howell asked.

''Drank like a giddy fish.'

'We all know that,' chorused the gentle children.

'He said, "See how a Christian can die"; an' he hadn't any conversation, 'cause someone or other –'

'Guessin' again, *as* usual,' McTurk sneered. 'Who?'

''Cynical man called Mandeville – said he was a silent parson in a tie-wig.'

'Right-ho! I'll take the silent parson with wig and 'purtenances. Taffy can have the dyin' Christian,' Stalky decided.

Howell nodded, and resumed: 'What about Swift, Beetle?'

''Died mad. Two girls. Saw a tree, an' said: "I shall die at the top." Oh yes, an' his private amusements were "ridiculous an' trivial".'

Howell shook a wary head. 'Dunno what that might let me in for with King. You can have it, Stalky.'

'I'll take that,' McTurk yawned. 'King doesn't matter a curse to me, an' he knows it. "Private amusements contemptible".' He breathed all Ireland into the last perverted word.

'Right,' Howell assented. 'Bags I the dyin' tree, then.'

''Cheery lot, these Augustans,' Stalky sighed. ''Any more of 'em been croakin' lately, Beetle?'

'My Hat!' the far-seeing Howell struck in. 'King always

gives us a stinker half-way down. What about Richardson –
that "Clarissa" chap, y'know?'

'I've found out lots about him,' said Beetle, promptly. 'He
was the "Shakespeare of novelists".'

'King won't stand that. He says there's only one Shakespeare.
'Mustn't rot about Shakespeare to King,' Howell objected.

'An' he was "always delighted with his own works",' Beetle
continued.

'Like you,' Stalky pointed out.

'Shut up. Oh yes, an' –' he consulted some hieroglyphics on
a scrap of paper – 'the – the impassioned Diderot (dunno who
he was) broke forth: "O Richardson, thou singular genius!"'

Howell and Stalky rose together, each clamouring that he
had bagged that first.

'I *must* have it!' Howell shouted. 'King's never seen me
breakin' forth with the impassioned Diderot. He's *got* to! Give
me Diderot, you impassioned hound!'

'Don't upset the table. There's tons more. An' his genius was
"fertile and prodigal".'

'All right! *I* don't mind bein' "fertile and prodigal" for a
change,' Stalky volunteered. 'King's going to enjoy this exam.
If he was the Army Prelim. chap we'd score.'

'The Prelim. questions will be pretty much like King's stuff,'
Beetle assured them.

'But it's always a score to know what your examiner's keen
on,' Howell said, and illustrated it with an anecdote. ''Uncle of
mine stayin' with my people last holidays –'

'Your Uncle Diderot?' Stalky asked.

'No, you ass! Captain of Engineers. He told me he was up
for a Staff exam. to an old Colonel-bird who believed that the
English were the lost Tribes of Israel, or something like that.
He'd written tons o' books about it.'

'All Sappers are mad,' said Stalky. 'That's one of the things
the guv'nor *did* tell me.'

'Well, ne'er mind. My uncle played up, o' course. 'Said he'd
always believed it, too. And *so* he got nearly top-marks for
field-fortification. 'Didn't know a thing about it, either, he said.'

'Good biznai!' said Stalky. 'Well, go on, Beetle. What about
Steele?'

'Can't I keep anything for myself?'

'Not *much*! King'll ask you where you got it from, and you'd show off, an' he'd find out. This ain't your silly English Literature, you ass. It's our marks. Can't you see that?'

Beetle very soon saw it was exactly as Stalky had said.

Some days later a happy, and therefore not too likeable, King was explaining to the Reverend John in his own study how effort, zeal, scholarship, the humanities, and perhaps a little natural genius for teaching, could inspire even the mark-hunting minds of the young. His text was the result of his General Knowledge paper on the Augustans and *King Lear*.

'Howell,' he said, 'I was not surprised at. He *has* intelligence. But, frankly, I did not expect young Corkran to burgeon. Almost one might believe he occasionally read a book.'

'And McTurk too?'

'Yes. He had somehow arrived at a rather just estimate of Swift's lighter literary diversions. They *are* contemptible. And in the "Lear" questions – they were all attracted by Edgar's character – Stalky had dug up something about Aubrey on Tom-a-Bedlams from some unknown source. Aubrey, of all people! I'm sure I only alluded to him once or twice.'

'Stalky among the prophets [16] of "English"! And he didn't remember where he'd got it either?'

'No. Boys are amazingly purblind and limited. But if they keep this up at the Army Prelim., it is conceivable the Class may not do itself discredit. I told them so.'

'I congratulate you. Ours is the hardest calling in the world, with the least reward. By the way, who are they likely to send down to examine us?'

'It rests between two, I fancy. Martlett – with me at Balliol – and Hume. *They* wisely chose the Civil Service. Martlett has published a brochure on Minor Elizabethan Verse – journeyman work, of course – enthusiasms, but no grounding. Hume I heard of lately as having infected himself in Germany with some Transatlantic abominations about Shakespeare and Bacon. He was Sutton.' (The Head, by the way, was a Sutton man.)

King returned to his examination-papers and read extracts from them, as mothers repeat the clever sayings of their babes.

'Here's old Taffy Howell, for instance – apropos to Diderot's eulogy of Richardson. "The impassioned Diderot broke forth: 'Richardson, thou singular genius!'"'

It was the Reverend John who stopped himself, just in time, from breaking forth. He recalled that, some days ago, he had heard Stalky on the stairs of Number Five, hurling the boots of many fags at Howell's door and bidding the 'impassioned Diderot' within 'break forth' at his peril.

'Odd,' said he, gravely, when his pipe drew again. 'Where did Diderot say that?'

'I've forgotten for the moment. Taffy told me he'd picked it up in the course of holiday reading.'

'Possibly. One never knows what heifers the young are ploughing with. Oh! How did Beetle do?'

'The necessary dates and his handwriting defeated him, I'm glad to say. I cannot accuse myself of having missed any opportunity to castigate that boy's inordinate and intolerable conceit. But I'm afraid it's hopeless. I think I touched him somewhat, though, when I read Macaulay's stock piece on Johnson. The others saw it at once.'

'Yes, you told me about that at the time,' said the Reverend John, hurriedly.

'And our esteemed Head having taken him off maths for this précis-writing – whatever that means! – has turned him into a most objectionable free-lance. He was without any sense of reverence before, and promiscuous cheap fiction – which is all that his type of reading means – aggravates his worst points. When it came to a trial he was simply nowhere.'

'Ah, well! Ours is a hard calling – specially if one's sensitive. Luckily, I'm too fat.' The Reverend John went out to bathe off the Pebble Ridge, girt with a fair linen towel whose red fringe signalled from half a mile away.

There lurked on summer afternoons, round the fives-court or the gym, certain watchful outcasts who had exhausted their weekly ration of three baths, and who were too well known to Cory the bathman to outface him by swearing that they hadn't. These came in like sycophantic pups at walk, and when the

Reverend John climbed the Pebble Ridge, more than a dozen of them were at his heels, with never a towel among them. One could only bathe off the Ridge with a House Master, but by custom, a dozen details above a certain age, no matter whence recruited, made a 'House' for bathing, if any kindly Master chose so to regard them. Beetle led the low, growing reminder: 'House! House, sir? We've got a House now, Padre.'

'Let it be law as it is desired,' boomed the Reverend John. On which word they broke forward, hirpling over the unstable pebbles and stripping as they ran, till, when they touched the sands, they were as naked as God had made them, and as happy as He intended them to be.

It was half-flood – dead-smooth, except for the triple line of combers, a mile from wing to wing, that broke evenly with a sound of ripping canvas, while their sleek rear-guards formed up behind. One swam forth, trying to copy the roll, rise, and dig-out of the Reverend John's sidestroke, and manoeuvred to meet them so that they should crash on one's head, when for an instant one glanced down arched perspectives of beryl, before all broke in fizzy, electric diamonds, and the pulse of the main surge slung one towards the beach. From a good comber's crest one was hove up almost to see Lundy on the horizon. In its long cream-streaked trough, when the top had turned over and gone on, one might be alone in mid-Atlantic. Either way it was divine. Then one capered on the sands till one dried off; retrieved scattered flannels, gave thanks in chorus to the Reverend John, and lazily trailed up to five-o'clock call-over, taken on the lower cricket field.

'Eight this week,' said Beetle, and thanked Heaven aloud.

'Bathing seems to have sapped your mind,' the Reverend John remarked. 'Why did you do so vilely with the Augustans?'

'They *are* vile, Padre. So's *Lear*.'

'The other two did all right, though.'

'I expect they've been swottin',' Beetle grinned.

'I've expected that, too, in my time. But I want to hear about the "impassioned Diderot", please.'

'Oh, that was Howell, Padre. You mean when Diderot broke

forth: "Richardson, thou singular genius"? He'd read it in the holidays somewhere.'

'I *beg* your pardon. Naturally, Taffy would read Diderot in the holidays. Well, I'm sorry I can't lick you for this; but if any-one ever finds out anything about it, you've only yourself to thank.'

Beetle went up to College and to the Outer Library, where he had on tap the last of a book called *Elsie Venner*, by a man called Oliver Wendell Holmes – all about a girl who was interestingly allied to rattlesnakes. He finished what was left of her, and cast about for more from the same hand, which he found on the same shelf, with the trifling difference that the writer's Christian name was now Nathaniel,[17] and he did not deal in snakes. The authorship of Shakespeare was his theme – not that Shakespeare with whom King oppressed the Army Class, but a low-born, poaching, ignorant, immoral village lout who could not have written one line of any play ascribed to him. (Beetle wondered what King would say to Nathaniel if ever they met.) The real author was Francis Bacon,[18] of Bacon's Essays, which did not strike Beetle as any improvement. He had 'done' the essays last term. But evidently Nathaniel's views annoyed people, for the margins of his book – it was second-hand, and the old label of a public library still adhered – flamed with ribald, abusive, and contemptuous comments by various hands. They ranged from 'Rot!' 'Rubbish!' and such like to crisp counter-arguments. And several times someone had written: 'This beats Delia'.[19] One copious annotator dis-sented, saying: 'Delia is supreme in this line', 'Delia beats this hollow'. 'See Delia's Philosophy, page so and so.' Beetle grieved he could not find anything about Delia (he had often heard King's views on lady-writers as a class) beyond a statement by Nathaniel, with pencilled exclamation-points rocketing all round it, that 'Delia Bacon discovered in Francis Bacon a good deal more than Macaulay.' Taking it by and large, with the kind help of the marginal notes, it appeared that Delia and Nathaniel between them had perpetrated every conceivable outrage against the Head-God of King's idolatry: and King was particular about his idols. Without pronouncing on the merits of the controversy, it occurred to Beetle that a well-mixed dose of

Nathaniel ought to work on King like a seidlitz powder.[20] At this point a pencil and a half sheet of impot-paper came into action, and he went down to tea so swelled with Baconian heresies and blasphemies that he could only stutter between mouthfuls. He returned to his labours after the meal, and was visibly worse at prep.

'I say,' he began, 'have you ever heard that Shakespeare never wrote his own beastly plays?'

''Fat lot of good to us!' said Stalky. 'We've got to swot 'em up just the same. Look here! This is for English parsin' tomorrow. It's *your* biznai.' He read swiftly from the school *Lear* (Act II Scene 2) thus:

> STEWARD: 'Never any:
> It pleased the King, his master, very late,
> To strike at me, upon his misconstruction;
> When he, conjunct, an' flatterin' his displeasure,
> Tripped me behind: bein' down, insulted, railed,
> And put upon him such a deal of man,
> That worthy'd him, got praises of the King
> For him attemptin' who was self-subdued;
> And, in the fleshments of this dread exploit,
> Drew me on here.

'Now then, my impassioned bard, *construez*! That's Shakespeare.'

''Give it up! He's drunk,' Beetle declared at the end of a blank half minute.

'No, he isn't,' said Turkey. 'He's a steward – on the estate – chattin' to his employers.'

'Well – look here, Turkey. You ask King if Shakespeare ever wrote his own plays, an' he won't give a dam' what the steward said.'

'I've not come here to play with ushers,' was McTurk's view of the case.

'I'd do it,' Beetle protested, 'only he'd slay *me*! He don't love me when I ask about things. I can give you the stuff to draw him – tons of it!' He broke forth into a précis, interspersed with praises, of Nathaniel Holmes and his commentators – especially the latter. He also mentioned Delia, with sorrow that he had not read her. He spoke through nearly the whole of prep; and the upshot of it was that McTurk relented and promised to approach King next 'English' on the authenticity of Shakespeare's plays.

The time and tone chosen were admirable. While King was warming himself by a preliminary canter round the Form's literary deficiencies, Turkey coughed in a style which suggested a reminder to a slack *employé* that it was time to stop chattering and get to work. As King began to bristle, Turkey inquired: 'I'd be glad to know, sir, if it's true that Shakespeare did not write his own plays at all?'

'Good God!' said King most distinctly. Turkey coughed again piously. 'They all say so in Ireland, sir.'

'Ireland – Ireland – Ireland!' King overran Ireland with one blast of flame that should have been written in letters of brass for instruction today. At the end, Turkey coughed once more, and the cough said: 'It is Shakespeare, and not my country, that you are hired to interpret to me.' He put it directly, too: 'An' is it true at all about the alleged plays, sir?'

'It is not,' Mr King whispered, and began to explain, on lines that might, perhaps, have been too freely expressed for the parents of those young (though it gave their offspring delight), but with a passion, force, and wealth of imagery which would have crowned his discourse at any university. By the time he drew towards his peroration the Form was almost openly applauding. Howell noiselessly drummed the cadence of 'Bonnie Dundee' on his desk; Paddy Vernon framed a dumb: 'Played! Oh, *well* played, sir!' at intervals; Stalky kept tally of the brighter gems of invective; and Beetle sat aghast but exulting among the spirits he had called up. For though their works had never been mentioned, and though Mr King said he had merely glanced at the obscene publications, he seemed to know a tremendous amount about Nathaniel and Delia – especially Delia.

'I told you so!' said Beetle, proudly, at the end.

'What? *Him!* I wasn't botherin' myself to listen to him an' his Delia,' McTurk replied.

Afterwards King fought his battle over again with the Reverend John in the Common Room.

'Had I been that triple ass Hume, I might have risen to the bait. As it is, I flatter myself I left them under no delusions as to Shakespeare's authenticity. Yes, a small drink, please. Virtue has gone out of me [21] indeed. But *where* did they get it from?'

'The devil! The young devil,' the Reverend John muttered, half aloud.

'I could have excused devilry. It was ignorance. Sheer, crass, insolent provincial ignorance! I tell you, Gillett, if the Romans had dealt faithfully with the Celt, *ab initio*, this – this would never have happened.'

'Quite so. I should like to have heard your remarks.'

'I've told 'em to tell me what they remember of them, with their own conclusions, in essay form next week.'

Since he had loosed the whirlwind, the fair-minded Beetle offered to do Turkey's essay for him. On Turkey's behalf, then, he dealt with Shakespeare's lack of education, his butchering, poaching, drinking, horse-holding, and errand-running as Nathaniel had described them; lifted from the same source pleasant names, such as 'rustic' and 'sorry poetaster', on which last special hopes were built; and expressed surprise that one so ignorant could have done 'what he was attributed to'. His own essay contained no novelties. Indeed, he withheld one or two promising 'subsequently transpireds' for fear of distracting King.

But, when the essays were read, Mr King confined himself wholly to Turkey's pitiful, puerile, jejune, exploded, unbaked, half-bottomed thesis. He touched, too, on the 'lie in the soul', which was, fundamentally, vulgarity – the negation of Reverence and the Decencies. He broke forth into an impassioned defence of 'mere atheism', which he said was often no more than mental flatulence – transitory and curable by knowledge of life – in no way comparable, for essential enormity, with the debasing pagan abominations to which Turkey had delivered himself. He ended with a shocking story about one Jowett, who seemed to have held some post of authority where King came from, and who had told an atheistical undergraduate that if he could not believe in a Personal God by five that afternoon he would be expelled – as, with tears of rage in his eyes, King regretted that he could not expel McTurk. And Turkey blew his nose in the middle of it.

But the aim of education being to develop individual judgment, King could not well kill him for his honest doubts about Shakespeare. And he himself had several times quoted, in respect to other poets: 'There lives more faith in honest doubt, Believe me, than in half the creeds.' So he treated Turkey in Form like a coiled puff-adder; and there was a tense peace among the Augustans.[22] The only ripple was the day before the Army Examiner came, when Beetle inquired if he 'need take this exam., sir, as I'm not goin' up for anything.' Mr King said there was great need – for many reasons, none of them flattering to vanity.

As far as the Army Class could judge, the Examiner was not worse than his breed, and the written 'English' paper ran closely on the lines of King's mid-term General Knowledge test. Howell played his 'impassioned Diderot' to the Richardson lead; Stalky his parson in the wig; McTurk his contemptible Swift; Beetle, Steele's affectionate notes out of the spunging-house to 'Dearest Prue', all in due order. There were, however, one or two leading questions about Shakespeare. A boy's hand shot up from a back bench.

'In answering Number Seven – reasons for Shakespeare's dramatic supremacy,' he said, 'are we to take it Shakespeare *did* write the plays he is supposed to have written, sir?'

The Examiner hesitated an instant. 'It is generally assumed that he did.' But there was no reproof in his words. Beetle began to sit down slowly.

Another hand and another voice: 'Have we got to say we believe he did, sir? Even if we do not?'

'You are not called upon to state your beliefs. But we can go into that at *viva voce* this afternoon – if it interests you.'

'Thank you, sir.'

'What did you do that for?' Paddy Vernon demanded at dinner.

'It's the lost tribes of Israel game, you ass,' said Howell.

'To make sure,' Stalky amplified. 'If he was like King, he'd have shut up Beetle an' Turkey at the start, but he'd have thought King gave us the Bacon notion. Well, he didn't shut 'em up; so they're playin' it again this afternoon. If he stands it then, he'll be sure King gave us the notion. Either way, it's dead-safe for us – an' King.'

At the afternoon's *viva voce*, before they sat down to the Augustans, the Examiner wished to hear, 'with no bearing on the examination, of course,' from those two candidates who had asked him about Question Seven. Which were they?

'Take off your gigs, you owl,' said Stalky between his teeth. Beetle pocketed them and looked into blurred vacancy with a voice coming out of it that asked: 'Who – what gave you that idea about Shakespeare?' From Stalky's kick he knew the question was for him.

'Some people say, sir, there's a good deal of doubt about it nowadays, sir.'

'Ye-es, that's true, but –'

'It's his knowin' so much about legal phrases.' Turkey was in support – a lone gun barking somewhere to his right.

'That is a crux, I admit. Of course, whatever one may think privately, officially Shakespeare *is* Shakespeare. But how have *you* been taught to look at the question?'

'Well, Holmes says it's impossible he could –'

'On the legal phraseology alone, sir,' McTurk chimed in.

'Ah, but the theory is that Shakespeare's experiences in the society of that day brought him in contact with all the leading intellects.' The Examiner's voice was quite colloquial now.

'But they didn't think much of actors then, sir, did they?' This was Howell cooing like a cushat dove. 'I mean –'

The Examiner explained the status of the Elizabethan actor in some detail, ending: 'And that makes it the more curious, doesn't it?'

'And this Shakespeare was supposed to be writin' plays and actin' in 'em *all* the time?' McTurk asked, with sinister meaning.

'Exactly what I – what lots of people have pointed out. Where did he get the time to acquire all this special knowledge?'

'Then it looks as if there was something in it, doesn't it, sir?'

'That,' said the Examiner, squaring his elbows at ease on the desk, 'is a very large question which –'

'Yes, sir!' – in half-a-dozen eagerly attentive keys . . .

For decency's sake a few Augustan questions were crammed in conscience-strickenly, about the last ten minutes. Howell took them since they involved dates, but the answers, though highly marked, were scarcely heeded. When the clock showed six-thirty the Examiner addressed them as 'Gentlemen'; and said he would have particular pleasure in speaking well of this Army Class, which had evinced such a genuine and unusual interest in English Literature, and which reflected the greatest credit on their instructors. He passed out: the Form upstanding, as custom was.

'He's goin' to congratulate King,' said Howell. 'Don't make a row! "Don't – make – a – noise – Or else you'll wake the Baby"' . . .

Mr King of Balliol, after Mr Hume of Sutton had compli-mented him, as was only just, before all his colleagues in Common Room, was kindly taken by the Reverend John to his study, where he exploded on the hearth-rug.

'He – he thought *I* had loosed this – this rancid Baconian rot among them. He complimented me on my breadth of mind – my being abreast of the times! You heard him? That's how they think at Sutton. It's an open stye! A lair of bestial! They have a chapel there, Gillett, and they pray for their souls – their *souls!*'

'His particular weakness apart, Hume was perfectly sincere about what you'd done for the Army Class. He'll report in that sense, too. That's a feather in your cap, and a deserved one. He said their interest in Literature was unusual. That is *all* your work, King.'

'But I bowed down in the House of Rimmon while he Baconized all over me! – poor devil of an usher that I am! You heard it! I ought to have spat in his eye! Heaven knows I'm as conscious of my own infirmities as my worst enemy can be; but what have I done to deserve this? What *have* I done?'

'That's just what I was wondering,' the Reverend John replied. 'Have you, perchance, done anything?'

'Where? How?'

'In the Army Class, for example.'

'Assuredly not! My Army Class? I couldn't wish for a better – keen, interested enough to read outside their allotted task – intelligent, receptive! They're head and shoulders above last year's. The idea that I, forsooth, should, even by inference, have perverted their minds with this imbecile and unspeakable girls'-school tripe that Hume professes! *You* at least know that I have my standards; and in Literature and in the Classics, I hold *maxima debetur pueris reverentia*.'[23]

'It's singular, not plural, isn't it?' said the Reverend John. 'But you're absolutely right as to the principle! ... Ours is a deadly calling, King – specially if one happens to be sensitive.'

⦃ A Friend of the Family ⦄

A Legend of Truth

Once on a time, the ancient legends tell,
Truth, rising from the bottom of her well,
Looked on the world, but, hearing how it lied,
Returned to her seclusion horrified.
There she abode, so conscious of her worth,
Not even Pilate's Question [1] called her forth,
Nor Galileo, [2] kneeling to deny
The Laws that hold our Planet 'neath the sky.
Meantime, her kindlier sister, whom men call
Fiction, [3] did all her work and more than all,
With so much zeal, devotion, tact, and care,
That no one noticed Truth was otherwhere.

Then came a War when, bombed and gassed and mined,
Truth rose once more, perforce, to meet mankind,
And through the dust and glare and wreck of things,
Beheld a phantom on unbalanced wings,
Reeling and groping, dazed, dishevelled, dumb,
But semaphoring direr deeds to come.
Truth hailed and bade her stand; the quavering shade,
Clung to her knees and babbled, 'Sister, aid!
I am – I was – thy Deputy, and men
Besought me for my useful tongue or pen
To gloss their gentle deeds, and I complied,
And they, and thy demands, were satisfied.
But this –' she pointed o'er the blistered plain,
Where men as Gods and devils wrought amain –
'This is beyond me! Take thy work again.'

Tables and pen transferred, she fled afar,
And Truth assumed the record of the War . . .

A Friend of the Family

She saw, she heard, she read, she tried to tell
Facts beyond precedent and parallel –
Unfit to hint or breathe, much less to write,
But happening every minute, day and night.
She called for proof. It came. The dossiers grew.
She marked them, first, 'Return. This can't be true.'
Then, underneath the cold official word:
'This is not really half of what occurred.'

She faced herself at last, the story runs,
And telegraphed her sister: 'Come at once.
Facts out of hand. Unable overtake
Without your aid. Come back for Truth's own sake!
Co-equal rank and powers if you agree.
They need us both, but you far more than me!'

A Friend of the Family

There had been rather a long sitting at Lodge 'Faith and Works', 5837 E.C.,[4] that warm April night. Three initiations and two raisings, each conducted with the spaciousness and particularity that our Lodge prides itself upon, made the Brethren a little silent, and the strains of certain music had not yet lifted from them.

'There are two pieces that ought to be barred for ever,' said a Brother as we were sitting down to the 'banquet'. '"Last Post" is the other.'

'I can just stand "Last Post". It's "Tipperary" breaks me,' another replied. 'But I expect everyone carries his own firing-irons inside him.'

I turned to look. It was a sponsor for one of our newly raised Brethren – a fat man with a fish-like and vacant face, but evidently prosperous. We introduced ourselves as we took our places. His name was Bevin, and he had a chicken farm near Chalfont St Giles, whence he supplied, on yearly contract, two or three high-class London hotels. He was also, he said, on the edge of launching out into herb-growing.

'There's a demand for herbs,' said he; 'but it all depends upon your connections with the wholesale dealers. *We* ain't systematic enough. The French do it much better, especially in those mountains on the Swiss an' Italian sides. They use more herbal remedies than we do. Our patent-medicine business has killed that with us. But there's a demand still, if your connections are sound. I'm going in for it.'

A large, well-groomed Brother across the table (his name was Pole, and he seemed some sort of professional man) struck in with a detailed account of a hollow behind a destroyed village near Thiepval, where, for no ascertainable reason, a certain rather scarce herb had sprung up by the acre, he said, out of the overturned earth.

'Only you've got to poke among the weeds to find it, and there's any quantity of bombs an' stuff knockin' about there still. They haven't cleaned it up yet.'

'Last time *I* saw the place,' said Bevin, 'I thought it 'ud be that way till Judgement Day. You know how it lay in that dip under that beet-factory. I saw it bombed up level in two days – into brick-dust mainly. They were huntin' for St Firmin Dump.' He took a sandwich and munched slowly, wiping his face, for the night was close.

'Ye-es,' said Pole. 'The trouble is there hasn't been any judgement taken or executed. That's why the world is where it is now. We didn't need anything but justice – afterwards. Not gettin' that, the bottom fell out of things, naturally.' [5]

'That's how I look at it too,' Bevin replied. 'We didn't want all that talk afterwards – we only wanted justice. What *I* say is, there *must* be a right and a wrong to things. It can't all be kiss-an'-make-friends, no matter what you do.'

A thin, dark brother on my left, who had been attending to a cold pork pie (there are no pork pies to equal ours, which are home-made), suddenly lifted his long head, in which a pale blue glass eye swivelled insanely.

'Well,' he said slowly. '*My* motto is "Never again." Ne-ver again for me.'

'Same here – till next time,' said Pole, across the table. 'You're from Sydney, ain't you?'

'How d'you know?' was the short answer.

'You spoke.' The other smiled. So did Bevin, who added: '*I* know how your push talk, well enough. Have you started that Republic of yours down under yet?'

'No. But we're goin' to. *Then* you'll see.'

'Carry on. No one's hindering,' Bevin pursued.

The Australian scowled. 'No. We know they ain't. And – and – that's what makes us all so crazy angry with you.' He threw back his head and laughed the spleen out of him. 'What *can* you do with an Empire that – that don't care what you do?'

'I've heard that before,' Bevin laughed, and his fat sides shook. 'Oh, I know *your* push inside-out.'

'When did you come across us? My name's Orton – no relation to the Tichborne one.'

'Gallip'li – dead mostly. My battalion began there. We only lost half.'

'Lucky! They gambled *us* away in two days. 'Member the hospital on the beach?' asked Orton.

'Yes. An' the man without the face – preaching,' said Bevin, sitting up a little.

'Till he died,' said the Australian, his voice lowered.

'*And* afterwards,' Bevin added, lower still.

'Christ! Were you there that night?'

Bevin nodded. The Australian choked off something he was going to say, as a Brother on his left claimed him. I heard them talk horses, while Bevin developed his herb-growing projects with the well-groomed Brother opposite.

At the end of the banquet, when pipes were drawn, the Australian addressed himself to Bevin, across me, and as the company re-arranged itself, we three came to anchor in the big anteroom where the best prints are hung. Here our Brother across the table joined us, and moored alongside.

The Australian was full of racial grievances, as must be in a young country; alternating between complaints that his people had not been appreciated enough in England, or too fulsomely complimented by an hysterical Press.

'No-o,' Pole drawled, after awhile. 'You're altogether wrong. We hadn't time to notice anything – we were all too busy fightin' for our lives. What *your* crowd down under are suffering from is growing-pains. You'll get over 'em in three hundred years or so – if you're allowed to last so long.'

'Who's going to stoush us?' Orton asked fiercely.

This turned the talk again to larger issues and possibilities – delivered on both sides straight from the shoulder without malice or heat, between bursts of song from round the piano at the far end. Bevin and I sat out, watching.

'Well, *I* don't understand these matters,' said Bevin at last. 'But I'd hate to have one of your crowd have it in for me for anything.'

'Would you? Why?' Orton pierced him with his pale, artificial eye.

'Well, you're a trifle – what's the word? – vindictive? – spiteful? At least, that's what *I*'ve found. I expect it comes from drinking stewed tea with your meat four times a day,' said Bevin. 'No! I'd hate to have an Australian after me for anything in particular.'

Out of this came his tale – somewhat in this shape:

It opened with an Australian of the name of Hickmot or Hickmer – Bevin called him both – who, finding his battalion completely expended at Gallipoli, had joined up with what stood of Bevin's battalion, and had there remained, unrebuked and unnoticed. The point that Bevin laboured was that his man had never seen a table-cloth, a china plate, or a dozen white people together till, in his thirtieth year, he had walked for two months to Brisbane to join up. Pole found this hard to believe.

'But it's true,' Bevin insisted. 'This chap was born an' bred among the black fellers, as they call 'em, two hundred miles from the nearest town, four hundred miles from a railway, an' ten thousand from the grace o' God – out in Queensland near some desert.'

'Why, of course. We come out of everywhere,' said Orton. 'What's wrong with that?'

'Yes – but – Look here! From the time that this man Hickmot was twelve years old he'd ridden, driven – what's the word? – conducted sheep for his father for thousands of miles on end, an' months at a time, alone with these black fellers that you daren't show the back of your neck to – else they knock your head in. That was all that he'd ever done till he joined up. He – he – didn't *belong* to anything in the world, you understand. And he didn't strike other men as being a – a human being.'[6]

'Why? He was a Queensland drover. They're all right,' Orton explained.

'I dare say; but – well, a man notices another man, don't he? You'd notice if there was a man standing or sitting or lyin' near you, wouldn't you? So'd any one. But you'd never notice Hickmot. His bein' anywhere about wouldn't stay in your mind. He just didn't draw attention any more than anything else that happened to be about. Have you got it?'

'Wasn't he any use at his job?' Pole inquired.

'I've nothing against him that way, an' I'm – I was his platoon sergeant. He wouldn't volunteer specially for any doings, but he'd slip out with the party and he'd slip back with what was left of 'em. No one noticed him, and he never opened his mouth about any doings. You'd think a man who had lived the way he'd lived among black fellers an' sheep would be noticeable enough in an English battalion, wouldn't you?'

'It teaches 'em to lie close; but *you* seem to have noticed him,' Orton interposed, with a little suspicion.

'Not at the time – but afterwards. If he was noticeable it was on account of his *un*noticeability – same way you'd notice there not being an extra step at the bottom of the staircase when you thought there was.'

'Ye-es,' Pole said suddenly. 'It's the eternal mystery of personality. "God before Whom ever lie bare –" Some people can occlude their personality like turning off a tap. I beg your pardon. Carry on!'

'Granted,' said Bevin. 'I think I catch your drift. I used to think I was a student of human nature before I joined up.'

'What was your job – before?' Orton asked.

'Oh, I was *the* young blood of the village. Goal-keeper in our soccer team, secretary of the local cricket and rifle – oh, lor'! – clubs. Yes, an' village theatricals. My father was the chemist in the village. *How* I did talk! *What* I did know!' He beamed upon us all.

'*I* don't mind hearing you talk,' said Orton, lying back in his chair. 'You're a little different from some of 'em. What happened to this dam' drover of yours?'

'He was with our push for the rest of the war – an' I don't think he ever sprung a dozen words at one time. With his upbringing, you see, there wasn't any subject that any man knew about he *could* open up on. He kept quiet, and mixed with his backgrounds. If there was a lump of dirt, or a hole in the ground, or what was – was left after anythin' had happened, it would be Hickmot. That was all he wanted to be.'

'A camouflager?' Orton suggested.

'You have it! He was the complete camouflager all through.

That's him to a dot. Look here! He hadn't even a nickname in his platoon! And then a friend of mine from our village, of the name of Vigors, came out with a draft. Bert Vigors. As a matter of fact, I was engaged to his sister. And Bert hadn't been with us a week before they called him "The Grief". His father was an oldish man, a market-gardener – high-class vegetables, bit o' glass, an' – an' all the rest of it. Do you know anything about that particular business?'

'Not much, I'm afraid,' said Pole, 'except that glass is expensive, and one's man always sells the cut flowers.'

'Then you *do* know something about it. It is. Bert was the old man's only son, an' – *I* don't blame him – he'd done his damnedest to get exempted – for the sake of the business, you understand. But he caught it all right. The tribunal wasn't takin' any the day he went up. Bert was for it, with a few remarks from the patriotic old was-sers on the bench. Our county paper had 'em all.'

'That's the thing that made one really want the Hun in England for a week or two,' said Pole.

'*Mwor osee!* The same tribunal, havin' copped Bert, gave unconditional exemption to the opposition shop – a man called Margetts, in the market-garden business, which he'd established *since* the war, with his two sons who, everyone in the village knew, had been pushed into the business to save their damned hides. But Margetts had a good lawyer to advise him. The whole case was frank and above-board to a degree – our county paper had it all in, too. Agricultural produce – vital necessity; the plough mightier than the sword; an' those ducks on the bench, who had turned down Bert, noddin' and smilin' at Margetts, all full of his cabbage and green peas. What happened? The usual. Vigors' business – he's sixty-eight, with asthma – goes smash, and Margetts and Co. double theirs. So, then, that was Bert's grievance, an' he joined us full of it. That's why they called him "The Grief". Knowing the facts, I was with him; but being his sergeant, I had to check him, because grievances are catchin', and three or four men with 'em make Companies – er – sticky. Luckily Bert wasn't handy with his pen. He had to cork up his grievance mostly till he came

across Hickmot, an' Gord in Heaven knows what brought those
two together. No! *As* y'were. I'm wrong about God! I always
am. It was Sheep. Bert knew's much about sheep as I do – an'
that's Canterbury lamb – but he'd let Hickmot talk about 'em
for hours, in return for Hickmot listenin' to his grievance.
Hickmot 'ud talk sheep – the one created thing he'd ever open
up on – an' Bert 'ud talk his grievance while they was waiting to
go over the top. I've heard 'em again an' again, and, of course, I
encouraged 'em. Now, look here! Hickmot hadn't seen an English house or a field or a road or – or anything any civ'lized man
is used to in all his life! Sheep an' blacks! Market-gardens an'
glass an' exemption-tribunals! An' the men's teeth chatterin'
behind their masks between rum-issue an' zero. Oh, there was
fun in Hell those days, wasn't there, boys?'

'Sure! Oh, sure!' Orton chuckled, and Pole echoed him.

'Look here! When we were lying up somewhere among those
forsaken chicken-camps back o' Doullens, I found Hickmot
making mud-pies in a farmyard an' Bert lookin' on. He'd made
a model of our village according to Bert's description of it.
He'd preserved it in his head through all those weeks an' weeks
o' Bert's yap; an' he'd coughed it all up – Margetts' house and
gardens, old Mr Vigors' ditto; both pubs; my father's shop,
everything that he'd been told by Bert done out to scale in mud,
with bits o' brick and stick. Haig ought to have seen it; but as
his sergeant I had to check him for misusin' his winkle-pin [7] on
dirt. 'Come to think of it, a man who runs about uninhabited
countries, with sheep, for a livin' must have gifts for mappin'
and scalin' things somehow or other, or he'd be dead. *I* never
saw anything like it – *all* out o' what Bert had told him by word
of mouth. An' the next time we went up the line Hickmot
copped it in the leg just in front of me.'

'Finish?' I asked.

'Oh, no. Only beginnin'. That was in December, somethin'
or other, '16. In Jan'ry Vigors copped it for keeps. I buried
him – snowin' blind it was – an' before we'd got him under the
whole show was crumped. I wanted to bury him again just to
spite 'em (I'm a spiteful man by nature), but the party wasn't
takin' any more – even if they could have found it. But, you

see, we had buried him all right, which is what they want at home, and I wrote the usual trimmin's about the chaplain an' the full service, an' what his captain had said about Bert bein' recommended for a pip, an' the irreparable loss an' so on. That was in Jan'ry '17. In Feb'ry some time or other I got saved. My speciality had come to be bombin's and night-doings. Very pleasant for a young free man, but – there's a limit to what you can stand. It takes all men differently. Noise was what started me, at last. I'd got just up to the edge – wonderin' when I'd crack an' how many of our men I'd do in if it came on me while we were busy. I had that nice taste in the mouth and the nice temperature they call trench-fever, an' – I had to feel inside my head for the meanin' of every order I gave or was responsible for executin'.[8] *You* know!'

'We do. Go on!' said Pole in a tone that made Orton look at him.

'So, you see, the bettin' was even on my drawin' a V.C. or getting Number Umpty rest-camp or – a firing party before breakfast. But Gord saved me. (I made friends with Him the last two years of the war. The others went off too quick.) They wanted a bombin'-instructor for the training-battalion at home, an' He put it into their silly hearts to indent for me. It took 'em five minutes to make me understand I was saved. Then I vomited, an' then I cried. *You* know!' The fat face of Bevin had changed and grown drawn, even as he spoke; and his hands tugged as though to tighten an imaginary belt.

'I was never keen on bombin' myself,' said Pole. 'But bombin'-instruction's murder!'

'I don't deny it's a shade risky, specially when they take the pin out an' start shakin' it, same as the Chinks used to do in the woods at Beauty, when they were cuttin' 'em down. But you live like a home defence Brigadier, besides week-end leaf. As a matter o' fact, I married Bert's sister soon's I could after I got the billet, an' I used to lie in our bed thinkin' of the old crowd on the Somme an' – feelin' what a swine I was. Of course, I earned two V.C.s a week behind the traverse in the exercise of my ord'nary duties, but that isn't the same thing. An' yet I'd only joined up because – because I couldn't dam' well help it.'

'An' what about your Queenslander?' the Australian asked.

'*Too de sweet! Pronto!* We got a letter in May from a Brighton hospital matron, sayin' that one of the name of Hickmer was anxious for news o' me, previous to proceedin' to Roehampton for initiation into his new leg. Of course, we applied for him by return. Bert had written about him to his sister – my missus – every time he wrote at all; an' any pal o' Bert's – well, *you* know what the ladies are like. I warned her about his peculiarities. She wouldn't believe till she saw him. He was just the same. You'd ha' thought he'd show up in England like a fresh stiff on snow – but you never noticed him. You never heard him; and if he didn't want to be seen he wasn't there. He just joined up with his background. I knew he could do that with men; but how in Hell, seein' how curious women are, he could camouflage with the ladies – my wife an' my mother to wit – beats *me*! He'd feed the chickens for us; he'd stand on his one leg – it was off above the knee – and saw wood for us. He'd run – I mean he'd hop – errands for Mrs B. or mother; our dog worshipped him from the start, though I never saw him throw a word to him; and – *yet* he didn't take any place anywhere. You've seen a rabbit – you've seen a pheasant – hidin' in a ditch? 'Put your hand on it sometimes before it moved, haven't you? Well, that was Hickmot – with two women in the house crazy to find out – find out – anything about him that made him human. *You* know what women are! He stayed with us a fortnight. He left us on a Sat'day to go to Roehampton to try his leg. On Friday he came over to the bombin' ground – not sayin' anything, *as* usual – to watch me instruct my Suicide Club, which was only half an hour's run by rail from our village. He had his overcoat on, an' as soon as he reached the place it was *mafeesh*[9] with him, as usual. Rabbit-trick again! You never noticed him. He sat in the bomb-proof behind the pit where the duds accumulate till it's time to explode 'em. Naturally, that's strictly forbidden to the public. So he went there, an' no one noticed him. When he'd had enough of watchin', he hopped off home to feed our chickens for the last time.'

'Then how did *you* know all about it?' Orton said.

'Because I saw him come into the place just as I was goin'

down into the trench. Then he slipped my memory till my train went back. But it would have made no difference what our arrangements were. If Hickmer didn't choose to be noticed, he *wasn't* noticed. Just for curiosity's sake I asked some o' the Staff Sergeants whether they'd seen him on the ground. Not one – not one single one had – or could tell me what he was like. An', Sat'day noon, he went off to Roehampton. We saw him into the train ourselves, with the lunch Mrs B. had put up for him – a one-legged man an' his crutch, in regulation blue, khaki warm an' kit-bag. Takin' everything together, per'aps he'd spoken as many as twenty times in the thirteen days he'd been with us. I'm givin' it you straight as it happened. An' now – look here! – this is what *did* happen.

'Between two and three that Sunday morning – dark an' blowin' from the north – I was woke up by an explosion an' people shoutin' "Raid!" The first bang fetched 'em out like worms after rain. There was another some minutes afterwards, an' me an' a Sergeant in the Shropshires on leaf told 'em all to take cover. They did. There was a devil of a long wait an' there was a third pop. Everybody, includin' me, heard aeroplanes. I didn't notice till afterwards that –'

Bevin paused.

'What?' said Orton.

'Oh, I noticed a heap of things afterwards. What we noticed first – the Shropshire Sergeant an' me – was a rick well alight back o' Margetts' house, an', with that north wind, blowin' straight on to another rick o' Margetts'. It went up all of a whoosh. The next thing we saw by the light of it was Margetts' house with a bomb-hole in the roof and the rafters leanin' sideways like – like they always lean on such occasions. So we ran there, and the first thing we met was Margetts in his split-tailed nightie callin' on his mother an' damnin' his wife. A man always does that when he's cross. Have you noticed? Mrs Margetts was in her nightie too, remindin' Margetts that he hadn't completed his rick insurance. An' that's a woman's lovin' care all over. Behind them was their eldest son, in trousers an' slippers, nursin' his arm an' callin' for the doctor. They went through us howlin' like *flammenwerfer* casualties [10] – right up the street to the surgery.

'Well, there wasn't anything to do except let the show burn out. We hadn't any means of extinguishing conflagrations. Some of 'em fiddled with buckets, an' some of 'em tried to get out some o' Margetts' sticks, but his younger son kept shoutin', "Don't! Don't! It'll be stole! It'll be stole!" So it burned instead, till the roof came down, top of all – a little, cheap, dirty villa. In *reel* life one whizbang would have shifted it; but in our civil village it looked that damned important and particular you wouldn't believe. We couldn't get round to Margetts' stable because of the two ricks alight, but we found someone had opened the door early an' the horses was in Margetts' new vegetable piece down the hill which he'd hired off old Vigors to extend his business with. I love the way a horse always looks after his own belly – same as a Gunner. They went to grazin' down the carrots and onions till young Margetts ran to turn 'em out, an' then they got in among the glass frames an' cut themselves. Oh, we had a regular Russian night of it, everybody givin' advice an' fallin' over each other. When it got light we saw the damage. House, two ricks an' stable *mafeesh*; the big glasshouse with every pane smashed and the furnace-end of it blown clean out. All the horses an' about fifteen head o' cattle – butcher's stores from the next field – feeding in the new vegetable piece. It was a fair clean-up from end to end – house, furniture, fittin's, plant, an' all the early crops.'

'Was there any other damage in the village?' I asked.

'I'm coming to it – the curious part – but I wouldn't call it damage. I was renting a field then for my chickens off the Merecroft Estate. It's accommodation-land, an' there was a wet ditch at the bottom that I had wanted for ever so long to dam up to make a swim-hole for Mrs Bevin's ducks.'

'Ah!' said Orton, half turning in his chair, all in one piece.

'S'pose I was allowed? Not me. Their Agent came down on me for tamperin' with the Estate's drainage arrangements. An' all I wanted was to bring the bank down where the ditch narrows – a couple of cartloads of dirt would have held the water back for half-a-dozen yards – not more than that, an' I could have made a little spill-way over the top with three boards – same as in trenches. Well, the first bomb – the one that woke me up –

had done my work for me better than I could. It had dropped just under the hollow of the bank an' brought it all down in a fair landslide. I'd got my swim-hole for Mrs Bevin's ducks, an' I didn't see how the Estate could kick at the Act o' God, d'you?'

'And Hickmot?' said Orton, grinning.

'Hold on! There was a Parish Council meetin' to demand reprisals, of course, an' there was the policeman an' me pokin' about among the ruins till the Explosives Expert came down in his motor car at three p.m. Monday, an' he meets all the Margetts off their rockers, howlin' in the surgery, an' he sees my swim-hole fillin' up to the brim.'

'What did he say?' Pole inquired.

'He sized it up at once. (He had to get back to dine in town that evening.) He said all the evidence proved that it was a lucky shot on the part of one isolated Hun 'plane goin' home, an' we weren't to take it to heart. I don't know that anybody but the Margetts did. He said they must have used incendiary bombs of a new type – which he'd suspected for a long time. I don't think the man was any worse than God intended him to be. I don't *reelly*. But the Shropshire Sergeant said –'

'And what did *you* think?' I interrupted.

'I didn't think. I knew by then. I'm not a Sherlock Holmes; but havin' chucked 'em an' chucked 'em back and kicked 'em out of the light an' slept with 'em for two years, an' makin' my livin' out of them at that time, I could recognize the fuse of a Mills bomb when I found it. I found all three of 'em. 'Curious about that second in Margetts' glasshouse. Hickmot mus' have raked the ashes out of the furnace, popped it in, an' shut the furnace door. It operated all right. Not one livin' pane left in the putty, and all the brickwork spread round the yard in streaks. Just like that St Firmin village we were talking about.'

'But how d'you account for young what's-his-name gettin' his arm broken?' said Pole.

'Crutch!' said Bevin. 'If you or me had taken on that night's doin's, with one leg, we'd have hopped and sweated from one flank to another an' been caught half-way between. Hickmot didn't. I'm as sure as I'm sittin' here that he did his doings quiet and comfortable at his full height – he was over six feet –

and no one noticed him. This is the way *I* see it. He fixed the
swim-hole for Mrs Bevin's ducks first. We used to talk over
our own affairs in front of him, of course, and he knew just
what she wanted in the way of a pond. So he went and made it
at his leisure. Then he prob'ly went over to Margetts' and lit
the first rick, knowin' that the wind 'ud do the rest. When
young Margetts saw the light of it an' came out to look, Hickmot
would have taken post at the back-door an' dropped the young
swine with his crutch, same as we used to drop Huns comin' out
of a dug-out. *You* know how they blink at the light? Then he
must have walked off an' opened Margetts' stable door to save
the horses. They'd be more to him than any man's life. Then
he prob'ly chucked one bomb on top o' Margetts' roof, havin'
seen that the first rick had caught the second and that the
whole house was bound to go. D'you get me?'

'Then why did he waste his bomb on the house?' said Orton.
His glass eye seemed as triumphant as his real one.

'For camouflage, of course. He was camouflagin' an air-raid.
When the Margetts piled out of their place into the street, he
prob'ly attended to the glasshouse, because that would be
Margetts' chief means o' business. After that – I think so, because otherwise I don't see where all those extra cattle came
from that we found in the vegetable piece – he must have
walked off an' rounded up all the butcher's beasts in the next
medder, an' driven 'em there to help the horses. And when he'd
finished everything he'd set out to do, I'll lay my life an' kit he
curled up like a bloomin' wombat not fifty yards away from the
whole flamin' show – an' let us run round him. An' when he'd
had his sleep out, he went up to Roehampton Monday mornin'
by some train that he'd decided upon in his own mind weeks
an' weeks before.'

'Did he know all the trains then?' said Pole.

'Ask me another. I only know that if he wanted to get from
any place to another without bein' noticed, he did it.'

'And the bombs? He got 'em from you, of course,' Pole went
on.

'What do *you* think? He was an hour in the park watchin' me
instruct, sittin', as I remember, in the bomb-proof by the dud-

hole, in his overcoat. He got 'em all right. He took neither more nor less than he wanted; an' I've told you what he did with 'em – one – two – *an'* three.'

''Ever see him afterwards?' said Orton.

'Yes. 'Saw him at Brighton when I went down there with the missus, not a month after he'd been broken in to his Roehampton leg. You know how the boys used to sit all along Brighton front in their blues, an' jump every time the coal was bein' delivered to the hotels behind them? I barged into him opposite the Old Ship, an' I told him about our air-raid. I told him how Margetts had gone off his rocker an' walked about starin' at the sky an' holdin' reprisal-meetin's all by himself; an' how old Mr Vigors had bought in what he'd left – tho' of course I said what *was* left – o' Margetts' business; an' how well my swim-hole for the ducks was doin'. It didn't interest him. He didn't want to come over to stay with us any more, either. We were a long, long way back in his past. You could see that. He wanted to get back with his new leg, to his own Godforsaken sheep-walk an' his black fellers in Queensland. I expect he's done it now, an' no one has noticed him. But, by Gord! He *did* leak a little at the end. He did that much! When we was waitin' for the tram to the station, I said how grateful I was to Fritz for moppin' up Margetts an' makin' our swim-hole all in one night. Mrs B. seconded the motion. We couldn't have done less. Well, then Hickmot said, speakin' in his queer way, as if English words were all new to him: "Ah, go on an' bail up in Hell," he says. "Bert was my friend." That was all. I've given it you just as it happened, word for word. *I'*d hate to have an Australian have it in for *me* for anything I'd done to *his* friend. Mark *you*, I don't say there's anything *wrong* with you Australians, Brother Orton. I only say they ain't like us or anyone else that I know.'

'Well, do you want us to be?' said Orton.

'No, no. It takes all sorts to make a world, as the sayin' is. And now' – Bevin pulled out his gold watch – 'if I don't make a move of it I'll miss my last train.'

'Let her go,' said Orton serenely. 'You've done some lorryhoppin' in your time, haven't you – Sergeant?'

'When I was two an' a half stone lighter, Digger,' Bevin smiled in reply.

'Well, I'll run you out home before sun-up. I'm a haulage-contractor now – London and Oxford. There's an empty of mine ordered to Oxford. We can go round by your place as easy as not. She's lyin' out Vauxhall-way.'

'My Gord! An' see the sun rise again! 'Haven't seen him since I can't remember when,' said Bevin, chuckling. 'Oh, there was fun sometimes in Hell, wasn't there, Australia?'; and again his hands went down to tighten the belt that was missing.

We and They

Father, Mother, and Me,
  Sister and Auntie say
All the people like us are We,
  And everyone else is They.
And They live over the sea,
  While We live over the way,
But – would you believe it? – They look upon We
  As only a sort of They! [11]

We eat pork and beef
  With cow-horn-handled knives.
They gobble Their rice off a leaf,
  Are horrified out of Their lives;
And They who live up a tree,
  And feast on grubs and clay,
(Isn't it scandalous?) look upon We
  As a simply disgusting They!

We shoot birds with a gun.
  They stick lions with spears.
Their full-dress is un –.
  We dress up to Our ears.
They like Their friends for tea.
  We like Our friends to stay;
And, after all that, They look upon We
  As an utterly ignorant They!

We eat kitcheny food.
  We have doors that latch.
They drink milk or blood,
  Under an open thatch.
We have Doctors to fee.
  They have Wizards to pay.
And (impudent heathen!) They look upon We
  As a quite impossible They!

All good people agree,
  And all good people say,

Debits and Credits

All nice people, like Us, are We
    And everyone else is They:
But if you cross over the sea,
    Instead of over the way,
You may end by (think of it!) looking on We
    As only a sort of They!

⅀ On the Gate ⅀

A Tale of '16[1]

If the Order Above be but the reflection of the Order Below[2] (as that Ancient[3] affirms, who had some knowledge of the Order), it is not outside the Order of Things that there should have been confusion also in the Department of Death. The world's steadily falling death-rate, the rising proportion of scientifically prolonged fatal illnesses, which allowed months of warning to all concerned, had weakened initiative throughout the Necrological Departments. When the War came, these were as unprepared as civilized mankind; and, like mankind, they improvised and recriminated in the face of Heaven.

As Death himself observed to St Peter[4] who had just come off The Gate[5] for a rest: 'One does the best one can with the means at one's disposal but –'

'*I* know,' said the good Saint sympathetically. 'Even with what help I can muster, I'm on The Gate twenty-two hours out of the twenty-four.'

'Do you find your volunteer staff any real use?' Death went on. 'Isn't it easier to do the work oneself than –'

'One must guard against that point of view,' St Peter returned, 'but I know what you mean. Office officializes the best of us ... What is it *now*?' He turned to a prim-lipped Seraph who had followed him with an expulsion-form for signature. St Peter glanced it over. 'Private R. M. Buckland,' he read, 'on the charge of saying that there is no God. 'That all?'

'He says he is prepared to prove it, sir, and – according to the Rules –'

'If you will make yourself acquainted with the Rules, you'll find they lay down that "the fool says in his heart,[6] there is no

235

God". That decides it; probably shell-shock. Have you tested his reflexes?'

'No, sir. He kept *on* saying that there –'

'Pass him in at once! Tell off someone to argue with him and give him the best of the argument till St Luke's[7] free. Anything else?'

'A hospital-nurse's record, sir. She has been nursing for two years.'

'A long while,' St Peter spoke severely. 'She may very well have grown careless.'

'It's her civilian record, sir. I judged best to refer it to you.' The Seraph handed him a vivid scarlet docket.

'The next time,' said St Peter, folding it down and writing on one corner, 'that you get one of these – er – tinted forms, mark it Q. M. A. and pass bearer at once. Don't worry over trifles.' The Seraph flashed off and returned to the clamorous Gate.

'Which Department is Q. M. A.?' said Death. St Peter chuckled.

'It's not a department. It's a Ruling. "*Quia multum amavit*".[8] A most useful Ruling. I've stretched it to . . . Now, I wonder what that child actually did die of.'

'I'll ask,' said Death, and moved to a public telephone near by. 'Give me War Check and Audit: English side: non-combatant,' he began. 'Latest returns . . . Surely you've got them posted up to date by now . . . Yes! Hospital Nurse in France . . . No! *Not* "nature and aliases". I said – what – was – nature – of – illness? . . . Thanks.' He turned to St Peter. 'Quite normal,' he said. 'Heart-failure after neglected pleurisy following over-work.'

'Good!' St Peter rubbed his hands. 'That brings her under the higher allowance – G. L. H. scale – "Greater love hath no man –"[9] But *my* people ought to have known that from the first.'

'Who is that clerk of yours?' asked Death. 'He seems rather a stickler for the proprieties.'

'The usual type nowadays,' St Peter returned. 'A young Power in charge of some half-baked Universe. Never having dealt with life yet, he's somewhat nebulous.'

Death sighed. 'It's the same with my old Departmental Heads. Nothing on earth will make my fossils on the Normal Civil Side realize that we are dying in a new age. Come and look at them. They might interest you.'

'Thanks, I will, but – Excuse me a minute! Here's my zealous young assistant on the wing once more.'

The Seraph had returned to report the arrival of overwhelmingly heavy convoys at The Gate, and to ask what the Saint advised.

'I'm just off on an inter-departmental inspection which will take me some time,' said St Peter. 'You *must* learn to act on your own initiative. So I shall leave you to yourself for the next hour or two, merely suggesting (I don't wish in any way to sway your judgement) that you invite St Paul,[10] St Ignatius (Loyola[11] I mean) and – er – St Christopher[12] to assist as Supervising Assessors on the Board of Admission. Ignatius is one of the subtlest intellects we have, and an officer and a gentleman to boot. I assure you' – the Saint turned towards Death – 'he revels in dialectics. If he's allowed to prove his case, he's quite capable of letting off the offender. St Christopher, of course, will pass anything that looks wet and muddy.'

'They are nearly all that now, sir,' said the Seraph.

'So much the better; and – as I was going to say – St Paul is an embarrass – a distinctly strong colleague. Still – we all have our weaknesses. Perhaps a well-timed reference to his seamanship in the Mediterranean – by the way, look up the name of his ship, will you? Alexandria register, I think – might be useful in some of those sudden maritime cases that crop up. I needn't tell *you* to be firm, of course. That's your besetting – er – I mean – reprimand 'em severely and publicly, but –' the Saint's voice broke – 'oh, my child, *you* don't know what it is to need forgiveness.[13] Be gentle with 'em – be very gentle with 'em!'

Swiftly as a falling shaft of light the Seraph kissed the sandalled feet and was away.

'Aha!' said St Peter. 'He can't go far wrong with that Board of Admission as I've – er – arranged it.'

They walked towards the great central office of Normal Civil Death, which, buried to the knees in a flood of temporary structures, resembled a closed cribbage-board among spilt dominoes.

They entered an area of avenues and cross-avenues, flanked by long, low buildings, each packed with seraphs working wing to folded wing.

'Our temporary buildings,' Death explained. ''Always being added to. This is the War-side. You'll find nothing changed on the Normal Civil Side. They are more human than mankind.'

'It doesn't lie in *my* mouth to blame them,' said St Peter.

'No, I've yet to meet the soul you wouldn't find excuse for,' said Death tenderly; 'but then *I* don't – er – arrange my Boards of Admission.'

'If one doesn't help one's Staff, one's Staff will never help itself,' St Peter laughed, as the shadow of the main porch of the Normal Civil Death Offices darkened above them.

'This façade rather recalls the Vatican, doesn't it?' said the Saint.

'They're quite as conservative. 'Notice how they still keep the old Holbein uniforms? 'Morning, Sergeant Fell.[14] How goes it?' said Death as he swung the dusty doors and nodded at a Commissionaire, clad in the grim livery of Death, even as Hans Holbein[15] has designed it.

'Sadly. Very sadly indeed, sir,' the Commissionaire replied. 'So many pore ladies and gentlemen, sir, 'oo might well 'ave lived another few years, goin' off, as you might say, in every direction with no time for the proper obsequities.'

'Too bad,' said Death sympathetically. 'Well, we're none of us as young as we were, Sergeant.'

They climbed a carved staircase, behung with the whole millinery of undertaking at large. Death halted on a dark Aberdeen granite landing and beckoned a messenger.

'We're rather busy today, sir,' the messenger whispered, 'but I think His Majesty will see *you*.'

'Who *is* the Head of this Department if it isn't you?' St Peter whispered in turn.

'You may well ask,' his companion replied. 'I'm only –' he checked himself and went on. 'The fact is, our Normal Civil Death side is controlled by a Being who considers himself all that I am and more. He's Death as men have made him – in their own image.' He pointed to a brazen plate, by the side of a black-curtained door, which read: 'Normal Civil Death, K. G., K. T., K. P., P. C., etc.' 'He's as human as mankind.'

'I guessed as much from those letters. What do they mean?'

'Titles conferred on him from time to time. King of Ghosts; King of Terrors; King of Phantoms; Pallid Conqueror, and so forth. There's no denying he's earned every one of them. A first-class mind, but just a leetle bit of a sn –'

'His Majesty is at liberty,' said the messenger.

Civil Death did not belie his name. No monarch on earth could have welcomed them more graciously; or, in St Peter's case, with more of that particularity of remembrance which is the gift of good kings. But when Death asked him how his office was working, he became at once the Departmental Head with a grievance.

'Thanks to this abominable war,' he began testily, 'my N. C. D. has to spend all its time fighting for mere existence. Your new War-side seems to think that nothing matters *except* the war. I've been asked to give up two-thirds of my Archives Basement (E. 7–E. 64) to the Polish Civilian Casualty Check and Audit. Preposterous! Where am I to move my Archives? And they've just been cross-indexed, too!'

'As I understood it,' said Death, 'our War-side merely applied for desk-room in your basement. They were prepared to leave your Archives *in situ*.'

'Impossible! We may need to refer to them at any moment. There's a case now which is interesting Us all – a Mrs Ollerby. Worcestershire by extraction – dying of an internal hereditary complaint. At any moment, We may wish to refer to her dossier, and how *can* We if Our basement is given up to people over whom We exercise no departmental control? This war has been made excuse for slackness in every direction.'

'Indeed!' said Death. 'You surprise me. I thought nothing made any difference to the N. C. D.'

'A few years ago I should have concurred,' Civil Death replied. 'But since this – this recent outbreak of unregulated mortality there has been a distinct lack of respect toward certain aspects of Our administration. The attitude is bound to reflect itself in the office. The official is, in a large measure, what the public makes him. Of course, it is only temporary reaction, but the merest outsider would notice what I mean. Perhaps *you* would like to see for yourself?' Civil Death bowed towards St Peter, who feared that he might be taking up his time.

'Not in the least. If I am not the servant of the public, what am I?' Civil Death said, and preceded them to the landing. 'Now, this' – he ushered them into an immense but badly lighted office – 'is our International Mortuary Department – the I.M.D. as we call it. It works with the Check and Audit. I should be sorry to say offhand how many billion sterling it represents, invested in the funeral ceremonies of all the races of mankind.' He stopped behind a very bald-headed clerk at a desk. 'And yet We take cognizance of the minutest detail, do not We?' he went on. 'What have We here, for example?'

'Funeral expenses of the late Mr John Shenks Tanner,' the clerk stepped aside from the red-ruled book. 'Cut down by the executors on account of the War from £173:19:1 to £47:18:4. A sad falling off, if I may say so, Your Majesty.'

'And what was the attitude of the survivors?' Civil Death asked.

'Very casual. It was a motor-hearse funeral.'

'A pernicious example, spreading, I fear, even in the lowest classes,' his superior muttered. 'Haste, lack of respect for the Dread Summons, carelessness in the Subsequent Disposition of the Corpse and –'

'But as regards people's real feelings?' St Peter demanded of the clerk.

'That isn't within the terms of our reference, Sir,' was the answer. 'But we *do* know that as often as not, they don't even buy black-edged announcement-cards nowadays.'

'Good Heavens!' said Civil Death swellingly. 'No cards! I must look into this myself. Forgive me, St Peter, but we Servants of Humanity, as you know, are not our own masters. No cards, indeed!' He waved them off with an official hand, and immersed himself in the ledger.

'Oh, come along,' Death whispered to St Peter. 'This is a blessed relief!'

They two walked on till they reached the far end of the vast dim office. The clerks at the desks here scarcely pretended to work. A messenger entered and slapped down a small autophonic reel.

'Here you are!' he cried. 'Mister Wilbraham Lattimer's last dying speech and record. He made a shockin' end of it.'

'Good for Lattimer!' a young voice called from a desk. 'Chuck it over!'

'Yes,' the messenger went on. 'Lattimer said to his brother: "Bert, I haven't time to worry about a little thing like dying these days, and what's more important, *you* haven't either. You go back to your Somme doin's, and I'll put it through with Aunt Maria. It'll amuse her and it won't hinder you." That's nice stuff for your boss!' The messenger whistled and departed. A clerk groaned as he snatched up the reel.

'How the deuce am I to knock this into official shape?' he began. 'Pass us the edifying Gantry Tubnell. I'll have to crib from him again, I suppose.'

'Be careful!' a companion whispered, and shuffled a typewritten form along the desk. 'I've used Tubby twice this morning already.'

The late Mr Gantry Tubnell must have demised on approved departmental lines, for his record was much thumbed. Death and St Peter watched the editing with interest.

'I can't bring in Aunt Maria *any* way,' the clerk broke out at last. 'Listen here, everyone! She has heart-disease. She dies just as she's lifted the dropsical Lattimer to change his sheets. She says: "Sorry, Willy! I'd make a dam' pore 'ospital nurse!" Then she sits down and croaks. Now *I* call that good! I've a great mind to take it round to the War-side as an indirect casualty and get a breath of fresh air.'

'Then you'll be hauled over the coals,' a neighbour suggested.

'I'm used to that, too,' the clerk sniggered.

'Are you?' said Death, stepping forward suddenly from behind a high map-stand. 'Who are you?' The clerk cowered in his skeleton jacket.

'I'm not on the Regular Establishment, Sir,' he stammered.

I'm a – Volunteer. I – I wanted to see how people behaved when they were in trouble.'

'Did you? Well, take the late Mr Wilbraham Lattimer's and Miss Maria Lattimer's papers to the War-side General Reference Office. When they have been passed upon, tell the Attendance Clerk that you are to serve as probationer in – let's see – in the Domestic Induced Casualty Side – 7 G.S.'

The clerk collected himself a little and spoke through dry lips.

'But – but I'm – I slipped in from the Lower Establishment, Sir,' he breathed.

There was no need to explain. He shook from head to foot as with the palsy; and under all Heaven none tremble save those who come from that class which 'also believe and tremble'.[16]

'Do you tell Me this officially, or as one created being to another?' Death asked after a pause.

'Oh, non-officially, Sir. Strictly non-officially, so long as you know all about it.'

His awe-stricken fellow-workers could not restrain a smile at Death having to be told about anything. Even Death bit his lips.

'I don't think you will find the War-side will raise any objection,' said he. 'By the way, they don't wear that uniform over there.'

Almost before Death ceased speaking, it was ripped off and flung on the floor, and that which had been a sober clerk of Normal Civil Death stood up an unmistakable, curly-haired, bat-winged, faun-eared Imp of the Pit. But where his wings joined his shoulders there was a patch of delicate dove-coloured feathering that gave promise to spread all up the pinion. St Peter saw it and smiled, for it was a known sign of grace.

'Thank Goodness!' the ex-clerk gasped as he snatched up the Lattimer records and sheered sideways through the skylight.

'Amen!' said Death and St Peter together, and walked through the door.

'Weren't you hinting something to me a little while ago about *my* lax methods?' St Peter demanded, innocently.

'Well, if one doesn't help one's Staff, one's Staff will never help itself,' Death retorted. 'Now, I shall have to pitch in a stiff demi-official asking how that young fiend came to be taken on in the N.C.D. without examination. And I must do it before the N.C.D. complain that I've been interfering with their departmental transfers. *Aren't* they human? If you want to go back to The Gate I think our shortest way will be through here and across the War-Sheds.'

They came out of a side-door into Heaven's full light. A phalanx of Shining Ones swung across a great square singing:

To Him Who made the Heavens abide, yet cease not from their
motion,
To Him Who drives the cleansing tide twice a day round ocean –
Let His Name be magnified in all poor folk's devotion! [17]

Death halted their leader, and asked a question.

'We're Volunteer Aid Serving Powers,' the Seraph explained, 'reporting for duty in the Domestic Induced Casualty Department – told off to help relatives, where we can.'

The shift trooped on – such an array of Powers, Honours, Glories, Toils, Patiences, Services, Faiths and Loves as no man may conceive even by favour of dreams. Death and St Peter followed them into a D.I.C.D. Shed on the English side where, for the moment, work had slackened. Suddenly a name flashed on the telephone-indicator. 'Mrs Arthur Bedott, 317, Portsmouth Avenue, Brondesbury. Husband badly wounded. One child.' Her special weakness was appended.

A Seraph on the raised dais that overlooked the Volunteer Aids waiting at the entrance, nodded and crooked a finger. One of the new shift – a temporary Acting Glory – hurled himself from his place and vanished earthward.

'You may take it,' Death whispered to St Peter, 'there will be a sustaining epic built up round Private Bedott's wound for his wife and Baby Bedott to cling to. And here –' they heard wings that flapped wearily – 'here, I suspect, comes one of our failures.'

A Seraph entered and dropped, panting, on a form. His plumage was ragged, his sword splintered to the hilt; and his face still worked with the passions of the world he had left, as his soiled vesture reeked of alcohol.

'Defeat,' he reported hoarsely, when he had given in a woman's name. 'Utter defeat! Look!' He held up the stump of his sword. 'I broke this on her gin-bottle.'

'So? We try again,' said the impassive Chief Seraph. Again he beckoned, and there stepped forward that very Imp whom Death had transferred from the N.C.D.

'Go *you*!' said the Seraph. 'We must deal with a fool according to her folly.[18] Have you pride enough?'

There was no need to ask. The messenger's face glowed and his nostrils quivered with it. Scarcely pausing to salute, he poised and dived, and the papers on the desks spun beneath the draught of his furious vans.

St Peter nodded high approval. '*I* see!' he said. 'He'll work on her pride to steady her. By all means – "if by all means", as my good Paul[19] used to say. Only it ought to read "by any manner of possible means". Excellent!'

'It's difficult, though,' a soft-eyed Patience whispered. 'I fail again and again. I'm only fit for an old-maid's tea-party.'

Once more the record flashed – a multiple-urgent appeal on behalf of a few thousand men, worn-out body and soul. The Patience was detailed.

'Oh, me!' she sighed, with a comic little shrug of despair, and took the void softly as a summer breeze at dawning.

'But how does this come under the head of Domestic Casualties? Those men were in the trenches. I heard the mud squelch,' said St Peter.

'Something wrong with the installation – as usual. Waves are always jamming here,' the Seraph replied.

'So it seems,' said St Peter as a wireless cut in with the muffled note of someone singing (sorely out of tune), to an accompaniment of desultory poppings:

'Unless you can love as the Angels love With the breadth of Heaven be –'

'*Twickt!*' It broke off. The record showed a name. The waiting Seraphs stiffened to attention with a click of tense quills.

'As you were!' said the Chief Seraph. 'He's met her.'

'Who is she?' said St Peter.

'His mother. You never get over your weakness for romance,' Death answered, and a covert smile spread through the Office.

'Thank Heaven, I don't. But I really ought to be going –'

'Wait one minute. Here's trouble coming through, I think,' Death interposed.

A recorder had sparked furiously in a broken run of S.O.S.s that allowed no time for inquiry.

'Name! Name!' an impatient young Faith panted at last. 'It *can't* be blotted out.' No name came up. Only the reiterated appeal.

'False alarm!' said a hard-featured Toil, well used to mankind. 'Some fool has found out that he owns a soul. 'Wants work. *I*'d cure him! . . .'

'Hush!' said a Love in Armour, stamping his mailed foot. The office listened.

''Bad case?' Death demanded at last.

'Rank bad, Sir. They are holding back the name,' said the Chief Seraph. The S.O.S. signals grew more desperate, and then ceased with an emphatic thump. The Love in Armour winced. 'Firing-party,' he whispered to St Peter. ''Can't mistake that noise!'

'What is it?' St Peter cried nervously.

'Deserter; spy; murderer,' was the Chief Seraph's weighed answer. 'It's out of my department – now. No – hold the line! The name's up at last.'

It showed for an instant, broken and faint as sparks on charred wadding, but in that instant a dozen pens had it written. St Peter with never a word gathered his robes about him and bundled through the door, headlong for The Gate.

'No hurry,' said Death at his elbow. 'With the present rush your man won't come up for ever so long.'

''Never can be sure these days. Anyhow, the Lower Establishment will be after him like sharks. He's the very type they'd want for propaganda. Deserter – traitor – murderer. Out of my way, please, babies!'

A group of children round a red-headed man who was telling them stories, scattered laughing. The man turned to St Peter.

'Deserter, traitor, murderer,' he repeated. 'Can *I* be of service?'

'You can!' St Peter gasped. 'Double on ahead to The Gate and tell them to hold up all expulsions till I come. Then,' he shouted as the man sped off at a long hound-like trot, 'go and picket the outskirts of the Convoys. Don't let anyone break away on any account. Quick!'

But Death was right. They need not have hurried. The crowd at The Gate was far beyond the capacities of the Examining Board even though, as St Peter's Deputy informed him, it had been enlarged twice in his absence.

'We're doing our best,' the Seraph explained, 'but delay is inevitable, Sir. The Lower Establishment are taking advantage of it, as usual, at the tail of the Convoys. I've doubled all pickets there, and I'm sending more. Here's the extra list, Sir – Arc J., Bradlaugh C.,[20] Bunyan J.,[21] Calvin J.[22] Iscariot J. reported to me just now, as under your orders, and took 'em with him. Also Shakespeare W. and –'

'Never mind the rest,' said St Peter. 'I'm going there myself. Meantime, carry on with the passes – don't fiddle over 'em – and give me a blank or two.' He caught up a thick block of Free Passes, nodded to a group in khaki at a passport table, initialled their Commanding Officer's personal pass as for 'Officer and Party', and left the numbers to be filled in by a quite competent-looking Quarter-master-Sergeant. Then, Death beside him, he breasted his way out of The Gate against the incoming multitude of all races, tongues, and creeds that stretched far across the plain.

An old lady, firmly clutching a mottle-nosed, middle-aged Major by the belt, pushed across a procession of keen-faced *poilus*, and blocked his path, her captive held in that terrible mother-grip no Power has yet been able to unlock.

'I found him! I've got him! Pass him!' she ordered.

St Peter's jaw fell. Death politely looked elsewhere.

'There are a few formalities,' the Saint began.

'With Jerry in this state? Nonsense! How like a man! My boy never gave me a moment's anxiety in –'

'Don't, dear – don't!' The Major looked almost as uncomfortable as St Peter.

'Well, nothing compared with what he *would* give me if he weren't passed.'

'Didn't I hear you singing just now?' Death asked, seeing that his companion needed a breathing-space.

'Of course you did,' the mother intervened. 'He sings beautifully. And that's *another* reason! You're bass, aren't you now, darling?'

St Peter glanced at the agonized Major and hastily initialled him a pass. Without a word of thanks the Mother hauled him away.

'Now, under what conceivable Ruling do you justify that?' said Death.

'I.W. – the Importunate Widow.²³ It's scandalous!' St Peter groaned. Then his face darkened as he looked across the great plain beyond The Gate. 'I don't like this,' he said. 'The Lower Establishment is out in full force tonight. I hope our pickets are strong enough –'

The crowd here had thinned to a disorderly queue flanked on both sides by a multitude of busy, discreet emissaries from the Lower Establishment who continually edged in to do business with them, only to be edged off again by a line of watchful pickets. Thanks to the khaki everywhere, the scene was not unlike that which one might have seen on earth any evening of the old days outside the refreshment-room by the Arch at Victoria Station, when the Army trains started. St Peter's appearance was greeted by the usual outburst of cock-crowing²⁴ from the Lower Establishment.

'Dirty work at the cross-roads,' said Death dryly.

'I deserve it!' St Peter grunted, 'but think what it must mean for Judas.'

He shouldered into the thick of the confusion where the pickets coaxed, threatened, implored, and in extreme cases bodily shoved the wearied men and women past the voluble and insinuating spirits who strove to draw them aside.

A Shropshire Yeoman had just accepted, together with a forged pass, the assurance of a genial runner of the Lower Establishment that Heaven lay round the corner, and was being stealthily steered thither, when a large hand jerked him back, another took the runner in the chest, and someone thundered: 'Get out, you crimp!' The situation was then vividly explained to the soldier in the language of the barrack-room.

'Don't blame *me*, Guv'nor,' the man expostulated. 'I 'aven't seen a woman, let alone angels, for umpteen months. I'm from Joppa. Where 'you from?'

'Northampton,' was the answer. 'Rein back and keep by me.'

'What? You ain't ever Charley B. that my dad used to tell about? I thought you always said –'

'I shall say a deal more soon. Your Sergeant's talking to that woman in red. Fetch him in quick!'

Meantime, a sunken-eyed Scots officer, utterly lost to the riot around, was being button-holed by a person of reverend aspect who explained to him that, by the logic of his own ancestral creed, not only was the Highlander irrevocably damned, but that his damnation had been predetermined before Earth was made.

'It's unanswerable – just unanswerable,' said the young man sorrowfully. 'I'll be with ye.' He was moving off, when a smallish figure interposed, not without dignity.

'Monsieur,' it said, 'would it be of any comfort to you to know that *I* am – I was – John Calvin?' At this the reverend one cursed and swore like the lost Soul he was, while the Highlander turned to discuss with Calvin, pacing towards The Gate, some alterations in the fabric of a work of fiction called the *Institutio*.

Others were not so easily held. A certain Woman,[25] with loosened hair, bare arms, flashing eyes and dancing feet, shepherded her knot of waverers, hoarse and exhausted. When the taunt broke out against her from the opposing line: 'Tell 'em what you were! Tell 'em if you dare!' she answered unflinchingly, as did Judas, who, worming through the crowd like an Armenian carpet-vendor, peddled his shame aloud that it might give strength to others.

'Yes,' he would cry, 'I am everything they say, but if *I'm* here it must be a moral cert for *you*, gents. This way, please. Many mansions,[26] gentlemen! Go-ood billets! Don't you notice these low people, Sar. *Plees* keep hope, gentlemen!'

When there were cases that cried to him from the ground – poor souls who could not stick it but had found their way out with a rifle and a boot-lace, he would tell them of his own end, till he made them contemptuous enough to rise up and curse him. Here St Luke's imperturbable bedside manner backed and strengthened the other's almost too oriental flux of words.

In this fashion and step by step, all the day's Convoy were piloted past that danger-point where the Lower Establishment are, for reasons not given us, allowed to ply their trade. The pickets dropped to the rear, relaxed, and compared notes.

'What always impresses me most,' said Death to St Peter, 'is the sheeplike simplicity of the intellectual mind.' He had been watching one of the pickets apparently overwhelmed by the arguments of an advanced atheist who – so hot in his argument that he was deaf to the offers of the Lower Establishment to make him a god – had stalked, talking hard – while the picket always gave ground before him – straight past the Broad Road.

'He was plaiting of long-tagged epigrams,'[27] the sober-faced picket smiled. 'Give that sort only an ear and they'll follow ye gobbling like turkeys.'

'And John held his peace through it all,' a full fresh voice broke in. '"It may be so," says John. "Doubtless, in your belief, it *is* so," says John. "Your words move me mightily," says John, and gorges his own beliefs like a pike going backwards. And that young fool, so busy spinning words – words – words – that he trips past Hell Mouth without seeing it! ... Who's yonder, Joan?'

'One of your English. 'Always late. Look!' A young girl with short-cropped hair pointed with her sword across the plain towards a single faltering figure which made at first as though to overtake the Convoy, but then turned left towards the Lower Establishment, who were enthusiastically cheering him as a leader of enterprise.

'That's my traitor,' said St Peter. 'He has no business to report to the Lower Establishment before reporting to Convoy.'

The figure's pace slackened as he neared the applauding line. He looked over his shoulder once or twice, and then fairly turned tail and fled again towards the still Convoy.

'Nobody ever gave me credit for anything I did,' he began, sobbing and gesticulating. 'They were all against me from the first. I only wanted a little encouragement. It was a regular conspiracy, but *I* showed 'em what I could do! *I* showed 'em! And – and –' he halted again. 'Oh, God! What are you going to do with *me*?'

No one offered any suggestion. He ranged sideways like a doubtful dog, while across the plain the Lower Establishment murmured seductively. All eyes turned to St Peter.

'At this moment,' the Saint said half to himself, 'I can't recall any precise ruling under which –'

'My own case?' the ever-ready Judas suggested.

'No-o! That's making too much of it. And yet –'

'Oh, hurry up and get it over,' the man wailed, and told them all that he had done, ending with the cry that none had ever recognized his merits; neither his own narrow-minded people, his inefficient employers, nor the snobbish jumped-up officers of his battalion.

'You see,' said St Peter at the end. 'It's sheer vanity. It isn't even as if we had a woman to fall back upon.'

'Yet there was a woman or I'm mistaken,' said the picket with the pleasing voice who had praised John.

'Eh – what? When?' St Peter turned swiftly on the speaker. 'Who was the woman?'

'The wise woman of Tekoah,' came the smooth answer. 'I remember, because that verse was the private heart of my plays – some of 'em.'

But the Saint was not listening. 'You have it!' he cried. 'Samuel Two, Double Fourteen. To think that *I* should have forgotten! "For we must needs die and are as water spilled on the ground which cannot be gathered up again. Neither doth God respect any person, *yet* –" Here you! Listen to this!'

The man stepped forward and stood to attention. Someone took his cap as Judas and the picket John closed up beside him.

'"*Yet doth He devise means* (d'you understand that?) *devise means that His banished be not expelled from Him!*" This covers your case. I don't know what the means will be. That's for you to find out. They'll tell you yonder.' He nodded towards the now silent Lower Establishment as he scribbled on a pass. 'Take this paper over to them and report for duty there. You'll have a thin time of it; but they won't keep you a day longer than I've put down. Escort!'

'Does – does that mean there's any hope?' the man stammered.

'Yes – I'll show you the way,' Judas whispered. 'I've lived there – a very long time!'

'I'll bear you company a piece,' said John, on his left flank. 'There'll be Despair to deal with. Heart up, Mr Littlesoul!'

The three wheeled off, and the Convoy watched them grow smaller and smaller across the plain.

St Peter smiled benignantly and rubbed his hands.

'And now we're rested,' said he, 'I think we might make a push for billets this evening, gentlemen, eh?'

The pickets fell in, guardians no longer but friends and companions all down the line. There was a little burst of cheering and the whole Convoy strode away towards the not so distant Gate.

The Saint and Death stayed behind to rest awhile. It was a heavenly evening. They could hear the whistle of the low-flighting Cherubim, clear and sharp, under the diviner note of some released Seraph's wings, where, his errand accomplished, he plunged three or four stars deep into the cool Baths of Hercules; the steady dynamo-like hum of the nearer planets on their axes; and, as the hush deepened, the surprised little sigh of some new-born sun a universe of universes away. But their minds were with the Convoy that their eyes followed.

Said St Peter proudly at last: 'If those people of mine had seen that fellow stripped of all hope in front of 'em, I doubt if they could have marched another yard tonight. Watch 'em stepping out now, though! Aren't they human?'

'To whom do you say it?' Death answered, with something of a tired smile. 'I'm more than human. *I*'ve got to die some time or other. But all other created Beings – afterwards . . .'

'*I* know,' said St Peter softly. 'And that is why I love you, O Azrael!'

For now they were alone Death had, of course, returned to

his true majestic shape – that only One of all created beings who is doomed to perish utterly, and knows it.

'Well, that's *that* – for me!' Death concluded as he rose. 'And yet –' he glanced towards the empty plain where the Lower Establishment had withdrawn with their prisoner. '"Yet doth He devise means."'

The Supports

(*Song of the Waiting Seraphs.*)

FULL CHORUS:
To Him Who bade the Heavens abide yet cease not from their motion,
To Him Who tames the moonstruck tide twice a day round Ocean —
Let His Names be magnified in all poor folks' devotion!

POWERS AND GIFTS:
Not for Prophecies or Powers, Visions, Gifts, or Graces,
But the unregardful hours that grind us in our places
With the burden on our backs, the weather in our faces.

TOILS:
Not for any Miracle of easy Loaves and Fishes,
But for doing, 'gainst our will, work against our wishes —
Such as finding food to fill daily-emptied dishes.

GLORIES:
Not for Voices, Harps or Wings or rapt illumination,
But the grosser Self that springs of use and occupation,
Unto which the Spirit clings as her last salvation.

POWERS, GLORIES, TOILS, AND GIFTS:
(*He Who launched our Ship of Fools many anchors gave us,*
Lest one gale should start them all — one collison stave us.
   Praise Him for the petty creeds
   That prescribe in paltry needs,
Solemn rites to trivial deeds and, by small things, save us!)

SERVICES AND LOVES:
Heart may fail, and Strength outwear, and Purpose turn to Loathing,
But the everyday affair of business, meals, and clothing,
Builds a bulkhead 'twixt Despair and the Edge of Nothing.

PATIENCES:
(*Praise Him, then, Who orders it that, though Earth be flaring*
   And the crazy skies are lit
   By the searchlights of the Pit,
Man should not depart a whit from his wonted bearing.)

HOPES:

He Who bids the wild-swans' host still maintain their flight on
    Air-roads over islands lost –
    Ages since 'neath Ocean lost –
Beaches of some sunken coast their fathers would alight on –

FAITHS:

He shall guide us through this dark, not by new-blown glories,
But by every ancient mark our fathers used before us,
Till our children ground their ark where the proper shore is.

SERVICES, PATIENCES, FAITHS, HOPES, AND LOVES:

He Who used the clay that clings on our boots to make us,
Shall not suffer earthly things to remove or shake us:
    But, when Man denies His Lord,
    Habit without Fleet or Sword
    (Custom without threat or word)
Sees the ancient fanes restored – the timeless rites o'ertake us.

FULL CHORUS:

For He Who makes the Mountains smoke and rives the Hills asunder,[28]
    And, tomorrow, leads the grass –
    Mere unconquerable grass –
Where the fuming crater was, to heal and hide it under,
    He shall not – He shall not –
Shall not lay on us the yoke of too long Fear and Wonder!

{ The Eye of Allah }

Untimely[1]

Nothing in life has been made by man for man's using
But it was shown long since to man in ages
Lost as the name of the maker of it,

Who received oppression and scorn for his wages —
Hate, avoidance, and scorn in his daily dealings —
Until he perished, wholly confounded.

More to be pitied than he are the wise
Souls which foresaw the evil of loosing
Knowledge or Art before time, and aborted
Noble devices and deep-wrought healings,
Lest offence should arise.

Heaven delivers on earth the Hour that cannot be thwarted,
Neither advanced, at the price of a world or a soul, and its Prophet
Comes through the blood of the vanguards who dreamed — too soon
                                          — it had sounded.

The Eye of Allah

The Cantor [2] of St Illod's [3] being far too enthusiastic a musician to concern himself with its Library, the Sub-Cantor, who idolized every detail of the work, was tidying up, after two hours' writing and dictation in the Scriptorium. The copying-monks handed him in their sheets – it was a plain Four Gospels ordered by an Abbot at Evesham – and filed out to vespers. John Otho, better known as John of Burgos, [4] took no heed. He was burnishing a tiny boss of gold in his miniature of the Annunciation for his Gospel of St Luke, which it was hoped that Cardinal Falcodi, the Papal Legate, [5] might later be pleased to accept.

'Break off, John,' said the Sub-Cantor in an undertone.

'Eh? Gone, have they? I never heard. Hold a minute, Clement.'

The Sub-Cantor waited patiently. He had known John more than a dozen years, coming and going at St Illod's, to which monastery John, when abroad, always said he belonged. The claim was gladly allowed for, more even than other Fitz Otho's, he seemed to carry all the Arts under his hand, and most of their practical receipts under his hood.

The Sub-Cantor looked over his shoulder at the pinned-down sheet where the first words of the Magnificat [6] were built up in gold washed with red-lac for a background to the Virgin's hardly yet fired halo. She was shown, hands joined in wonder, at a lattice of infinitely intricate arabesque, round the edges of which sprays of orange-bloom seemed to load the blue hot air that carried back over the minute parched landscape in the middle distance.

'You've made her all Jewess,' said the Sub-Cantor, studying the olive-flushed cheek and the eyes charged with foreknowledge.

'What else was Our Lady?' John slipped out the pins. 'Listen,

Clement. If I do not come back, this goes into my Great Luke, whoever finishes it.' He slid the drawing between its guard-papers.

'Then you're for Burgos again – as I heard?'

'In two days. The new Cathedral yonder – but they're slower than the Wrath of God, those masons – is good for the soul.'

'*Thy* soul?' The Sub-Cantor seemed doubtful.

'Even mine, by your permission. And down south – on the edge of the Conquered Countries – Granada way – there's some Moorish diaper-work that's wholesome. It allays vain thought and draws it toward the picture – as you felt, just now, in my Annunciation.'

'She – it was very beautiful. No wonder you go. But you'll not forget your absolution, John?'

'Surely.' This was a precaution John no more omitted on the eve of his travels than he did the recutting of the tonsure which he had provided himself with in his youth, somewhere near Ghent. The mark gave him privilege of clergy at a pinch, and a certain consideration on the road always.

'You'll not forget, either, what we need in the Scriptorium. There's no more true ultramarine[7] in this world now. They mix it with that German blue. And as for vermilion –'

'I'll do my best always.'

'And Brother Thomas' (this was the Infirmarian in charge of the monastery hospital) 'he needs –'

'He'll do his own asking. I'll go over his side now, and get me re-tonsured.'

John went down the stairs to the lane that divides the hospital and cook-house from the back-cloisters. While he was being barbered, Brother Thomas (St Illod's meek but deadly persistent Infirmarian) gave him a list of drugs that he was to bring back from Spain by hook, crook, or lawful purchase. Here they were surprised by the lame, dark Abbot Stephen, in his fur-lined night-boots. Not that Stephen de Sautré was any spy; but as a young man he had shared an unlucky Crusade, which had ended, after a battle at Mansura, in two years' captivity among the Saracens at Cairo where men learn to walk softly. A fair huntsman and hawker, a reasonable disciplinarian, but a man of science above all, and a Doctor of Medicine under one Ranulphus, Canon of St Paul's, his heart was more in the monastery's hospital work than its religious. He checked their list interestedly, adding items of his own. After the Infirmarian had withdrawn, he gave John generous absolution, to cover lapses by the way; for he did not hold with chance-bought Indulgences.

'And what seek you *this* journey?' he demanded, sitting on the bench beside the mortar and scales in the little warm cell for stored drugs.

'Devils, mostly,' said John, grinning.

'In Spain? Are not Abana and Pharphar –?' [8]

John, to whom men were but matter for drawings, and well-born to boot (since he was a de Sanford on his mother's side), looked the Abbot full in the face and – 'Did *you* find it so?' said he.

'No. They were in Cairo too. But what's your special need of 'em?'

'For my Great Luke. He's the master-hand of all Four when it comes to devils.'

'No wonder. He was a physician. You're not.'

'Heaven forbid! But I'm weary of our Church-pattern devils.[9] They're only apes and goats and poultry conjoined. 'Good enough for plain red-and-black Hells and Judgement Days – but not for me.'

'What makes you so choice in them?'

'Because it stands to reason and Art that there are all musters of devils in Hell's dealings. Those Seven, for example, that were haled out of the Magdalene. They'd be she-devils – no kin at all to the beaked and horned and bearded devils-general.'

The Abbot laughed.

'And see again! The devil that came out of the dumb man. What use is snout or bill to *him*? He'd be faceless as a leper. Above all – God send I live to do it! – the devils that entered the Gadarene swine. They'd be – they'd be – I know not yet what they'd be, but they'd be surpassing devils. I'd have 'em diverse as the Saints themselves. But now, they're all one pattern, for wall, window, or picture-work.'

'Go on, John. You're deeper in this mystery than I.'

'Heaven forbid! But I say there's respect due to devils, damned tho' they be.'

'Dangerous doctrine.'

'My meaning is that if the shape of anything be worth man's thought to picture to man, it's worth his best thought.'

'That's safer. But I'm glad I've given you Absolution.'

'There's less risk for a craftsman who deals with the outside shapes of things – for Mother Church's glory.'

'Maybe so, but John' – the Abbot's hand almost touched John's sleeve – 'tell me, now, is – is she Moorish or – or Hebrew?'

'She's mine,' John returned.

'Is that enough?'

'I have found it so.'

'Well – ah well! It's out of my jurisdiction, but – how do they look at it down yonder?'

'Oh, they drive nothing to a head in Spain – neither Church nor King, bless them! There's too many Moors and Jews to kill them all, and if they chased 'em away there'd be no trade nor farming. Trust me, in the Conquered Countries, from Seville to Granada, we live lovingly enough together – Spaniard, Moor, and Jew. Ye see, *we* ask no questions.'

'Yes – yes,' Stephen sighed. 'And always there's the hope, she may be converted.'

'Oh yes, there's always hope.'

The Abbot went on into the hospital. It was an easy age before Rome tightened the screw as to clerical connections. If the lady were not too forward, or the son too much his father's beneficiary in ecclesiastical preferments and levies, a good deal was overlooked. But, as the Abbot had reason to recall, unions between Christian and Infidel led to sorrow. None the less, when John with mule, mails, and man, clattered off down the lane for Southampton and the sea, Stephen envied him.

He was back, twenty months later, in good hard case, and loaded down with fairings. A lump of richest lazuli, a bar of orange-hearted vermilion, and a small packet of dried beetles which make most glorious scarlet, for the Sub-Cantor. Besides that, a few cubes of milky marble, with yet a pink flush in them, which could be slaked and ground down to incomparable background-stuff. There were quite half the drugs that the Abbot and Thomas had demanded, and there was a long deep-red cornelian necklace for the Abbot's Lady – Anne of Norton. She received it graciously, and asked where John had come by it.

'Near Granada,' he said.

'You left all well there?' Anne asked. (Maybe the Abbot had told her something of John's confession.)

'I left all in the hands of God.'

'Ah me! How long since?'

'Four months less eleven days.'

'Were you – with her?'

'In my arms. Childbed.'

'And?'

'The boy too. There is nothing now.'

Anne of Norton caught her breath.

'I think you'll be glad of that,' she said after a while.

'Give me time, and maybe I'll compass it. But not now.'

'You have your handwork and your art and – John – remember there's no jealousy in the grave.'

'Ye-es! I have my Art, and Heaven knows I'm jealous of none.'

'Thank God for that at least,' said Anne of Norton, the always ailing woman who followed the Abbot with her sunk eyes. 'And be sure I shall treasure this' – she touched the beads – 'as long as I shall live.'

'I brought – trusted – it to you for that,' he replied, and took leave. When she told the Abbot how she had come by it, he said nothing, but as he and Thomas were storing the drugs that John handed over in the cell which backs on to the hospital kitchen-chimney, he observed, of a cake of dried poppy-juice: 'This has power to cut off all pain from a man's body.'

'I have seen it,' said John.

'But for pain of the soul there is, outside God's Grace, but

one drug; and that is a man's craft, learning, or other helpful
motion of his own mind.'[10]

'That is coming to me, too,' was the answer.

John spent the next fair May day out in the woods with the
monastery swineherd and all the porkers; and returned loaded
with flowers and sprays of spring, to his own carefully kept
place in the north bay of the Scriptorium. There, with his
travelling sketch-books under his left elbow, he sunk himself
past all recollections in his Great Luke.

Brother Martin, Senior Copyist (who spoke about once a
fortnight), ventured to ask, later, how the work was going.

'All here!' John tapped his forehead with his pencil. 'It has
been only waiting these months to – ah God! – be born. Are ye
free of your plain-copying, Martin?'

Brother Martin nodded. It was his pride that John of Burgos
turned to him, in spite of his seventy years, for really good
page-work.

'Then see!' John laid out a new vellum – thin but flawless.
'There's no better than this sheet from here to Paris. Yes!
Smell it if you choose. Wherefore – give me the compasses and
I'll set it out for you – if ye make one letter lighter or darker
than its next, I'll stick ye like a pig.'

'Never, John!' the old man beamed happily.

'But I will! Now, follow! Here and here, as I prick, and in
script of just this height to the hair's-breadth, ye'll scribe the
thirty-first and thirty-second verses of Eighth Luke.'

'Yes, the Gadarene Swine! "*And they besought him that he
would not command them to go out into the abyss. And there was a
herd of many swine*"' – Brother Martin naturally knew all the
Gospels by heart.

'Just so! Down to "*and he suffered them*". Take your time to
it. My Magdalene has to come off my heart first.'

Brother Martin achieved the work so perfectly that John
stole some soft sweetmeats from the Abbot's kitchen for his
reward. The old man ate them; then repented; then confessed
and insisted on penance. At which, the Abbot, knowing there
was but one way to reach the real sinner, set him a book
called *De Virtutibus Herbarum* to fair-copy. St Illod's had

borrowed it from the gloomy Cistercians, who do not hold with pretty things, and the crabbed text kept Martin busy just when John wanted him for some rather specially spaced letterings.

'See now,' said the Sub-Cantor improvingly. 'You should not do such things, John. Here's Brother Martin on penance for your sake –'

'No – for my Great Luke. But I've paid the Abbot's cook. I've drawn him till his own scullions cannot keep straight-faced. *He*'ll not tell again.'

'Unkindly done! And you're out of favour with the Abbot too. He's made no sign to you since you came back – never asked you to high table.'

'I've been busy. Having eyes in his head, Stephen knew it. Clement, there's no Librarian from Durham to Torre fit to clean up after you.'

The Sub-Cantor stood on guard; he knew where John's compliments generally ended.

'But outside the Scriptorium –'

'Where I never go.' The Sub-Cantor had been excused even digging in the garden, lest it should mar his wonderful book-binding hands.

'In all things outside the Scriptorium you are the master-fool of Christendie. Take it from me, Clement. I've met many.'

'I take everything from you,' Clement smiled benignly. 'You use me worse than a singing-boy.'

They could hear one of that suffering breed in the cloister below, squalling as the Cantor pulled his hair.

'God love you! So I do! But have you ever thought how I lie and steal daily on my travels – yes, and for aught you know, murder – to fetch you colours and earths?'

'True,' said just and consicence-stricken Clement. 'I have often thought that were I in the world – which God forbid! – I might be a strong thief in some matters.'

Even Brother Martin, bent above his loathed *De Virtutibus*, laughed.

*

But about mid-summer, Thomas the Infirmarian conveyed to John the Abbot's invitation to supper in his house that night, with the request that he would bring with him anything that he had done for his Great Luke.

'What's toward?' said John, who had been wholly shut up in his work.

'Only one of his "wisdom" dinners. You've sat at a few since you were a man.'

'True: and mostly good. How would Stephen have us –?'

'Gown and hood over all. There will be a doctor from Salerno – one Roger,[11] an Italian. Wise and famous with the knife on the body. He's been in the Infirmary some ten days, helping me – even me!'

''Never heard the name. But our Stephen's *physicus* before *sacerdos*, always.'

'And his Lady has a sickness of some time. Roger came hither in chief because of her.'

'Did he? Now I think of it, I have not seen the Lady Anne for a while.'

'Ye've seen nothing for a long while. She has been housed near a month – they have to carry her abroad now.'

'So bad as that, then?'

'Roger of Salerno will not yet say what he thinks. But –'

'God pity Stephen! . . . Who else at table, beside thee?'

'An Oxford friar. Roger is his name also. A learned and famous philosopher. And he holds his liquor too, valiantly.'

'Three doctors – counting Stephen. I've always found that means two atheists.'

Thomas looked uneasily down his nose. 'That's a wicked proverb,' he stammered. 'You should not use it.'

'Hoh! Never come you the monk over me, Thomas! You've been Infirmarian at St Illod's eleven years – and a lay-brother still. Why have you never taken orders, all this while?'

'I – I am not worthy.'

'Ten times worthier than that new fat swine – Henry Who's-his-name – that takes the Infirmary Masses. He bullocks in with the Viaticum, under your nose, when a sick man's only faint from being bled. So the man dies – of pure fear. Ye know it!

I've watched your face at such times. Take Orders, Didymus. You'll have a little more medicine and a little less Mass with your sick then; and they'll live longer.'

'I am unworthy – unworthy,' Thomas repeated pitifully.

'Not you – but – to your own master you stand or fall. And now that my work releases me for awhile, I'll drink with any philosopher out of any school. And Thomas,' he coaxed, 'a hot bath for me in the Infirmary before vespers.'

When the Abbot's perfectly cooked and served meal had ended, and the deep-fringed naperies were removed, and the Prior had sent in the keys with word that all was fast in the Monastery, and the keys had been duly returned with the word, 'Make it so till Prime,' the Abbot and his guests went out to cool themselves in an upper cloister that took them, by way of the leads, to the South Choir side of the Triforium. The summer sun was still strong, for it was barely six o'clock, but the Abbey Church, of course, lay in her wonted darkness. Lights were being lit for choir-practice thirty feet below.

'Our Cantor gives them no rest,' the Abbot whispered. 'Stand by this pillar and we'll hear what he's driving them at now.'

'Remember all!' the Cantor's hard voice came up. 'This is the soul of Bernard himself, attacking our evil world. Take it quicker than yesterday, and throw all your words clean-bitten from you. In the loft there! Begin!'

The organ broke out for an instant, alone and raging. Then the voices crashed together into that first fierce line of the '*De Contemptu Mundi*'. [12]

'*Hora novissima – tempora pessima*' – a dead pause till the assenting *sunt* broke, like a sob, out of the darkness, and one boy's voice, clearer than silver trumpets, returned the long-drawn *vigilemus*.

'*Ecce minaciter, imminet Arbiter*' [13] (organ and voices were leashed together in terror and warning, breaking away liquidly to the '*ille supremus*'). Then the tone-colours shifted for the prelude to – '*Imminet, imminet, ut mala terminet –*'

'Stop! Again!' cried the Cantor; and gave his reasons a little more roundly than was natural at choir-practice.

'Ah! Pity o' man's vanity! He's guessed we are here. Come away!' said the Abbot. Anne of Norton, in her carried chair, had been listening too, further along the dark Triforium, with Roger of Salerno. John heard her sob. On the way back, he asked Thomas how her health stood. Before Thomas could reply the sharp-featured Italian doctor pushed between them. 'Following on our talk together, I judged it best to tell her,' said he to Thomas.

'What?' John asked simply enough.

'What she knew already.' Roger of Salerno launched into a Greek quotation to the effect that every woman knows all about everything.

'I have no Greek,' said John stiffly. Roger of Salerno had been giving them a good deal of it, at dinner.

'Then I'll come to you in Latin. Ovid hath it neatly. *"Utque malum late solet immedicabile cancer –"* [14] but doubtless you know the rest, worthy Sir.'

'Alas! My school-Latin's but what I've gathered by the way from fools professing to heal sick women. *"Hocus-pocus –"* but doubtless you know the rest, worthy Sir.'

Roger of Salerno was quite quiet till they regained the dining-room, where the fire had been comforted and the dates, raisins, ginger, figs, and cinnamon-scented sweetmeats set out, with the choicer wines, on the after-table. The Abbot seated himself, drew off his ring, dropped it, that all might hear the tinkle, into an empty silver cup, stretched his feet towards the hearth, and looked at the great gilt and carved rose in the barrel-roof. The silence that keeps from Compline to Matins had closed on their world. The bull-necked Friar watched a ray of sunlight split itself into colours on the rim of a crystal salt-cellar; Roger of Salerno had re-opened some discussion with Brother Thomas on a type of spotted fever that was baffling them both in England and abroad; John took note of the keen profile, and – it might serve as a note for the Great Luke – his hand moved to his bosom. The Abbot saw, and nodded permission. John whipped out silver-point and sketch-book.

'Nay – modesty is good enough – but deliver your own opinion,' the Italian was urging the Infirmarian. Out of courtesy to the foreigner nearly all the talk was in table-Latin; more formal and more copious than monk's patter. Thomas began with his meek stammer.

'I confess myself at a loss for the cause of the fever unless – as Varro[15] saith in his *De Re Rustica* – certain small animals which the eye cannot follow enter the body by nose and mouth, and set up grave diseases. On the other hand, this is not in Scripture.'

Roger of Salerno hunched head and shoulders like an angry cat. 'Always *that*!' he said, and John snatched down the twist of the thin lips.

'Never at rest, John,' the Abbot smiled at the artist. 'You should break off every two hours for prayers, as we do. St Benedict was no fool. Two hours is all that a man can carry the edge of his eye or hand.'

'For copyists – yes. Brother Martin is not sure after one hour. But when a man's work takes him, he must go on till it lets him go.'

'Yes, that is the Demon of Socrates,'[16] the Friar from Oxford rumbled above his cup.

'The doctrine leans toward presumption,' said the Abbot. 'Remember, "Shall mortal man be more just than his Maker?"'[17]

'There is no danger of justice'; the Friar spoke bitterly. 'But at least Man might be suffered to go forward in his Art or his thought. Yet if Mother Church sees or hears him move anyward, what says she? "No!" Always "No."'

'But if the little animals of Varro be invisible' – this was Roger of Salerno to Thomas – 'how are we any nearer to a cure?'

'By experiment' – the Friar wheeled round on them suddenly. 'By reason and experiment. The one is useless without the other. But Mother Church –'

'Ay!' Roger de Salerno dashed at the fresh bait like a pike. 'Listen, Sirs. Her bishops – our Princes – strew our roads in Italy with carcasses that they make for their pleasure or wrath. Beautiful corpses! Yet if I – if we doctors – so much as raise the skin of one of them to look at God's fabric beneath, what

266

says Mother Church? "Sacrilege! Stick to your pigs and dogs, or you burn!"'

'And not Mother Church only!' the Friar chimed in. '*Every* way we are barred – barred by the words of some man, dead a thousand years, which are held final. Who is any son of Adam that his one say-so should close a door towards truth? I would not except even Peter Peregrinus, my own great teacher.'

'Nor I Paul of Aegina,' Roger of Salerno cried. 'Listen, Sirs! Here is a case to the very point. Apuleius affirmeth, if a man eat fasting of the juice of the cut-leaved buttercup – *sceleratus* we call it, which means "rascally"' – this with a condescending nod towards John – 'his soul will leave his body laughing.[18] Now this is the lie more dangerous than truth, since truth of a sort is in it.'

'He's away!' whispered the Abbot despairingly.

'For the juice of that herb, I know by experiment, burns, blisters, and wries the mouth. I know also the *rictus*, or pseudo-laughter on the face of such as have perished by the strong poisons of herbs allied to this ranunculus. Certainly that spasm resembles laughter. It seems then, in my judgement, that Apuleius, having seen the body of one thus poisoned, went off at score and wrote that the man died laughing.'

'Neither staying to observe, nor to confirm observation by experiment,' added the Friar, frowning.

Stephen the Abbot cocked an eyebrow toward John.

'How think *you*?' said he.

'I'm no doctor,' John returned, 'but I'd say Apuleius in all these years might have been betrayed by his copyists. They take short-cuts to save 'emselves trouble. Put case that Apuleius wrote the soul *seems to* leave the body laughing, after this poison. There's not three copyists in five (*my* judgement) would not leave out the "seems to". For who'd question Apuleius? If it seemed so to him, so it must be. Otherwise any child knows cut-leaved buttercup.'

'Have you knowledge of herbs?' Roger of Salerno asked curtly.

'Only, that when I was a boy in convent, I've made tetters

round my mouth and on my neck with buttercup-juice, to save going to prayer o' cold nights.'

'Ah!' said Roger. 'I profess no knowledge of tricks.' He turned aside, stiffly.

'No matter! Now for your own tricks, John,' the tactful Abbot broke in. 'You shall show the doctors your Magdalene and your Gadarene Swine and the devils.'

'Devils? Devils? *I* have produced devils by means of drugs; and have abolished them by the same means. Whether devils be external to mankind or immanent, I have not yet pronounced.' Roger of Salerno was still angry.

'Ye dare not,' snapped the Friar from Oxford. 'Mother Church makes Her own devils.'

'Not wholly! Our John has come back from Spain with brand-new ones.' Abbot Stephen took the vellum handed to him, and laid it tenderly on the table. They gathered to look. The Magdalene was drawn in palest, almost transparent, grisaille, against a raging, swaying background of woman-faced devils, each broke to and by her special sin, and each, one could see, frenziedly straining against the Power that compelled her.

'I've never seen the like of this grey shadow work,' said the Abbot. 'How came you by it?'

'*Non nobis!*[19] It came to me,' said John, not knowing he was a generation or so ahead of his time in the use of that medium.

'Why is she so pale?' the Friar demanded.

'Evil has all come out of her – she'd take any colour now.'

'Ay, like light through glass. *I* see.'

Roger of Salerno was looking in silence – his nose nearer and nearer the page. 'It is so,' he pronounced finally. 'Thus it is in epilepsy – mouth, eyes, and forehead – even to the droop of her wrist there. Every sign of it! She will need restoratives, that woman, and, afterwards, sleep natural. No poppy-juice, or she will vomit on her waking. And thereafter – but I am not in my Schools.' He drew himself up. 'Sir,' said he, 'you should be of Our calling. For, by the Snakes of Aesculapius, you *see*!'

The two struck hands as equals.

'And how think you of the Seven Devils?' the Abbot went on. These melted into convoluted flower- or flame-like bodies, ranging in colour from phosphorescent green to the black purple of outworn iniquity, whose hearts could be traced beating through their substance. But, for sign of hope and the sane workings of life, to be regained, the deep border was of conventionalized spring flowers and birds, all crowned by a kingfisher in haste, atilt through a clump of yellow iris.

Roger of Salerno identified the herbs and spoke largely of their virtues.

'And now, the Gadarene Swine,' said Stephen. John laid the picture on the table.

Here were devils dishoused, in dread of being abolished to the Void, huddling and hurtling together to force lodgment by every opening into the brute bodies offered. Some of the swine fought the invasion, foaming and jerking; some were surrendering to it, sleepily, as to a luxurious back-scratching; others, wholly possessed, whirled off in bucking droves for the lake beneath. In one corner the freed man stretched out his limbs all restored to his control, and Our Lord, seated, looked at him as questioning what he would make of his deliverance.

'Devils indeed!' was the Friar's comment. 'But wholly a new sort.'

Some devils were mere lumps, with lobes and protuberances – a hint of a fiend's face peering through jelly-like walls. And there was a family of impatient, globular devillings who had burst open the belly of their smirking parent, and were revolving desperately toward their prey. Others patterned themselves into rods, chains and ladders, single or conjoined, round the throat and jaws of a shrieking sow, from whose ear emerged the lashing, glassy tail of a devil that had made good his refuge. And there were granulated and conglomerate devils, mixed up with the foam and slaver where the attack was fiercest. Thence the eye carried on to the insanely active backs of the downward-racing swine, the swineherd's aghast face, and his dog's terror.

Said Roger of Salerno, 'I pronounce that these were begotten of drugs. They stand outside the rational mind.'

'Not these,' said Thomas the Infirmarian, who as a servant of the Monastery should have asked his Abbot's leave to speak. 'Not *these* – look! – in the bordure.'

The border to the picture was a diaper of irregular but balanced compartments or cellules, where sat, swam, or weltered, devils in blank, so to say – things as yet uninspired by Evil – indifferent, but lawlessly outside imagination. Their shapes resembled, again, ladders, chains, scourges, diamonds, aborted buds, or gravid phosphorescent globes – some wellnigh star-like.

Roger of Salerno compared them to the obsessions of a Churchman's mind.

'Malignant?' the Friar from Oxford questioned.

'"Count everything unknown for horrible,"' Roger quoted with scorn.

'Not I. But they are marvellous – marvellous. I think –'

The Friar drew back. Thomas edged in to see better, and half opened his mouth.

'Speak,' said Stephen, who had been watching him. 'We are all in a sort doctors here.'

'I would say then' – Thomas rushed at it as one putting out his life's belief at the stake – 'that these lower shapes in the bordure may not be so much hellish and malignant as models and patterns upon which John has tricked out and embellished his proper devils among the swine above there!'

'And that would signify?' said Roger of Salerno sharply.

'In my poor judgement, that he may have seen such shapes – without help of drugs.'

'Now who – *who*,' said John of Burgos, after a round and unregarded oath, 'has made thee so wise of a sudden, my Doubter?'

'I wise? God forbid! Only John, remember – one winter six years ago – the snow-flakes melting on your sleeve at the cookhouse-door. You showed me them through a little crystal, that made small things larger.'

'Yes. The Moors call such a glass the Eye of Allah,'[20] John confirmed.

'You showed me them melting – six-sided. You called them, then, your patterns.'

'True. Snow-flakes melt six-sided. I have used them for diaper-work often.'

'Melting snow-flakes as seen through a glass? By art optical?' the Friar asked.

'Art optical? *I* have never heard!' Roger of Salerno cried.

'John,' said the Abbot of St Illod's commandingly, 'was it — is it so?'

'In some sort,' John replied, 'Thomas has the right of it. Those shapes in the bordure were my workshop-patterns for the devils above. In *my* craft, Salerno, we dare not drug. It kills hand and eye. My shapes are to be seen honestly, in nature.'

The Abbot drew a bowl of rose-water towards him. 'When I was prisoner with — with the Saracens after Mansura,' he began, turning up the fold of his long sleeve, 'there were certain magicians — physicians — who could show —' he dipped his third finger delicately in the water — 'all the firmament of Hell, as it were, in —' he shook off one drop from his polished nail on to the polished table — 'even such a supernaculum as this.'

'But it must be foul water — not clean,' said John.

'Show us then — all — all,' said Stephen. 'I would make sure — once more.' The Abbot's voice was official.

John drew from his bosom a stamped leather box, some six or eight inches long, wherein, bedded on faded velvet, lay what looked like silver-bound compasses of old box-wood, with a screw at the head which opened or closed the legs to minute fractions. The legs terminated, not in points, but spoon-shapedly, one spatula pierced with a metal-lined hole less than a quarter of an inch across, the other with a half-inch hole. Into this latter John, after carefully wiping with a silk rag, slipped a metal cylinder that carried glass or crystal, it seemed, at each end.

'Ah! Art optic!' said the Friar. 'But what is that beneath it?'

It was a small swivelling sheet of polished silver no bigger than a florin, which caught the light and concentrated it on the lesser hole. John adjusted it without the Friar's proffered help.

'And now to find a drop of water,' said he, picking up a small brush.

'Come to my upper cloister. The sun is on the leads still,' said the Abbot, rising.

They followed him there. Halfway along, a drip from a

gutter had made a greenish puddle in a worn stone. Very carefully, John dropped a drop of it into the smaller hole of the compass-leg, and, steadying the apparatus on a coping, worked the screw in the compass-joint, screwed the cylinder, and swung the swivel of the mirror till he was satisfied.

'Good!' He peered through the thing. 'My Shapes are all here. Now look, Father! If they do not meet your eye at first, turn this nicked edge here, left- or right-handed.'

'I have not forgotten,' said the Abbot, taking his place. 'Yes! They are here – as they were in my time – my time past. There is no end to them, I was told . . . There *is* no end!'

'The light will go. Oh, let me look! Suffer me to see, also!' the Friar pleaded, almost shouldering Stephen from the eye-piece. The Abbot gave way. His eyes were on time past. But the Friar, instead of looking, turned the apparatus in his capable hands.

'Nay, nay,' John interrupted, for the man was already fiddling at the screws. 'Let the Doctor see.'

Roger of Salerno looked, minute after minute. John saw his blue-veined cheek-bones turn white. He stepped back at last, as though stricken.

'It is a new world – a new world and – Oh, God Unjust! – I am old!'

'And now Thomas,' Stephen ordered.

John manipulated the tube for the Infirmarian, whose hands shook, and he too looked long. 'It is Life,' he said presently in a breaking voice. 'No Hell! Life created and rejoicing – the work of the Creator. They live, even as I have dreamed. Then it was no sin for me to dream. No sin – O God – no sin!'

He flung himself on his knees and began hysterically the *Benedicite omnia Opera*.

'And now I will see how it is actuated,' said the Friar from Oxford, thrusting forward again.

'Bring it within. The place is all eyes and ears,' said Stephen.

They walked quietly back along the leads, three English counties laid out in evening sunshine around them; church upon church, monastery upon monastery, cell after cell, and the bulk of a vast cathedral moored on the edge of the banked shoals of sunset.

When they were at the after-table once more they sat down, all except the Friar who went to the window and huddled bat-like over the thing. 'I see! I see!' he was repeating to himself.

'He'll not hurt it,' said John. But the Abbot, staring in front of him, like Roger of Salerno, did not hear. The Infirmarian's head was on the table between his shaking arms.

John reached for a cup of wine.

'It was shown to me,' the Abbot was speaking to himself, 'in Cairo, that man stands ever between two Infinities – of greatness and littleness. Therefore, there is no end – either to life – or –'

'And *I* stand on the edge of the grave,' snarled Roger of Salerno. 'Who pities *me*?'

'Hush!' said Thomas the Infirmarian. 'The little creatures shall be sanctified – sanctified to the service of His sick.'

'What need?' John of Burgos wiped his lips. 'It shows no more than the shapes of things. It gives good pictures. I had it at Granada. It was brought from the East, they told me.'

Roger of Salerno laughed with an old man's malice. 'What of Mother Church? Most Holy Mother Church? If it comes to Her ears that we have spied into Her Hell without Her leave, where do we stand?'

'At the stake,' said the Abbot of St Illod's, and, raising his voice a trifle, 'You hear that? Roger Bacon, heard you that?'

The Friar turned from the window, clutching the compasses tighter.

'No, no!' he appealed. 'Not with Falcodi – not with our English-hearted Foulkes made Pope. He's wise – he's learned. He reads what I have put forth. Foulkes would never suffer it.'

'"Holy Pope is one thing, Holy Church another,"' Roger quoted.

'But, I – *I* can bear witness it is no Art Magic,' the Friar went on. 'Nothing is it, except Art optical – wisdom after trial and experiment, mark you. I can prove it, and – my name weighs with men who dare think.'

'Find them!' croaked Roger of Salerno. 'Five or six in all the

273

world. That makes less than fifty pounds by weight of ashes at the stake. I have watched such men – reduced.'

'I will not give this up!' The Friar's voice cracked in passion and despair. 'It would be to sin against the Light.'

'No, no! Let us – let us sanctify the little animals of Varro,' said Thomas.

Stephen leaned forward, fished his ring out of the cup, and slipped it on his finger. 'My sons,' said he, 'we have seen what we have seen.'

'That it is no magic but simple Art,' the Friar persisted.

''Avails nothing. In the eyes of Mother Church we have seen more than is permitted to man.'

'But it was Life – created and rejoicing,' said Thomas.

'To look into Hell as we shall be judged – as we shall be proved – to have looked, is for priests only.'

'Or green-sick virgins on the road to sainthood who, for cause any mid-wife could give you –'

The Abbot's half-lifted hand checked Roger of Salerno's outpouring.

'Nor may even priests see more in Hell than Church knows to be there. John, there is respect due to Church as well as to Devils.'

'My trade's the outside of things,' said John quietly. 'I have my patterns.'

'But you may need to look again for more,' the Friar said.

'In my craft, a thing done is done with. We go on to new shapes after that.'

'And if we trespass beyond bounds, even in thought, we lie open to the judgment of the Church,' the Abbot continued.

'But thou knowest – *knowest!*' Roger of Salerno had returned to the attack. 'Here's all the world in darkness concerning the causes of things – from the fever across the lane to thy Lady's – thine own Lady's – eating malady. Think!'

'I have thought upon it, Salerno! I have thought indeed.'

Thomas the Infirmarian lifted his head again; and this time he did not stammer at all. 'As in the water, so in the blood must they rage and war with each other! I have dreamed these ten years – I thought it was a sin – but my dreams and Varro's are true! Think on it again! Here's the Light under our very hand!'

'Quench it! You'd no more stand to roasting than – any other. I'll give you the case as Church – as I myself – would frame it. Our John here returns from the Moors, and shows us a hell of devils contending in the compass of one drop of water. Magic past clearance! You can hear the faggots crackle.'

'But thou knowest! Thou hast seen it all before! For man's poor sake! For old friendship's sake – Stephen!' The Friar was trying to stuff the compasses into his bosom as he appealed.

'What Stephen de Sautré knows, you his friends know also. I would have you, now, obey the Abbot of St Illod's. Give to me!' He held out his ringed hand.

'May I – may John here – not even make a drawing of one – one screw?' said the broken Friar, in spite of himself.

'Nowise!' Stephen took it over. 'Your dagger, John. Sheathed will serve.'

He unscrewed the metal cylinder, laid it on the table, and with the dagger's hilt smashed some crystal to sparkling dust which he swept into a scooped hand and cast behind the hearth.

'It would seem,' said he, 'the choice lies between two sins. To deny the world a Light which is under our hand, or to enlighten the world before her time.[21] What you have seen, I saw long since among the physicians at Cairo. And I know what doctrine they drew from it. Hast *thou* dreamed, Thomas? I also – with fuller knowledge. But this birth, my sons, is untimely. It will be but the mother of more death, more torture, more division, and greater darkness in this dark age. Therefore I, who know both my world and the Church, take this Choice on my conscience. Go! It is finished.'

He thrust the wooden part of the compasses deep among the beech logs till all was burned.

The Last Ode[22]
(Nov. 27, B.C. 8)
Horace, Ode 31, Bk V

As watchers couched beneath a Bantine oak,
   Hearing the dawn-wind stir,
Know that the present strength of night is broke
   Though no dawn threaten her
Till dawn's appointed hour – so Virgil died,
Aware of change at hand, and prophesied

Change upon all the Eternal Gods had made
   And on the Gods alike –
Fated as dawn but, as the dawn, delayed
   Till the just hour should strike –

A Star new-risen above the living and dead;
   And the lost shades that were our loves restored
As lovers, and for ever. So he said;
   Having received the word . . .

Maecenas waits me on the Esquiline:
   Thither tonight go I . . .
And shall this dawn restore us, Virgil mine,
   To dawn? Beneath what sky?

⚏ The Gardener ⚏

One grave to me was given,
　One watch till Judgement Day;
And God looked down from Heaven
　And rolled the stone away.

One day in all the years,
　One hour in that one day,
His Angel saw my tears,
　And rolled the stone away! [1]

Everyone in the village knew [2] that Helen Turrell did her duty by all her world, and by none more honourably than by her only brother's unfortunate child. The village knew, too, that George Turrell had tried his family severely since early youth, and were not surprised to be told that, after many fresh starts given and thrown away, he, an Inspector of Indian Police, had entangled himself with the daughter of a retired non-commissioned officer, and had died of a fall from a horse a few weeks before his child was born. Mercifully, George's father and mother were both dead, and though Helen, thirty-five and independent, might well have washed her hands of the whole disgraceful affair, she most nobly took charge, though she was, at the time, under threat of lung trouble which had driven her to the South of France. She arranged for the passage of the child and a nurse from Bombay, met them at Marseilles, nursed the baby through an attack of infantile dysentery due to the carelessness of the nurse, whom she had had to dismiss, and at last, thin and worn but triumphant, brought the boy late in the autumn, wholly restored, to her Hampshire home.

All these details were public property, for Helen was as open as the day, and held that scandals are only increased by hushing them up. She admitted that George had always been rather a black sheep, but things might have been much worse if the mother had insisted on her right to keep the boy. Luckily, it seemed that people of that class would do almost anything for money, and, as George had always turned to her in his scrapes, she felt herself justified – her friends agreed with her – in cutting the whole non-commissioned officer connection, and giving the child every advantage. A christening, by the Rector, under the name of Michael, was the first step. So far as she knew herself, she was not, she said, a child-lover, but, for all his faults, she had been very fond of George, and she pointed out that little Michael had his father's mouth to a line; which made something to build upon.

As a matter of fact, it was the Turrell forehead, broad, low, and well-shaped, with the widely spaced eyes beneath it, that Michael had most faithfully reproduced. His mouth was somewhat better cut than the family type. But Helen, who would concede nothing good to his mother's side, vowed he was a Turrell all over, and, there being no one to contradict, the likeness was established.

In a few years Michael took his place, as accepted as Helen had always been – fearless, philosophical, and fairly good-looking. At six, he wished to know why he could not call her 'Mummy', as other boys called their mothers. She explained that she was only his auntie, and that aunties were not quite the same as mummies, but that, if it gave him pleasure, he might call her 'Mummy' at bedtime, for a pet-name between themselves.

Michael kept his secret most loyally, but Helen, as usual, explained the fact to her friends; which when Michael heard, he raged.

'Why did you tell? *Why* did you tell?' came at the end of the storm.

'Because it's always best to tell the truth,' Helen answered, her arm round him as he shook in his cot.

'All right, but when the troof's ugly I don't think it's nice.'

'Don't you, dear?'

'No, I don't, and' – she felt the small body stiffen – 'now you've told, I won't call you "Mummy" any more – not even at bedtimes.'

'But isn't that rather unkind?' said Helen softly.

'I don't care! I don't care! You've hurted me in my insides and I'll hurt you back. I'll hurt you as long as I live!'

'Don't, oh, don't talk like that, dear! You don't know what—'

'I will! And when I'm dead I'll hurt you worse!'

'Thank goodness, I shall be dead long before you, darling.'

'Huh! Emma says, "'Never know your luck".' (Michael had been talking to Helen's elderly, flat-faced maid.) 'Lots of little boys die quite soon. So'll I. *Then* you'll see!'

Helen caught her breath and moved towards the door, but the wail of 'Mummy! Mummy!' drew her back again, and the two wept together.

At ten years old, after two terms at a prep. school, something or somebody gave him the idea that his civil status was not quite regular. He attacked Helen on the subject, breaking down her stammered defences with the family directness.

''Don't believe a word of it,' he said, cheerily, at the end. 'People wouldn't have talked like they did if my people had been married. But don't you bother, Auntie. I've found out all about my sort in English Hist'ry and the Shakespeare bits. There was William the Conqueror to begin with, and — oh, heaps more, and they all got on first-rate. 'Twon't make any difference to you, my being *that* — will it?'

'As if anything could —' she began.

'All right. We won't talk about it any more if it makes you cry.' He never mentioned the thing again of his own will, but when, two years later, he skilfully managed to have measles in the holidays, as his temperature went up to the appointed one hundred and four he muttered of nothing else, till Helen's voice, piercing at last his delirium, reached him with assurance that nothing on earth or beyond could make any difference between them.

The terms at his public school and the wonderful Christmas, Easter, and Summer holidays followed each other, variegated and glorious as jewels on a string; and as jewels Helen treasured them. In due time Michael developed his own interests, which ran their courses and gave way to others; but his interest in

Helen was constant and increasing throughout. She repaid it with all that she had of affection or could command of counsel and money; and since Michael was no fool, the War took him just before what was like to have been a most promising career.

He was to have gone up to Oxford, with a scholarship, in October. At the end of August he was on the edge of joining the first holocaust of public-school boys who threw themselves into the Line; but the captain of his O.T.C.,[3] where he had been sergeant for nearly a year, headed him off and steered him directly to a commission in a battalion so new that half of it still wore the old Army red, and the other half was breeding meningitis through living overcrowdedly in damp tents. Helen had been shocked at the idea of direct enlistment.

'But it's in the family,' Michael laughed.

'You don't mean to tell me that you believed that old story all this time?' said Helen. (Emma, her maid, had been dead now several years.) 'I gave you my word of honour – and I give it again – that – that it's all right. It is indeed.'

'Oh, *that* doesn't worry me. It never did,' he replied valiantly. 'What I meant was, I should have got into the show earlier if I'd enlisted – like my grandfather.'

'Don't talk like that! Are you afraid of its ending so soon, then?'

'No such luck. You know what K. says.'

'Yes. But my banker told me last Monday it couldn't *possibly* last beyond Christmas – for financial reasons.'

''Hope he's right, but our Colonel – and he's a Regular – says it's going to be a long job.'

Michael's battalion was fortunate in that, by some chance which meant several 'leaves', it was used for coast-defence among shallow trenches on the Norfolk coast; thence sent north to watch the mouth of a Scotch estuary, and, lastly, held for weeks on a baseless rumour of distant service. But, the very day that Michael was to have met Helen for four whole hours at a railway-junction up the line, it was hurled out, to help make good the wastage of Loos,[4] and he had only just time to send her a wire of farewell.

In France luck again helped the battalion. It was put down

near the Salient, where it led a meritorious and unexacting life, while the Somme [5] was being manufactured; and enjoyed the peace of the Armentières and Laventie sectors when that battle began. Finding that it had sound views on protecting its own flanks and could dig, a prudent Commander stole it out of its own Division, under pretence of helping to lay telegraphs, and used it round Ypres at large.

A month later, and just after Michael had written Helen that there was nothing special doing and therefore no need to worry, a shell-splinter dropping out of a wet dawn killed him at once. The next shell uprooted and laid down over the body what had been the foundation of a barn wall, so neatly that none but an expert would have guessed that anything unpleasant had happened. [6]

By this time the village was old in experience of war, and, English fashion, had evolved a ritual to meet it. When the postmistress handed her seven-year-old daughter the official telegram to take to Miss Turrell, she observed to the Rector's gardener: 'It's Miss Helen's turn now.' He replied, thinking of his own son: 'Well, he's lasted longer than some.' The child herself came to the front-door weeping aloud, because Master Michael had often given her sweets. Helen, presently, found herself pulling down the house-blinds one after one with great care, and saying earnestly to each: 'Missing *always* means dead.' Then she took her place in the dreary procession that was impelled to go through an inevitable series of unprofitable emotions. The Rector, of course, preached hope and prophesied word, very soon, from a prison camp. Several friends, too, told her perfectly truthful tales, but always about other women, to whom, after months and months of silence, their missing had been miraculously restored. Other people urged her to communicate with infallible Secretaries of organizations who could communicate with benevolent neutrals, who could extract accurate information from the most secretive of Hun prison commandants. Helen did and wrote and signed everything that was suggested or put before her.

Once, on one of Michael's leaves, he had taken her over a

munition factory, where she saw the progress of a shell from blank-iron to the all but finished article. It struck her at the time that the wretched thing was never left alone for a single second; and 'I'm being manufactured into a bereaved next of kin,' she told herself, as she prepared her documents.

In due course, when all the organizations had deeply or sincerely regretted their inability to trace, etc., something gave way within her and all sensation – save of thankfulness for the release – came to an end in blessed passivity. Michael had died and her world had stood still and she had been one with the full shock of that arrest. Now she was standing still and the world was going forward, but it did not concern her – in no way or relation did it touch her. She knew this by the ease with which she could slip Michael's name into talk and incline her head to the proper angle, at the proper murmur of sympathy.

In the blessed realization of that relief, the Armistice [7] with all its bells broke over her and passed unheeded. At the end of another year she had overcome her physical loathing of the living and returned young, so that she could take them by the hand and almost sincerely wish them well. She had no interest in any aftermath, national or personal, of the war, but, moving at an immense distance, she sat on various relief committees and held strong views – she heard herself delivering them – about the site of the proposed village War Memorial.

Then there came to her, as next of kin, an official intimation, backed by a page of a letter to her in indelible pencil, a silver identity-disc, and a watch, to the effect that the body of Lieutenant Michael Turrell had been found, identified, and re-interred in Hagenzeele Third Military Cemetery [8] – the letter of the row and the grave's number in that row duly given.

So Helen found herself moved on to another process of the manufacture – to a world full of exultant or broken relatives, now strong in the certainty that there was an altar upon earth where they might lay their love. These soon told her, and by means of time-tables made clear, how easy it was and how little it interfered with life's affairs to go and see one's grave.

'*So* different,' as the Rector's wife said, 'if he'd been killed in Mesopotamia, or even Gallipoli.'

The agony of being waked up to some sort of second life drove Helen across the Channel, where, in a new world of abbreviated titles, she learnt that Hagenzeele Third could be comfortably reached by an afternoon train which fitted in with the morning boat, and that there was a comfortable little hotel not three kilometres from Hagenzeele itself, where one could spend quite a comfortable night and see one's grave next morning. All this she had from a Central Authority who lived in a board and tar-paper shed on the skirts of a razed city full of whirling lime-dust and blown papers.

'By the way,' said he, 'you know your grave, of course?'

'Yes, thank you,' said Helen, and showed its row and number typed on Michael's own little typewriter. The officer would have checked it, out of one of his many books; but a large Lancashire woman thrust between them and bade him tell her where she might find her son, who had been corporal in the A.S.C. His proper name, she sobbed, was Anderson, but, coming of respectable folk, he had of course enlisted under the name of Smith; and had been killed at Dickiebush, in early 'Fifteen. She had not his number nor did she know which of his two Christian names he might have used with his alias; but her Cook's tourist ticket expired at the end of Easter week, and if by then she could not find her child she should go mad. Whereupon she fell forward on Helen's breast; but the officer's wife came out quickly from a little bedroom behind the office, and the three of them lifted the woman on to the cot.

'They are often like this,' said the officer's wife, loosening the tight bonnet-strings. 'Yesterday she said he'd been killed at Hooge. Are you sure you know your grave? It makes such a difference.'

'Yes, thank you,' said Helen, and hurried out before the woman on the bed should begin to lament again.

Tea in a crowded mauve and blue striped wooden structure, with a false front, carried her still further into the nightmare. She paid her bill beside a stolid, plain-featured Englishwoman, who, hearing her inquire about the train to Hagenzeele, volunteered to come with her.

'I'm going to Hagenzeele myself,' she explained. 'Not to Hagenzeele Third; mine is Sugar Factory, but they call it La Rosière now. It's just south of Hagenzeele Three. Have you got your room at the hotel there?'

'Oh yes, thank you. I've wired.'

'That's better. Sometimes the place is quite full, and at others there's hardly a soul. But they've put bathrooms into the old Lion d'Or - that's the hotel on the west side of Sugar Factory - and it draws off a lot of people, luckily.'

'It's all new to me. This is the first time I've been over.'

'Indeed! This is my ninth time since the Armistice. Not on my own account. *I* haven't lost anyone, thank God - but, like everyone else, I've a lot of friends at home who have. Coming over as often as I do, I find it helps them to have someone just look at the   the place and tell them about it afterwards. And one can take photos for them, too. I get quite a list of commissions to execute.' She laughed nervously and tapped her slung Kodak. 'There are two or three to see at Sugar Factory this time, and plenty of others in the cemeteries all about. My system is to save them up, and arrange them, you know. And when I've got enough commissions for one area to make it worth while, I pop over and execute them. It *does* comfort people.'

'I suppose so,' Helen answered, shivering as they entered the little train.

'Of course it does. (Isn't it lucky we've got window-seats?) It must do or they wouldn't ask one to do it, would they? I've a list of quite twelve or fifteen commissions here' - she tapped the Kodak [9] again - 'I must sort them out tonight. Oh, I forgot to ask you. What's yours?'

'My nephew,' said Helen. 'But I was very fond of him.'

'Ah, yes! I sometimes wonder whether *they* know after death? What do you think?'

'Oh, I don't - I haven't dared to think much about that sort of thing,' said Helen, almost lifting her hands to keep her off.

'Perhaps that's better,' the woman answered. 'The sense of loss must be enough, I expect. Well, I won't worry you any more.'

The Gardener

Helen was grateful, but when they reached the hotel Mrs Scarsworth (they had exchanged names) insisted on dining at the same table with her, and after the meal, in the little, hideous salon full of low-voiced relatives, took Helen through her 'commissions' with biographies of the dead, where she happened to know them, and sketches of their next of kin. Helen endured till nearly half-past nine, ere she fled to her room.

Almost at once there was a knock at her door and Mrs Scarsworth entered; her hands, holding the dreadful list, clasped before her.

'Yes – yes – *I* know,' she began. 'You're sick of me, but I want to tell you something. You – you aren't married, are you? Then perhaps you won't . . . But it doesn't matter. I've *got* to tell someone. I can't go on any longer like this.'

'But please –' Mrs Scarsworth had backed against the shut door, and her mouth worked dryly.

'In a minute,' she said. 'You – you know about these graves of mine I was telling you about downstairs, just now? They really *are* commissions. At least several of them are.' Her eye wandered round the room. 'What extraordinary wall-papers they have in Belgium, don't you think? . . . Yes. I swear they are commissions. But there's *one*, d'you see, and – and he was more to me than anything else in the world. Do you understand?'

Helen nodded.

'More than anyone else. And, of course, he oughtn't to have been. He ought to have been nothing to me. But he *was*. He *is*. That's why I do the commissions, you see. That's all.'

'But why do you tell me?' Helen asked desperately.

'Because I'm *so* tired of lying. Tired of lying – always lying – year in and year out. When I don't tell lies I've got to act 'em and I've got to think 'em, always. *You* don't know what that means. He was everything to me that he oughtn't to have been – the one real thing – the only thing that ever happened to me in all my life; and I've had to pretend he wasn't. I've had to watch every word I said, and think out what lie I'd tell next, for years and years!'

285

'How many years?' Helen asked.

'Six years and four months before, and two and three-quarters after. I've gone to him eight times, since. Tomorrow'll make the ninth, and – and I can't – I *can't* go to him again with nobody in the world knowing. I want to be honest with someone before I go. Do you understand? It doesn't matter about *me*. I was never truthful, even as a girl. But it isn't worthy of *him*. So – so I – I had to tell you. I can't keep it up any longer. Oh, I can't!'

She lifted her joined hands almost to the level of her mouth, and brought them down sharply, still joined, to full arms' length below her waist. Helen reached forward, caught them, bowed her head over them, and murmured: 'Oh, my dear! My dear!' Mrs Scarsworth stepped back, her face all mottled.

'My God!' said she. 'Is *that* how you take it?'

Helen could not speak, and the woman went out; but it was a long while before Helen was able to sleep.

Next morning Mrs Scarsworth left early on her round of commissions, and Helen walked alone to Hagenzeele Third. The place was still in the making, and stood some five or six feet above the metalled road, which it flanked for hundreds of yards. Culverts across a deep ditch served for entrances through the unfinished boundary wall. She climbed a few wooden-faced earthen steps and then met the entire crowded level of the thing in one held breath. She did not know that Hagenzeele Third counted twenty-one thousand dead already. All she saw was a merciless sea of black crosses, bearing little strips of stamped tin at all angles across their faces. She could distinguish no order or arrangement in their mass; nothing but a waist-high wilderness as of weeds stricken dead, rushing at her. She went forward, moved to the left and the right hopelessly, wondering by what guidance she should ever come to her own. A great distance away there was a line of whiteness. It proved to be a block of some two or three hundred graves whose headstones had already been set, whose flowers were planted out, and whose new-sown grass showed green. Here she could see clear-cut letters at the ends of the rows, and, referring to her slip, realized that it was not here she must look.

A man knelt behind a line of headstones – evidently a gardener, for he was firming a young plant in the soft earth. She went towards him, her paper in her hand. He rose at her approach and without prelude or salutation asked: 'Who are you looking for?'

'Lieutenant Michael Turrell – my nephew,' said Helen slowly and word for word, as she had many thousands of times in her life.

The man lifted his eyes and looked at her with infinite compassion before he turned from the fresh-sown grass toward the naked black crosses.

'Come with me,' he said, 'and I will show you where your son lies.'

When Helen left the Cemetery she turned for a last look. In the distance she saw the man bending over his young plants; and she went away, supposing him to be the gardener.[10]

The Burden

One grief on me is laid
   Each day of every year,
Wherein no soul can aid,
   Whereof no soul can hear:
Whereto no end is seen
   Except to grieve again –
Ah, Mary Magdalene,
   Where is there greater pain?

To dream on dear disgrace
   Each hour of every day –
To bring no honest face
   To aught I do or say:
To lie from morn till e'en –
   To know my lies are vain –
Ah, Mary Magdalene,
   Where can be greater pain?

To watch my steadfast fear
   Attend my every way
Each day of every year –
   Each hour of every day:
To burn, and chill between –
   To quake and rage again –
Ah, Mary Magdalene,
   Where shall be greater pain?

One grave to me was given –
   To guard till Judgment Day –
But God looked down from Heaven
   And rolled the Stone away!
One day of all my years –
   One hour of that one day –
His Angel saw my tears
   And rolled the Stone away! [11]

Notes

Introduction

1. Morton Cohen (ed.), *Rudyard Kipling to Rider Haggard: The Record of a Friendship* (1964), p. 140.

2. Robert Wolf, 'Chiefly Debits', *Nation*, 27 November 1926, pp. 509–10; Edmund Wilson, 'Kipling's Debits and Credits', *New Republic*, 6 October 1926, pp. 194–5; Jerome K. Jerome, quoted by Morton Cohen, op. cit., p. 65; Max Beerbohm, 'On the Shelf', *see* Vasant Shane, *Rudyard Kipling, Activist and Artist* (1976), p. 5.

   For other early reviews of Kipling see Roger Lancelyn Green (ed.), *Kipling: The Critical Heritage* (1971).

3. T. S. Eliot, 'Kipling Redivivus', *Athenaeum*, 9 May 1919, p. 297.

4. *See* Morton Cohen, op. cit., p. 135.

5. Charles Carrington, *Rudyard Kipling: His Life and Work* (1955), p. 503.

6. *fortunate hour*: Rudyard Kipling, *Something of Myself* (1937), p. 12.

7. M. H. Hirst, 'Rudyard Kipling's "Debits and Credits"', *Central Literary Magazine*, January 1927, p. 13.

8. Angus Wilson, *The Strange Ride of Rudyard Kipling. His Life and Work* (1979), p. 435.

9. J. M. S. Tompkins, *The Art of Rudyard Kipling* (1959), p. 167.

10. *Something of Myself*, p. 136.

11. John Rouse, 'The Literary Reputation of Rudyard Kipling', unpublished Ph.D. thesis, University of New York (1964); 'Mr Kipling and the New Decameron', *Saturday Review*, 7 August 1920, p. 114.

12. C. A. Bodelsen, *Aspects of Kipling's Art* (1964), pp. 53–72. *See also* Elliot L. Gilbert, *The Good Kipling: Studies in the Short Story* (1972), pp. 168–87.

13. Roger Lancelyn Green, op. cit., p. 104.

14. *Something of Myself*, p. 209.

15. J. M. S. Tompkins, op. cit., p. 4.

16. *Something of Myself*, p. 209.
17. ibid., p. 207.
18. C. S. Lewis, 'Kipling's World', *They Asked for a Paper* (1962), p. 73; Lord Radcliffe, quoted in Lord Birkenhead, *Rudyard Kipling* (1980), p. 337. For an account of Kipling's late manner, see Bodelsen, op. cit., pp. 87–123.
19. Carrington, op. cit., p. 493.
20. *Quia multum amavit: see* Luke 7: 47: 'Her sins, which are many, are forgiven, for she loved much'.
21. J. M. S. Tompkins, op. cit., p. 212.
22. *See* note 2 above.
23. Lisa A. F. Lewis, 'Some Links Between the Stories in Kipling's "Debits and Credits"', *English Literature in Transition*, 25 (1982–3), p. 76; W. W. Robson in Andrew Rutherford (ed.), *Kipling's Mind and Art* (1964), p. 265; C. A. Bodelsen, op. cit., p. 122.
24. J. M. S. Tompkins, op. cit., pp. 158–9.
25. Lisa Lewis, op. cit., pp. 75–6.
26. Charles Carrington, op. cit., p. 470.

The Enemies to Each Other

First published *MacLean's Magazine* (with two illustrations by D. G. Summers), 15 July 1924, entitled 'A New Version of What Happened in the Garden of Eden'. There is a fragmentary manuscript of 'The Enemies to Each Other', marked by Kipling as 'How the Peacock kept his Tail', in the Durham manuscripts of *Debits and Credits*.

1. *With Apologies ... Mirza Mirkhond*: Kipling apologizes to 'the Shade of Mirza Mirkhond' on the title-page of this story because 'The Enemies to Each Other' is an imitation of the Persian historian's florid and bombastic style in *The Rauzat-us-Safa* ('The Garden of Purity'), a history of the world beginning with the creation and ending in the year 1505. Mirkhond Mohammed bin Khawand-Shah bin Hahmud (1433–98) lived and worked at Herat in Afghanistan. There is a translation of *The Rauzat-us-Safa* in the library at Bateman's, and the first three pages of Kipling's story resemble the section of Mirkhond's book entitled 'Summary of the History of Adam the Pure'. But while the language and syntax resemble Rehatsek's translation of Mirkhond, Kipling reworks Mirkhond's view of creation into something more arche-

typal than historical. In Kipling's tale the conflict between Adam and Eve – a state of both hate and love – demonstrates hopeless emotional strife, the insoluble incompatibilities of separate human natures. In *Rewards and Fairies* Kipling had explored open imaginative ways of dealing with emotional strife and resolving it, reinventing Biblical prototypes. In 'The Enemies to Each Other' he portrays the other side of the archetype: conflict that is unchangeable, eternal and fixed.

2. *Abu Ali Jafir ...*: Kipling's rewriting of Genesis draws together figures from Judaism, Christianity and Islam.

3. *Archangel Jibrail*: the Islamic Archangel who is believed to act as intermediary between God and man, and as bearer of revelation to the Prophets. In the Bible Gabriel is the counterpart.

4. *Archangel Michael*: usually represented as a warrior, and believed to be helper of the Church's armies against the Heathen. *See* Revelation 7: 7. In the Koran Mikha'el is the counterpart.

5. *Archangel Azrael*: the angel of death. In the Koran Izra'il is the counterpart.

6. *Tayif*: a city in Saudi Arabia near Mecca, and a sanctuary.

7. *Eblis*: the Devil; Satan.

8. *My Compassion ... Wrath*: see Genesis 8: 21–2. This reference to God's mercy is a touchstone throughout the volume. *See* 'Yet doth He devise means that His banished be not expelled from Him' (p. 250); 'Marvellous mercy and infinite love' (p. 177).

9. *Get ye ... to the other*: see Genesis 3: 15: 'And I will put enmity between thee and the woman, and between thy seed and her seed; it shall bruise thy head, and thou shalt bruise his heel.'

10. *Serendib*: Ceylon.

11. *Quabil and Habil (Cain and Abel)*: see Genesis 4: 2.

12. *Our Curse and Our Blessing*: see Genesis 3: 16–19.

Sea Constables: A Tale of '15

'The Changelings' was first published in *Debits and Credits*, 'Sea Constables: A Tale of 15' in *Metropolitan Magazine* (with two illustrations by Anton Otto Fischer), September 1915 and 'The Vineyard' in the *Sunday Express*, 19 September 1926.

The Changelings

1. *I was ... grocer's clerk*: Here the reference to the civilian professions of the First World War servicemen points a contrast to Kipling's earlier Indian soldier stories. Formerly he had dealt with a professional army, now he turns to the effects on the lives of middle-aged men of their sudden forced entry into the war. This poem recalls Number xxxvii of W. E. Henley's poem-sequence, *Echoes* (*1872–1889*), volume entitled *A Book of Verses* (1888), which begins:

> Or ever the knightly years were gone
> With the old world to the grave
> I was a king in Babylon
> And you were a Christian slave.

2. *pied craft*: camouflaged ships.
3. *Hoisted us Heavens-high*: *see* Psalm 108: 26.

Sea Constables

4. *Cheer up ... 'Soon be dead*: Harbord suggests this is an echo of a song of the period whose chorus ends: 'Cheer up, cully, you'll soon be dead./It's a short life and a gay one.'
5. *Don't talk shop . . .*: a criticism frequently levelled against Kipling's stories, but seen by Edmund Wilson as part of Kipling's own particular brand of Modernism. (*See Introduction*, p. 18.)
6. *Vesiga soup*: Nicholas Freeling's *Cook Book* (1972) has a commentary on this story as its last chapter. According to Freeling Vesiga 'came from Russia and had to do with the spine of the sturgeon'. (He believes it was the spine marrow.) This is confirmed by the manuscript where Kipling makes a joke about the hind legs of sturgeons.
7. *Damnation to all neutrals!*: This is the preface to the tale that follows concerning the treatment of a 'neutral' who trades petrol to the enemy during the war. Kipling also criticized neutrals in two poems, 'The Question' (1916) and 'The Holy War' (1917). *See Definitive Edition* pp. 327; 289. Harbord points out that the sense of outrage created by the callous sinking of merchant ships by German U-Boat commanders during the First World War is implicit in the background of this story.
8. *bride of Antigua*: in the manuscript of the story the limerick is

complete and reads as follows: 'There was a young bride of Antigua/Who said to her spouse, "What a pig you are!"/He replied "Oh my Queen/Is it manners you mean/Or do you refer to my figuar?"'

9. *Isn't it extraordinary ... weeks?*: *See* note 1 (above).

10. *sprudel*: according to Harbord this is equivalent to 'a dose of salts'.

11. *I was surprised ... word*: The story measures the point at which the pressures of war cause men to behave in ways that would be unacceptable in peace, cf. the title of the poem, 'The Changelings'.

The Vineyard

12. *At the eleventh hour he came*: The reference here is to the New Testament parable. *See* Matthew 10: 1–16.

'In the Interests of the Brethren'

'Banquet Night' was first published in *Debits and Credits* and 'In the Interests of the Brethren' in *Story-Teller Magazine* and *Metropolitan Magazine* (with two illustrations by Dalton Stevens), December 1918. Separate issue, 1918.

'Banquet Night'

1. *King Solomon ... stone*: In 1929 Kipling presented to his Lodge in Lahore a gavel composed of stones from the quarries for the building of King Solomon's Temple in Jerusalem. For Kipling and Freemasonry see Albert Frost, 'Rudyard Kipling's Masonic Allusions', *Kipling Journal* (October 1942); Basil Bazley, 'Freemasonry in Kipling's Works', *Kipling Journal* (December 1949); B. A. Smith, 'Some Masonic References in Rudyard Kipling's Works', *Transactions of the Somerset Master's Lodge* (1926); Brother H. Carr, 'Kipling and the Craft', *Transactions of the Quatuor Coronati Lodge* (1964).

2. *Felling and floating*: for the building of Solomon's temple see 1 Kings 5–7.

3. *Garments from Bozrah*: see Isaiah 63.

4. *Hyssop and Cedar*: see 1 Kings 4: 33.

5. *the Bramble, the Fig and the Thorn*: see Judges 9: 7–20.

6. *Joppa beach*: *see* 2 Chronicles 2: 16.

7. *shook hands*: a special handshake enables Masons who have not previously met to identify each other.

8. *Louis ... Treize*: Louis XIII of France (1601–43).

9. *A Man from Messines*: a battle in France in 1917 which was part of the Ypres Salient.

10. *Faith and Works 5837*: 'The Janeites' (p. 120), 'A Madonna of the Trenches' (p. 177) and 'A Friend of the Family' (p. 218) are also located in this fictional lodge.

11. *All Ritual ... fly to it*: a crucial aspect of Kipling's belief, and one of the main themes of this story.

12. *... the Spirit ... that giveth life*: Freemasonry contains many of the elements of Christianity. Compare here, for example, 2 Corinthians 3: 6: '... for the letter killeth, but the spirit giveth life'.

13. *I noticed Peter Gilkes ... Iowa*: Smith (*see* note 1 above) notes that these references show the depth of Kipling's background knowledge of Masonry: 'Gilkes and Wilson were among their great leaders ... Dunkerley was an illegitimate son of George II ... and Anthony Sayer the first Grand Master ... The Grand Lodge of Iowa was founded in 1840, and around 1850 it began to collect rare items, of Masonic books especially, which have made their library into one of the best collections of its kind in the English-speaking world. Not one English Mason in ten thousand would be expected to know this, yet Kipling threw in this little detail to emphasize the importance of the picture in question' (pp. 33–4).

14. *ashlar*: square-hewn stone.

15. *the only practical creed ... children*: The story demonstrates that in addition to his conviction that ritual is a necessary element in preserving men under stress, Kipling's love of Freemasonry was also centred in the companionship and security to men of all race, caste and creed.

16. *Hespere panta fereis*: Sappho fragment: 'Evening Star that bringest back all that Dawn hath scattered far ...' J. M. Edmonds (ed.), *Lyra Graeca* (1922), p. 285.

17. *a paraphrase from Micah*: *see* Micah 4: 8: 'He hath shewed thee, O man, what is good; and what doth the Lord require of thee, but to do justly, and to love mercy, and to walk humbly with thy God?'

18. '*Entered Apprentices' Song*': a Masonic hymn by Matthew Birkhead collected in Edmonstoune Duncan, *The Minstrelsy of England*, vol. 2, p. 179. There are three levels of Craft Masonry – Entered Apprentice, Fellow-Craft and Master-Mason.

19. *Revelations of St John*: St John's Gospel is a key text for the Freemasons. Much of Masonic work is a symbolic search for the unknown God.

The United Idolaters

'To the Companions' and 'The Centaurs' were first published in *Debits and Credits*. 'The United Idolaters' was first published in *MacLean's Magazine* (with one illustration by D. G. Summers), 1 June 1924; *Nash's Magazine* and *Hearst's International Magazine* (each with three illustrations by James Montgomery Flagg), June 1924.

To the Companions

1. *Horace, Ode 17, Bk V*: (*See also* 'Horace, Odes', pp. 119, 141, 201, 276). Kipling recorded his love of Horace in his autobiography where he writes: 'C– [F. W. Haslam] taught me to loathe Horace for two years; to forget him for twenty, and then to love him for the rest of my days and through many sleepless nights.' See also *Kipling's Horace* edited by C. E. Carrington (1978). This is an edition of the fifty-five epigrams which appear in the margins of Kipling's own copy of Horace's *Odes*. Carrington writes: 'Some are free translations from Horace; some are critical comments or glosses; and some his own developments of a Horatian theme.' In 'Regulus', a late Stalky story, published in *A Diversity of Creatures*, King's Latin set read an imitation of 'the fifth Ode of Horace's Third Book' written by Kipling himself. The controversy among classicists prompted by Kipling's imitation led him to publish (for fun): 'Q. Horati Flacci Carminum Librum Quintum a Rudyardo Kipling et Carlo Graves Anglice Redditum ...' in collaboration with A. D. Godley, Public Orator at Oxford, in 1922.

The United Idolaters

2. *the College*: This story is a continuation of the adventures of *Stalky and Co*. The original stories were published in 1899, with an additional tale 'Regulus' (*see* note 1 above) published eighteen years later. 'The United Idolaters' and 'The Propagation of

Knowledge' are less exaggerated in tone than their predecessors, and display less overt didactic intention.

3. *myall-wood*: scented acacia wood.

4. *See* 'Slaves of the Lamp' – *Stalky and Co* (author's note).

5. *Uncle Remus*: Brer Terrapin and Tar Baby are characters from the *Uncle Remus* stories (1883) of Joel Chandler Harris (1848–1908).

6. *painted or and sable*: the heraldic words for gold and black.

7. *Hypatia*: Charles Kingsley's historical novel (1853). The account of Mary Magdalen in this book is very like Helen Turrell's fate in 'The Gardener'. *See* p. 227.

8. *Brer Terrapin . . . Art*: see *Introduction*, p. 9.

9. *If you're anxious . . . aesthetic line*: Gilbert and Sullivan's operetta *Patience* (1904).

10. *Bishop Odo*: half-brother to William the Conqueror, who made him bishop of Bayeux in 1049. Bishop Odo died in 1097.

11. *House of Rimmon*: *see* 2 Kings 5: 18.

The Centaurs

12. *the young Centaur-colts*: half-man, half-horse.

13. *Chiron*: King of the Centaurs, who in later myths is depicted as wise and kindly, and famous for his knowledge of archery, music and medicine. Chiron was immortal; but he was accidentally wounded by one of Hercules' shafts and was in such pain that he exchanged his immortality for death.

The Wish House

'Late Came the God' and 'Rahere' were first published in *Debits and Credits*. 'The Wish House' was first published in *MacLean's Magazine* (with two illustrations by Roy Fischer), 15 October 1924.

'Late Came the God'

1. *Till the stones . . . ached for her*: the poem introduces the theme of the story: the strength of women's love and their capacity to bear suffering. *See Introduction*, pp. 19–26.

2. *she called on the Night*: *see* Judges 6: 36–40.

The Wish House

3. *Mrs Ashcroft*: some commentators claim that Kipling borrowed several of her features from Chaucer's Wife of Bath. In his autobiography Kipling is characteristically evasive about this: 'The review said that I had revived Chaucer's Wife of Bath even to the 'mormal on her shinne'. And it looked just like that too! There was no possible answer, so, breaking my rule not to have commerce with any paper, I wrote to the *Manchester Guardian* and gave myself "out – caught to leg".' In fact, it was Chaucer's Cook, and not his Wife of Bath who had the 'mormal on her shinne'.

4. *easy, ancient Sussex*: the story is an extraordinary mixture of old and new, of supernatural and realist elements. W. W. Robson was one of the first to draw attention to this story, and his analysis remains one of the most perceptive.

5. *cherubim ... charabancs*: buses or coaches.

6. *a Token*: an apparition or spectre (dialect), possibly also a *doppel-ganger* (double). The 'Token' represents the child's demand for belief and trust in the irrational and the imaginative.

7. *hoppin'*: hop-picking (author's note).

8. *'Let me take everythin' bad ... for love's sake'*: It is possible that Kipling's ideas were influenced by Catholic beliefs of the 'Way of Exchange'. *See* Richard Griffiths, *The Reactionary Revolution: The Catholic Revival in French Literature, 1870–1914* (1966), pp. 156–7. 'Of all the doctrines related to suffering which were preached at the time, that of vicarious suffering or mystical substitution was the one which held the attention of Catholic writers ... In taking on these sufferings for the world, man is imitating and to a certain extent supplementing the sufferings of Christ on the Cross ... People may take on suffering for the community in which they live, or for the salvation of those near and dear to them ... In the cases of all these forms of expiation, an essential element is the free will of the sufferer.' Harbord quotes Nevill Coghill's discussion of the Christian theory of co-inherence in *Light on C. S. Lewis* (1965), p. 64: 'Lewis claimed to possess this power and had used it to ease the suffering of his wife, a cancer victim: "You mean," I said, "that the pain left her, and that you felt it in your body?" "Yes," he said, "in my legs. It was crippling. But it relieved hers."' *See also* J. R. Thrane, 'The Role of the Token in "The Wish House"', *Kipling Journal*, March

1973, p. 7: 'the story's "pattern" corresponds closely – not exactly – to that of the so-called "Calvinistic" Protestant interpretation of the Atonement that is sometimes called "Penal Theory". In it Christ's willing death is seen less as a meritorious, exemplary substitute for the punishment due to fallen man, and far more as a vicarious endurance by the Son of that punishment itself.' The bases for such a belief are to be found in Galatians 6:2 and in Colossians 1:24.

9. *It do count . . . de pain?*: see *Introduction*, pp. 20–21.

Rahere

10. *Rahere, King Henry's Jester*: Rahere, also a character in *Rewards and Fairies*, was a courtier turned priest who founded St Bartholomew's Hospital. According to tradition, he was inspired to do this after seeing a family of lepers in the London streets. *See* Frederick F. Cartwright, *A Social History of Medicine* (1977), p. 25. Kipling chose to draw on another tradition that Rahere was King Henry's jester.

11. *a Horror of Great Darkness*: see Genesis 15: 12: 'And when the sun was going down, a deep sleep fell upon Abram; and, lo, an horror of great darkness fell upon him.' Throughout Kipling's writings there are powerful evocations of spiritual darkness: a fear of mental and spiritual fragmentation, and of death. *See* 'The Gate of the Hundred Sorrows' in *Plain Tales from the Hills*; 'At the End of the Passage' in *Life's Handicap*; 'The House Surgeon' in *Actions and Reactions*.

12. *perfect Love*: as in 'Late Came the God' and 'The Wish House', love and suffering are linked in this poem: the eye of love transforms the leper – 'faceless, fingerless, obscene' – into something without 'blemish'.

The Janeites

'The Survival' and 'Jane's Marriage' were first published in *Debits and Credits*. 'The Janeites' was first published in the *Story-Teller Magazine* and *Hearst's International Magazine* (with four illustrations in colour by Harry Dunn), May 1924.

The Survival

1. *And Gods for Gods make room*: a recurrent theme in Kipling's writings: that even the gods are not immune from time. Kim, we are told, 'accepted this new God without emotion. He knew already a few score'. Similarly in 'Weland's Sword', *Puck of Pook's Hill*, Puck is unperturbed by the passing of the gods: 'I'd seen too many Gods charging into Old England to be upset about it'. It is precisely because of this interchangeability of the gods that Kipling assigns to every soul the right to choose between different racial creeds. What is important is not the gods but the predicament of suffering humanity. This point is most powerfully made in the epigraph to the fourteenth chapter of *Kim*:

> My brother kneels (so saith Kabir)
>   To stone and brass in heathen wise,
> But in my brother's voice I hear
>   My own unanswered agonies.
> His god is as his Fates assign,
> His prayer is all the world's – and mine.

2. *the Lodge of Instruction*: see 'In the Interests of the Brethren', note 10.

3. *Brother Anthony ... Brother Humberstall*: the narrator, Brother Anthony and Brother Humberstall all tell parts of this story. This kind of multiple narration is characteristic of Kipling's late manner.

4. *Lazarus*: the man Jesus is said to have raised from the dead. *See* John 6: 1–45.

5. *Lar Pug Noy*: Lapugnoy, seven miles from La Basse.

6. *this Secret Society woman ... this Jane*: The story and the poem which follows is, in one respect, Kipling's tribute to Jane Austen. Carrington notes that Kipling 'would never pass through Winchester without reflecting that, after Stratford, it was the holiest place in England, for the sake of Jane Austen and Izaak Walton'. But, at the same time, in 'The Janeites' the theme of Jane Austen's writings is subservient to Kipling's investigation of the way in which bonds are formed – and a brotherhood created – between men who share experience, albeit that of Masonry, the war or the reading of Jane Austen. In addition to this, as Harbord points out, the story offers an excellent account of the working of heavy artillery in France in 1918, and pays tribute to the men who manned the guns.

7. *a nactuary*: an actuary: an expert in statistics, especially someone who calculates risks and premiums.

8. *Bradbury*: one pound note.

9. *Tilniz an' trap-doors*: Tilneys and trap-doors. See *Northanger Abbey*, chapter 11.

10. *perookier*: wig-maker.

11. *Imshee kelb*: get out, you dog (author's note)

12. *some Abbey or other*: *Northanger Abbey* (1818)

13. *the Reverend Collins . . . Lady Catherine De Bugg . . . Miss Bates*: the Reverend Collins and Lady Catherine de Bourgh in *Pride and Prejudice* (1813); Miss Bates in *Emma* (1816).

14. *Laura . . . Miss What's-her-Name . . . Captain T'other Bloke*: There is a 'Laura Place' in both *Northanger Abbey* and *Persuasion*; Anne Elliot and Captain Wentworth in *Persuasion* (1818).

15. *obese*: he meant to say 'obscene'.

Jane's Marriage

16. *Sir Walter*: Walter Scott (1771–1832).

17. *Henry*: Henry Fielding (1707–54).

18. *Tobias*: Tobias Smollett (1721–71)

19. *Miguel*: Miguel de Cervantes (1547–1616).

The Prophet and the Country

'The Portent' and 'Gow's Watch' were first published in *Debits and Credits*. 'The Prophet and the Country' was first published in *Hearst's International Magazine* (with three illustrations by David Robertson), October 1924.

The Portent

1. *That Virtue springs from iron within*: Throughout his writings Kipling shows himself fascinated by what, in a phrase borrowed from Rider Haggard, he termed 'breaking strain': the point at which the over-stretched body and mind give way. Kipling first used the expression in 'A Bank Fraud', *Plain Tales from the Hills*. *See also* 'In the Same Boat', *A Diversity of Creatures*; 'Uncovenanted Mercies', *Limits and Renewals*, and 'Hymn of Breaking Strain', *Rudyard Kipling's Verse, Definitive Edition*, p. 384.

2. *beeves*: oxen.

3. *the magneto*: the broken steel spring of the magneto symbolizes the

spiritual despair that permeates both the frame and the story itself. Bodelsen links this story with 'My Sunday at Home', *The Day's Work*; 'The Puzzler', *Actions and Reactions*; 'The Vortex', *A Diversity of Creatures*, and 'Aunt Ellen', *Limits and Renewals*, as 'farcical tales' in which 'their real point is not the sequence of fantastic happenings that constitutes the action, but a spiritual experience that they are an attempt to express'.

4. *Ethnology*: the science of human races, their relations to one another and their characteristics.

5. *The Man Without a Country*: a story by Edward Everett Hale.

6. *Prohibition*: The Volstead Act was passed in the U.S.A. and instituted in 1918. It prohibited the sale and consumption of alcohol.

7. *the Movies*: Tompkins sees Tarworth's projected anti-Prohibition film as a demonstration of 'the wonderful language and procedures of the American Movie industry'.

8. *artificially virg'nized*: in this story Kipling cautions against forms of extremism in national life.

9. *Parphar*: see II Kings 5: 10–12.

10. *the Black Hawk War*: the 1832 war against the Red Indians in Wisconsin.

11. *Ezekiel . . . Chebar*: see Ezekiel 1: 1.

12. *The Wages of Sin!*: see Romans 6: 23.

13. *Yellowstone Park*: a large park in Wyoming.

14. *ships that pass in the night*: from *Tales of a Wayside Inn* (1863) by Longfellow (1807–82).

Gow's Watch

15. *Gow's Watch*: On 30 September 1911 Haggard recorded in his Diary: 'Kipling read me two of his plays'. These have not been identified, but 'Gow's Watch' may be one of the fragments that survive. Both this extract – Act IV Scene 4 – and the one that follows 'A Madonna of the Trenches' in this volume – Act V Scene 3 – deal with a soldier-courtier named Gow, and are a pastiche of Jacobean drama. The other extant plays by Kipling are *The Harbour Watch*, written by Kipling and his daughter Elsie, and produced in London in 1913 (the manuscript is now in the British Library); and *Upstairs* – this was never produced (the typescript is now in the Berg Collection, New York Public Library).

16. *bombards*: a primitive type of cannon.
17. *puissance*: force or power.

The Bull that Thought

'The Bull that Thought' was first published in *Cosmopolitan Magazine* (with three illustrations by John R. Flanagan), December 1924. 'Alnaschar and the Oxen' was first published in *Debits and Credits*.

The Bull that Thought

1. *I had attacked the distance several times*: Kipling's fascination for cars is featured both in his stories (*see*, for example, 'They', *Traffics and Discoveries*) and in his autobiography, *Something of Myself*, pp. 176–8.
2. *a Mistral*: a cold north or north-west wind in the Mediterranean provinces of France.
3. *Blue de Luxe*: an express train.
4. *the foam and pulse of Youth renewed*: see Introduction, pp. 12–14.
5. *tisane*: a light champagne.
6. *Carpentier*: Georges Carpentier (1894–1975), French boxer.
7. *Apis*: the bull is named after the Egyptian bull-god.
8. *Arles*: a town about fifty miles from Marseilles famous for its almost perfect Roman arena which is used for bull-fighting.
9. *the Republic*: the Third Republic (1871–1940).
10. *Minotaur*: a Cretan monster, half-man, half-bull.
11. *Foch*: Ferdinand Foch (1851–1929), Marshal of France.
12. *Like the audience . . . to him*: Harbord cites a possible source for the story. In 1890 a bull named Lechuzo displayed such skill, and fought so stylishly, that he was never killed after the fights, as is the custom. Then one day he apparently lost interest, jumped the walls of the arena, and began to graze in the town square outside. A wealthy Andalusian bought him and took him back to his farm.
13. *a certain Rabelaisian abandon*: François Rabelais, French humorist and satirist, famous for *Gargantua* (1534).
14. *Cyrano*: Cyrano de Bergerac (1619–55). A French soldier wounded in the Spanish War who became a dramatist and novelist thereafter. *See* the *Oxford Companion to the Theatre* (1983), p. 709: 'In *Cyrano de Bergerac* (1898) . . . he achieved a marvellous fusion of romantic bravura, lyric love and theatrical craftsmanship, and

its success was overwhelming. It became a perennial favourite, not only in France, but in England and America, where something of its quality was apparent even through a pedestrian translation, *L'Aiglon* (the *Eaglet*, 1900), in which Bernhardt played the ill-fated son of Napoleon . . .'

15. *Molière*: 1622–73. French dramatist.

Alnaschar and the Oxen

16. *Alnaschar*: cf. 'The Tale of Al-Ashar, The Barber's Fifth Brother', *Tales From Ten Thousand and One Nights*. Alnaschar sits with a tray of glass-ware for sale. Dreaming of the immense profits he hopes to make and how he will spend them, he suddenly kicks out and breaks all the glass, splintering his dreams. *See* N. J. Dawood's translation (1954), pp. 61–8.

17. *Sussex cattle . . . dew*: an (ironic?) link with the fighting bulls of the Camargue.

18. *Lobengula*: King of the Matabele (1833–94).

19. *Mithras*: A Persian sun god, worshipped by some Romans, including characters in *Puck of Pook's Hill*, where Kipling ties Mithraism in with Freemasonry, and 'The Church that was at Antioch', *Limits and Renewals*, where Kipling shows how some Christian ceremonies derived from it. *See* Curnow, *The Mysteries of Mithras* (1902).

A Madonna of the Trenches

'Gipsy Vans' and 'Gow's Watch' were first published in *Debits and Credits*. 'A Madonna of the Trenches' was first published in *MacLean's Magazine* (with two illustrations by F. R. Gruger), 15 August 1924.

Gipsy Vans

1. *Unless you come . . . away*: The contempt for the conventional expressed in this poem prefaces the exploration of the positive aspects of the uncovenanted and the illegal in the story which follows.

A Madonna of the Trenches

2. *Swinburne*: Like Robert Browning, Swinburne (1837–1909) was an acknowledged influence on Kipling's poetry. Kipling writes in his autobiography: 'Swinburne's poems I must have come across first at my Aunt's. He did not strike my very young mind as "anything in particular" till I read *Atalanta in Calydon . . .*'

3. *the Lodge of Instruction*: *see* note 10 to 'In the Interests of the Brethren'.

4. *the Tyler's Room*: the 'Tyler' is the door-keeper of a Masonic Lodge.

5. *Sampoux*: In the magazine edition it was 'Fampoux', a real place, mentioned (as are most of the battlefields in *Debits and Credits*) in Kipling's history of his son's regiment, *The Irish Guards in the Great War* (1923). When collected, the initial was changed: it probably derives from the Sambres Canal, not far from Arras, combined with Fampoux.

6. *what advantage . . . if the dead didn't rise*: *see* 1 Corinthians 25: 32: 'If after the manner of men I have fought with beasts at Ephesus, what advantageth it me, if the dead rise not?' Like 'The Wish House' and 'The Gardener' in this volume, 'A Madonna of the Trenches' is a tale of love and death, but in this story the vision of love is also linked with the idea of the resurrection. *See Introduction* pp. 22–3.

7. *Whatever a man . . . love*: *see* the epigraph to this story from Swinburne's 'Les Noyades'.

8. *'Tisn't fair . . . all me life*: The persistent but puzzled allusions throughout the story to the resurrection of the body emphasize how incomprehensible these ideas are, particularly as they are expressed by the shocked and sceptical young narrator. Clem's apparent 'conversion' as a result of it all, and at the same time his refusal to accept the full implications of what he has seen, is imaged in the story's implicit equation of 'shell-shock' with 'belief', and shows the need for the intervention of the 'mercy and love' mentioned in the epigraph and in the story itself.

9. *a bit of a gatherin' in 'er breast*: In this volume Grace Ashcroft in 'The Wish House' and Anne of Norton in 'The Eye of Allah' are also dying of cancer. *See Introduction* pp. 7–8.

10. *poy-looz*: nickname for the French Infantrymen, derived from *poilu*.

11. *the Angels of Mons*: reputed to have appeared in the sky during the British withdrawal from Mons in August 1914, and to have protected the British soldiers throughout the retreat.

12. *Armine, . . . by marriage*: Harbord notes interestingly that this is the only Kipling story with a shock at the end.

Gow's Watch

13. *Gow's Watch*: *see* note 15 to 'The Prophet and the Country'.

The Propagation of Knowledge

'The Birthright' was first published in *Debits and Credits*. 'The Propagation of Knowledge' was first published in *Strand Magazine* (with five illustrations by C. E. Brick), and *McCall's Magazine* (with one illustration by F. M. Flagg), January 1926.

The Birthright

1. *We have such wealth . . . gems and gold!*: a pastiche of some modes of Renaissance English verse to preface a Stalky story concerning the study of English literature.

The Propagation of Knowledge

2. *pearls . . . before . . . swine*: *see* Matthew 7: 6.
3. *epigonoi*: *see* O.E.D.: 'One of a later (and less distinguished) generation'.
4. *Harrison Ainsworth and Marryat*: whose novels are described by King as promiscuous cheap fiction' (p. 206). William Harrison Ainsworth (1805–82); Captain Frederick Marryat (1792–1848).
5. *Surtees*: Robert Smith Surtees (1805–64), sporting novelist.
6. *Allow me to observe . . . hint*: a quotation from chapter sixty-five of Marryat's *Peter Simple* (1834).
7. *Dr Johnson . . . Macaulay*: this is a reference to the life of Johnson which Macaulay wrote for the *Encyclopaedia Britannica* in 1856.
8. *Admirable Crichton*: the hero of Ainsworth's *Crichton* (1837). This novel includes a bullfight scene (cf. 'The Bull that Thought'), and a scene in an alchemist's laboratory (cf. 'The Eye of Allah').
9. *old Du Maurier . . . Punch*: *see Punch*, vol. 72, p. 202 (5 May 1877).
10. *the Head's . . . Library*: Kipling himself was excused games at school and allowed the run of the headmaster's library. It was here

he began the wide-ranging and eclectic reading that continued all his life.

11. *Curiosities of Literature*: by Isaac d'Israeli (1766–1848), published in 1791–1823.

12. *not without dust and heat*: a quotation from Milton's *Areopagitica* (1644).

13. *This evening he fell on ... funny*: see *Curiosities of Literature*, pp. 292–4.

14. *They had drinkin'-horns ... about it*: see *Curiosities of Literature*, p. 293.

15. *Aubrey*: John Aubrey (1626–97).

16. *Stalky among the prophets*: see 1 Samuel 20.

17. *Nathaniel*: Nathaniel Holmes (1815–1901) who published *The Authorship of Shakespeare* (1886).

18. *Francis Bacon*: 1561–1626. The story plays ironically on the much-debated belief that Shakespeare's plays had in fact been written by Bacon.

19. *Delia*: Delia Salter Bacon (1811–59) who published *The Philosophy of the Plays of Shakespeare Unfolded* (1857).

20. *a seidlitz powder*: a laxative compounded of two powders mixed separately with water and then poured together to effervesce.

21. *Virtue has gone out of me*: see Mark 5: 20.

22. *a tense peace among the Augustans*: an allusion to Saintsbury's *Peace of the Augustans*, 1916.

23. *maxima debetur pueris reverentia*: the greatest respect is due to young persons (author's note). From Juvenal, *Satire* xiv.

A Friend of the Family

'A Legend of Truth' and 'We and They' were first published in *Debits and Credits*. 'A Friend of the Family' was first published in *MacLean's Magazine* (with two illustrations by A. C. Valentine), 15 June 1924.

A Legend of Truth

1. *Pilate's Question*: see John 18:37–8.

2. *Galileo*: 1564–1642, Italian mathematician, astronomer, physicist.

3. *Truth ... Fiction*: see 'A Matter of Fact', *Many Inventions*, an earlier working of a similar theme.

A Friend of the Family

4. *Lodge 'Faith and Works', 5837 E. C.: see* 'In the Interests of the Brethren', note 10.

5. *'Ye-es,' said Pole . . . naturally: see Introduction*, p. 15.

6. *He – he didn't belong . . . a human being*: the theme of loneliness pervades Kipling's writings, and is often linked with the fear of breakdown and isolation. The defensive feelings of the outcast and the angle of vision that sees everything askew yet deeply are reflected in stories from 'To be Filed for Reference', *Plain Tales from the Hills* to 'The Tender Achilles', *Limits and Renewals*.

7. *winkle-pin*: instrument for extracting spent cartridges from a firearm.

8. *I had to feel inside my head . . . executin'*: In a number of stories in *Debits and Credits* and *Limits and Renewals* Kipling examines the new mental horrors provided by the war. The *descente aux enfers* had been imaginatively anticipated in the stories of psychic and psychological trauma. *See* 'The Phantom Rickshaw', *Wee Willie Winkie*, and 'In the Same Boat', *A Diversity of Creatures*.

9. *mafeesh*: the end, finish (Arabic).

10. *flammenwerfer casualties*: the victims of a flame-throwing gun.

We and They

11. *But – would you believe it? . . . They!*: This is reminiscent of early statements in Kipling's Anglo-Indian stories and poems – including the often misquoted 'What should they know of England whom only England know' ('The English Flag', *Definitive Edition*, p. 221) – concerning racist beliefs.

On the Gate: A Tale of '16

'On the Gate: A Tale of '16' was first published in *McCall's Magazine* (with one illustration by E. F. Ward), June 1926. There is a fragmentary manuscript marked by Kipling 'The Department of Death' in the Durham manuscripts of *Debits and Credits*. 'The Supports' was first published in *Hutchinson's Story Magazine*, July 1919. Separate issue, 1919.

On the Gate: A Tale of '16

1. *On the Gate: A Tale of '16*: The story was begun in April 1916 according to Kipling's wife's diary where it is referred to as 'his St

Peter story'. On 22 May 1918, Haggard recorded in his dairy: 'Also he [Kipling] read me a quaint story about Death and St Peter, written in modern language, almost in slang, which his wife would not let him publish. It would have been caviare to the General if he had, because the keynote of it is infinite mercy extending even to the case of Judas.'

2. *If the Order Above ... Below*: This curious wording inverts what we would expect here, but enforces the theme of the poem, 'The Supports', which follows the story: an attempt to locate religion firmly in the world of ordinary reality. According to Dionysius the Areopagite, an authority on the orders of angels, there are nine of these: seraphim, cherubim, thrones, dominions, virtues, powers, principals, archangels, angels.

3. *that Ancient*: either Hermes Trismegistos or Roger Bacon (1214–94). *See* H. Stanley Redgrove, *Alchemy Ancient and Modern* (1911), p. 39: 'The first name which is found in the history of alchemy is that of Hermes Trismegistos ... we are told that Alexander the Great found the tomb of Hermes in a cave near Hebron. The tomb contained an emerald table – "The Smaragdine table" – on which were inscribed thirteen sentences in Phoenician characters of which the first two are: (a) I speak not fictitious things, but what is true and most certain. (b) What is below is like that which is above, and what is above is like that which is below, to accomplish the miracle of one thing.'

4. *St Peter*: leader of the Apostles, founder of the Christian church in Rome. Traditionally seen as keeper of the gate of heaven. *See* Matthew 16: 18, 19.

5. *The Gate*: of Heaven. The story is a celestial fantasy which takes the form of a conversation between Azrael, the angel of death, and St Peter. Byron's 'Vision of Judgement' (1821) is an analogue, possibly even a source, for this story.

6. *the fool says in his heart*: see Psalm 14:1.

7. *St Luke*: St Paul speaks of him as 'our beloved Luke, the physician', Colossians 4: 14.

8. *Quia multum amavit*: There is implicit reference here to the incident of the woman anointing Christ's feet. *See* Luke 7: 47: 'Her sins, which are many, are forgiven, for she loved much'.

9. *Greater love hath no man*: see John 15:13: 'Greater love hath no man than this, that a man lay down his life for his friends'.

10. *St Paul*: Until his conversion to Christianity, Paul was known as Saul, and famous for his persecution of the Christians. After

sudden conversion on the road to Damascus, Paul became an apostle. His subsequent career is related in the Acts of the Apostles.

11. *St Ignatius Loyola*: 1491–1556. Spanish theologian and one of the most influential figures in the Catholic Reformation of the sixteenth century; founder of the Jesuits in Paris in 1534.

12. *St Christopher*: martyr. According to the legend St Christopher used to transport travellers across a river. One night when he was carrying a child the child suddenly became so heavy that St Christopher could hardly get across the river. 'You have been carrying the whole world. I am Jesus Christ, the king you seek' the child told him.

13. *oh, my child . . . forgiveness*: a reference to St Peter's denial of Christ. *See* Matthew 26: 69–75.

14. *Sergeant Fell*: word-play on *Hamlet* Act V: 'This fell sergeant death is swift in his arrest'.

15. *the grim livery of death . . . Holbein*: Hans Holbein, painter (1497–1593). The reference here is to 'The Dance of Death', designed by Holbein and cut by Lützelberger, 1523–6.

16. *also believe and tremble*: see James 2:19.

17. *To Him who made . . . devotion!*: see p. 253.

18. *a fool . . . folly*: see Proverbs 26: 4.

19. *By all means . . . Paul*: see Corinthians 9: 22.

20. *Bradlaugh*: Charles Bradlaugh (1833–91), British radical and atheist, a freethinker in the tradition of Voltaire and Thomas Paine, prominent throughout the second half of the nineteenth century for his championship of individual liberties.

21. *Bunyan*: John Bunyan (1628–88), English minister and author of *The Pilgrim's Progress* (1678), the book that was the most characteristic expression of the Puritan religious outlook.

22. *Calvin*: John Calvin (1509–64), theologian; one of the most prominent Protestant reformers of the sixteenth century. He formulated the rigorous doctrine of predestination.

23. *Importunate Widow*: see Luke 18: 1–8.

24. *cock-crowing*: see Matthew 26: 74.

25. *A certain Woman*: Mary Magdalene: referred to by some as a prostitute who was converted to Christianity by Jesus and became one of His most devoted followers thereafter. *See* Luke 7: 47.

26. *Many mansions*: see John 14:2.

27. *plaiting of long-tagged epigrams*: Bunyan's occupation whilst in prison. *See Grace Abounding*, published in 1666. *See Everyman's*

Dictionary of Literary Biography, compiled by Cousin & Browning (1958), p. 96.

The Supports

28. *He Who makes . . . asunder*: *see* Psalm 104: 32 and Micah 1: 4.

The Eye of Allah

'Untimely' and 'The Last Ode' were first published in *Debits and Credits*. 'The Eye of Allah' was first published in *Strand Magazine* (with four illustrations by F. Marania) and *McCall's Magazine* (with one illustration by Arthur E. Becher), September 1920. Televised by the B.B.C. on 21 December 1960.

Untimely

1. *Untimely*: the poem introduces the theme of the story: the problem of scientific progress in a world that is unable to deal with it. 'Marklake Witches', *Rewards and Fairies*, and 'The Eye of Allah' show how the 'thinking' of a rational pragmatic society leads to the destruction of two powerful imaginative inventions – the stethoscope and the microscope.

The Eye of Allah

2. *The Cantor*: *see* Abbot Gasquet, *English Monastic Life* (1904), pp. 61; 86; 112: 'The Cantor . . . was naturally the instructor of music and trained [the novices] . . . In many monasteries he also had to teach the boys of the cloister school to read . . . The Infirmarian . . . must be gentle . . . and good-tempered, kind, compassionate to the sick . . . was always to keep in his cupboard a good supply of ginger, cinnamon, peony etc. . . . All monks wore 'night-boots'. These were probably fur-lined cloth-protectors for the feet, which served [the purpose of] keeping them warm and rendering their footfall inaudible during . . . the greater silence . . . from Compline to Prime.' The story is set in the past, but undated. 'Roger . . . A learned and famous philosopher' (p. 263) is probably a reference to Roger Bacon, a Franciscan friar who published a work on optics and who lived and worked in Oxford. (*See* **Charles**

Singh, *From Magic to Science* (1928).) In a lecture on this story, Lisa Lewis commented that at the beginning of the story, John is illuminating a text for Cardinal Falcodi, the Papal Legate in England. Almost two years later, 'about midsummer', the Abbot's dinner-guests speak of Falcodi 'made Pope' (Pope Clement IV, 1265–68). This enables us to date the story in 1266 or 1267. Lisa Lewis also noted the extraordinary range of this story: 'Three different societies – England, Spain and Italy and three different professions – artist, monk and doctor.'

3. *St Illod*: There is no such saint in the calendar, the nearest being St Illtyd. Lisa Lewis suggested that the Abbey was probably somewhere near Winchester, since John Otho goes to Southampton to set sail for Spain. She also suggested that the monks in the story were Benedictines. *See The Benedictines in England*, British Library Series No. 3 (1980); Dom David Knowles, *The Monastic Order in England* (1966).

4. *John of Burgos*: or John Fitz (meaning 'son of') Otho. *See* Matthew Paris, *History of England* (1235–73), translated into modern English by the Reverend J. A. Giles (1853); *Cambridge Mediaeval History*, volume VI, p. 265.

5. *the Papal Legate*: the ecclesiastic deputed to represent the Pope.

6. *Magnificat*: a song of praise from Luke 1: 46–55, included in the Evening Prayer Service of the Church of England.

7. *ultramarine*: the colour of blue pigment derived from lapis lazuli.

8. *Albana and Pharphar*: see II Kings 5: 12.

9. *But I'm weary of our Church-pattern devils*: John of Burgos sets out to revitalize Christian iconography. The anarchic creative energy of his images exemplifies the mode of imagination advocated in 'The Bull that Thought'.

10. *But for pain ... own mind*: In the stories up to *Rewards and Fairies* the theme of 'a man's craft' (his job or profession) is very important. The characters gain self-knowledge, self-respect and a kind of personal salvation through their work.

11. *Roger*: Scientists of the school of Salerno had pioneered the study of anatomy and surgery. There is a manuscript of a work on surgery in the Bodleian Library by the Italian Roger of Salerno who was a real historical character. *See* Loren McKinney, *Illustrations in Mediaeval Manuscripts*, Wellcome Historical Medical Library (1965), pp. 113, 115, 157, 162.

12. *De Contemptu Mundi*: hymn no. 226, A[ncient] and M[odern], 'The world is very evil' (author's note).

13. *Ecce minaciter, imminet Arbiter*: The judge arrives in angry mood.
14. *Utque malum . . . cancer*: Ovid, *Metamorphoses II*, 825–6. The reference is to the swift spreading of the cancer to the as yet uninfected parts of the body.
15. *Varro*: a reference to the twelfth chapter of Varro's second book on farming written in 27 B.C. (M. Terentii Varronis, *Rerum Rusticarum Libri Tres*.)
16. *Socrates*: the Athenian philosopher (469–399 B.C.).
17. *Shall mortal man . . . Maker?*: see Job 4: 17.
18. *Apuleius affirmeth . . . laughing*: see Pseudo-Apuleius, *Herbarium Apuleii: Leechdoms, Wortcunning and Starcraft of Early England*, (ed.) Cockayne, volume 1 (1864).
19. *Non nobis*: see Psalm 115.
20. *a little crystal . . . Eye of Allah*: the first microscopes – single lens – were used in the mid-fifteenth century. Lisa Lewis suggests that the microscope described in the story is a compass microscope with a lieberkuhn mirror invented around 1600, and that Kipling modified this to accord with what he imagined the thirteenth century would have produced.
21. *To deny the world . . . her time*: see note 1 above. As Charles Carrington has pointed out (*Kipling Journal*, 1966, pp. 27–8) the notion of breaking a scientific instrument probably came from Isaac d'Israeli's *Curiosities of Literature*. See also 'The Propagation of Knowledge', note 11.

'The Last Ode'

22. *The Last Ode*: see 'The United Idolaters', note 1. The date beneath the poem's title is the date of Horace's death; Maecenas was Horace's patron and had died just before Horace.

The Gardener

'The Gardener' was first published in *McCall's Magazine* (with one illustration by Arthur E. Becher), April 1925. 'The Burden' was first published in *Debits and Credits*.

On 14 March 1925 Kipling wrote to Rider Haggard from France: 'Went off at once to Rouen Cemetery (11,000 graves) and collogued with the Head Gardener and the contractors. One never gets over the shock of this dead sea of arrested lives.' According to Carrington, on the evening Kipling wrote this letter he began to write 'the story of Helen Turrell and her nephew and the gardener in the great 20,000 cemetery'. Kipling finished the story at Lourdes on 22 March. *See* Charles Carrington, *Rudyard Kipling, His Life and Work* (1955), p. 497.

The Gardener

1. *Epigraph*: *see* note 11.
2. *Everyone in the village knew*: *see* Introduction pp. 23–26. As Tompkins points out the narrative is strictly ironic: 'the language of Helen's lie is used so that we may assess the cost of it'. (Michael is Helen's illegitimate child and not her nephew.) In 'Some Echoes of Austen', *English Literature in Transition*, 29, 1986, p. 80, Lisa Lewis notes that in 'The Gardener' Kipling came the closest he had ever come to the style of Jane Austen: 'For what [Helen Turrell] tells us is not so much the inner truth of her story but an encoded truth, as it would be told by one woman to another in a small community where discretion is deeply valued.' *See also* 'The Janeites', note 6.
3. *O.T.C.*: Officers Training Corps.
4. *Loos*: Battle of, September 1915.
5. *the Somme*: there were battles on this front between 1916 and 1918.
6. *The next shell . . . happened*: the circumstances of Michael's death closely resemble those of Kipling's son John who was killed in the Battle of Loos on 27 September 1915, aged 18. In John's case, however, the body was never recovered.
7. *the Armistice*: signed 11.00 a.m. on 11 November 1918.
8. *Hagenzeele Third Military Cemetery*: this is not a real war cemetery. Kipling wrote the official booklet of the Imperial War Graves Commission, *The Graves of the Fallen*, 1919.
9. *twelve or fifteen commissions . . . the Kodak*: Birkenhead's biography records that Kipling photographed a son's grave for an elderly lady from Durham when he visited the Flanders battlefields in 1920.
10. *supposing him to be the gardener*: Here the context and the wording recall John 20: 15, and the possible identification of Christ and 'the gardener'. *See* Introduction, p. 25. On the other hand, as W. W. Robson points out, 'the gardener' could be a Belgian gardener

313

who says 'son' by way of habit, as most people visiting the cemetery would be searching for the graves of their sons. Other commentators have suggested that 'the gardener' is the dead young man, or his father. For further discussion of the various alternatives *see* Mrs G. H. Newsom, 'Ways of looking at "The Gardener"', *Kipling Journal*, March 1978; Bruce E. Wallis, 'The Resurrection Motif in Kipling's "The Gardener"', *Studies in Short Fiction*, 1973.

The Burden

11. *But God looked down ... away!*: The reference here is to Mary Magdalene who went to Christ's tomb and found it empty. Mark 16: 9 states that she was the first person to whom Christ appeared after his resurrection. *See also* references to Mary Magdalene in 'On the Gate' and 'The Eye of Allah' (pp. 248, 258).

FOR THE BEST IN PAPERBACKS, LOOK FOR THE

In every corner of the world, on every subject under the sun, Penguin represents quality and variety – the very best in publishing today.

For complete information about books available from Penguin – including Pelicans, Puffins, Peregrines and Penguin Classics – and how to order them, write to us at the appropriate address below. Please note that for copyright reasons the selection of books varies from country to country.

In the United Kingdom: For a complete list of books available from Penguin in the U.K., please write to *Dept E.P., Penguin Books Ltd, Harmondsworth, Middlesex, UB7 0DA*

In the United States: For a complete list of books available from Penguin in the U.S., please write to *Dept BA, Penguin, 299 Murray Hill Parkway, East Rutherford, New Jersey 07073*

In Canada: For a complete list of books available from Penguin in Canada, please write to *Penguin Books Canada Ltd, 2801 John Street, Markham, Ontario L3R 1B4*

In Australia: For a complete list of books available from Penguin in Australia, please write to the *Marketing Department, Penguin Books Australia Ltd, P.O. Box 257, Ringwood, Victoria 3134*

In New Zealand: For a complete list of books available from Penguin in New Zealand, please write to the *Marketing Department, Penguin Books (NZ) Ltd, Private Bag, Takapuna, Auckland 9*

In India: For a complete list of books available from Penguin, please write to *Penguin Overseas Ltd, 706 Eros Apartments, 56 Nehru Place, New Delhi, 110019*

In Holland: For a complete list of books available from Penguin in Holland, please write to *Penguin Books Nederland B.V., Postbus 195, NL–1380AD Weesp, Netherlands*

In Germany: For a complete list of books available from Penguin, please write to *Penguin Books Ltd, Friedrichstrasse 10 – 12, D–6000 Frankfurt Main 1, Federal Republic of Germany*

In Spain: For a complete list of books available from Penguin in Spain, please write to *Longman Penguin España, Calle San Nicolas 15, E–28013 Madrid, Spain*

RUDYARD KIPLING IN PENGUIN CLASSICS

Already published and forthcoming titles

'The most complete man of genius I have ever known' – Henry James

'For my own part I worshipped Kipling at thirteen, loathed him at seventeen, enjoyed him at twenty, despised him at twenty-five, and now again rather admire him. The one thing that was never possible, if one had read him at all, was to forget him' – George Orwell

Also published in Penguin
Rudyard Kipling: His Life and Work
A literary biography by Charles Carrington

John Aubrey	**Brief Lives**
Francis Bacon	**The Essays**
James Boswell	**The Life of Johnson**
Sir Thomas Browne	**The Major Works**
John Bunyan	**The Pilgrim's Progress**
Edmund Burke	**Reflections on the Revolution in France**
Thomas de Quincey	**Confessions of an English Opium Eater**
	Recollections of the Lakes and the Lake Poets
Daniel Defoe	**A Journal of the Plague Year**
	Moll Flanders
	Robinson Crusoe
	Roxana
	A Tour Through the Whole Island of Great Britain
Henry Fielding	**Jonathan Wild**
	Joseph Andrews
	The History of Tom Jones
Oliver Goldsmith	**The Vicar of Wakefield**
William Hazlitt	**Selected Writings**
Thomas Hobbes	**Leviathan**
Samuel Johnson/	**A Journey to the Western Islands of**
James Boswell	**Scotland/The Journal of a Tour to the**
	Hebrides
Charles Lamb	**Selected Prose**
Samuel Richardson	**Clarissa**
	Pamela
Adam Smith	**The Wealth of Nations**
Tobias Smollet	**Humphry Clinker**
Richard Steele and	Selections from the **Tatler** and the **Spectator**
Joseph Addison	
Laurence Sterne	**The Life and Opinions of Tristram Shandy,**
	Gentleman
	A Sentimental Journey Through France and Italy
Jonathan Swift	**Gulliver's Travels**
Dorothy and William	**Home at Grasmere**
Wordsworth	

PENGUIN CLASSICS

Netochka Nezvanova Fyodor Dostoyevsky

Dostoyevsky's first book tells the story of 'Nameless Nobody' and introduces many of the themes and issues which will dominate his great masterpieces.

Selections from the Carmina Burana A verse translation by David Parlett

The famous songs from the *Carmina Burana* (made into an oratorio by Carl Orff) tell of lecherous monks and corrupt clerics, drinkers and gamblers, and the fleeting pleasures of youth.

Fear and Trembling Søren Kierkegaard

A profound meditation on the nature of faith and submission to God's will which examines with startling originality the story of Abraham and Isaac.

Selected Prose Charles Lamb

Lamb's famous essays (under the strange pseudonym of Elia) on anything and everything have long been celebrated for their apparently innocent charm; this major new edition allows readers to discover the darker and more interesting aspects of Lamb.

The Picture of Dorian Gray Oscar Wilde

Wilde's superb and macabre novella, one of his supreme works, is reprinted here with a masterly Introduction and valuable Notes by Peter Ackroyd.

A Treatise of Human Nature David Hume

A universally acknowledged masterpiece by 'the greatest of all British Philosophers' – A. J. Ayer